A CHANCE ENCOUNTER

Rae Shaw

2021

Spare Time Press

For Mum and Dad

Part One

DUPLICITY

1

Julianna

Autumn

She raised her fists, swept her arm back and slaked her anger with a punch. By the time she'd worked up a sweat, she'd dealt with Alex's fake smiles, his smirking lips and the dimple in his chin. The punch bag continued to dance on its rope, shaken by the force of her blows, then limped to a sway, the crimson cover sticky in places.

The album was empty. She had no more photos to tape to the shabby leather. She had punched her way through the wedding ones, and the honeymoon snaps, shredding them with her knuckles and kicking feet. There was always the weekend in Paris.

Another jab. Another kick. Forget Paris. Forget the walk along the Champs Elysees. The kiss under the Eiffel Tower. The nice Parisian who had caught them cuddling on the banks of the Seine and added a shot to the collection. She punished her wrapped knuckles, the blistered heel of her bare foot. Every inch of her had to hurt.

What mattered, what had to be expunged, was the night she had propelled him out of the front door with one powerful kick up the ass. The satisfaction of seeing his smile disintegrating, replaced by fury and humiliation, was worth the unneighbourly curtain twitches. What she felt had been there on his face for everyone to see. That was what gave her the idea for trashing photographs.

Julianna began each day in the cellar. It wasn't much of a basement, more of a claustrophobic sliver under the mews house. To hide the crumbling brickwork, she had hung curtains rescued from charity shops across the walls and, to cushion her feet, she had laid a threadbare rug over the concrete floor, but it lacked any substance and occasionally her knees jarred as she hopped about on her toes.

The punch bag therapy lasted ten minutes. She buried her face in a towel and heaved a sigh of relief. There were more photos, things she could aim at, but nothing could remove the bitterness, the memory of finding the necklace on her bedside table, planted there because he had given up waiting for her to find out the truth.

She wanted to see things clearly again. But nobody would understand how hard it felt trying to recapture that skill, not even those she counted as friends or family.

During her police training, and the subsequent more in depth assessment she had undertaken when she worked for the intelligence services, her mentors had told her she was "insightful", "observant", able to "read between the lines and see the detail hidden in the big picture". Oh, the irony of that excellent appraisal; the buzz it had given her equal to kickboxing. Alex had taken her out to an exclusive restaurant and applauded her with his usual wit and languid remarks. Again, she had missed the signs.

He'd taken that bitch to the same restaurant.

She had amassed numerous theories as to her failings. The obvious was her husband had drained her of her precious abilities. She had gone soft on him, pandered to what he needed, and in the end, all that self-effacing effort meant nothing to him. She quit working for government, those secret agencies that Hollywood romanticised in spy films when in reality they relied on hard graft and few rewards. What good was she? The numpty on the money laundering desk who couldn't even spot her husband's duplicity wasn't going to "see" the things criminals hid.

To her surprise, the misery of handing in her notice was salvaged by somebody she had heard of, but never met. Alex's alumni friend, Jackson Haynes, had headhunted her and brought her to work for him at Haynes Financial Services, a thriving business that bought and sold lesser companies; it also happened to excel at exposing fraudsters.

She had the most unusual set of roles in the company and no authentic job title. It was exactly what she liked about it, although the job had yet to thrive in the direction she desired. There again, the circumstances weren't right for pushing through her ambitions. God forbid somebody put her in charge of anything and promoted her to management. She wasn't ready to deal with people. Not yet.

Versatility was the key to her success. Depending where she was needed, she migrated between tasks, such as fraud investigations, and occasionally the chauffeur's seat of an executive car where she doubled as a protection officer. She enjoyed driving the high-powered car with its reinforced bodywork. The black paintwork reflected the rows of skyscrapers. The leather seat gently creaked under her legs. Together, she and the car crawled through the city traffic. Driving was tolerable, sitting around waiting for something to happen wasn't. She passed the time listening to the radio and finished a book of ten-minute crosswords. Each one took six minutes – she felt cheated.

However, her feelings toward Haynes were ambivalent. The man was impenetrable, a bastion protected by rigorous deportment. She rarely drove him, mostly she ferried the wife, and the kids. When she had driven him, he had stretched out on the back seat, engaged in telephone conversations or absorbed in thought. If she caught his eye in the rear-view mirror, he admonished her with a glare. She was supposed to be invisible, something that hit her hard. Invisible during a covert investigation was one thing but being ignored by the people she was supposed to protect was tough.

Neither was she convinced by Jackson's highbrow ethics. Why was a financier patronising a charity for those lost to the dark world of trafficking? Was he the romantic hero rescuing fallen women, as he might appear to some of his loyal employees, or using the foundation for his own machinations? After she had cruised through the probationary period, she started to wonder more about his wife and why Hettie stuck with Jackson.

Mrs Haynes had a regular driver, Tess, but Julianna was the back-up. Chauffeuring meant keeping a diplomatic distance while Mrs Haynes went about her daily life, but Julianna had a woeful tendency to put on superhero capes and leap into action when nobody asked or expected it of her. She rather liked the criticism. She wore it as a badge of honour.

The call from headquarters instructed her to pick up Mrs Haynes from the emergency department of the local hospital. The eldest child, a boy named Noah, was at home with the nanny, Lara – another loyal servant who practised martial arts in her spare time. However, the new baby, Evey, went everywhere with Mrs Haynes because of the need to feed her. Julianna drove as quickly as the congestion allowed and parked in a taxi bay outside the minor injuries unit.

Stripped of a layer of foundation, Mrs Haynes's heavy-lidded eyes shadowed her alabaster cheeks; a small part of her renowned beauty lost to exhaustion. A row of strips sealed the wound on her forehead. She fingered it, tutting to herself. While Mrs Haynes slipped into the backseat, fussing, Julianna strapped the baby carrier in next to her. Evey smelt of baby wipes.

Julianna was about to leave the busy hospital car park when her mobile beeped. She read the text message. 'We're to swing by and pick up your husband from the office,' she told Mrs Haynes.

'Why's he bothering...' Hettie muttered in dismay, her voice drowned out by the wail of a siren.

Why wasn't she pleased? Wasn't it what she wanted – her husband by her side? In fact, why hadn't he rushed off to the hospital already? Julianna was still trying to piece together the Haynes marriage. She rarely saw them together, since they were apart during the day, which was when Julianna was assigned to be a chauffeur. Most of the time her superiors, Gary Maybank and Chris Moran, drove the couple in the evenings. Mr Haynes was extremely protective of his wife and kids and the level of security around the Haynes family was high. Julianna had seen the confidential reports and understood why. She doubted Mrs Haynes had a clue about the constant threats.

She parked outside the monolithic building. Mr Haynes strode across the pavement and handed Julianna his laptop case, which she placed in the boot space next to the baby's buggy. There was dried blood on the handles of the buggy.

'Home, sir?'

Mr Haynes nodded and sat in the front. The car pulled away and he twisted in his seat to look at his wife. Julianna caught his expression out of the corner of her eye. Why the scowl?

'Is she asleep?' He cocked his head at the baby carrier hidden behind where he sat.

'Yes,' Mrs Haynes said.

'What happened?'

'We went for a walk. I tripped, okay? Stupid heel broke off and I fell against a tree. My phone got smashed on the way down. The roots had torn up the paving stone and my heel was caught in the gap.'

The phone would be replaced by the end of the day. It was a minor inconvenience. Operating a well-oiled machine was the key to Haynes's business practices, and his home life.

'Lara said you were bleeding everywhere. So, what happened, Hettie?'

'I don't know. I don't … remember.'

Julianna tightened her grip on the steering wheel and stayed focused on the car bumper she was following. Seriously, the man had no bedside manner. He wasn't worried about his wife, he was annoyed at the intrusion into his working day. Perhaps a few of his photographs on the punch bag…

'She called an ambulance because you froze. You freaked her out. An ambulance for a little cut on the head.'

Not one word of comfort or concern had passed his lips. Unbelievable.

'Don't, Jackson. I didn't ask for the ambulance. Lara, she's never seen me lose it. I haven't done it for months and months.' There was a low sob, quite distant; Mrs Haynes was far away. Julianna bit on her lip and stayed silent. *None of my business.*

'She probably thought you were concussed. The symptoms are similar. Are you all right?'

Julianna rolled her eyes at the belated show of compassion.

'Yes. I came out of it in one of those cubicles. They gave me oxygen and I suppose it helped me. There's blood on Evey's buggy.'

'Lara can clean it up.'

'You didn't have to leave work,' Mrs Haynes said.

His profile twitched. 'Yes, I did. You're going to need sorting out, aren't you?'

And what the hell did he mean by sorting out? It made Julianna's blood run cold hearing him speak that way. The man was an ass.

Jackson, now facing forward, was tapping his fingers on his lap and glancing at his wristwatch from time to time. In the rear-view mirror, Mrs Haynes brushed aside a lock of hair; her hand was trembling.

She was afraid.

A few minutes later Julianna pulled up outside the Holland Park whitewashed house with its three floors and battery of CCTV cameras focused on the windows and doors. Jackson carried the baby carrier indoors.

'I won't be needing you again.' Hettie climbed out of the car.

Jackson held the front door open for his wife. She hobbled on her broken heel and rushed past without a glance in his direction. With a kick of his foot, he slammed the door shut.

Julianna sped off back to Haynes' headquarters, her driving duties finished for the day. Her supervisor, Chris Moran, owed her an explanation about Hettie's marriage. Hasty, misplaced sentiment, intrusive: those were Julianna's flaws, but she wasn't going to let somebody else occupy her punch bag if she could help it, and she liked Hettie; the woman was blessed with dazzling looks and talent, and something else, which frustrated Julianna because words couldn't describe what she felt. The feelings Julianna could express magnanimously regarding herself were bitterness and envy. Compassion, too, if she dug deep enough, although it wasn't an emotion she wore on her sleeve.

She relayed the incident in the car to the security chief in an abbreviated fashion. He scratched his bald patch and tilted his chair back with his long legs. His desk was a well-guarded corner plot in the team's open plan office in the basement. Lunchtime, and they were alone. Her stomach rumbled as she reached the point about the blood on the buggy's handles.

Chris interrupted her. 'I should have briefed you on her phobia of blood before today. Sorry, I thought you'd been told.'

'That wasn't what bothered me, Chris. She didn't look happy. The way he spoke to her, it sounded like he was, well, going to bite her head off… or something.'

Chris groaned and his chair landed back on the front legs with a jolt. 'Look, take my word for it, they love each other. Crazy mad love. It's just their way. Don't read into what they say to each other. It's a minefield. Don't go there. I don't and I've been with Mr Haynes for years.'

'He didn't show much sympathy—'

'Julianna, leave it!' The bark was a familiar rebuke. He was an ex-copper, too.

Chris was nominally her line manager. He pulled rank when it came to what she did for the company; whether it was helping the forensic accountants or bodyguard duties, Chris had the final say. She couldn't afford to risk upsetting the status quo.

'New guy in forensics – Mark Clewer.' Chris slid a folder across the table. 'He's been checked out. If he needs help, then you're the contact.'

She opened the manila folder and read the first few lines of the report. 'He doesn't start until Monday.'

He turned away and waved a dismissive hand. 'Haynes hand-picked him. Just do your stuff, Julianna. It's what we employed you for.'

Her stuff. She wasn't sure exactly what her stuff entailed anymore.

Chris had told her to leave the couple alone. But her palms itched, like a scab needing to be picked. In the celebrity press, Mrs Haynes appeared on Mr Haynes's arm, smiling and playing her part beautifully. Maybe that was all she was to him: a beautiful object or a trophy wife whom he adored for the sake of good publicity. It didn't help her conscience knowing that there were young children in the Haynes household – what if they witnessed the unpleasant truths about their parents' behind the scenes relationship? Julianna was determined to re-establish her credentials as an investigator, even if it was only in the privacy of her own mind.

For the rest of the week, she wasn't asked to drive Mrs Haynes. The opportunities for spying were few.

The intelligence service had recruited her from the Metropolitan's Serious Fraud division. They had needed her brains – her brawn was under appreciated – to help track the money hidden by terrorists and organised crime, but she had been trained to do undercover operations. Nothing glamorous, just routine sur-veillances, which were generally tedious and uneventful. By Friday, she had formulated a plan. Her weekends were typically free time, however she was on the reserve list. One of the security guards who worked the night shift at Jackson's Surrey estate wanted time off at short notice. Julianna volunteered to do the shift.

Heading south out of the City of London in her ancient personal vehicle, Julianna approached the estate with a smidgen of trepidation at her treasonous plot. The secluded house was Georgian and well-maintained, and a substantial property compared to the townhouse in Holland Park where the couple lived during the week. Fasleigh House was a squire's sanctuary, and with its extensive network of security cameras and fences, it posed few issues for the team based in the gatehouse.

Tom Draper, the other guard on duty, was already there when Julianna rolled up. He briefed her, then buried his ginger mop in a bike magazine. She drummed her fingers on the table, wondering when to make her move. She hadn't been this excited in a long time. Adrenaline accelerated her heartbeats to a manageable pace. She was ready.

'I thought I saw something on the monitor, over by the perimeter fence.' She waggled her finger at the screen.

'Probably a rabbit or fox. Happens,' he said, without looking up.

'I'll go check. Better safe than sorry.' She picked up a torch.

'If all you want is fresh air, just say so. It's not as if anything ever happens here. Stay away from the house though,' he said, still focused on the photo of a Harley-Davidson.

'I'm sure I saw something odd.' Pretence was better than appearing foolish.

She collected a pair of binoculars and hurried into the garden. She skirted around the perimeter wall and performed a cursory hunt for the benefit of the cameras. Ruse completed, she snuck into the shrubbery and trained the binoculars on the large bay window at the back of the house. There were no curtains drawn or blinds lowered, the house was lit up like a Christmas tree. Choosing a bush to perch behind, she had an excellent view of the sitting room.

They were both there. He was lifting the baby out of her arms; Mrs Haynes had been feeding the child. He left the room with Evey. Hettie rested her head against the couch. The room relied on the dim light of lamps, which projected tentacle rays, reflecting off surfaces and zigzagging over the glass-top coffee table. The shadows obscured the finer details. Hettie was bathed in a warm glow where the beams crossed. Her hair was bundled into a bird's nest bun. She was relaxed, lounging in baggy pants, quite unlike the upmarket attire she wore when out and about. Her eyelids drooped. Then, abruptly, she stirred.

The binoculars nearly slipped out of Julianna's hands. Mrs Haynes was wide awake. A small smile descended over her face. Her bra remained tangled around her waist. She hadn't bothered to replace the cup over her breast. Her nipple was invisible under the t-shirt.

Mrs Haynes, Hettie, *goddammit, what to call the woman*, turned to face the other end of the room, which wasn't visible to Julianna. She giggled and covered her open mouth with her hand. With little decorum, she slid along the leather sofa until she was flat on her back and opened her arms, creating the space to receive him.

Watching the lovers embrace with roving hands and intertwined limbs, Julianna gorged on the fortune of another. Alex had not shown one instance of the passion she was witnessing across the immaculate lawn. As Chris said, they had their ways. They were adroit lovers. In the privacy of their home, they put aside formalities and frolicked like teenagers.

And what was she? A concerned individual undertaking a covert act of surveillance or a voyeur, spying on her boss as if he was a common criminal? Any of her mentors would have slapped her wrist and told her she had missed the bigger picture. Haynes was a CEO and not a romantic hero who smothered his wife in an open display of unbridled affection. The conversation she had overheard in the car earlier in the week now made perfect sense. Hettie Haynes wasn't afraid of her husband. She knew exactly what "sorting out" meant. Her hand hadn't been shaking with fear, but excitement. Jackson had dashed home to comfort his wife, but chose to appear aloof and detached in the presence of his newest driver. An intensely private man who hated the limelight and, having created a tough boss image at work, he wasn't going to ruin his reputation by fawning over his wife in the middle of the day. It made more sense than the ridiculous post-Alex scenario Julianna had hurriedly concocted.

The blow, when she allowed herself to feel it, was a devastating as the one she had given Alex. Still on her knees, she bent over, hugging the flayed pit of her stomach and thought of the hours she would need to spend in the cellar.

Backing away into the darkness, she stumbled over hidden roots before finding a path. She hated what she had become. Hated the idea she had lost it. Wiping the perspiration from her brow, the dirt from her knees, she switched off the light and punched the keypad code for the gatehouse.

Draper made no comment on her prolonged absence.

'You were right – foxes.' She pretended to read a book for the rest of the shift. She didn't turn a page.

The stupid exercise she had engaged in had backfired badly. Far from demonstrating exemplary investigative skills, she'd misinterpreted the facts, insinuated emotions that weren't there and come up with her version of a carefree wife ridiculed by an uninspiring husband. It was exactly why she had left her last job. She wasn't fit for purpose any longer.

Blaming Alex was wrong too. Her natural cynicism had dragged her into this cock-up. She should just do her job – driving fast cars in slow traffic interspersed with measly surveillance operations. It wasn't on the scale of anti-terrorism or serious international money laundering, but it paid the mortgage and, without Alex's income, she was struggling.

2
Mark

The elevator doors opened to reveal Jackson Haynes, a man best known for sporting a tailor-made suit with monographed pockets and gold cufflinks, and not sweatpants and t-shirt. He leaned against the mirrored wall, towel coiled around his neck, and swept aside a lock of damp hair with his manicured hand. Girded with the kind of muscles that belonged on a dedicated athlete, Jackson boasted without requiring the use of words. He acknowledged Mark with a curl of his thin lips.

Mark felt inadequate and small. He would never be that fit nor was he the kind of person who spent every morning lifting weights and running nowhere on a treadmill. Apparently his boss was just that and Mark's heart sank a little as he wondered if he should take up a new hobby to impress Jackson.

Wiping his sweaty face with the edge of the towel, Jackson waved him into the lift. It should be an auspicious start and Mark needed plenty of good omens. He wore his grandfather's watch; a scratched talisman he kept with him in breach of his belief that superstitions were utter nonsense.

'Mark. Your first day?' Jackson stepped to one side. Mark's hands were full and he hung his briefcase off his little finger.

'Yes,' Mark replied. Should he have added an ingratiating "sir"? Strike a balance, he decided. Keep it formal, polite, but casual, too. He tapped his floor button, just managing to reach it with his thumb, then propped his briefcase between his feet. His arms ached from carrying the cardboard box.

'I must try the gym.' It wasn't his thing. He liked to frequent the terraces of a football stadium back in Manchester, but now, away from familiar territory, downtime was about the comfy sofa and a bottle of beer. Without a car, he was lumbered with public transport and attacks of inertia.

'You're an early starter, why not?' Jackson said.

True, but then that was because sleep wasn't always forthcoming. He stifled a yawn. He searched Jackson's face for some trace of fatigue and was disappointed – there wasn't a shadow blemishing his skin.

'Mornings are nice and quiet for working,' he said instead.

Jackson guffawed. 'Not in my house. Evey was screaming the place down, then Noah.'

Mark had forgotten about the pregnancy. He usually fixated on her emerald eyes and not her swollen belly. 'Congratulations on the birth of your daughter.'

'Hettie, the poor girl, is shattered with constant feeding. Things are settling down now she's past six weeks. Thankfully. Speaking of settling in, Hettie and I would like you to join us for a quiet evening meal at Fasleigh. I'll email you the details. Some friends of mine to introduce you to.'

Mark bounced up onto the balls of his feet. The weight of the cardboard box forgotten for a moment. 'That would be fantastic.'

The lift jolted and the doors opened.

Jackson's lips smiled. His shrewd cornflower eyes didn't. He possessed an aristocratic sharpness in all of his features; youthful good-looks chiselled with faint lines of wisdom.

His boss held the lift doors open while he gathered his possessions. 'Thanks again, er, Mr Haynes. I look forward to it.' Meeting Jackson Haynes in any circumstance was always a step in the right direction. At least so far. 'Send my regards to Hettie.'

'Will do.' Jackson punched a button and disappeared behind the lift doors.

The invite to dinner was born out of a meeting months ago when Mark had indulgently pawed Hettie in a West End bar. Jackson hadn't been there and she had arrived with a gaggle of girlfriends. A hen night or something. Mark had wandered in with a group of unremarkable work colleagues, who had subsequently made their excuses and left him glued to the big screen, pint in hand, watching a lengthy analysis of a football match. He had been a little drunk. Sidling up to Hettie, filled with optimism that he might pull such a gorgeous woman, he had failed to notice the wedding ring on her finger or Gary Maybank eyeballing him from the side-lines. She had bought him a drink and taken his business card, which had disappeared into her purse. As she had risen from the bar seat to re-join her friends, he put his arm around her waist to steady her. Gary had charged across the floor and rugby tackled him to the floor. Hettie had been mortified and berated Gary for leaping in when it wasn't necessary. Her apologies had embarrassed Mark because his intentions hadn't been honourable – he fancied her rotten. She was too sweet to hang out in those kinds of bars – Jackson owned a snazzy nightclub somewhere, didn't he?

That was how he met Hettie. How he caught Jackson's attention and became her accountant. Gary might have been scolded by Hettie but later she told Jackson about the drunk in the bar who slotted his arm around his pregnant wife. Mark should have been sporting a black eye after the encounter, but instead everything snowballed into a peculiar job interview.

Mark bounded into his new office and nearly collided with the cleaner. She jumped and clutched a gloved hand to her chest.

'Bloody hell,' she said. 'You shouldn't do that, creeping into rooms.'

'Sorry. Didn't mean to startle you.' He sidestepped the cleaning trolley.

She snorted. 'Oh, not to worry. I'm just not use to anyone being about at this time of day.' A waft of fresh bleach and stale tobacco followed her as she moved about the small office.

'A necessity of your job.' He placed the cardboard box and laptop case on the desk.

She was a talker – not what he wanted first thing in the morning. He opted for minimal responses. She clucked her tongue and bustled around the room with a duster. The dots on her sleeve blurred as she chased phantom cobwebs. The bare room was spotless.

'This room has been clear for a couple of weeks. So it's yours now?'

'Yes, new job, so an early start. I expect it'll wear off.' Desperate for his routine caffeine fix, he followed her out of the door into the communal office in search of a drink.

She weaved the cleaning trolley between the cubicles, heading towards the service lift, and left him by the vending machine. He returned to his office and place the Styrofoam cup on the desk. Rummaging in the cardboard box, he removed a strip of shiny black plastic embossed with his name and slid it into the empty slot on the outside of the door:

MARK CLEWER

He stood back to admire it, then, returning to the office, he spotted picture hooks along one wall. He hung two framed pictures opposite his desk. One he'd brought with him from Manchester, the other was a more recent acquisition: a small watercolour painted specifically for him. The artist's signature in the corner of the painting was barely visible: "H Haynes".

At nine o'clock, Mark gave a briefing to his new colleagues – an enthusiastic team of three. Their commitment was important; he would have to prove himself worthy if he wanted the best projects landing on his desk. Their work was split into two areas: internal embezzlement and dodgy clients with suspicious accounts: money laundering was usually top of the list. The latter was something with which he was familiar, but he didn't explain to the others why.

Mark had moved to London in self-imposed exile after the incident in Manchester. Snapped up by a specialist recruiter, the spell at Daneswan, a small subsidiary, led to a change in fortune and a swift transfer to Haynes' top-notch forensic accountancy team; a reward for tidying up Mrs Haynes's account. He had been promised the forensic role by the one man who could ensure he would get it: Jackson Haynes.

Mark's first case was an internal one and involved the car fleet manager. The man accused of embezzling was responsible for keeping the fuel tanks topped up; a routine internal audit had flagged discrepancies. Mark read the file and made notes. It wasn't the first time he had seen this type of fraud. The audacity of some never surprised him; criminals lurked in all the dark corners of life. The manager would likely lose his job. Many corporations would go out of their way to hide unwanted publicity, but not so at Haynes

Financials: the perpetrators were publicly vilified in court. Mark imagined Jackson had had a hand in shaping the policy.

However, to make his case, Mark needed the illegal act to be witnessed. A paper trail alone wouldn't be as convincing as a photograph or audio account of the illicit transactions. Mark wasn't cut out for hanging around petrol stations with a long lens camera. For one thing, he lacked a car. He needed a field operative to catch the man red-handed. The suggestion by one of the team was to speak to the head of the security team, Chris Moran, and ask for one of his operatives. The meeting concluded, and alone at his desk, he pulled up Moran's profile and accompanying mug shot in the company directory – a torpedo shaped head with a granite face. Mark suspected the request would be granted with a begrudging glare.

His mobile sang an unmelodious tune, which he had specifically picked for a purpose. She had to ring him, on his first day. He flicked the mobile to speaker phone then slid it a good distance away from his hand. His fingers clutched a pen.

'Mum.'

'I rang you yesterday.' No hello or how are you. Bloody typical.

'What do you want, Mum?'

'When are you going to send me the two hundred you promised?' She whined like a teenager.

Always money. It wasn't as if he was rolling in it. According to her, she hadn't a penny left even with the two jobs she worked. Lawyers cost, she liked to remind him, which was a gripe at his preferred profession. He never regretted his choice of career. Numbers were more polite than words.

'Give me a chance, will you. It's my first day. I'm trying to make an impression.'

A lengthy pause. She wasn't impressed. Deidre had to be the most important person in his life.

'Fine.' She sniffed. The fake disappointment washed over Mark. She couldn't act.

'I'll transfer some money this evening. Just a hundred though. I've taken out a deposit on a new apartment.' He instantly regretted mentioning the flat.

'Another one? You're always moving.'

Away from you, he nearly said. Instead, he chewed the end of the pen. 'It's on the bus route. If you want me to splash out and buy a car…'

'No, no. Save your money, darling.'

The "darling" made his toes curl. He hated it. Hated the falseness of her tone, the way she delivered affection in little packages as if it made up for all the crap she threw at him.

'Don't forget to find a solicitor. There must be good ones in London. Better than up here.'

'God, Mum. It doesn't make any difference.' He punctuated each word staccato style. 'If anything, they'll be more expensive.'

Deidre clung to the hope new evidence was around the corner. She fruitlessly pursued missing connections, the names of her husband's backstabbing mates who supposedly had slithered away to secret hideouts in London. Mark's optimism had vanished years ago. Nobody spoke up for his father. Whoever held the clues to Bill Clewer's guilt or innocence remained shamelessly silent or petrified. The whole bunch of them were scared, not of the law, but of what life had turned them into – career criminals. Clearing his father's name wasn't top of anyone's list.

'Well, let's hope that means something.' She didn't bother to say goodbye.

Releasing his grip on the pen, Mark reached for the office telephone and dialled a number.

She had taken up residence in his head – a grating echo of her voice – and the reverberations refused to budge. Grabbing his overcoat, Mark escaped to a cafe two streets away. He substituted the irritating sound with the remorseless milieu of traffic, then the eruption of steam pulsing out of the coffee machine intervened.

The queue snaked its way around the chairs and tables to the counter. He picked up partial conversations; the ear bashing of an absent colleague or problematic client, the slump in the stock markets. He ordered a coffee, then waited for his panini to be toasted before spotting an empty table. He made a beeline for it. A young woman pivoted on her seat and jolted his arm. The coffee spilt out of his cup and splashed her leg and table.

'Oh God! So sorry,' she said. The hem of her short skirt was high and the stream of coffee ran along the elastic lace of her hold-up.

Mark froze. The blunt tip of her nose stuck out from under her fringe of mocha curls. Her melodious voice had lost its adolescent tones.

His little sister Ellen had just spilt his coffee over her leg.

She winced with her head still bowed, apparently oblivious to his identity. 'Oh shit.'

If he walked out of the café right then, she might never notice him. She was more interested in dabbing the spillage with her napkin.

But this was his sister.

'Are you okay, Ellen?' he asked.

She went rigid, just as he had done. Without looking up, she said, 'Mark?'

He moved around the table and faced her.

The unsightly spots and limp hair – the companions of an undeveloped teenager – were absent. In their place, a young woman had emerged. It was Ellen, but not the girl he remembered. That girl had been a sallow, almost pitiful child, who had slunk about the house with a permanent scowl. Now she had wavy hair, which she had cut short, and her eyebrows were shaped into crescents, arching over mahogany irises. Her fingernails were elongated by extensions that glittered as she swept her hand over her leg. The portrait of maturity continued with her pencil skirt and jacket: the classic tailoring worn in nearly every office of the City of London. She'd always had the potential to blossom into something attractive, but he'd never anticipated that an office suit would do the trick.

'That must have hurt.' He backed away, opting for anything that avoided a kiss or a hug. 'I'll get some ice for you.'

Mark hijacked the front of the queue to ask for ice. The disapproving barista slammed a plastic cup of ice down on the counter. Mark wrapped a few cubes up in a napkin and handed it to Ellen.

'Keep it on. The longer the better.'

Her hand shook as she pressed the napkin onto the stained patch.

Another wince. 'It's cold,' she murmured.

'Good.' Mark took the seat opposite her. He had lost a quarter of his drink to her leg and the table.

She shot him a glance and smiled. *Heavens, she's changed beyond recognition. What had happened since they' last met? When had they last met?*

'Three years ago,' she said. 'I know that's what you're thinking. You're blinking like crazy trying to work it out.'

'Three!' He believed her. It probably was that long. Christmases, birthdays, none of those kinds of occasions warranted special attention in the Clewer household. Except, of course, Dad's birthday. They had been made to honour that and keep it like a holy day. The last Christmas Ellen would have been home, Mark had gone skiing; a disastrous attempt at reconciliation with his now ex-girl-friend.

She shrugged. 'Mum hasn't spoken to me in months.'

'Lucky girl.' He poked his panini and checked it wasn't too hot. One burning was enough.

Ellen abandoned the wet napkin on the table and stirred her tea. She ignored the sarcasm. 'So, why are you here? I mean, here in London?' she asked.

The extent of their disconnected lives was made real in that one question. He'd been in London for months. 'Work. When did you leave home?'

'A year ago.'

He stared straight at her, wide-eyed with shock; they made eye contact for the first time since he'd sat down. He was conscious his eyes might convey surprise, hers were wary.

'Fu—' he ended the expletive and looked away. 'Mum doesn't talk about you.'

And he never asked after her, that much was now apparent to Ellen who gave another little dismissive shrug. If she was bothered, she hid it well, and Ellen knew exactly how to use emotional dis-plays to get her own way. He hadn't forgotten her theatrical tan-trums and feinted attempts at self-harming. Although, in hindsight, he now recognised it has the most successful approach for handling their mother.

Social services had described it as a cry for help. Her little experiments had gone badly wrong – the razor wasn't blunt. However, the twelve-year-old Ellen hadn't persuaded them otherwise. According to Deidre, who considered Social Services an unnecessary interference, they had lectured her about priorities, rebutting her claims that Ellen was just a typical difficult kid. Ellen had never been typical. An indignant Deidre already had to deal with the gossip about her husband; she would never be able to face her neighbours – Deidre had wailed this at Ellen, as if her daughter cared. Mark had shrugged off the humiliation; he had been busy making other plans.

What Social Services achieved had been to encourage their mother to notice Ellen. For a while, Deidre had practised how to be a parent and insisted that if anybody bullied her kids, they should say their dad was innocent. Mark had brushed things aside by talking about appeals. Ellen had never said a thing one way or the other. People formed their own opinion of what had happened and hers had been decided a long time ago.

Ellen had continued to cut herself repeatedly as a teenager. Why she did this was something Mark had never been told by Deidre, but it explained why outsiders kept tabs on Ellen. When Deidre had been told Social Services were considering taking them into care, she had been horrified. Ellen had seemed keen on the idea, but they sent her to a special CAMHS unit for a month instead. Having packed his bags, Mark had gone to Oxford University on a scholarship. Deidre wanted him to study law and become a lawyer, obviously. He had chosen mathematics, then accountancy exams. Ellen, he imagined, had moped about the house on her own with Deidre and the living ghost of their father.

Now here she was, far away from Manchester. She smirked. 'It wouldn't cross her mind to mention me. I let her down. I'm a... terrible daughter.'

Mark grinned.

Ellen mimicked Deidre really well. 'I'm stupid and selfish for leaving.'

Once he might have agreed with that counterproductive assessment. He edged away from the past. 'She doesn't rate me much better.'

'But you talk to her.'

'I talk about… well, you know, the usual.'

'Dad.'

The conversation dried up. One word was all it took. There were no skeletons in the cupboard for the Clewer siblings. The biggest skeleton was an elephant who danced around in front of them and neither of them would acknowledge it.

'So.' Mark pursed his lips. 'What's with the fancy clothes? I'd always assumed you'd be wearing jeans and up to your knees in a muddy field.'

She laughed. 'Oh, how I wish.' The smile slipped away. 'Can't afford to go down that road. So I'm a personal assistant.'

'Oh dear,' he said, sympathetically. He had won the scholarship. It sucked that she hadn't had the same opportunities. 'Not what you hoped for.'

'No. Definitely not. Not that I'm putting down PAs. Sterling work given the shit they have to put up with from the stupid, lazy bastards called their bosses. Sorry. Today has been shit. I do stuff in my spare time with a local charity.'

'In a city? Don't you need open fields?'

'Urban archaeology is more fun. Every time a construction company puts down foundations, they dig up some remains. But unless it turns out to be a national treasure, they cover it up and build on top. You?'

'Forensic accountancy.'

'Oh?' She wasn't the only one unfamiliar with the profession. Hardly anyone Mark met knew what it entailed.

'I work for a mergers and acquisitions conglomerate. My boss buys up smaller companies, those in finance and accountancy, restructures them, sells some, keeps others. He's something of a money-making machine. Financial stuff isn't always squeaky clean. We go after employees who embezzle company money for personal gain. Or there are the crooked clients. Money launderers. Fraudulent deals. And also private cases that are brought to our attention for investigation.'

'Don't the police deal with that kind of thing?' She picked apart her sandwich and removed the lettuce. Mark stopped a smile from forming. She had never taken to salad; Ellen hadn't changed that much.

'Once they know about it but how do they find out, eh? In any case, not every client we investigate turns out to be bad, just crap at filing paperwork or understanding the system. It's more about ethics. The company I work for doesn't want to be aiding and abetting criminals by helping them fiddle their books. We audit randomly, pick up on suspicious transactions and do some research. It's harder to cover your tracks when an audit is unannounced. Most of the time, though, things are legit.'

'Sounds intriguing. Bit like archaeology; digging up the dirt, so to speak.'

Mark chewed on a mouthful of panini. She had grown up, embraced some witticisms and added charm, things she had lacked as a gawky child. Was she really standing on her own two feet? It was hard to imagine Ellen existing comfortably without some kind of emotional prop. She sank her teeth into her sandwich and he glanced at his watch. He should stay a little longer and try to engage with her.

'Interesting analogy. We're not a big team but the work is varied. We also help with due diligence for new acquisitions. Checking up and auditing their financial systems. As I said, varied.' He swallowed the last of his coffee.

'More interesting than my job. I never know what my boss wants from me. Some days he can be friendly, others a complete bastard. Depends on whether he's arguing with his wife or shagging his bit on the side. Nice thing about artefacts is that they don't bitch or bark. They just tell stories.' She pulled more lettuce from her sandwich and squished it into her napkin. Still a messy eater, too. Were they really from the same nest, or had Deidre planted her in their home from somewhere else? Relating to Ellen was the equivalent to building a bridge across a chasm. She was somewhere on the other side in the distance.

'Tough,' he said, tapping his foot under the table.

'God, he's a twat, Mark. It's a goddamn PR company. I wouldn't want him to represent me. Ego inflated idiot.' She stopped. 'Sorry, I'm ranting. I just can't get it out of my system sometimes.'

'Get what out of your system?'

'I don't know. Emotions. Just accepting things as they are.'

Something Mark could relate to. 'I know.' He leaned forward, pushing aside his empty cup. 'Nobody else out there for you?'

She blushed and waved a dismissive hand. 'No. Just Nicky. We're bedsit neighbours. He keeps an eye out for me, just like a bro...' She covered her mouth. 'Sorry. That's sounds awful. I mean, a friend.'

Mark accepted the rebuke. He hadn't been a brother to her, not in the way she might have expected. There again, if he had been a big sister, then perhaps the story might have been different. Perhaps she might not have ended up in a psych unit after making criss-cross patterns on her arms. He couldn't blame her for finding somebody to replace him, and Dad. They both needed a better father.

'A good friend then?'

'We jog together. Go to the local pub for a drink now and again. That kind of stuff. Nothing... he's gay.'

Mark laughed. 'I'm not judging you, Ellen. If you had a boyfriend, I'm not going to give him the third degree.'

'And you? Girlfriend?'

He shook his head. 'Had. We parted company when I moved down here. Mutual decision to end it.' The breakup had hardly broken his heart, it hadn't even caused a splinter. 'Look. I really have to go.' He rose to his feet and brushed the crumbs off his jacket.

She was busy examining her leg.

'That okay?' he asked.

She smoothed her skirt over the damp patch. 'Sure.' For a fleeting moment, he saw a different girl peering up at him, a younger version but with the same opaque eyes and peppering of pinprick freckles around her nose. Ellen was hiding underneath the elegant officer worker and she was hurting, just like him. He couldn't just walk away again.

He fished out one of his newly minted business cards and scribbled his mobile number and address on the back. He handed it to her.

Squinting, she deciphered the scrawl. 'Islington. How nice.' And wrote hers down on a separate card.

Just the address and her work telephone number. The message was clear; her trust had to be earned if she was going to give him her personal unlisted number. She guarded it carefully to avoid Deidre's interference.

He slid it into his back pocket. 'How about you come over for dinner one evening? We can catch up properly.'

She radiated sunshine peeping out from a gloomy cloud. As if it hurt, she ducked her eyes down and the fleeting brilliance evaporated. 'Sure. Absolutely.' She needed and despised him in one efficient bundle of emotions. Most people would implode with the combination, but Ellen specialised in contradictions.

What now? Shake hands? Slap her on the back like his cousin, Alfie, whom he met from time to time. When in Manchester, Mark preferred to visit Uncle Tim. For those very occasional weekends that other house had been everything a home should be — tranquil with the odd outburst of appropriate laughter. The envy was almost unbearable.

He bent and she expectantly tilted her cheek towards his lips. The peck was swift, a minutiae glance, and she blushed. A connection had been made and he couldn't let it die a death. If there was a reason for lassoing her back into his life, it was because Ellen presented a useful advantage: she was accomplished at manipulating Deidre.

3

Ellen

I met my brother today. By accident. He spilt his coffee over me.

Ellen waited half an hour for a reply, which wasn't unusual. She pottered about the bedsit, listening out for the familiar chirping that she'd assigned to his profile. Eventually, she heard it over the microwave. Hot noodles in a bowl… delicious.

Are you okay!?

She smiled. She expected his concern. She liked it.

Yes.

She typed quickly, eager to tell him her news.

He's working in the city, not too far from my office. I was running an errand, stopped for lunch in this cafe and I knocked his coffee cup. He didn't recognise me!

She curled her legs underneath her and slurped on a coke. The bedsit was piping hot. She had dispensed with her work clothes and slipped on a pair of ragged edged shorts and t-shirt. The red mark on her thigh was visible, but it didn't hurt. The faint white lines of her scars lurked beneath it. She hated looking at them. What an idiot she had been to think they would fade into nothing. By the time she started marking her arms, she had learnt how to do it properly and those ones hardly showed at all.

Back then, she had been a skinny sixteen-year-old hiding underneath baggy hoodies and cropped jeggings. Waiting to bloom, her mother had told Mrs Asani, the next-door neighbour, almost apologetically. Mrs Asani's daughter had beautiful brown eyes and smiled a lot at the soccer-mad boy who had lived opposite them. Ellen had worked out smiling wasn't the best approach but had said nothing to her besotted rival. Neighbours had been a useful distraction from other things. Mark rarely came home and when he did, he constantly argued with Deidre about appeals and expensive solicitors.

Big brother! Must be exciting for you, sweetie.

Ah, Freddie, always saw the good in everything. It was why she liked him. Ever since she'd first chatted to him on Facebook, she had sought to garner his friendship. She'd had to lie to get into the private Facebook group. After a few weeks, the guilt at her deception gnawed and kept her awake at night. The truth was important, so she confessed to him – she wasn't a victim of a crime, she was the daughter of a murderer. She had told him she found out about her father's sentence on her twelfth birthday. Told him how she had run away still dressed in her grubby school uniform, carrying a faded satchel on the crook of her elbow, and nearly colliding with the advertising board outside the local newsagents. The board had an image emblazoned across it of the front cover of the Manchester Evening News, a grainy photo beneath the headline – **LIFE FOR LOCAL MAN JAILED FOR COWARDLY MURDER.** He had resembled a gorilla with his five o'clock shadow and hunched shoulders, and nothing like the dad she'd once adored. She had kicked over the stand and stamped on it until the shopkeeper shouted abuse at her. Later, she had gone home and opened her two presents: a see-through plastic bag of make-up to hide her "ridiculous amount of acne" – Deidre said this to Ellen's face – and a Barbie doll from Uncle Tim, who had forgotten she wasn't a little girl, although at least he had tried.

She had experienced a string of social workers in rapid succession and had presented, in a highly orchestrated manner, enough worrying issues for them. It wasn't always nice attention. Their patience had dwindled when she had played up, and consequently she had been sent to a special unit for a month to learn, as her social worker had framed it, more about herself. Ellen had found out nothing she hadn't already known – she was very good at keeping secrets.

Freddie, far from berating her about her lie, was very sympathetic to her circumstances. He had immediately bounced a message back clearly stating she was a victim, just like anyone else. A victim of her father's wrongdoing. An indirect victim, but one nevertheless. His reassurance was astounding. She poured out her fears, her hatred and loneliness to Freddie and he absorbed it all without judging her.

After exchanging messages with Freddie, she had built sufficient trust and revealed who her father was and where she lived, the name of the town, not her actual address – she wasn't that stupid. Freddie had gone silent for a while, which upset and worried her. She had paced her pokey bedroom, ignored her mother's calls for dinner, and prayed he wouldn't block her. He had replied to her message a few days later, apologising for not responding; he had been out of the country and busy. He had set about reassuring Ellen that she was special, and her opinions mattered, and she shouldn't allow anyone else to convince her otherwise, especially her mother.

Her friend was so unlike her parents. He sent her "listening" messages – open-ended questions followed by soft advice. He referred to her as sweetie. A strange endearment because from anyone else, it would have been creepy. It helped that Freddie Z, as he was known on Facebook, was a trained counsellor who ran a victim support group. Somehow, unlike the social workers she shunned, he knew how to handle Ellen, who struggled to accept that her destiny had been determined by her father stabbing a man to death. When that poor sod's heart had been pierced by the blade, hers had been too.

From then on, she had relinquished her maternally depleted mother of any semblance of parental responsibility and gave it to Freddie. He read her messages, which he insisted she use in an encrypted service, and he answered them in a considerate fashion, but not always immediately. He teased out her ambitions, especially her love of history and archaeology. And her fears.

She had dreaded visiting days. Mark used to tag along, but after he had left home he insisted on going on his own, if he bothered to go at all. On her last visit, approaching the imposing prison gates, she had nearly retched. Hearing the keys clang and the doors slam behind them, she had been convinced she would be shut in with those violent men and left there as some kind of punishment for keeping her secret, the one Mark knew nothing about. Ellen had been watched the whole way by security cameras and the gnarled men with their faded tattoos and creased uniforms. In the visitors' room, they had ogled her breasts; the one part of her that seemed to grow disproportionately to the rest of her shapeless body.

'Remember he's innocent,' Deidre had whispered.

'Then why is he still here?'

After that awful encounter with her father, who hadn't looked her in the eyes and bundled cigarette packets into his pockets, Ellen decided she wouldn't visit him anymore.

She had spent the last summer holiday in Manchester volunteering for a local archaeology trust that excavated urban sites; something worthwhile and enjoyable, and the time away from Deidre had brought her into adulthood with the belief her fate lay in her own hands and nobody else's. Freddie had suggested she leave home and seek out the excitement of London, and new adventures. Get out and meet people, he had typed.

She had packed her bags on her eighteenth birthday, any hope of studying archaeology shattered by the lack of money. She refused to cry when she had tottered up the costs of going to university, instead she had hatched a different plan – raise the money herself. Announcing to Deidre that she was leaving home to find work in London as a secretary or administrator or something, Ellen had braced herself for the anticipated tirade of disappointment. Instead, Deidre had spoken with icy precision from behind a veil of cigarette smoke.

'Selfish. Idiotic. Girl.'

Ellen hadn't minded the idiot. With a good batch of exam results, she wasn't stupid. However, the selfish had riled to the point of fury. Leave her, the little voice in her head screamed. Let Deidre dedicate her life to proving her husband's innocence, something that had consumed her since Ellen's twelfth birthday.

How's London, sweetie? Freddie had written the day after she had arrived.

Great. Liberating. I've a little bedsit in a sea of bedsits. I've met this guy called Nicky. He's living above me and moved in at the same time. He's lovely.

Lovely?

She had ignored the hint of jealousy.

Don't fret. He's gay.

It had been a couple of hours before he sent a reply.

Be careful, sweetie. People aren't always what they seem.

She had agreed. She knew exactly what he meant.

Freddie steadfastly remained her pillar, her secret daddy. If anyone else asked what she meant by seeking advice, she referred to her professional counsellor, Mr Z. He was so much better than social workers at teasing out her problems, so much more interested in her life than her own mother.

Freddie was the best.

She gulped down her diet coke. Freddie wanted to know everything about her abrupt meeting, what she and Mark talked about, how it felt to have her brother back in her life. He was such a curious bloke.

She typed furiously.

Forensic accountant?

Ellen explained as briefly as possible what Mark had told her. It wasn't the best explanation, but Freddie was quick as well as curious.

Like a copper, but for a company?

Yes. He works for Haynes Financials. It's on his business card.

She flipped the card over to examine the corporate logo.

She waited. Minutes ticked. She switched on the television and channel hopped. It happened sometimes. Freddie had other clients and she shouldn't monopolise his time every evening. She was one of many girls he helped. Boys, too, he frequently pointed out. She knew, given how secretive he was about his work, that they had been abused. At least her father wasn't like that. He wasn't that kind of nasty man. Bill Clewer orchestrated things but had never got his hands dirty. Until that one day of extreme violence.

Good for him.

His brevity signalled the end. He was too busy now to message her.

I'm meeting him for dinner.

Have a good time.

She sent him a barrage of silly emojis. It was how she ended all of their conversations, lampooning their relationship in a series of codified affections. Freddie wasn't really her dad, just a bloke who cared.

4
Julianna

Julianna strolled into Mark's office, having announced her arrival with a rattle of the door handle. He rose to greet her, offering a firm handshake, then a chair at the table.

Mark had an affable face, which delivered a genial, if brief smile. His skin was slightly swarthy, as if he had inherited some distant gene from a hot country, like Spain or Southern France, which had lost a little of its dominance under the weak English sun. He had chocolate hair to match the olive skin and cappuccino eyes that were dusted with speckles of light. When he opened his mouth and spoke, he was pure Mancunian. It didn't ruin his image. The northern accent added a little twist of surprise. She wondered what he would make of her nutmeg skin tone and ironed straight hair. Her ethnicity went further west than Cornwall, to her grandfather in Trinidad.

Given he was a businessman, and not royalty, Jackson liked to vet newcomers to an unnecessary extent. However, she had learnt nothing about Mark from her privileged position of being on Haynes' security team. Mark's file was innocuous, almost sanitised, which seemed odd, because he clearly knew Hettie Haynes: the evidence was hanging on the wall of his office.

'Thanks for dropping by. I hope you can clear this one up quickly for us.' Mark opened his dossier. For the next half an hour they formulated a plan to capture the offending employee.

'Let's catch the idiot in the act.' She smirked, pleased that the case was more than a little background check. She would book the long lens out of the store cupboard and buy some gum to chew — something not permitted when driving.

Julianna flipped shut her notepad and scanned the room, before returning once again to the painting. It couldn't be ignored.

'Your predecessor left quickly. Ill-health, unfortunately for him. You're new to the company?' she asked, tentatively, watching to see if Mark resisted the line of interrogation.

'Not quite. I worked as an accountant at Daneswan, a subsidiary of this firm. This internal post came up and I grabbed the opportunity to transfer.' A cordial response and encouraging. She edged further, determined to fill in the blanks.

'And promotion, no doubt.' She wished she had tried asking awkward questions with Alex. Her mistake was giving him the benefit of the doubt whenever he arrived home late from work. She had bought his excuses like a naïve teenager instead of an intelligence officer. Any one of her mentors would have been disappointed with her infatuation with a gallant man with no backbone. Alex had laughed in her face when he confessed to adultery. He had basked in his achievement, while denigrating his and Julianna's love life with puerile jibes.

Bastard.

She had to get over him.

'Yes. My office floor space seems to have quadrupled in size,' Mark said sardonically, waving his hands at the less than spacious room; his smile broadened. He had an eye-catching grin and it held her attention, which she supposed was his intention. A well-packaged man with good dress sense. Something to applaud; she had a penchant for smart uniforms, which must run in her family – Alex was dashing in a tux. Mark assumed a confident manner, but perhaps a little wary, too; he twirled his pen between fidgeting fingers. There had to be more to Mark than charm. She would wait. In her opinion, people eventually showed their true colours after a couple of meetings. Except Alex. He might as well have studied drama at Oxford rather than law. And Jackson, too. Damn them both.

She walked over to the two pictures hanging side by side on the wall. One was of a bloody hand clutching a thorny rose and the other a paler watercolour showing a sapling with variegated ivy strangling its boughs and branches. The swirly signature of the artist was in the bottom corner.

'One of Mrs Haynes'.' She raised an eyebrow. 'You bought it from her gallery?'

There was an awkward pause. 'Er. No. A gift. It's called 'The Bower''.' He blushed and squirmed in his seat. He obviously hadn't expected anyone to look that closely.

Julianna was the kind of inquisitive so-and-so that did look. Details were everything, and not to be missed. Like a delicate painting, the brush strokes revealed the nature of the artist as much as the composition.

'A bower is also a lady's apartment. A stark contrast to the other picture. She wouldn't like that one.' She gestured at the gory rose picture.

Mark stood next to her, scratching his chin. 'Why not?'

'Oh. Blood, you know. She has a phobia about blood.' Julianna turned in time to see his eyes widen. 'Shit, you didn't know. I thought, having a gift, you knew her well. Don't mention I said that, will you?' The lie worked well; his mouth twitched nervously, weighing her up, no doubt.

'No, of course not. I'm more of a friend of Mr Haynes,' he said, slowly, a marked emphasis on "mister".

Another one of Jackson Haynes's friends. She hated the old boys' network. There must be some secret cadre with a connection to Oxford; Alex had been at Christchurch.

Mark had only recently arrived in London, initially working at a different, smaller office, then suddenly he had been transferred to headquarters. The gift of the painting must have happened prior to his move. Where had Hettie met him? She was a talented artist who'd studied at the Royal Academy of Fine Arts. Before her marriage to Jackson, she fulfilled commissions for famous clients. She didn't just give her artwork away to anyone and Mark probably couldn't afford to buy one of her pictures.

As for Mrs Haynes, Julianna listened into the quiet conversations held in the back of the car and, as expected, offered no counsel. Hettie wasn't always comfortable with the lack of privacy; she would attempt to codify her remarks and her eyes would flutter back and forth, occasionally glancing at the rear-view mirror to check whether Julianna was paying any attention to her phone calls.

Julianna maintained her professionalism under duress – if only she could speak up and ask Hettie outright about Mark.

She tapped her finger on the folder Mark had handed her. 'Well, I best follow this up.' The meeting ended with another brisk handshake. 'Good to meet you, Mark.'

She hesitated at the door for one last inspection of the painting and her new colleague – his fawn cheeks tinged with a hint of shame. Far from advertising his connection to Hettie Haynes, he had played it down, claiming Jackson was his friend, not Hettie. The lady's bower, the secret apartment, was the clue to why a new employee had that painting hanging in his office. Chris had given her Mark's personnel record a week ago. That bugged her too. Maybe it was so Jackson could use Julianna to keep an eye on his wife's admirer. Cheeky of him, but probably in character.

From now on, she would pay more attention to Mark Clewer. She bristled with delight – somehow, she had created a mission of her own. What the remit was, she would devise during the project.

5
Mark

The unique ringtone again. Hearing it gave him a few seconds to stopper a groan. He let it ring long enough to wrap a towel around his waist and dig out the phone from his trouser pocket. Shaking his head, he sprinkled the bathmat with water. He could ignore her, but she was as stubborn as a limpet on a wave-battered rock.

'Mark. I tried to ring you yesterday evening.'

'Mum. I'm fine. The new job is going good and—'

'When are you going to visit? I haven't seen you in months. You're overdue to visit. Not just me, but Dad too. He's been asking about you.'

He wrote to his father regularly, read the replies, but that was it. The distant father and son relationship didn't extend to phone calls or visits.

'Have they moved him again?' He wiped the condensation off the mirror. There were dark shadows under his eyes and a fine dusting of bristles on his chin. The late night session in the pub had stretched on into the small hours.

'No. It depresses him so much when he gets moved at short notice.' At one point they shipped him to the North East and Deidre had jacked in one of her jobs to free up time to visit him.

'I'll try to come one weekend.' Mark switched to speaker phone and dried himself. He had no plans to travel north in the coming weeks.

'Good.' Her voice lifted out of the doldrums. 'Have you found a new solicitor? You said you'd find another to launch a fresh appeal.'

Mark pressed his lips together. She had fired the last one for incompetence.

'Mark?' She echoed against the tiles. 'You're in London now. There have to be good lawyers in London.'

There were good lawyers in Manchester. 'We can't afford them, Mum.' *We, no, that should be you, Mum.* He tossed the towel aside and went into the bedroom.

'Eight years. Eight bleedin' years. They won't even consider paroling him.'

That was how long he had maintained his plea of innocence. *A guilty man would have quit by now, surely?* His mother repeated this mantra to every solicitor she hired.

'You know he won't get parole while he continues to maintain his innocence. You know that. No acceptance of guilt, no parole. We need fresh evidence to launch a new appeal.' He picked a shirt out of the wardrobe. A script wasn't necessary when explaining things to Deidre; a recorded message would do just as easily.

'What about that witness?'

Witness! The elusive witness. *Put a sock in it, Mum.*

He never told people at work about his father. Guilt or innocence didn't matter; the man was in prison. London provided plenty of lawyers, but Mark didn't know where to begin to find the right one. Given Deidre's interfering ways, it would have to be somebody with thick skin who could dig through conflicting evidence in the hope of finding something countless others had missed. They would also have to charge peanuts.

'Mum, don't cry. I'll sort something out.' Mark flopped onto the bed. He listened without paying any attention. The familiar sensations plagued him: blood turned to ice; muscles, rigid; dry eyes fixed on that spot on the ceiling; bottled anger corked. He hated telling necessary lies. They blossomed and grew and hid the reality he feared to face. The story of his father might not be complete and there were plenty of pieces missing, but joining up the dots wouldn't mend his relationship with Deidre.

Ellen had cried off, left him alone to deal with lawyers and the mountain of paperwork. He dearly wanted the situation resolved. More especially, he wanted to end the farcical pretence of supporting his parasitic mother. Ellen owed him.

6
Ellen

Ellen cast her eye about his apartment: open plan, spacious and minimalist. 'You've not been here long?'

'Two months.' Mark dropped the door keys on the kitchen work-top. 'Does it show?'

'To be honest some men, especially those living alone, don't go for much about the place. Others are downright untidy. I know you're not the untidy type, but this sparse?' His old bedroom in Manchester was now a storage room filled with boxes and boxes of Bill Clewer's things. Deidre refused to throw them out.

'I like objects to have a purpose. I don't need superfluous stuff, like ornaments. I might buy a few more pieces of furniture.'

In other words, he was constantly on the move. Sunlight burst through the corner window and fanned out. He drew the blinds down. There was an L-shaped settee, a matching armchair, which faced the wall-mounted television that appeared to be his sole form of enter-tainment, and six chairs around a dining table, which seemed a little excessive for one man. The dazzling kitchen units were too white, and clean. Both of them had learnt self-sufficiency at a young age.

She kicked off her heels. 'Under floor heating?'

'Yep.'

'Very nice. Cosy.' She wriggled her toes.

He opened a cupboard door in the kitchen and pulled out pans. She stretched out on the sofa and left him to it.

The soup tasted a tad salty but was otherwise good. The crusty bread was still fresh. 'Nice,' she said between slurps.

'So, you've not contacted Mum—'

'No.' She had anticipated Deidre. The challenge was derailing

Mark's insensitive probing while giving him the opportunity to befriend her. 'Don't want to go there.'

'She's struggling—'

'Don't care.' She left the spoon in the bowl. 'Look, Mark, it's lovely catching up with you. But Mum is off the agenda. And Dad. I want to get to know you.' She locked onto his gaze and figured he would cave if she held it long enough.

His mild frown evaporated quickly. 'What's there to know? I'm an accountant. I'm boring. I watch football on Saturdays.'

Ellen picked up her spoon. 'I can't believe how old you look—'

'Cheers.'

'I mean, come on, you were a teenager when you left home. Now, you're this man.' A man who had lost the chubby cheekbones of adolescence and replaced them with slightly gaunt ones. If he ate soup every day, it might explain the weight loss. He had the olive skin of their maternal grandparents who had emigrated from Southern France when hippies wore flared dungarees. For some reason, her skin tone was less pronounced, a paler facsimile. Sepia suited Mark.

A few cubes of carrot bobbed on the surface. She tasted chicken. It wasn't his fault; she hadn't mentioned the vegetarianism. When she had arrived in London she started cutting out meat. Dieting was a popular fad, something to chat about over lunch with the girls in the office, and she picked vegetarian because it was easier than some of the other ones – low carb, high protein, this and that – the choice had nothing to do with ethics.

'Something wrong?' he asked.

She shook her head. 'No. Just we're a bit like strangers, aren't we? I feel like I'm going on a date with my own brother.'

'I suppose. I always remember you as this sad girl who hid in her room.'

A painfully accurate description. 'Had my reasons.'

'Yes. You did.' Mark reached over and took her hand. He squeezed it. 'Sorry. That's all I want to say. Okay? I ignored you. I ignored everyone. I just wanted to get out.'

She slid her hand under the table. 'We both did. I had to wait longer.' She shrugged, dismissively. Six years. Her own private prison sentence. 'And now we're both in London.'

He leaned back in his chair. 'Tell me about your work.'

Neutral territory and a wise option. She moaned, she couldn't help it. He offered advice, good advice, which surprised her. Why had she assumed he wasn't knowledgeable about dealing with people. He had his own team, he explained.

He fetched cheese from the fridge. She helped herself to thick slices and smeared butter over the crackers.

Mark fidgeted in his seat, toying with his crackers.

'What?' she asked.

'You've banned me from talking about them.'

'When I'm ready. That's what I'm saying. I'm not ready. Don't let's spoil this evening with them.' She flicked a breadcrumb at his face. 'Cheer up.'

He laughed. The crumb fight continued for a few minutes. They had had them as kids; the memory was pleasant.

'Let's watch a movie,' he said.

She curled up on the settee and Mark parked himself in the arm-chair. He was impatient to tell her things. She had rebuffed him, but for how long would she be able to hold him off? She didn't want to hear about appeals and solicitors. There were no doubts in her head about her father. The younger Ellen had overheard the arguments about his "business dealings" through doors and walls. There were other things that she noticed: his coming home late without explanation and the envelopes of cash he handed to Deidre when Ellen wasn't sup-posed to be looking. The white powder that dusted the coffee table. Using her fingertip, an eleven-year-old Ellen had traced patterns in it until a scowling Deidre wiped it away with a brisk flick of her wrist.

Clues were everywhere. If you were small and curious, they were easy to stumble upon. Mark's analytical mind operated on numbers. This murderer didn't use numbers. Or words. Ellen had found things out by accident, like searching for pennies in her father's coat pocket and finding bigger things.

Mark picked something mindless and forgettable to watch. The perfect choice.

Returning home to her tiny bedsit, which she now hated, Ellen fired up her iPad and sent a message to Freddie.

Mark wants to talk about them. Him.

The reply came swiftly. Is that still painful for you?

Yes.

It wasn't the memories. She had plenty of those. It was the battles she had fought to make herself heard. She had dared to breach her containment. She had screamed, scratched and cut her way out. For one month she had tried being a mute because, she had naively assumed, people listened better to silent children. Talkative ones were constantly hushed. She had practised every trick, hoping to distract Deidre from her futile efforts to free her father, and none of them, not one fucking thing, had worked.

Have you ever thought how hard it is for Mark?

She hadn't. It wasn't the response she was expecting from her friend and it read like a rebuke. While Ellen lived with their mother, Mark, as the closest thing to a responsible adult in Deidre's life, had borne the brunt of her desperate need to prove her husband's innocence. Mark had propped up her belief for so long he was unable, or unwilling, to break free. Ellen fingered the edge of the tablet. How to explain what Deidre had done to Mark?

She typed. He's her puppet.

That can't be easy for him. He's trying to hold things together. How's the appeal going?

I don't know. Nowhere, I guess.

Then, don't worry. You don't want your father out, do you?

No!

Then, Mark's okay?

She hesitated. He's okay.

If he isn't, you'll know. If that day comes when you've nobody, then come to me in Ireland.

She stared wide-eyed at the screen. It was the first time he had suggested they meet up, and given a hint of where he lived. She liked the idea he was Irish and it explained his easy going appeal.

Why? she asked tentatively.

There are great digs in my area. You can get your hands filthy.

She laughed. Dirty man.

Humour was good. It softened destructive edges and eased tension, like a crumb fight.

Ellen pounded on the door. 'Nicky!'

The boom of the bass beat weakened, and the door opened a crack.

'Ellie, hun.' Nicky waved her in with a beaming smile. 'I thought you were out.'

She pushed the door shut with her bottom. 'I should get one of those broomsticks with an extension so I can bang on the ceiling.'

He laughed. 'Little old ladies do that.'

'Little old ladies are generally deaf. I'm not.'

He swaggered across the room, sashaying his hips. The effeminate mannerism was the only one Nicky possessed. The rest of him was pure masculinity. From his beefy shoulders to his lithe calves with their pronounced tendons and chiselled muscles, Nicky exuded youthfulness, which, given he was close to thirty, was especially impressive.

Ellen stole an apple from the fruit bowl on the kitchen counter. His bedsit was identical to hers, even the kitchen units were the same, except his were stained and one of the handles had come loose. He might be proud of his body, but Nicky wasn't keen on exercising it with housework. Somewhere, buried under abandoned clothes and fitness magazines, were his dumb-bells and fluorescent pink trainers.

'So, tell me. How did it go with big bro?'

She swallowed a mouthful of apple. 'Better than I thought. He didn't know I'm a vegetarian. In fact, he doesn't know much about me at all.' She perched on the end of the sofa next to a lingering odour of take-aways.

'Hardly surprising, is it?'

'It was a bit like a blind date.'

Nicky covered his mouth in feigned horror. His burnished eyes sparkled with merriment. 'You're dating and it's not *me*. I'm heartbroken.'

'I'm dating my brother, yes. That's how sad my life is.'

They both laughed.

The translucent t-shirt revealed what she liked best about him, as did the knee-length shorts that hung awkwardly low on his pelvis. He yanked them up and immediately, they dropped back to below his hipbones. The ribbons of his groin muscles rose up to meet the brace of parallel abs. She couldn't imagine him in a suit and tie. Nicky was born for the grunge look and it reminded her why he was forbidden fruit. She turned away and spun the apple on her palm. One bite and she had lost her appetite.

'We didn't talk about family,' she said.

'You mean the unmentionables.'

Not long after they met – colliding halfway up the stairs, then spilling out their gripes over a coffee – she had told him about her dad being in jail and her mother's obsession. Nicky was irresistible in nature and treated friends and lovers with equality when it came to advice and companionship. He was the real-life teddy bear who talked and hugged, but never went any further. When they went running together, he concentrated on the pavement and breathing. He pushed her, dragging her the extra mile especially if she complained that her legs would dissolve. When she'd suggested he should be a personal trainer, he'd blushed. 'Too personal.' The shyness surprised her.

He worked as a barista three streets away. Ellen had never had bitter coffee at Nicky's flat.

'He's still doing her bidding.' Ellen held out the apple. 'Sorry. You finish it.'

'You're taking sides again.' Nicky's observation stung. He took the apple but didn't bite into it.

'There are sides. He should quit defending the indefensible.' Mark's belief in their dad's innocence was unfathomable. As far as she was concerned, Bill Clewer had lied and Mark was aiding this duplicity by keeping his head in the sand, year after year, hoping it would all go away.

'You can be friends, though. Go on dates.' Nicky leaned on the kitchen surface. Picking up a knife, he slowly began to pare the apple and the peel came away in one serpentine coil. A small knife, too. It could fit in his pocket.

'I want to be part of a family, Nicky. I want somebody to care about me.' A miserly whine and she regretted the implication that she couldn't look after herself. She had always looked after herself. She was sick of the responsibility.

'You've always got me.' He put the knife and apple down and

drew her into his embrace. They were strong arms with tattoos extending from shoulder to wrists. He could crush her if he wanted to. His thrumming heartbeats were little more than pitter patters against her chest. Hers thundered with confusion.

'Why did you have to be gay?' She had asked that question many times.

'Why did you have to be a girl?' The usual response.

She pushed him away and changed tack. 'How is the world of men?'

'Horrendous.' He swept his hand across his brow. 'I've not been laid in days.'

'No bikers on the horizon?'

The walls of Nicky's bedsit were covered with posters of motorbikes. And men. Men on bikes to be precise. Men wearing leathers or tattooed from neck to ankle. He wasn't that interested in the bikes.

'Oh, there are always bikers, honey. Always. I've just been working tedious extra shifts.'

More giggles. He chopped the apple into quarters and handed one back to her. 'Eat. You look like a wraith.'

'I'm fine. I've been running every day.'

'Good for you. But remember to eat.'

Freddie lectured her too. Frequently. Thin girls aren't attractive. Men like boobs and bums.

Nicky didn't know about Freddie. Nobody knew about him. She liked keeping it a secret; a trait that must run in the family. One day Freddie would be obsolete and she would stop sending messages and he wouldn't need to know why. She fancied meeting him first and thanking him in person for propping her up when everyone else watched her fall down.

She ate the apple, not because she was hungry, but because Nicky had asked her to, and she needed friends. And she would meet Mark again because he was family. Real family. It was time to let him back in and have him prove to her that he was man enough to look after her. Freddie had competition.

7

Julianna

The first time Julianna met Mark, she had gone away convinced he was hiding something, perhaps an obsession for Hettie, and that was the reason why Chris had dumped his file right in Julianna's line of sight.

During their second meeting they fine-tuned their tactics for trapping the fleet car manager. Mark called her Mrs Baptiste. There never had been a Mrs Alex Woodfall, only Ms Julianna Baptiste; she had proudly kept her family name. It was unfortunate error, but not uncommon. She corrected him, including the pronunciation, perhaps too sharply, then found herself blurting out the reason; Alex's sordid affair with his secretary. Mark sympathised with a few appropriate questions. Was it long ago? Nearly eighteen months. Divorced? A quickie, neither of them wanted to go to court. She even admitted she had literally thrown Alex out of the front door.

'Formidable. Black belt in something?' Mark asked.

'Yes. A few of them.'

She liked his honesty and directness, the way he spoke what was on his mind instead of sugar coating it. She also noted he stared at her when he shouldn't. She tried to act like an adult and not squirm in her seat.

Snapping shots of the carpool manager at the petrol station, she ruminated on the painting of the bower, which hung right in front of Mark's desk; the abstract depiction of a lady's chamber hidden amongst leaves and branches. An allegory alluding to a covert love affair? Or was he simply expressing an infatuation with his boss's wife, which wasn't exactly healthy either. Each time she thought of the bower, she played out possible scenes until they reached some unsavoury conclusion. At that point, stuck in a car conducting a rather tedious stakeout, she realised she was still jealous of Hettie. Mark might have a fondness for the boss's wife, but she was beyond his reach and he wasn't a fantasist. All he had of hers was a painting on the wall. It struck Julianna as ludicrous, almost insulting, to think she wanted him for herself. Then, what the heck, why shouldn't she have some fun in life. It wasn't as if she planned to recreate the Paris weekend.

The next visit to his office, they went through the photographs she had taken.

She had an itch that needed scratching, the subliminal kind of curiosity that she often had before questioning a suspect. Alone with Mark in his office was a good opportunity to find out what he thought of Haynes.

'So, Mr Haynes has really taken you under his wing. He's invited you to the Opportunitas fundraiser. Most employees are way down the pecking order for an invitation.'

He had stopped writing when she mentioned the fundraiser. 'How did you know about the invite?'

'I'm on the security team, remember? I get to see the list of invitees. Your name was on it.' Including a blank space for an extra person to accompany him. Julianna wasn't on that particular list; she would be otherwise engaged that night. She needed the extra money.

He tapped his pen on the paper and shrugged. 'It's because I was Hettie's accountant. I helped sort out a problem she was having with overseas payments. She has a gallery… but you know that.'

She picked up a photograph and pretended to look at it. 'I thought you worked at Daneswan?'

'I did. It's no big deal, okay, he offered me the opportunity to help with Hettie's accounts. She's brilliant at art, but rubbish at numbers. She won't let Jackson get involved. She likes her independence.'

The painting on the wall of Mark's office was a reward; it made sense, more personal than a bonus payment. But why had Mark told her it was Haynes who was his friend? 'You met Haynes, and he gave you—'

'No.' Mark retrieved the photograph from her. 'It all started because I chatted up Hettie in a wine bar. I didn't know who she was, I just bumped into her, and thought… well, I didn't pay attention to the man keeping an eye on her. She took my business card with her.'

Julianna tried hard not to smile. Poor Mark, hoping that a business card might forge more than a working relationship. 'She would have given it to Jackson, and he, obviously, knows Daneswan, since he owns it.'

'I had an interview, and he gave me Hettie's account. Officially, it was all through Daneswan. Nothing private about it.' There was a marked irritation in his voice.

'He likes you then. Jackson has invited you to his house for dinner, too.' She bit her lip. 'That's on a list somewhere too. I don't mean to pry.' She did, she was hopelessly in love with prying. 'I just assumed you met him somewhere, maybe in the past. What a lucky guy you are, falling on your feet here.'

'Lucky? I suppose. I don't think Jackson depends on luck.' He wasn't paying attention to the photographs.

'No, you're right. He doesn't. Not if Hettie's involved.'

He was staring at the watercolour on the wall, his dark eyes focused, his mind somewhere else.

He took a call, arranging to meet somebody called Ellen. He apologised to her, this Ellen, for not knowing she was a vegetarian and suggested a fish restaurant. A new woman in his life, Julianna surmised. She hid her disappointment. It was probably for the best. Emotional attachments with work colleagues should be avoided. Still, it was an unfortunate turn of events.

A hiatus descended while Mark was dispatched on training courses and Chris hijacked Julianna for bodyguard duties. She drove the Hayneses to a midday appointment at Hettie's doctor. They spoke about a recent dinner party and Mark's name popped up. Julianna's grip on the steering wheel tightened. She avoided rear-view mirror glimpses, and focused her acute hearing on the conversation instead.

'You invited Mark. Why?' Hettie asked.

'You know why,' Jackson said, in an off-hand manner.

'I don't. You know I don't understand these games you play with people. It's cruel. If you'd help—'

Jackson spoke softly. 'It's for the best. He has to find out for himself. I'm just keeping an eye on things.'

The frustrating snippets of information seemed almost for Julianna's benefit, not Hettie's.

'He thinks you're his friend. Our friend. I don't like it,' Hettie said.

'He's a grown man. I'm giving him opportunities, contacts. It's his choice if he uses them.'

Julianna's heart skipped a beat when he mentioned contacts. She flicked the A/C vent towards her face and hoped the icy blast masked her reaction.

Hettie made no attempt to lower her voice. 'But now you say his sister is involved.'

'Ellen? She's on the fringe. Chris pointed out the family is partly estranged. In any case, she's barely out of her teens.'

Julianna smothered a gasp. His sister! So she had overheard Mark arranging to meet his sister. It made a difference. A big difference. If he was free…

'Well,' Hettie said markedly, 'I'm just saying all this because I like Mark. He's a good accountant. I gave him a painting when you took him off me for this new job.'

'Good with numbers, yes. People? He needs more guidance. He needs to meet the right people.'

'And what if he meets the wrong people? Isn't that just as dangerous after what happened?'

Jackson made a "pfft" sound. 'I made sure the police didn't expose him. I need him to stay sharp, though.'

Against her wishes, the hairs on the back of Julianna's neck stood on end.

'Well, don't let this get out of hand, Jackson, or I shall be very cross.'

The conversation went no further: they had arrived at the clinic. Jackson had engineered everything: Mark had contacted Julianna because he had been given her name by Chris, Jackson's confidante and spy in the office. And, maybe, instead of Jackson telling Hettie to hush, he had allowed Julianna to eavesdrop, leaving her hungry to know more.

The whole business of the painting was nothing, a quirky detail she could now discard.

The final project meeting with Mark was prior to the fundraiser; he had complied a report for the police. He flirted with her again. Not overtly, or even consciously. She assimilated those nuances and acknowledged the appeal remained intact even after the conversation in the car. Hettie might have encouraged Julianna's curiosity, provoked a touch of rivalry, but now Julianna was independently possessive of Mark. She liked the idea she fancied a man with a mystery to solve and it made the seduction doubly thrilling. Unlike Alex, she would invest very little of herself in Mark. She had nothing to lose.

8
Mark

Winter

Every October the Haynes foundation, Opportunitas, held its fund-raising event at the Savoy Hotel. Jackson cast aside business rivalries and invited executives, clients and dignitaries to hobnob with rent-by-the-hour celebrities. Mark didn't fit into any of those categories. Not fitting in was becoming a feature of his life in London. The dinner party was a practice run for the charity ball, and Mark attended out of both curiosity and a need to hone his social skills to the next level.

The exclusive party was held, naturally, at Fasleigh House, the vast mansion Jackson inhabited at the weekends, and which required a train journey and a chauffeur driven car to reach. The soiree involved formal black-tie attire, yet still managed to be bizarrely pedestrian and relaxed. Much of that was down to Hettie.

The food was exquisitely delicious, each dish orchestrated to lead to the next and served by choreographed caterers who swooped along the table when the clatter of cutlery subsided, signifying the end of a course.

'Mark,' Hettie said softly, leaning across the polished oak. 'Missing your favourite client?'

'Of course. How's my replacement doing?' Mark said, awkwardly wishing he was still her personal accountant.

A baby's cry cut through the merriment. An unashamedly resplendent Hettie announced her apologies and swept out, her golden dress and sequins glittering under the lamplight.

She brought the restless child into the dining room and Mark, unable to look away, watched her breastfeed the baby. She didn't bother to cover her breast and the small fingers thrashed, clawing tiny nails into her mother's flesh. Hettie's lack of embarrassment clashed with everyone else's discomfort. Except Mark felt none of it. He was in awe of her confidence; the display of maternal instinct riding roughshod over etiquette.

Hettie's eyelids drooped. The baby lay in her arms, satiated and placid. The group decamped for coffee in the sitting room and Jackson retrieved his sleeping daughter from the exhausted Hettie and returned her upstairs. The atmosphere changed when Jackson returned. She curled up with her head on his lap. The conversation then meandered around the room, never anchoring itself to one person or theme. From Jackson's personal accountant, Edmund, to the shrill-voiced art dealer, whose name Mark cared to forget, then back to the retired police inspector, Graham, who fiddled with his wedding ring and never mentioned his absent wife. Of the dozen people surrounding the Hayneses, only Mark worked for Haynes Financial.

The eclectic group had nothing in common, no obvious connections. Drawn together by one man, they possessed the wit to maintain polite discourse without ever touching on personal matters. Their words danced and weaved, never revealing why they were friends of Jackson. Hettie slept. If anyone found it rude, they all had the decency to keep quiet. Mark struggled to stay focused. From the outside looking in, he wanted to belong, but they weren't his crowd. He had no crowd.

Graham, the policeman, wasn't comfortable either.

'First time here?' Mark asked him while the others chatted.

'What? No, no.' Graham drained his wine glass. 'A few times now. I help out with Opportunitas; bit of liaising with my former colleagues. Missing persons stuff, mostly. Jackson has his circle of friends. I'm like you, just one of them; pop up now and again. He has excellent caterers.' He patted his portly stomach.

Following the Fasleigh party, Mark slipped off Jackson's radar; Mark wasn't worthy after all. Consequently he hadn't expected an invitation to the Winter Ball, especially one hand-delivered to his desk by Jackson's PA.

Handing the embossed invitation to the doorman of the grand hotel, Mark entered the function suite and, catching his reflection in a mirror, adjusted his bowtie. The air hummed with voices, laughter and distant music. Waiters drifted through the throng with champagne and canapés on platters. The buffet, which was laid out on a golden cloth, was a work of art: spirals of carrots, twirls of greenery impregnated with pink salmon, and beads of caviar. The centre piece, an ice sculpture of a swan, was melting under the lights. People were snapping selfies with their phones. Jackson had paid for the food out of his own pocket. Eating it seemed calamitous, an insult; nobody wanted to ruin the culinary backdrop. Mark popped a cherry tomato in his mouth.

Straightening himself up, he circulated, building repartee using executive style soundbites. The invitation was for two – but he hadn't brought Ellen along. Although they had rekindled a functional relationship, they were different creatures when it came to social occasions. Mark closed in on himself; Ellen unfolded. She also drank a lot.

During a meal out, she had consumed a whole bottle of red wine, quaffed it like cordial. He had picked up the bill. The next time he had picked a cheaper vintage. She didn't notice.

For four weeks, he had entertained her and as long as they steered away from the elephant in the room, they got on fine. The elephant stomped about in Mark's head most days, but Ellen was adamant it wasn't for discussion. Her glibness riled him. Ellen brushed her mother under the rug and, for good measure, threw her entire childhood under it too – not for discussion – and boyfriends, who needed them? She had talked about Nicky, work and digging and had a way of making frivolity seem important; a foil for his tendency to be sombre and serious.

Instead of bringing her to the ball, he had insisted she attended a wedding somewhere in Oxfordshire. A friend of a friend from work. She wasn't keen. He had coaxed her into going with a bribe: money for a dress.

'You might meet somebody,' he had said.

It had prompted the usual defence. 'Why would I want to meet a somebody?' Good point. It was the sort of thing he might say. Why tie your life to someone else?

Ellen had gone in the end with this friend. She would thank him afterwards.

His first tour of the ballroom confirmed that Jackson relied on an eclectic web of friends and contacts to support his charity. Mark shook hands with Jackson's property developer, a lazy-eyed man who spoke at length about the cost of running women's refuges in the heart of a major city. Then Jackson's personal accountant, the elegant Edmund, whom Mark had met at Jackson's dinner party sauntered over to greet Mark, who was smiling from the nose down. Thankfully, Edmund didn't want to talk shop. The other party guest was the police inspector, Saddler, who had brought along his narrow-hipped wife. Her nose twitched like a playful rabbit and she giggled over an empty glass of bubbly. The sequin-festooned dress, which hung off her shoulders, was as limp as her nervous handshake. She opened her mouth to say something but the policeman scowled and reeled her off in a different direction.

After a second circuit, Mark spied a familiar face standing by the wall. She was dressed no differently to an invitee but she wasn't a guest; a coil of wire trailed down from behind one ear and she had no drink in her hand. She scanned the room, eyes roving, never dwelling on one person for more than a second, except for him. Whether she was doing it deliberately, Mark couldn't tell, but her pattern of observations definitely included looking at him. Curiosity got the better of him and he sauntered over to her to lean his shoulder against the wall. He folded his arms and cocked his head to one side.

'Hi, Mark.' Her attempt at nonchalance failed. She fidgeted with her earpiece.

'Julianna. Haven't seen you for a couple of weeks. What have you been up to?'

'Oh, this and that. Keep doing weekend work for extra money. Tonight being an example.'

She was avoiding eye contact now, so overtly, he nearly laughed out loud. For an expert in blending into her environment, she wasn't trying very hard. He shouldn't mock. Julianna had a challenging job marking the Haynes family wherever they went. Hettie in particular wasn't keen on the extra layers of protection. She had griped to Mark when he queried the cost of CCTV cameras in the gallery. Not for the art, she had glowered, for me. Jackson prized his wife beyond any artwork.

'Where is she?' he asked.

'Over there. Chris is back by the door.'

She gestured and he spotted her. Hettie Haynes had bounced back from pregnancy brilliantly. Her dress, a turquoise number with silver slithers, was moulded around her hourglass hips and bountiful breasts. She shook hands, moved, spoke and shook hands again. The perfect hostess.

'She doesn't look as tired as last time I saw her,' he said absent-mindedly.

'She weaned the kid on to solids and since then the kid's been sleeping like a baby should. Sleeping.'

Mark raised an eyebrow at Julianna's knowledge of Hettie's breast-feeding status.

'Drove her last week and she made a point of saying how much better things were now that she has several successive hours sleep a night.' She turned her face fractionally to Mark's. 'I don't ask, she just spews this stuff out.'

'You're not keen on babies then.' Mark couldn't imagine Julianna spewing anything. Babies were different.

It wasn't intended as a question, but Julianna pursed her lips, then smirked. 'Not other people's; I can't help it.'

He tapped his nose a few times. 'I'll not tell her. Diplomacy suits you.'

'Comes with the job. One mustn't get too attached to the client.'

'He wasn't in the car then?'

She laughed. 'Oh no. Definitely a different atmosphere when he's in the car.'

Jackson would monopolise any conversation and make it his own. It explained her snark.

'She's on the move. I'll have to change location. Wouldn't do to lose her; that would be a serious black mark.' Julianna toyed with the piece of wire around her neck.

'String you up by the balls?' Mark chortled, then abruptly cringed.

A smiley-faced Julianna rescued him. 'Well, more likely my nipples, don't you think?' she said slyly and with a pronounced wink. She walked, purposely and carefully, to the other side of the room.

Mark raked his fingers through his hair. What a tease she had become since their first meeting. Was it a genuine attempt at provoking him into action? He needed more evidence. He rolled back the conversation to what she had said about Hettie. Each time he met somebody familiar with Jackson and Hettie Haynes he wondered how well they knew the couple. Julianna undoubtedly had insider information and was bound to secrecy about it.

A familiar voice spoke by his ear. 'Mark, enjoying the evening?'

Mark shifted from his position against the wall and turned to face Jackson. The man was imposing; it didn't matter whether he was seated or standing, he occupied space that couldn't be seen, only felt, and it wasn't due to his height, although he was taller than Mark, but simply through his demeanour and those piercing eyes. Jackson Haynes maintained the uncanny ability to present both a ruthless and charming smile at the same time. Mark had been caught lounging by a wall looking disinterested and Jackson would want to know why. Mark decided the best policy was honesty.

'Yes, thank you. Resting my back and chatting to Julianna Baptiste. We've done some work together. However, she has to keep tabs on Hettie, so she's vaporised, spy-like into the horde.' He gestured with his empty wine glass towards the far end of the room.

'My wife likes her.' Jackson trained his eyes on Hettie before moving his focus back to Mark. 'Come, there's somebody I'd like you to meet.'

Mark followed Jackson through the bustling room towards the smaller antechamber with more chairs and a thinner crowd. There, Mark was introduced to a man who was the spitting image of Jackson.

'Mark Clewer, my brother, Luke,' Jackson said. Mark shook hands with the facsimile. 'And this is the lovely Sophia, Luke's partner.'

More handshakes and with introductions completed, Jackson wandered away.

There was an awkward pause. 'I take it you work for Jackson?' the Jackson clone asked, except Luke was shorter, and sparser about the shoulders and thighs.

'Yes. Forensic accountancy team.'

Mark grabbed a fresh glass of wine off a passing waiter. The couple declined the top up.

'So what do you two do?' Mark asked, spinning out the conversation on a weak thread, one he immediately regretted.

'I'm a barrister and Sophia is a solicitor. Ah, not a fan of our profession.' Luke offered a half-hearted chuckle.

The flash of mild disgust was brief – milliseconds – but noted.

'Christ, I'm sorry, I must appear very rude. You'd think I was used to it being an accountant. All we need is an estate agent and we could start a club for thieving bastards who shaft people.' Given the hardening of Luke's face, he had failed with his injection of humour. If only people were like formulas. Numbers in, numbers out. No guarded words or dancing around issues that weren't up for discussion or might cause offence. He had been let down by lawyers; it wasn't a statement of disrespect, only the truth.

Sophia continued to smile. Mark knocked back a mouthful of alcohol. Women, why were they so persistent?

'Don't worry,' said Sophia. 'Since Luke is a prosecution barrister he's used to being despised by the criminal underclass. I, on the other hand, do legal aid defence. Makes for some interesting end of day conversations.'

Mark chewed on his lip. If she wasn't put off by his ill-conceived remark, would she help him out with finding a solicitor? It was worth raking up the sordid family history to find out.

'I, unfortunately, have been involved in many protracted legal battles on behalf of my father; none of them had any good outcomes. I'm in search of a new solicitor to help with his appeal. My mum won't have anything to do with the last one.' Mark had procrastinated for weeks about his father's appeal status. The documentation, including statements and police reports, had been sent down to his flat, the boxes dumped in the corner of his guest room.

'Sounds stressful,' Sophia said sympathetically. Luke was staring over her head. He had vacated the conversation.

'Luke, Sophia, you came after all.' Hettie was hidden behind Luke and she greeted her brother-in-law and his partner with a swift kiss on each of their cheeks. Mark looked away, embarrassed. She hadn't touched him, or even acknowledged his presence.

'Couldn't stay away. Sophia's pro-bono work for sex workers puts her at the top of Jackson's guest list,' Luke said.

Sophia blushed.

'And so she should be,' said Hettie. 'Mark, how are you?' She quickly ran her hand down his sleeve and touched the cheap cuff-link. He was uncomfortably warm and the bow-tie was strangling him. He wished they were alone like they used to be when he met her.

Was Julianna watching them? Had she seen the little gesture of familiarity? Would it bother her? It meant nothing, of course; Hettie was a tactile person. What if that was why Jackson had Hettie followed everywhere – the possessive husband seeking any excuse to find fault with his wife? All those meetings Mark had had in her gallery, going over her accounts. She was never alone.

'Good.' A lie – why had he come tonight? 'I'm delighted to be here.'

'No companion?' Hettie asked.

'At a wedding.'

'Pity. You didn't go with her?'

'And miss this?' Miss what? He had little money to offer Opportunitas and no connection to its charity work. All he had done was meet a few people, smile and shake hands. What exactly was Jackson expecting him to do? He didn't want to discuss Ellen with Hettie, who sensibly directed the conversation back to the evening's events.

Jackson's shadow man, Chris Moran, appeared at her side and whispered in her ear.

'Speech time, folks. I've been ordered, no rephrase that, requested to direct you to the main salon for the obligatory thank yous.' Hettie nudged her brother-in-law. 'I have to go corral the guests.'

Sophia offered to help. Hettie weaved between people, smiling and gesturing to the double doors.

'At least Jackson is short and to the point,' Luke said. Jackson's succinct style of speaking was known in the workplace, too.

Luke was right, Jackson's salutations and gratitude was brief and delivered in a congenial tone. After a round of applause, many guests left. With no taxi ordered, Mark wondered if he should make his way home, or wait to see if things took a different tack now that the formal proceedings were over.

As if to read his mind, the familiar deep voice of his host spoke in his ear. 'Don't leave yet.'

Turning to look over his shoulder, Mark saw Jackson usher a departing couple toward the exit. Jackson ebbed and flowed amongst his guests in a tidal fashion, his voice, more than anything, carried through the crowd.

The diehard guests congregated near the buffet having midnight snacks – the swan had lost its fine neck and head. Mark helped himself to a vol-au-vent. Sophia appeared at his side, without Luke.

'Look, I may not be the right person, but if you want to send me details of your father's case, I'll look it over. Maybe I can help or recommend somebody else,' she said with a gentle southern drawl similar to Julianna's Cornish one.

Her suggestion stunned Mark. 'Why? You don't know me.'

She touched his arm. He didn't flinch. 'Because, Mark, kindred spirits need to stick together, don't they?' She retracted her hand.

'Kindred?'

'Helping the innocent or wrongly accused is something of a calling. Few lawyers are willing to stick at it.'

'I'm not a lawyer. I mean, it's a family matter.'

She gave a small shrug. 'And you're a friend of Jackson's. Need I say any more. Let me get a pen and paper and I'll write my email address down for you. Send me the judgement summary. Let me help you.' She spoke with a sincerity that flummoxed Mark. First Jackson had taken Mark under his wing, now Sophia. He didn't want pity or sympathy. He wanted the whole damn business resolved once and for all.

'If you have that calling, I'm not going to say no.' Immediately, he regretted his insolence. 'Thank you, is what I meant to say. You see, Dad's case isn't…. we're talking a life sentence…'

Sophia loaded her plate with sprigs of salad leaves. 'If he's innocent, does it matter? I've defended those accused of murder. Rape. The law is fallible. It fucks up when it shouldn't. People like me, and you, we shouldn't be dissuaded by what others think. Okay?'

A crusader. A passionate believer in putting things right. Sophia didn't understand Mark's motives weren't so pure. He was the dutiful son, nothing more. He hoped for innocence, if only because it would justify the cost, and the years of dealing with an insufferable mother. Ellen, even if she didn't want to hear the truth, deserved it too.

'Okay. Thank you,' he said with sincerity.

Luke joined them, looping his arm around his girlfriend and the conversation diverted into safer territory. Hettie approached them with shallow steps. Her eyelids were heavy, as if the mascara was laden with lead.

'How are you bearing up' Sophia asked.

'My feet are killing me,' she whispered.

'Why don't you sit down?'

Hettie blushed and rolled her eyes up to the ceiling. 'Because...' She peered over her shoulder. There was no sign of Jackson.

Mark didn't understand marriage, why somebody had to have that control, that level of influence over another. Wasn't love about equality? 'You need permission to sit down?' he scoffed.

'No!' Hettie said firmly. 'He would send me for a rest; up in our suite. He knows I'm not back up to strength yet. I've had tonsillitis. Evey is far more demanding than Noah ever was during the night. No, that would be it. For the whole night, so to speak, well probably.' She lowered her head, and leaned toward the group. 'The kids are with the nanny.'

'Oh.' Sophia's mouth stayed open.

Luke laughed, loudly. 'Oh, Hettie, I'm sorry.'

'Fuck. Me and my gob.' Hettie groaned. 'I'm not even bloody well drinking. And my tits are leaking. I'm going to need to express soon.'

Mark had filled his evening with regrettable misunderstandings. 'You should rest. You do look tired,' he said. 'Julianna is hovering. She thinks you've passed your bedtime.'

Julianna's expression of boredom remained her chief definition.

'She wants me to sit down,' said Hettie. 'Once I'm tucked upstairs she's off duty and can hit the bar before it closes. Oh sorry, guys, I'm beat. Watch. See how long it takes him to notice my arse taking up residence on one of those comfortable chairs.' She pointed to the corner of the room.

Her little audience watched with muted hilarity as she carefully nestled in the chosen chair. A few minutes later Jackson honed in on his wife. He bent down and whispered in her ear. Helping her up to her feet, he signalled to Julianna and she escorted Hettie to the lobby. As Hettie passed close to her amused admirers, she gave a small wave and a grin. She didn't seem that unhappy. Perhaps he had whispered something unexpected to her.

Luke agreed with Mark's observation. 'She's got my big brother wrapped around her little finger. Nobody thinks it, but that's the secret of their relationship.'

Julianna returned from the penthouse suite minus her radio device and headed straight for the bar. At the buffet table, she built a mountain of food on her plate. Mark continued to chat to Luke and Sophia. The initial frostiness he felt toward the couple had evaporated. He should stop firing his emotions from the hip and concentrate on using his brain before opening his mouth.

Julianna stabbed at the food with a fork. Nobody was talking to her. Mark caught her eye and gestured. She shook her head. He insisted with a stern stare of disapproval, then a smile of welcome. Reluctantly, she came over to join him.

'Off duty?' Mark asked.

'Yes. She's gone to bed. Had to prop her up in the lift.' Julianna licked her lips. 'Sorry, ravenous.'

'Do you know Luke and Sophia?'

She didn't and he introduced her to Jackson's brother and partner.

'So you work together?' Sophia asked.

'We've done some work together,' Julianna said. 'I've a background in criminal investigations.' She turned to Mark. 'Have the files on that case gone to the prosecution?'

'Yep. The police will decide whether to charge the others involved.'

Luke raised an eyebrow. 'You investigate fraud?'

'This was a case of embezzlement. The company car fleet manager. Nothing original, he copied the scam after reading about it in the newspaper. Julianna did some covert surveillance and we caught him red-handed.'

'Car pool manager? How does he commit fraud?' Sophia asked.

'With a little help from his friends.' Julianna sipped on her wine before continuing. 'We wanted to catch the guy in the act to prove it. So I parked close by the filling station and watched, waited. Another humdrum day in the life of me, rather like playing bodyguard.'

'Complaining, Baptiste?'

Julianna cringed and edged sideways to allow Jackson to join the little circle.

'No sir, wouldn't dream of it. Talking about a surveillance job I did for Mark last month.'

Jackson shifted his attention from Julianna to Mark. 'An internal case?'

'The pool car manager.'

'Ah yes. I saw the dismissal notice.' Jackson nodded and tossed back a mouthful of spirits.

'Please explain,' said Sophia. 'I don't understand what he did.'

'It's simple,' Mark explained. 'He fills the pool cars with fuel, ready for them to go out again. There are several fuelling stations near to the private garage where the cars are parked overnight. He takes a few a day. He has a company fuel card. He can only buy fuel or oil, nothing else. Now and again, he meets a mate in the forecourt. His mate fills his car with fuel and is given an excellent discount on the pump total. He hands over cash and our embezzler pays for his mate's fuel with the company card and pockets the cash. Turns out he had lots of mates.'

Julianna joined in. 'Caught three on camera on separate days. Trouble was he was getting greedy. Mileage records and fuel consumption didn't match up and the whole thing was exposed.'

'Crafty,' Sophia said.

'Stupid,' said Jackson. 'Did he profess his innocence?' he asked Mark.

'God, yes. He went through quite a long list of explanations until we showed him the photos and then he caved in. Unfortunately, he won't give the identities of his mates.'

'He's afraid of them,' said Julianna. 'Not sure if "mates" is the correct definition. He's probably embroiled with some local villains and it got out of hand.'

Luke cleared his throat. 'In any case, they could claim that they simply gave him the money to pay the cashier. They won't mention the fuel card. Plead ignorance. It's much harder to prosecute them.'

'So you wouldn't prosecute them?' Mark was disappointed. The real criminals never got caught.

Luke shook his head. 'Waste of money.'

Mark lifted his glass. 'The case was made by Julianna. So thank you, Mrs Baptiste, for your humdrum day in a car!'

'Ms Baptiste,' she said swiftly.

The curtness was marked, even Jackson's head turned. Mark understood bitterness, how it crept out of the shadows and into everyday things. He had forgotten her marital status; she had mentioned her ex-husband during a meeting about the fuel scandal, had told him not to call her missus and that she preferred a neutral title. Or just Julianna. She had flashed him a pretty smile. It was the first hint that she liked him. He was convinced she liked him. Or wanted something from him.

'Are you okay?' Sophia asked Mark. 'You look flushed.'

'Fine. It's hot in here.' Julianna swallowed a mouthful of cheese. She looked up and realised her mistake.

How bloody embarrassing, for him as well as her.

Jackson purloined Mark for a trip to the bar. The two men, of near equal height, leaned against the counter and avoid each other's eyes. Mark estimated Jackson's bar tab would be substantial by the end of the night. He resisted smiling. Jackson's wealth went beyond numbers; there was a good measure of inherent philanthropy.

Jackson stooped a little over Mark's shoulder. 'How's Ellen? Recovered from her burn?' Jackson asked. The barman was quietly working his way through their order.

Mark speculated if everybody he met were Jackson's spies, then he remembered the quiet conversation at Fasleigh House the previous month. He had referred to the freak coffee spillage encounter with his sister, which Mark had used to illustrate life's strange twists of fate. In the fog of alcohol he had mentioned he hadn't seen his sister for a few years. Jackson had the ability to latch onto seemingly unimportant things and read beyond the headlines.

'Oh, it was superficial. She's at a wedding today.'

'Why not let her have some fun at my club. Bring her along the next time I'm there. I'll let you know when I'll be there next.' Jackson owned a ridiculously expensive nightclub in the West End. He used it to attract celebrities and then milked them for his fund-raisers.

Mark almost said no thanks. Ellen in a nightclub – would he have to be her chaperone, watch how much she drank, whom she talked to? It wasn't his idea of a fun night out and Ellen wouldn't take kindly to his big brother role. However, if he turned Jackson down, he doubted there would be a second chance.

'I'd be delighted to bring Ellen along, naturally. Honoured,' he said swiftly.

Jackson's motives for befriending Mark remained cloaked. Mark suspected it had something to do with what had happened at the Haydocks accountancy company, his previous employer. That incident hung on his heels no matter how hard he tried to shake off its legacy. To cover his tracks he had moved three times since arriving in London. Eventually, luck won out and rather like his chance encounter with Ellen in the coffee shop, he had had a similar one with Hettie in the wine bar. That fortuitous event had led to a personal interview with Jackson at his headquarters.

It had been a congenial, yet probing interview, in which Jackson had picked apart Mark's work at Daneswan, the accountancy firm that recruited him after he had left Manchester. Remarkably, Jackson hadn't asked about Haydocks. Battling the urge to confess what he had inadvertently unleashed all those months ago, he had opted to keep quiet and presented himself as loyal, hardworking. Trustworthy. It came as a surprise that the interview ended on a high point: Jackson asked him to tidy up his wife's accounts.

When they had shaken hands, Jackson had held it longer than he had expected. 'You won't be at Daneswan for much longer, Mark. You'll be moved here to my HQ and the Forensic Accountancy division as soon as there's an opening.'

The weird thing was Mark hadn't expressed any hint of wanting to shift into forensic accountancy. It excited him: delving into the dark world of fraud and embezzling and he had the right skills for the role. But Haynes Financial Services recruited the most experienced for those kinds of jobs. Mark lacked professional qualifications.

'Thank you,' he had said with a dry throat. He wanted to know why, but Jackson had steered him out of the door. 'My PA will put you in contact with my wife.' On the office threshold, Jackson had thumped his back, nearly knocking Mark off his feet.

Three months later, Jackson's promise had been delivered.

As the barman loaded the tray with drinks, offering to bring them over, Mark glanced over his shoulder, and caught the rosy cheeked Julianna staring at him. She hurriedly disposed of her empty plate on a nearby table. Her furtive evening of spying led Mark to wonder whether she cared for the Haynes family or not. He had always imagined the role of bodyguard as soulless and detached. Was she really prepared to step in and put her life on the line for them?

He and Jackson re-joined the group and helped distribute the drinks. He missed Hettie's frivolity.

'Hettie still tires easily,' Mark said. Julianna's eyes flashed bright under the halogens. He wasn't sure why he was thinking of Hettie when he was consciously looking at another woman.

Jackson pursed his lips. 'She's been overdoing it. Trying to run the gallery and nursing Evey at the same time. She's had trouble with the concept of owning a business and taking maternity leave.'

Sophia frowned. 'She told me she was going to get some art graduates in to provide extra help.'

'I pointed out that interns require a great deal of supervision.' Jackson fingered his glass, 'So I told her to appoint an experienced gallery manager as maternity cover.'

'I suspect that didn't go down well,' Luke said.

'No,' Jackson said, dryly, 'But I didn't give her a choice. So she found one.'

Mark recalled the lengthy discussions with Hettie about her wish to keep her business independent of her husband's conglomeration. 'She would have resisted that idea,' Mark said.

Jackson raised his glass to his lips and paused. 'She did. Briefly.'

Mark expected something on Julianna's face; a frown of disapproval on behalf of Hettie, but nothing, not even a shadow crossed her face. A true professional or an unconcerned individual?

Jackson continued. 'Since Frances started work last month Hettie's health has improved considerably. The doctors had threatened her with a tonsillectomy. That scared her too.'

She had a strong dislike of blood, so an operation would be a frightening prospect.

The dynamics of Jackson's marriage were not up for further discussion and he moved off with Luke and Sophia in tow, leaving Julianna with Mark.

He would always crave for Hettie, but he had to accept he had no place in her life. Once his client, always the boss's wife, she wasn't his friend. She would never be his lover.

He needed a distraction. A lure. Somebody to guide him away from the unattainable. No love, no commitment. Just companionship. Sex. God, he missed sex.

Julianna hadn't moved. She was waiting. Unlike Hettie, Julianna wasn't stunning, although her blended ethnicity brought out the best of her attractiveness. She had wavy black hair that didn't quite hold its place when she tied it back. The rogue locks added to rather than subtracted from her appeal. Her plump, and kissable, lips were a little wide, her cheekbones lofty, a hint of flatness to her nose and her chin angular and masculine. Her chocolate eyes were astounding. Beautiful, no. Attractive, yes. When it came to romance, he wondered if she was as impartial as he was. During one previous meeting, she had slipped out a few remarks about her ex, whom she detested with a loathing that was impressive, while inferring things that made him wonder if she missed some aspects of her marriage. Mark had no point of reference. He had no plans to marry.

'Still no replacement Mr Woodfall?' he asked tentatively.

'Nope. There isn't going to be another Mr Woodfall. Learnt my lesson,' she replied.

What had he to lose? Upset her and she would likely walk off. It wasn't as if their paths crossed regularly. He could live with the fallout.

'But, I think you miss Mr Woodfall in other ways, don't you?' he said softly.

She shoulders stiffened and as her eyes widened, her firm chin hung a fraction lower. The stunned expression made her even more attractive. Was he as worthy, as agreeable in appearance? Mark was honest enough to admit he had flaws: he wished his hair was lighter, his skin smoother.

'Possibly.' She spoke through a small parting of her lips.

It wasn't a no. So he shifted closer, making sure nobody was in earshot.

'That's a yes, Julianna. Admit it.'

She blushed and dropped her eyes. Fancy that, he thought, she wasn't that battle hardened.

He leaned into her ear. 'I'm not going to tell you what to do, but you weren't watching just her, were you?'

She snatched a rogue lock of hair and shoved it behind her ear. The silence answered him. No face slap, no stomping on his toes. She was a martial arts expert, something to which she had alluded when she described how she had thrown her husband out of the house, and she probably could make a humiliating point of it in front of the small gathering. But she hadn't. Her coyness had surprised him. She'd wanted him to ask.

Immediately there was a problem. 'My apartment is some distance away. It's late, so perhaps—'

'Mine isn't. The divorce was generous in that respect; I got the house.'

They left in a taxi without exchanging a word. They both knew what they wanted. He should feel ashamed, but he didn't. Life was about grabbing opportunities. Each chance encounter of his life had led him to a different place. This was just another one.

9

Julianna

Sitting by her side in the back of the cab, Mark had the decency to stay quiet. Turning to face him she slipped her hand across the seat and tangled her fingers through his and rested them on his lap.

'I'm not afraid of us doing this,' she said, softly. 'This is what I want. I'm over Alex.' Maybe she had just fibbed about Alex, but she wanted to make a point – she was with Mark and he could open up to her. He squeezed her hand in reply. He was remarkably calm, and slightly dopey from the alcohol.

The cab pulled over outside her mews house.

Shutting the front door, she kicked off her shoes. Mark copied her.

'Nice house. Has character, not like my flat.'

So far he had only seen the outside of the terrace house and the narrow hallway with its tiled floor. Character didn't extend to dodgy plumbing and electrics.

'It's small.' And pricey.

'It's a house. Allow yourself the honour of having two floors and stairs. I long for stairs.' He swept his arm up. She didn't need a hint. No script was needed either. The hesitation was due to nerves. It had been nearly two years since Alex last touched her.

'I have a cellar, too.' She instantly regretted mentioning the cellar. 'It's dark…'

He stepped toward her. 'We won't go down there then, because I'd rather see you.'

Mark was clearly plucking chat up lines out from his readymade stash. She didn't need them. Reaching up, she tugged on his bow-tie and pulled it apart.

'I've always wanted to do that.' She twisted the ribbon around her finger. 'Wreck a bow-tie.'

'Good job it's not elasticated. Anything else you'd like to dismantle?'

She grinned. 'Everything.'

'Feel free, but maybe not here. Somewhere more comfortable?' He raised his eyebrows.

Again, she held back, battling the doubts.

'You haven't done this in a while?' he asked.

She shook her head. 'No. Not since I left my husband.' She had lost all interest in sex. Burdened by Alex's lack of remorse, she saw no purpose in acting like him and using sex as an excuse for destroying what dignity she had left. But now a casual acquaintance had rekindled her natural desires; her choked needs were about to be made flesh again.

'I'm flattered that you picked me.' Mark swept a strand of hair out of her eyes.

The smallest of touches was sufficient to unfreeze frozen limbs. They were adults, Jackson had said so himself. Adults made choices and lived with the consequences. She rose up onto her tiptoes, meeting him at eye level. 'I didn't pick you. I want you.' She crossed in front of him to the bottom of the stairs. 'Also, my feet are killing me.' She led him upstairs.

Bathed in the Sunday morning light, Julianna woke first. Mark was snoring softly, one leg lying on top of the duvet and one arm draped across his brow. Their clothes were strewn across the floor. Creeping out of bed, she picked up his white shirt and slipped it on. It just reached the tops of her knees.

Downstairs, she made fresh coffee. She had no clue what he liked for breakfast. She checked the fridge for eggs and bacon. He wasn't a vegetarian, she knew that much about him, but little else. She's spent half the night having sex with a man she barely knew.

She carried the two mugs upstairs. Nudging the bedroom door open with her elbow, she slipped inside. Mark was sitting up in bed, the duvet patted over both his legs and his eyes bleary, but open.

'Ooh, smells good.'

'Here.' She put the mug on his bedside table, then carried her own to the other one.

'Thanks. You're wearing my shirt. That's brave of you.'

She smoothed the tails down and gave a twirl. 'It seemed like the thing to do, you know, wear your man's shirt. All actresses do it.'

'So we're in a film?'

She climbed back into bed and clasped her mug in her hands. 'I feel like I'm in one of those film noir movies. I should be drawing on a cigarette, plumes of smoke coiling above our heads. We're draped in dark shadows, engaged in enigmatic half-sentences about obscure things.'

He stared at her. 'Thank God, because I thought for a minute you were going to burst into song like Bette Midler or Barbara Streisand.' A broad smile spread his lips wider. He had a sweet, boyish smile.

She thumped his arm and nearly spilt her coffee.

'Ow.'

'So…' Another sip, another pause. 'We're here.'

'Yes.' He puffed out his cheeks in contemplation. He needed a shave. During the night, she'd touched those dark bristles with her lips.

'And… this is it?'

He frowned. 'It sounds terribly final.'

Relief bubbled up inside her. A peculiar sensation, because she was determined to be indifferent to everything they'd done.

Mark cleared his throat. 'I hadn't expected you to want what we did last night.'

'Meaning?' She thought they had done everything she wanted, and more.

'Kissing. Cuddling. Those kind of things.'

'Oh.' She had misjudged him again. 'Why not?'

'Because, we both know this isn't about love.' He watched her reaction closely. No blinking, just in case he missed the slightest hint that he had got it wrong.

She faltered, unable to speak. Julianna had never experienced sex like it before. Even before she met Alex, her previous bedfellows were amorous, but lacked any sense of adventure. Julianna sought an edge, a thrill to life. It was the reason she took up martial arts, learnt how to shoot a gun and kicked down doors. Love was Alex's gift, his promise, until he shattered it.

She swallowed a mouthful of scorching coffee. 'No, it's not about love. But it's not one night either, is it?'

He blinked. 'No.'

'We should get to know each other a bit better then. Over cooked breakfast?'

'Excellent idea.'

He showered while she cooked a brunch of sausages, eggs and toast. He had nothing else to wear apart from his tuxedo while she had the luxury of changing into jeans and a woollen sweater. The house was a couple of hundred years old and the heating was diabolically bad in cold weather. She couldn't afford to buy a new system. She had bought out Alex's half of the mortgage and could barely pay the taxes and utility bills. However, given its location, its value was shifting constantly upwards and she didn't want to sell. Mark was right – the house had character, it was all hers, and she had grown quite possessive of it.

'He was a successful lawyer. Extravagant,' she explained. 'I wanted something further out, he insisted on this location.'

'How did you two meet? University?'

She shook her head. 'I skipped Uni and went straight into the police force. Life in Cornwall was dull and I got impatient. I moved to London and joined the Met. Alex was working on a big property deal, which is how he gets his kicks, and I was investigating fraud. We were introduced by a mutual friend.' She glanced away, briefly. He understood: Alex was off topic.

'You've always been into fraud and corruption?'

She dipped her toast in the egg and swirled the yolk around. 'I got noticed. They thought I was wasted on the beat and I was transferred to the serious fraud office. I solve complex things. I should have gone to university perhaps; become an academic with my head in the clouds. Oxford, somewhere like that.' Her parents were surprised when she turned down an offer. It wasn't as if they couldn't afford to send her, but it wouldn't have been easy for them. 'You went?'

'I did. To Oxford and I read Mathematics.'

'You met Jackson... no sorry, that can't be right, you're too young.'

'No. I met Jackson because I chatted up his wife. Big mistake.' Mark's cheeks glowed. 'Somehow he got wind of my stupidity and invited me to meet him. Technically, I already worked for him at Daneswan, which he owns. Jackson owns these little accountancy firms. Eyes everywhere. Anyway, I thought he was going to rake me over the coals and fire me. He was charming. Hettie needed some advice and Jackson arranged for us to meet at her gallery. He liked me, I guess. After that, we exchanged emails about a few cases his forensic team were dealing with and he wanted my opinion. I suppose it was a test. Hence the transfer from Daneswan.'

None of what Mark had said was in his personnel file, the one that security kept.

'Jackson knew Alex at school.' She'd married an older man, as had Hettie. Only, Hettie had struck gold and Julianna had found rust. 'You weren't in the Bullingdon club, were you?'

He laughed. 'Heck, no. I got a scholarship. I'm a council house kid. Bread and butter pudding for tea if I was lucky.'

She smiled. 'Alex and Jackson met at a reunion. Different years, of course, but still old boys.' She despised the secret networks the public schools built. She should have seen the betrayal coming. Alex wanted a wife to parade at parties, a blonde bombshell with a plastic smile and not a frizzy-haired kick-boxing champion.

'Not my scene,' he said.

'So no secrets in your past?'

He slowly lowered his fork. 'Secrets?'

'Stuff, you know. Well, anything exciting.' She half-expected a bead of sweat to drip down his temple. In a few seconds, he had gone from relaxed to rigid. 'What?' she asked. His hand rested on the table, a span's width away from hers. She could touch it. Hold it. Something to jolt him out of his hiding place. He slipped his hand off the table and used the napkin to wipe his lips. He sighed, deeply. She waited patiently, containing her eagerness.

'My dad worked hard – he was a fitness trainer at a local boxing club. Helped kids keep off the streets. Everyone liked Bill Clewer. There was always food, clothes, a little money for holidays. He took me to see United play. We couldn't afford a season ticket, he had to beg and borrow to buy any tickets. Mum would have tea ready when we got home.'

'Just you?'

'Ellen, my sister, was a baby.'

'Then…' There had to be a then. He had painted a picture of contentment. Now, he had to blow it apart.

'Then, he got into petty crime. Robbing Peter to pay Paul kind of stuff. Shifting stolen goods or counterfeit ones out of the back of a van. No drugs, vice or violent acts, not at first. Later…' He slouched in his chair. He had left the top two buttons of his shirt undone and the tails hanging out. He hadn't shaved. Mark, unintentionally, bore a good resemblance to the caricature of a brat pack rogue. She had joked about the film noir. Mark wasn't flippant.

'So, he ended up on the wrong side of the law,' she said.

'He ended up in prison serving a life sentence for murder.' He fixed his dark eyes on hers and waited.

She once had the displeasure of meeting some of society's worst on a regular basis. She had seen crime scenes and dead bodies, interviewed traumatised victims, listened to their horror stories for hours, then heard the pathetic excuses given by the accused. Murder no longer shocked her like it once did, but Mark's revelation was a surprise.

'Who did he kill?' If he had murdered a woman, would Mark lose his appeal? She held her breath.

'Another guy.'

Julianna exhaled, softly, and leaned on her elbows attentively.

'Somebody he knew from a rival gang,' Mark said. 'He pleaded not guilty to murder. But the jury rejected the lesser charge of manslaughter on the advice of the judge. Dad claimed he had gone to negotiate a deal, something to their mutual benefit and it went bad. He says it was self-defence. He stood in court and said the other man attacked him and he fought back. Except…' Mark groaned and rubbed his eyes.

'The evidence didn't support him?' They both understood the importance of forensics; the sordid details, the indelible evidence of wrongdoing.

He nodded. 'There was a knife in the other man's hand. But,

critically, Dad said he was in the car with him, fighting him, but nothing found inside the car supports this. In fact, there were no fingerprints or fibres inside the car, and the only fibres recovered from Dad's clothing were on the outside and the driver's window was wound down, too. He'd been stabbed in the heart.'

'But the victim was holding a knife?'

Mark lips pressed together. Another nod.

'Could somebody have cleaned up afterwards, to make it look like your dad wasn't in the car?'

He pursed his lips, briefly. 'Possibly. To be honest, I've not read all the evidence. I was seventeen when it happened.'

Seventeen! 'You were a kid? This must have happened...'

'Nine years ago. Ellen was eleven. She has problems dealing with it. I left home, went to Oxford.' He slowly straightened up. 'Look. It's a pile of shit and I'm stuck with it because I'm their son. Dad has tried for years to reduce the sentence. Mum is still crusading to prove his innocence. She thinks there's a witness who can corroborate Dad's story. He had mates, people he went around with, and she thinks they're too afraid to speak up for him.'

'Have you found them, these witnesses?'

This time, he laughed. A dry, humourless chuckle. He had obviously fielded that question many times. 'No. It's nine years ago. Gangs change. People go to jail, come out of jail. One thing stays the same – silence.' He dropped into a disappointed whisper.

'And you want to clear him?' She nudged with her voice. 'Mark?'

He clenched a fist on the table. 'I want it to be over. I idolised him, Julianna. He was Dad. Is Dad. Fuck, I don't know. He could have managed a fitness centre and made something of himself. He writes to me. Dear son letters. All optimistic. He's full of his plans to open his own gym once he's released. He's going to help recovering drug addicts and alcoholics. He's already started in the prison gym and the officers are impressed with his attitude.'

'When does he get paroled?'

'He doesn't. Not until he admits—'

'His guilt.' Julianna collected up the dirty plates. Mark's secret was out and it wasn't horrendous. His father was a crook and possibly a murderer, but not a psychopath.

She admired Mark's loyalty, but ultimately, it was self-destructive. Over the last few weeks, his cheeks had appeared more and more gaunt as if he was sucking stress in and holding on to it tightly. One thing Julianna was certain about: Jackson knew about Bill Clewer. Mark had attracted Jackson's attention by chatting up Hettie in a bar. What did Jackson do when anyone, any stranger, paid attention to his wife? He had them checked out. Chris Moran would contact his network of law enforcers and private investigators and do a background check. Mark's past belonged to Jackson Haynes.

Jackson had given Mark a job. Out of pity? She doubted that. Hettie had called her husband heartless, which implied malicious intent. But why? Jackson wasn't involved in criminal gangs like Bill; he fought them using the work of his foundation. Opportunitas rescued victimised women and gave them new homes and jobs. They traced those that went missing and brought closure to anxious families whether the news was good or bad. From what she had learnt since she joined the company, Jackson wasn't as a cold-hearted as he seemed. He nurtured his employees through hard choices, but never treated them cruelly or sanctimoniously. It left Julianna only one option. There was more to Mark's past. Something he hadn't revealed, another even darker secret, possibly dangerous. But it didn't make sense: Jackson had allowed Mark contact with precious Hettie, and she had given him a present – a painting – and they had invited him to parties. Mark had a use and that had to be the reason why Jackson kept tabs on him. Now that was a puzzle worth solving and if her theory was correct, Jackson had set her up to solve it.

'I can understand if you don't want to see me again.' Mark rose to his feet and started to button his shirt up. 'I'm okay about it.'

'Well, I'm not,' Julianna said. 'You've been honest. I'm not going to tar you with the same brush as your dad.'

The relief on his face was palpable. The shadows under his eyes remained – he was tired – but there was a spark lit in them. She had seen that same sparkle last night.

'Thank you.' He swept her into his arms and kissed her until she flapped her arms and he released her. 'Don't flatten me.' He held up his hands in defence.

She wrinkled her nose. 'You need fresh clothes.' The comment signified the end of the conversation. Where they went next was unknown. She would wait. She had become good at waiting. Ever since she had left her last job, she'd loitered in a state of limbo.

She called for a taxi and after a few silent pauses on the doorstep they parted company with a brief hug. An odd sense of distance had descended.

'See you,' she said.

He waved and ducked inside the cab.

That was it for the day. Sex, breakfast and confessions. All that was left was the laundry. And daydreaming about Mark.

10

Ellen

Hurrying along the hotel corridor, Ellen's heels snagged on the frayed carpet and she nearly collided with a wall. Tottering for a second, she giggled. The childish response was due to adrenaline and nothing to do with the best man's embarrassing jokes. She glanced over her shoulder, half expecting him to come running after her. She wouldn't find that funny.

She had so nearly done it. Got laid, just like Nicky.

The best man's brother had strutted his stuff on the dance floor. Ellen's friend, Marsha, called him a buffoon behind his back. Ellen had ignored Marsha and danced with him because he looked super fit. It had been obvious that he was interested. He had said her dancing was "sick", which had amused her, because he was a terrible dancer. He had ground his hips against hers until she had to dash to the bathroom for a pee.

She had drunk far too much. When he, fuck, she didn't even know his name, when he had jerked his head toward the exit, she'd nodded, then whipped out her mobile and nearly called Mark as if she needed his permission.

Why? Freddie had a strict no phone calls policy. She didn't even know his number. But then she remembered where her brother was... hobnobbing with the hoi polloi. The cool corridor had cleared her head in a way a conversation with Mark couldn't. When they had reached Whathisname's room door, she had whispered, 'Sorry,' and bolted in the opposite direction.

A wave of nausea hit as she unlocked her door. With her head over the bowl, she retched the contents of three margaritas into the toilet, but not the red wine. Lying on the bed, her heels dangling off the edge, she closed her eyes and rode the merry-go-round. Around and around she spun until it happened again. She managed to reach the bathroom in time.

Splashing cold water on her flushed face helped alleviate the horrible feeling her insides were keen to be on the outside. She staggered across the room and undressed. Face down on the bed, drooling onto the pillow, she groaned. She had so nearly cracked. Freddie would have been disappointed if she had gone all the way with Whathisname. Freddie used to tell her virginity was a precious thing.

It had happened to her before – the yearning, then the flight. The dark-eyed boy across the road, whom Mrs Asani was convinced fancied her daughter, had invited Ellen into his room after school one day. She had wavered, fighting the fuzzy feel of excitement. He had been too impatient and when she had dithered, he'd shrugged his shoulders, 'Forget it'.

She couldn't though. If she had gone with him would she have regretted it? Eventually, she had told Freddie. It wasn't long after she first started communicating with him. She had been convinced right from the start he was a catholic priest. When she had described her urges and the boy across the road's invitation, he'd rattled on about sin. Her theory about Freddie's faith lasted long enough for her to visit a church. Everyone sang the hymns she didn't know, stood up, knelt, prayed for starving children and wars, but nothing about sin or sex.

She had told Freddie she didn't believe in God because God would stop people from murdering each other. That was when she had confessed she wasn't a victim of crime and told him who her father was. He had heard of the case, knew the name and accepted her back. But he stopped mentioning sin and God, so she shelved the priest theory. Then, he had changed, and started to get suggestive, almost goading her on.

Turning Whathisname down was the right decision. It wasn't due to sin, right or wrong. Sleeping with him would have been a stupid thing to do and swiftly regretted. That kind of relationship wasn't what she wanted. What she wanted was the same thing she had felt when she had cut herself, but without all the questions that came with it. Of course, she had the answers. However, they, those responsible adults who had ruled her life until she left home, hadn't known that and they'd treated her like an imbecile.

She floated into sleep on her merry-go-round. It wasn't a pleasant sensation. She should give up drinking.

The journey home on the train the next morning was uneventful. Her friend wasn't really sober. They were both delicate and not daring to speak in case something unspeakable came up with their words. How did alcoholics manage?

Back at home, she confessed to Freddie she had almost slept with a stranger. She typed the words out and, without reading them back, hit send. Clasping her hands in her lap, she waited for his response. After a few minutes, she gave up and headed upstairs to knock on Nicky's door.

'Hiya, kiddo, come in.'

Ellen navigated her way past the piles of un-ironed clothes, the weights and the empty takeaway cartons.

'For fuck's sake, Nicky.' She picked up the rubbish and dropped it into the trash can. 'Don't you want a boyfriend?'

'Yes. A very domesticated one. Good wedding?'

'Yes. I got very drunk and danced until three in the morning. The rest is a haze.' Why lie? There was no shame in saying no to sex. Nicky probably did, when it suited him. She had lied because she wanted sex to be an unimportant thing. Nicky didn't care who he did it with, why should she?

'So, you're okay?' he asked.

'Honestly, Nicky, I'm a bit hungover and emotional. Can we make some space in your pigsty and watch Netflix or something? I want company, that's all.' And, for the headache to go. She rubbed her temples.

'Sure, honey.' He removed a few things from the couch. 'Can't seem to keep on top of things.'

'Lazy queer!'

Nicky's eyes narrowed.

She shouldn't have said it. Only gay people used that word, didn't they? 'I... I...' She felt sick again. She turned to leave.

'Forget it. I'm just crabby. Hormones.' He grinned. 'I'm not lazy. I am queer, though.'

She laughed with relief and collapsed onto the couch. Nicky bounced onto the cushion next to her and picked up the TV remote.

Ellen fell asleep halfway through the film, her cheek against Nicky's shoulder. She woke to the enchanting aroma of coffee and hazelnut; one of Nicky's specials. She washed dishes in the sink while he pumped his weights up and down. It was a performance, without the usual boom of his beatbox, and just for her benefit. Sweat trickled down his face and his biceps bulged as he flexed his muscles. She never asked for anything more from him and he never expected anything in return, other than perhaps a spot of cleaning. Both of them would be embarrassed if they tried to made a thing of it. So sad, and frustrating: her first love was unattainable.

He wiped his face with a towel. 'I'm meeting somebody,' he said sheepishly. 'I should freshen up.'

'Not here?' She had done a reasonable job of cleaning his kitchen.

'No.' His cheeks glowed brighter.

Nicky's other life, the one he had before he had moved into the block, was as off topic as her own. He mentioned a rough time with gangs and drugs. He had broken free and maintained a squeaky clean lifestyle of exercise and diets. The fringe of this new life bled into the old one. If he had hinted at anything it was the bikers, or his brother, Jed. Jed Redder, the name made her laugh. Nicky hadn't laughed with her – the brothers didn't share the same father.

She had to stand on her tiptoes to kiss one of those flushed cheeks. Goodbye kisses on the lips were out-of-bounds.

Trooping downstairs, she leaned on the door of her flat to shut it. The room felt icy. Soulless. She had always planned to share a flat with some chirpy girl, but she hadn't met one yet. London seemed to lack what she sought. It was a huge disappointment. The negative vibes festered and grew with each passing week.

She checked her messages. Mark still hadn't called, but Freddie had replied.

You should feel proud of yourself.

There it was, as expected, a pat on the back.

The telephone buzzed. Mark was calling. Now she was fielding both men at the same time.

'Mark. Hi,' she said. 'Did you have a good time?'

'Yes. Very, in fact. Immeasurably better than I anticipated.' He sounded chirpy. It had to have been a good night for him; Mark preferred measurables. 'How did your wedding go?'

She stared at her iPad. Freddie wasn't always free. In fact, getting hold of him recently was often a struggle.

'I got exceedingly drunk. I'm now very hungover.'

He chuckled. 'Comes with it.'

'I guess.'

'Can we meet? I've got an idea to help you save some money.'

She pushed the iPad off her lap. 'Sure. I'm all for more money.'

'Good.'

They made arrangements to meet at his place. He was specific about that.

'I know you're not interested, or so you say, but there's a chance I might be getting help with Dad's appeal. Somebody who has connections.'

'You're right, I'm not interested. Don't expect me to contribute to the funds.'

'I guessed you'd say that. Oh, something else,' said Mark. 'Jackson Haynes, my boss, has invited us to his club one evening. Don't know when. Soon, possibly.'

How awful for both of them. If they shared one thing, it was a dislike of loudness and brash behaviour. Mark used to do Mrs Haynes's accounts. Ellen assumed her presence was important to Mark, if only because his boss had commanded it, and who said no to Jackson?

'Jackson Haynes is taking a keen interest in you. Us. Why?'

A sigh and a pause. 'Don't know.'

Liar. He had some inkling as to the reason. 'He doesn't know about Dad, does he?'

'I doubt it. I've not said anything. He might know about Haydocks though. It would be on my resume.'

'Haydocks?'

'Where I worked as an accountant after I graduated from Oxford.' He cleared his throat. 'It didn't exactly end well. It's why I left Manchester and came here to London.'

'Shit happens,' she said. What did he do – sleep with the wrong person? Forget to send off his tax returns? She discounted the second silly idea, but the first was definitely in Mark's territory. When they were kids, she had shared an adjoining wall with Mark's bedroom and what Deidre didn't know was best kept that way. The walls might not have had eyes, but Ellen had ears.

'Yeah.' He sighed. 'I fucked up.'

'I'm sorry.' What else could she say?

'I wanted a promotion. It went very wrong. It's probably wise, Ellen, to never take anyone at face value.'

'Jackson Haynes included?' And our father, what of his worth? She held her tongue. She had said it all before.

There was a pause. She'd hit another raw nerve. Everything she said today dropped mini bombshells on other people's sensibilities.

'Probably. He's got something on me, Ellen. I'm sure of it.'

'Good or bad?'

'It's not easy to answer. Sometimes doing the right thing looks bad.' Mark sighed again; he sounded like a deflating balloon. 'Don't worry, Ellen. It's nothing to do with you. Or Dad. It's just business. Money. Fucking money.'

'Why not leave? Get another job?'

'I don't want to. I like what I do. It's a dream job for me. In any case, I'm probably being paranoid about Haynes. Mum keeps—'

'Nope. Don't bring her up.' Ellen wasn't that patient. Mum was always lurking behind Mark's woes, just like Dad was behind hers.

He had to stop sighing. She found it irritatingly self-serving.

'Let's leave it at that. See you soon.' He rung off without waiting for a goodbye.

She threw the phone onto a cushion. 'Damn it.'

On the iPad she typed a message. I'm glad you think I made the right decision. Because it feels like nothing I do is right.

What's gone wrong?

Mark. Keeping secrets.

About the appeal?

No. Although he's getting help from somebody.

Really?

It won't make a difference. What he's more worried about is his new boss.

Haynes?

Yeah. And something to do with the last company he worked for. Haydocks.

There was a lengthy delay before Freddie dropped the next line.

Sorry. Phone call. Always somebody wanting my advice. He added a smiley. Haydocks? Not heard of it.

His last job in Manchester. He was very cagey about it. Said he'd fucked up on something and had to leave.

Mark must be battling his conscience. You kept your dignity and resisted temptation last night. Be proud.

The word proud jumped out of the screen. He was labouring a point.

She clutched her iPad. Another message from Freddie popped up, following straight on from the last. He had written a sermon about the importance of virginity. It wasn't the first time he'd lectured on the subject of playing safe, but he hadn't framed it with references to purity and abstinence. He came across as more sanctimonious than ever.

Freddie the priest was back. For fuck's sake, why now? She wished she had never told him. It wasn't about sex. Didn't he get it? She could so easily tell terrible fibs just to have somebody talk to her, touch her, heal her fractured heart. Her anger spilt over, down her arms into her fingertips.

I'm getting pissed again. You can't stop me. Can you?

Freddie?

An hour passed. She had drunk half a bottle of wine, which on top of a hangover was having a peculiar effect on her vision and stomach.

I can't, he replied, finally. I can worry about you. Wish you were here with me. I would hug you and tell you it's going to be fine, Ellen. Everything will be fine. Somebody special is out there waiting for you.

Ellen arrived at Mark's apartment in a sequinned dress and the same high-heels she'd worn to the wedding. The silver necklace adorning her neck had been a gift from Uncle Tim. She rarely took it out of its box; it reminded her of Manchester and another life.

Mark complimented her on her appearance. 'Stop looking glum.

You look fab.' He straightened his collar. No tie tonight.

She didn't want to go to Razzles. Just the name of the club was off-putting – how retro was it going to be? Jackson Haynes wasn't a young man, and hardly likely to sponsor a rave. Was the club a front for some dodgy deals, or a vanity project? And then there was Mark's determination to scrambled up the career ladder to escape something he had done at Haydocks.

'Mark, I'm not sure,' she said.

He poured her a glass of wine. 'Drink. Loosen up.' He left the glass on the kitchen counter. She eyed it suspiciously.

He tapped her arm. 'Before we go, I want to show you something.' He led her to a door. 'This is the spare room.'

It had a bed, but nothing else. What struck her was the space. Her bedsit could fit inside this one room. Stacked in the far corner were cardboard boxes with sealed lids.

'I know you're trying to save. I'm suggesting you move in with me.' He stood in front of the boxes.

'What... live with you?' She left her mouth hanging open. He had to be kidding; they hadn't been under the same roof for years.

'Temporarily, of course. But just think. I live closer to your work. You'll save on fares. Plus, I'm out, a lot.'

Meaning, he wasn't keen on spending time with her, which she found equally unappealing. 'I'll live with you? So, like, I'm going to cook and clean?'

'No!' He dragged her by her arm to another door. 'En-suite. Your own. We'll have a rota for cleaning. Cooking, if you like.'

The bathroom was petite. However, it was clean. Spotless, in fact. He shut the door behind them.

She needed to save, and he probably worked long hours for Haynes. 'I can't pay you much.'

Mark moved, and she saw the labels on the boxes: *William Clewer. Appeal hearing.* Mark wasn't stupid: he had set a trap for her, and it was good one. A tempting one.

They returned to the living area.

'I'm trying to help you, Ellen.' He wrung his hands together. 'Give me what you can afford for rent.'

'So I can save, just that?'

'Yes. Go to university, whatever. Like I did.'

She hadn't anticipated he carried that guilt so heavily.

'Why, why now?' She gave the apartment a fresh appraisal: modern, simple and a good location. She could never afford it on her own. And she would rather share. Better her brother than a strange girl, even a chirpy girl.

A sudden flare of exasperation swept over his face. 'I want to get to know you.'

He was lying. He wanted something from her and she had a good idea what it was. Just because she had suffered living with their mother after he had left didn't make her a useful conduit for relaying the latest instalments of Mark's ineptness at managing the appeal. She and Deidre were utterly estranged and Mark knew it. In the end, she gave him the benefit of the doubt. He wasn't inept, merely useless at appearing sanguine.

'I'm not sure.' She sighed, adding in an indecisive eye roll to extend the ruse a little longer.

'Think about it, Ellie.'

He used to call her that when he bribed her with sweets. Two lollipops for each time she lied to Deidre about his whereabouts. The rate was five for Dad. Deidre was easier to fool.

'I have to give notice. The landlord's a crook—'

He smirked. 'Aren't they all.'

'And, I need my deposit back.'

'There's no rush. As I say, I'm spending my time elsewhere.' A hint. A bad one too. The place smelt of roses.

'I have friends...' Hardly any. She would miss Nicky.

'Friends can visit. You're a grown woman.'

Yes, I am. She said nothing. She would tell him her answer another time.

'Shall we go then?'

She was about to step into an exclusive, if possibly dated, night club. If she moved in Mark's circles, who knew what other fortunes might drop into her lap. He collected his jacket and had one last check in the mirror. Mark was more vain than she'd realised. On the way past the kitchen, she swallowed a mouthful of red wine to bolster her nerves.

Razzles turned out to be far from dated; the Mayfair venue featured all the trimmings of money with its velvet-clad decor, soft purple lighting, glazed floor, and seamless panelling. She immediately felt a buzz in the air, the energy of countless exhales mixed together. Unfortunately, the music was deafening and the bar ridiculously expensive. Mark bought the first round of drinks.

'There's Jackson.' He pointed to a tall man in a cordoned off area of the floor. An audience fanned out around him like a fast-flowing current avoiding a boulder. He wasn't alone; somebody, a brick-shaped man, filtered who got near.

Mark, his hand on her elbow, steered Ellen through the crowd, and they walked past the minder, who gave a curt nod to Mark.

A green-eyed, stunningly attractive woman hooked her arm through Mark's. 'You came.' Her pearl necklace was as white as her teeth.

'Hi, Hettie. You're perky,' Mark said. A liquid smile sped across his face, as if Mark was trying to harness all the charm of a James Bond star.

'First time in months that I've been here. I'm going to have fun. Even a drink or two.' She lifted a glass and it reflected her glossy lips.

Ellen was lost for a second in the magnetic appeal that came with celebrities. She'd seen this woman in a magazine, one of those with pictures and no substance. 'Pleasure to meet you.'

'Mark used to be my accountant. I miss him so much.' She squeezed Mark's arm. 'His replacement is so boring.'

Mark turned a shade of mellow pink. 'Hettie, you're too dazzling for me.'

'She dazzles everybody, doesn't she?' said the tall man blocking out the spotlight behind Hettie. 'Is this Ellen?'

Before she could offer it, Jackson Haynes scooped up Ellen's hand. She expected him to kiss the knuckles, Godfather style. Instead, he gave a momentary shake and released it. The impression he left lasted longer than that swift touch. He hadn't dropped his gaze.

'Mark said you're a keen archaeologist.'

There wasn't a question mark at the end of that sentence. He already knew a lot about her. Ellen shot a fiery glance at her brother. Now he had pink ears. What else had he revealed about her? 'Amateur and relatively untested. I'd like to study.'

'My brother Luke and I know somebody, a professor.' Jackson's eyes twinkled under the lights. 'He's well connected.'

Ellen said nothing again. Mark fidgeted with his beer glass.

She and Mark moved to explain to another new person who she was – always Mark's sister, but not everyone knew Mark. He was a newcomer too. The introductions grew quicker, less involved. She was an appendix, always attached to him and framed by his friendship with Jackson and Hettie. Mark's boss was surrounded by a skilled group of sycophants, fawners of wealth and power. She hid her disgust. She was a fish out of water and drowning. Although it was more like suffocating. She briefly bumped into Hettie again. Razzle dazzle Hettie with her charm and her effervescent spirit. A mother free from the chains of babies, she shone under the lights. Mark couldn't stop looking at her. So, he fancied his boss's wife. The infatuation might explain his desperate need to be part of Jackson's fan club.

As for Jackson Haynes, he had to have a hidden agenda regarding Mark. And her, too, because Haynes watched her almost as much as he tracked his wife about the club.

Ellen wasn't enjoying herself. While Mark hobnobbed his way up the social ladder, she drifted, aimlessly circulating. One bald man, who introduced himself as Graham, wanted to know what she had dug out of the ground. She should have listed shards of pottery, coins, smashed roof tiles, clay pipes amongst the unexplained, including the fragile pieces of an iron age weapon – her greatest find and now on display in a museum in Manchester. Instead, she blurted, 'Knives. I find knives.' She turned on her heels and hurried to the bathroom.

Razzles was a mistake. She wished she was somewhere quieter. Cooler, too. The swelter of bodies in close proximity burnt her skin. It seemed a ludicrous way to spend time – squeezed into a confined space and blasted with loud voices and music when you could be outside in the fresh air. Digging in the dirt was more fun, as was running with Nicky.

She finished another glass of wine, then weaved through the sea of bodies to Mark's side. 'I want to leave,' she whispered into his ear. She had to say it twice before he heard her correctly.

He glared. 'Leave. It's not even midnight.'

'I don't like it. The whole atmosphere is a tawdry, chauvinistic power play. I want to go.'

He heard her clearly that time.

'Who's your friend, Mark?' a bearded man asked, swaying, leering at her sparking sequins, especially the ones that decorated her bosom.

'My sister. Hands off.'

The intruder crashed into a table and his beer spilt over his shirt.

Jackson filled the empty space. 'Okay?'

'Sure,' Mark said. 'Hogan is a little worse for wear.' The stumbling Hogan was jettisoned from Jackson's inner sanctuary by the minder. Jackson grunted something incomprehensible but seemed satisfied.

'I'm afraid we have to go. Ellen is a little tired.' Mark's excuse ensured Ellen bore the brunt of her brother's annoyance.

'It's been a pleasure to have your company, Miss Clewer,' Jackson said pleasantly.

'Devera. Ellen Devera.'

Mark's body stiffened, just as she expected.

'My grandfather's name,' she said unnecessarily.

It was their mother's maiden name, too, but she wouldn't mention Deidre in the same breath as their beloved, late grandfather. She hadn't changed it legally. By not uttering *their* name, she maintained a distance from her immediate family.

Jackson's eyebrows furrowed. 'Perhaps you should take her home, Mark.'

'Too much drink,' Mark muttered, apologetically.

Ellen fumed; they treated her like a child. Mark bundled her through the crowd, passed the revellers to the exit.

The frosty atmosphere between them didn't thaw in the taxi. Mark took her to his apartment and the spare bed. She was too pissed to care where she slept. She sent a text to Nicky, warning him she wasn't going to join him for the Sunday morning run. She lay rigid and listened to Mark potter about as he readied himself for bed. This could be her home. She needed to save money; Mark's offer was too good to ignore.

She twisted on her side, drifting, never quite sure if she was awake or inebriated; she came face to face in the dim light with the boxes and witnessed the spectacle of her father perched on one of them, drumming his fingers on the lid. His sunken eyes formed dark pits, and below his ragged nose were his swollen lips. That was how she remembered him from the last visit – patched up bruises. Trapped alone with the vacant expression of an apparition, she grappled with nausea. He might as well be a ghost, except Bill wasn't dead.

'Go away,' she said to the shadow.

The hallucination wavered, then vanished.

In the morning, she called for a cab to take her home. Mark wasn't up. She left a note.

I'll move in with you if you get rid of those boxes. I don't want to see them.

11
Julianna

Julianna hot-desked nearly every day. She generally either hijacked a spare workstation in the security office in the basement, which was a ghastly pit with no windows, or she hopped upstairs to the floor where the internal auditors worked and borrowed one of their desks. She was typing up a lengthy report when her mobile rang.

'Julianna?'

Her heart sank slightly. 'Yep. What can I do for you, Chris?' She saved the document and closed the lid of her laptop.

'Sorry for the short notice, but Tess had to dash off with a vomiting bug—'

'That's what happens when you share a car with babies—'

He emitted a low rumbling that resembled laughter. 'Probably. I need you to collect Hettie from her gallery A.S.A.P. and take her home.'

'She's working?'

'Just this week. New exhibits going up. Tess is very apologetic.'

'I understand. I take it there's a car waiting downstairs?' Speed was essential. The boss wouldn't tolerate his wife being unmarked at a public venue. Julianna sped along as quickly as the traffic allowed. She parked outside the gallery and found Hettie in the back office, somewhat bemused by Julianna's appearance.

'Rabbit's hat? Tess in and you out?'

'Tess really isn't well. So, I jumped out of the rabbit hole,' Julianna said. 'Backup girl to the rescue.' But no cape; she didn't come with accessories.

'I thought she looked a little pale earlier. I'm about finished. I need to get home.'

Julianna helped Hettie lock up and set the surprisingly complex alarm system. The traffic was especially horrendous, and rain lashed the windscreen. Winter crept closer every day, adding to the sense of bleakness. The gloom spilt into the car. Not being able to see Hettie's face perhaps made Julianna unusually trusting. Why not come clean with her? It wasn't as if Hettie hankered after Mark. She had had some dealings with him, was possibly party to some information about his past, things Mark wasn't happy revealing to Julianna, but might have done with his attractive client.

'Mrs Haynes, I thought you should know, well...' Julianna lost momentum before she had uttered a complete sentence.

'Go on, Julianna. The road is long, as they say,' Hettie said, encouragingly.

'Mark Clewer and I are in a relationship.' Julianna exhaled and waited for a reply.

'Okay. He once was my accountant. It's not something that bothers me. I get the feeling that my previous dealings with Mark are bothering you though.' Hettie leaned towards the centre of the car and came into view of the mirror.

'We're not in love or anything.' There was nothing romantic about what she did with Mark in her bedroom, only that it served a mutual purpose. 'But I do care about him. Can we just be honest with each other, Mrs Haynes?'

'Sure, fire away.'

'I've being seeing Mark since the gala ball. But my question goes back to before them. To be blunt, I drove you and your husband to the clinic, remember?'

'Ah. We spoke about Mark in the car on the way, didn't we? Whoops.'

'Yes. You implied Jackson was being less than kind about how he was treating Mark.'

'I did?' Hettie feigned surprise. She had shifted back in her seat again, hiding whatever expression was painting her face. 'I probably over-egged it, that's all.'

'I know about his father being in prison for murder. I assume that was what you were referring to.'

'Yes, naturally,' Hettie said slowly. 'That's quite a lot to get to grips with, isn't it, on top of everything else. Poor Mark.'

On top of everything else? Hettie hadn't known about Mark's father. Julianna now knew she and Jackson had been discussing something else. Julianna had unwittingly told Hettie about Mark's father. Jackson would not be pleased. There again, Jackson had not laid down his own agenda and what was she expected to do with the sporadic amounts of information flying in her direction? Duck or charge at them?

'He's so frustrated by the lack of closure.' Damn Jackson's secretive nature. Julianna decided to go for bust. 'His mother insists on taking the case to appeal. She's driving him nuts.'

'Domineering, then. Oh dear.'

Julianna blinked. She hadn't expected such a harsh comment from Hettie. It implied Mark was weak-willed. Wasn't Hettie somewhat in the same boat with regard to Jackson? Pot calling kettle black?

The traffic moved off and Julianna tracked the leading car's brake lights.

'I guess she is. I've not met her.' Julianna wasn't keen to either. 'Or Ellen.'

'The sister? I have. At Razzles. Sweet girl. Out of her depth in London. I think her ambitions lie elsewhere. She's very keen to become an archaeologist. Jackson has this friend she should meet.'

Hettie was far more perceptive than she let people think. It was what made her a good artist. All those observations were filed away and brought to life in paints or inks, occasionally sculptures. She had talented hands and observant eyes, an excellent combination.

Julia pulled up outside the house. 'So, with regard to Mark, I shouldn't be worried about him? I mean, what Jackson implied was there was things he didn't know—'

'Your question poses a dilemma. If Jackson wanted you to know, he'd have said, wouldn't he? You see, I know that it's to do with Mark's job in Manchester, and that it troubles Jackson that Mark hasn't pieced things together – he doesn't think it's his responsibility to tell Mark. But frankly, beyond knowing that Mark hasn't, I've no clue as to what Mark is supposed to know. Jackson doesn't tell me everything. He is very protective of me, as you might have noticed.'

Julianna turned to face her. 'Doesn't it get too much, this cocoon he keeps you in? I'd feel smothered.'

Hettie's hand was on the door handle. 'Oh, that's why I love him. Married him. I crave that kind of control. I'm quite capable of doing things my way, don't get me wrong. People don't get to see all of Jackson, I do, somebody has to, and I will always have that advantage. I didn't tell him I was working today. He'll be a tad mad. It won't change anything between us, because love, whether you want it or not, generally has no limits. I must get in. Children calling.' She grabbed her briefcase. 'Don't browbeat Mark. He'll open up in his own time. He's got a lot on his plate, bless him.'

Trouble was, unless Julianna could get him to open up to her, their relationship was probably doomed to failure. On the way to her house, she picked up groceries. She wanted to cook something special for Mark; he was visiting.

She welcomed him in with a kiss and a glass of wine. From the way he shovelled food into his mouth, he was hungry for food, and probably something else, but he would have to be patient.

'The situation with Ellen? This moving in, has she agreed?' she asked, grappling with the spaghetti on her plate.

He shrugged. 'She's not exactly said no. I reckon, given her income, she should be able to save enough for the first year of living costs. I'm prepared to chip in, if she would let me. I don't think she likes the idea of loans.'

'Don't blame her. That's very generous of you.'

He spooled his spaghetti around a fork. 'I didn't treat her well when she was a kid. Ignored her.'

'She turned out all right. Can't be that bad.'

'I guess.' He paused, spaghetti dangling off his fork. 'I worry about her drinking. Her lack of friends. I took her to the club, but nothing came of it. She asked to leave. I thought she might get on with Hettie.'

By raking up family issues, Ellen was in danger of dragging Mark into a black hole, especially as the young woman refused to discuss anything to do with her parents, which riled Mark, obviously. He needed to share the burden with somebody. While Ellen might have cut herself free, Mark refused to. Or couldn't. Was there a difference?

'What happened when you left home? Did you not want to stay in contact with Ellen?'

'Student life is rather selfish. Then, I went back to Manchester, but avoided home. We've an uncle, Tim, Dad's brother. He's so different. He washed his hands of Dad long before the murder. He offered a sanctuary from it all. I'd occasionally see Ellen at his house. We weren't talking much, though.'

His appetite out did hers. He had eaten half his plate before Julianna had a chance to tackle hers. 'You lived elsewhere?'

'Salford, in lodgings. The job was demanding. A steep learning curve. Too steep. I discovered things I shouldn't have done.'

Julianna's ears were on fire. 'Oh,' she said, as nonchalantly as she could while her heart thumped heavily. She avoided Mark's eyes.

'Yeah.' He chewed slowly. 'Shit, basically. I uncovered criminal activities.'

'A client's?'

He swirled his wine around the glass before downing a generous mouthful. 'More complicated. I had to run for it when I realised I'd stirred a hornet's nest. Before I left, I downloaded heaps and sent it to the police. You see, I blew the whistle and legged it. To this day, the police don't know who sent them the stuff. I used a fake account and deleted it straight away.'

Julianna had a different training to Mark. One that went beyond unearthing falsified figures, tax evasion and phoney bank accounts. Hers went deeper into the dark net and covert communications. If the police wanted to know, they could find out. But she suspected they were more interested in what Mark had uncovered and considered chasing after the whistle-blower a waste of time.

'What was the name of the company you worked for?' she asked.

'Haydocks. Just one owner who is now locked behind bars facing charges of money laundering.'

'And the clients?'

Mark shrugged. 'I never uncovered the whole trail before things got a little dicey. I'm assuming they were drug dealers or something. They'd been using Haydocks to help them launder money for some time. Perhaps they'd got slack with the process. Something caught my eye and boom, it blew up, as they say.'

'Ellen knows nothing?'

'Nah. It's nothing to do with her. But, obviously, I kept quiet. Didn't even tell Tim why I left. Nobody came after me. I moved a few times just to be sure.'

Nobody came after Mark because of Jackson. Somehow, he had crushed the police investigation into Mark's involvement in case anything leaked out to the bad guys. The snippet of information she had overheard in the back of the car now slotted into the picture, another brush stroke made visible. 'And… that's it?'

He pivoted, his eyes darkening. She had pushed too hard.

'What's with the third degree?'

'Nothing,' she said, perhaps too sharply. 'Am I getting under your skin?'

'A tad. Frankly, it could easily have fucked up my career. Snitching seemed the honourable thing to do and the legal one. But clients want to trust their accountants. It's no secret that everyone cooks the books a little, don't they? Loopholes get exploited. Numbers fudged. It's the way of things.'

'So, you moved into forensic accountancy because you fancied more of the same? Isn't that the whole point of the job, uncovering illicit activities?'

'Except now I've got Jackson's backing. It's his name that comes knocking on people's doors, not mine. He's the crusader. I actually enjoy investigating fraud, and the like.'

'Is this why he employed you, do you think? He must have known about Haydocks.'

'Well, yeah, it's on my resume. Can't wipe out all those years and leave them blank on my employment record.'

'And within months of being in London, you end up working in his forensics team: your ideal job. When do you think he knew about you?'

Mark smirked. 'I met Hettie first, remember.'

Poking Mark to think was harder than she thought. He hadn't realised the lengths Jackson went to with his vetting process; Mark's lack of imagination and dogmatic style of work seemed to stymy his ability to think outside of the box.

'You met her, yes, and it was a lucky break for you. What if when she gave Jackson your business card, he already knew your name?'

He frowned, shaking his head. 'Jackson? Interested in me because I uncovered a money laundering operation in Manchester? Nah.' He resumed eating.

'Haydocks is a competitor of Jackson's, isn't it?'

He sighed and lowered his fork; she was annoying, she knew that was a problem. 'Not really. Look, it's more likely he read about the arrests in the newspapers. He never even asked about Haydocks in the interview.'

Julianna called that a red flag. The one thing Jackson should have raised in the interview was the thing he didn't. And yet Mark wasn't seeing why. What if Haydocks was known to Jackson for a different reason, and having Mark in his company was a useful asset because of it.

He twizzled his fork round and round, without lifting the spaghetti to his mouth. 'All the same,' he said, 'please don't say anything to anyone. I'm watching my back, that's all.' He was suspicious. Perhaps, it might make him open up more another time. Maybe he might tell her what made him decide to bring down Haydocks.

She lay down her knife. 'I won't say a thing about it at work. Honest. You're right, it's none of my business. But can I just say I'm proud of you, Mark. That took guts.'

She had recovered herself well; the shadow across his face lifted.

'Okay, tit for tat. Tell me something that you've kept secret.'

A fair request. 'My husband screwed my best friend.' Julianna poured them both two full glasses of wine.

'Friend? I thought she was his secretary?' Mark leaned forward on his elbows, keen to hear the dirt on her ex.

'Paralegal secretary. She and I studied at the same sixth form college down in Cornwall. I left home and she joined me in London. Best mates for years and then she got a job at this law firm where Alex worked and introduced us. It was how we met, Alex and me. Never crossed my mind back then that she would have her own designs on him. She was my bridesmaid.' Julianna stabbed at the pasta. 'And right under my bleedin nose.' She gave up and tossed aside the fork.

Mark collected the dishes and carried them through into the kitchen. She followed him.

'You couldn't have known—'

She cut him down with a glare. 'I'm a copper, or I was. I worked for the government in intelligence. And I couldn't even work out my husband was cheating on me with my best friend! It's galling, truly, fucking... Back-stabbing bitch. Betrayal by two important people in my life.' Downstairs was the punch bag. She needed it. Without it, objects would probably fly around the room and doors would be kicked in. Her anger wasn't directed at them, those two, but her failings. Her inadequacies.

He grabbed her flailing hand and drew it to his waist, forcing her into his embrace. 'You quit your job out of shame because you don't trust your instincts anymore. A bit like me, really, isn't it? Failing to notice Dad was a gangster. At least, the kind of hardnose criminal who gets involved in murder. It's easily done when it's about the people you love. Blind faith, eh.' He tipped her chin up.

She glanced over his shoulder, refusing to calm down. 'I suppose I don't expect much from others these days.'

'Except me, I hope.' Mark leaned back on the kitchen counter, taking her with him. He was warm and soft about the middle. He had put on weight since she first slept with him.

'I'd rather know the truth than a pretence at loving somebody again.' Her temples had ceased throbbing. There wasn't any doubt that Mark had a calming influence on her.

'Me, too. That why I'm still there, trying for resolution with Dad. I have to know categorically one way or the other. I have to know: did he lie to me, because he promised me he was innocent.'

'He did?' She hadn't known there was a promise involved.

'One of my lasts visits. I pinned him to his seat, metaphorically speaking, and looked him in his eyes.' Mark possessed dark pitted eyes. Black olives surrounded by saffron skin. She was now hungry with a different kind of appetite

'And?'

'He said he wasn't a hired assassin. Those words exactly.'

'Very precise.' Almost pedantically so. It seemed Mark was unaware of the potential ramifications of what his father had said.

She couldn't bear to tell him. She didn't want to be the one to smash a promise apart.

'Hence the legal wrangling. Mum doesn't need a promise. She just wants to walk down the streets and not feel humiliated.'

'Then let's hope Sophia can help you.' She smiled and he eased off with his arm lock.

'So what's for afters?' he asked sweetly.

'You.' Her smile broadened into a grin.

12

Mark

She landed on her bottom for the third time and even from a distance of several metres Mark could see she was laughing her head off. With some difficulty she got back on her feet and continued on her disastrous circuit. Her arms floated out to her sides and her knees kept knocking together as she attempted to push forward. Julianna might be a kick-boxer and karate expert, but she couldn't ice-skate with any grace. Eventually, she made her way over to Mark, who stood by the ringside, slurping on a can of coke.

'Sure you don't want to join me?' She leaned on the barrier, panting heavily.

'Absolutely.' What he was witnessing was cold, wet and guaranteed to embarrass. 'What's with the ice-skating?'

'It's on my bucket list of things to do before I die. This ice-rink is on my doorstep and why not?'

She had arranged to meet him nearby. Her idea, and a surprise; he wasn't sure it matched his expectations of a date. 'But why now?'

'It's you. You've made me come out of my doldrums, brought me back to life. I'm feeling motivated.' She kicked the skates against the side of the barrier.

He smirked. 'My screwing you to the bed makes you want to live out a childhood dream?'

She clung to the barrier. 'Don't, Mark. You make it sound vulgar and degrading. You know it's not like that for us.' She admonished him with a matronly, disapproving look. He guessed she had practised it as police officer. Thankfully, it fractured into a smile. The reprimand was gone before he could retaliate with a flinch.

'No. It's nothing like that.' Whether she heard over the thump of the background music, he didn't know. She pushed away with wobbly legs and arms swinging unproductively.

Mark rested his elbows on the barrier and watched Julianna continue her precarious tour of the ice-rink. Since their first bedroom encounter on the night of the ball they had been meeting regularly, at least once a week. The commitment was loose, non-binding, and either of them could cancel at short notice. The lack of formality suited both of them, or so it seemed. For how long though? Julianna, after her failed marriage, possibly wanted the sex to have meaning, some cathartic outpouring that would heal her. Mark's need was different. Julianna was a tantalising distraction, and a rather beautiful one, too.

He'd spent the weekend in Manchester, staying with Tim and cousin Alfie. They had taken him to a football match – the highlight of the day. Then, with no enthusiasm, he wore the mantle of a dutiful son and visited his mother, who was still living in the same house where she had built a shrine of faded photographs, threadbare football scarves and albums of newspapers, as if her husband was dead and not imprisoned. She even kept his clothes in the bedroom wardrobe. Mark sat in the armchair – Bill's old throne – and announced he had found a new solicitor. Sophia had taken custody of the boxes of documents.

'There's a new hunt for the witness,' he had told Deidre, explaining his progress.

She had poured the tea in celebration. Warm shades of colour filled her snowy face, but she would never thaw for him. She never congratulated him on his efforts. Her own were pitiful – Deidre dictated and harangued, but never got her hands dirty with lawyers unless she had to. If he had any admiration for his mother, it was her devotion to Bill's cause. Mark genuinely believed she loved his father. It wasn't the same for Mark. He wasn't able to feel like he used to.

As for meeting Ellen in London, he left his sister out of the conversation. Until Ellen was willing to engage with Deidre, it would only antagonise his mother. The rift was obvious by her continuing lack of concern for her daughter.

He had tuned out the rest of the day. Nothing of significance happened. She had hugged him and he had caught the train home. Back at his flat, he had contacted Ellen and told her the boxes were gone, and that she was welcome to move in. She still hadn't replied to his text, which worried him a little. He should visit her and find out who Nicky was.

Julianna fell over again. Somebody helped her back up on to her feet. She waved at him and set off again. Her balance and coordination were improving – a quick learner, not surprising given her natural athleticism. He stared across the sea of bodies tumbling round the rink, weaving and sliding. Why not give it a go? Hardly anyone was good at it. He went to collect a pair of boots.

13
Mark

'Mark?' Ellen whispered.

Mark pressed the phone closer to his ear. He blinked at the illuminated display on the alarm clock – midnight. 'What?'

'Please, something is wrong. Really wrong. I can't stop crying.' She sobbed, uncontrollably, to illustrate the point.

He rolled out of bed; he had only just got into it. The bedroom light stabbed his eyes, one in particular throbbed unpleasantly. Why now? Why couldn't he have one decent night's sleep and not have to rely on pills.

'Mark?' Her voice was dulled by something. He could guess what.

He walked out of his bedroom. A glass of water might help. 'Are you alone?'

Another pitiful sob. 'Yes.'

'So what's with the crying? Eh?'

He pictured her alone, tears streaking her face. She was diminutive in stature, like a small child. Only twenty years old. At her age he'd had the support of other students, a personal tutor and the pastoral care system of a large college. He had managed fine without it. Ellen was different though. Her fragility wasn't to do with a lack of motivation – she had left home and found a job without help – it was something else, some need to self-destruct when the pressure bore down on her. She was quite capable of crocodile tears, though. He balanced his sympathy accordingly.

She blew her nose. 'I invited this guy to my room—'

'Ellen!' He spluttered on the water. 'He hurt you?' Why wonder she was upset, she had done a foolish thing, except Julianna had done the same thing with him: invited him in and taken him to her bed. But this was his little sister whom he babysat as a teenager while his parents went to the pub. Should he hasten over there… and… what exactly? Hold her hand. They never held hands or hugged.

'No.' She dropped the slurring. 'Of course not.'

'Was it Nicky?'

'Nicky?' she said with a vocal sneer. 'He's not here. He's with his friend. That's why I called you,' she said feebly. Nicky was her hand-holder. Mark was way down on the reserve list. He rolled his eyes to the kitchen lights.

'This man you invited,' Mark couldn't care less about her sensibilities, 'did you fuck?'

'No!' she said indignantly. 'He's somebody I met out jogging. We've passed each other a few times. Caught our breath, you know, and chatted.' Her voice slurred again. 'He runs for an athletics club. Does marathons. The London marathon. I want to do it.'

'Jesus, Ellen,' he muttered. Things were far worse than he thought. He had underestimated Ellen's weakness for alcohol. He couldn't demand she move in with him, but the sooner the better. The issue was no longer about unity and handling Deidre – Ellen was too broken to cope with their mother – it was about providing her with stability. Julianna would understand and it wasn't as if she came to his flat often. They preferred hers as it was closer to the office.

If Ellen did take up his offer, he would have to ensure she understood there would be no inviting men around at short notice, regardless of their sexual orientation.

She hiccupped. 'I'm not that drunk.'

He didn't agree. 'You're absolutely sure that he didn't fuck you?' Would she know? Had he slipped her a pill or something?

She whispered, sheepishly. 'I did some things. A couple of things with him.'

Mark closed his eyes. 'Did he force you to do them?'

'No.' She seemed adamant on that; he had to believe her. 'He'll not be happy with me.'

'Why? I don't understand.'

'I was mad at him. He's so pompous sometimes and telling me that I'm good, when I know I'm bad, and that I should stay safe, like I'm a kid.'

Mark lowered his glass of water. The pain now was focused quite brilliantly on one spot and growing bigger by the minute. 'You're not making sense, Ellen.' The jogging friend was more than a passing acquaintance. This person was offering the kind of advice Mark would give and at the same time, preying on Ellen's vulnerabilities.

'He's a good friend, but he lives in Ireland.'

'Oh, for fuck's sake, Ellen. Stop winding me up. You're drunk. We'll talk when you're sober.'

'I'm not winding you up. He's been so good to me and there so few people out there for me when it matters.'

'I'm here, aren't I? Hardly that far away.'

She spoke the truth, though. For years, he had no clue about her friends. This Irishman, whoever he was, had encouraged her to do something sexual, something that she was ashamed to admit to, especially to her older brother. Where were her girlfriends? Women did this kind of stuff — hand holding and tissues. He should introduce Ellen to Julianna. Immediately, he dismissed the idea. He wanted to keep things as simple as possible with Julianna and the less complications, the better. He had already made an error taking Ellen to Razzles and expecting her to slot into that crowd. He had wasted the opportunity to make an impression with Haynes. If he had wanted to have a good time, he should have taken Julianna. What Ellen needed was somebody who talked about things she enjoyed doing, like marathons, or digging in the dirt for lost objects.

'You should have a shower, or something. If it helps.' He checked the wall clock; he'd an early meeting. 'I have to go to bed. You'll be okay, yes?'

She sniffed, drowsily.

He left the glass in the sink and padded back to his bedroom. 'Or perhaps, just go to sleep.' His efforts to reach out to her seemed futile. Why had he bothered? There were other more important things to discuss. 'You got the message about the boxes? The solicitor?' he asked.

'Yes. Deidre's happy, I assume.'

'No.' He guffawed. 'This is Mum.'

'Then burn them. Burn the fucking lot.' She spoke venomously, without one hint of drunkenness.

He didn't care for the familiar angry flare of her voice. 'This is the last time, though. I told her, that's it. If Sophia finds nothing new, then, yes, we'll burn it all. We'll light a bonfire somewhere. Okay?'

'I don't believe you. You'll never do it. You don't want to do it. You're just like her; head up your arse.'

'Sober up. The offer still stands, but you've got to get a grip on this… whatever this is or whoever is fucking with you.'

She hung up without saying goodbye.

Ellen had managed for years without him. He had made his offer and it was there on the table if she wanted it. At the end of the day, she was an adult and had made little effort to reach out to him for years. Why wouldn't he do the same? Let her play around with strangers, as long as they enjoyed it, did it matter? He wasn't an angel himself and his relationship with Julianna was casual and low-key. If Ellen drank, then it was her choice. Julianna would disagree, but then Julianna wasn't part of his family. And what was the point of families anyway? Mark had stepped into Bill's shoes and they didn't fit, which pleased Mark no end.

There were no more drunken calls from Ellen. Perhaps, he hoped, that one night had sobered her up. Young people made mistakes and Ellen was at that experimental stage. Mark had been through it and done things he regretted, both professionally and personally. He had more important things to consider, like staying in Jackson's eyeline, which was proving to be a challenge.

Mark rarely came across Jackson at work, which wasn't surprising, the man ruled a business empire and Mark's team was one small cog in the machine. Equally, he rarely bumped into Julianna. If they saw each other in the office building, they walked past each other with a cursory nod and perhaps a small smile of recognition. They'd agreed to keep things under the radar of their colleagues.

Things progressed with his new job, cases came and went, and they were mostly resolved without recourse to prosecutions. If

Mark assumed Jackson had forgotten about him, he was mistaken. At nine o'clock he was summoned for an impromptu meeting regarding an acquisition that Jackson was negotiating.

'Mark, come in.' Jackson waved Mark over the threshold into his grandiose office. There were others there, seated around the conference table, eyeing Mark with a mixture of curiosity and wariness. Departments were prone to rivalry, a bit like football teams – they all enjoyed the game but their side had to be the best. He wasn't familiar with this bunch of lawyers.

Jackson introduced the team managing the negotiations. 'We've entered due diligence with a smallish size company. There are discrepancies with their projections. It looks like they're spinning their financials incorrectly. Come and take a look. I want to know if these are irregularities or whether they're engaging in opportunistic accounting policies.'

Mark glanced over the latest financial statements, information provided by the other company. 'I can't tell from this. I'd need further information. It does look dubious to have these kinds of projections in the current economic climate.'

'Put aside what you're doing at the moment, Mark, I want you to concentrate on this. I'm tired of being screwed around by companies who think they can milk me for a high purchase price and then cover up their failings.' Jackson returned to his desk.

Mark took the remark as a dismissal and he followed the others out of the room.

'Wait, Mark,' Jackson said. 'Shut the door.'

'Sir.' Mark fingered his jacket buttons. Beneath the cool breeze of the air-conditioning, he was perspiring like a squeezed sponge.

'Please sit.' Jackson pointed at the nearest chair. 'I've been in contact with Luke. He's been helping Sophia with your father's appeal case.'

Mark's heart skipped forward a few beats. He had never discussed his father with Jackson or Hettie. However, he shouldn't be surprised; Jackson had eyes and ears everywhere. The introductions at the ball had been more contrived than he'd realised.

'I passed the documents to Sophia and she's been looking them over,' Mark said.

Jackson nodded. What else did he know about? Haydocks reared its demonic head again. 'More than looking them over, Mark. She and Luke have found the witness that the previous appeal failed to identify. They're going to see him.'

Words briefly escaped Mark. How had they managed where others had failed? 'Wow, that is good news.' He ran his trembling fingers through his hair. 'The last solicitor up in Manchester couldn't locate him.'

'Luke can be persuasive.' Jackson grinned. Luke shared his brother's tenacity, as well as appearance. 'I hope this works out for you and your father.'

'So do I. I'm planning to visit him later in the month. It's tough seeing him behind bars.'

'I can imagine,' Jackson said dryly. 'Your sister. Do you keep her in the loop?'

'Not really. We've had a little falling out.'

'Fix it, Mark. She's young. You're supposed to be the man in her life.'

Jackson's rebuke hit below the belt. Mark jerked, recoiling. Sometimes, his boss behaved like his mentor, which Mark appreciated as long as it remained in a limited capacity and preferably related to work. When it came to personal relationships, he wasn't so sure he wanted it. Jackson was in his mid-thirties – probably – and he had an old school approach to handling women. Julianna would struggle with the authoritarian type. Having met Hettie, heard her speak with great affection for her husband, Mark knew outward appearances weren't always a good measure of a man.

Regardless of Jackson's decent qualities, it was somewhat troubling being in debt to the Haynes family. If Jackson knew Mark had spied on his former boss, perhaps he wouldn't be so magnanimous.

'I'll reimburse them, Luke and Sophia,' said Mark. 'I'm grateful for their support. My father has always maintained his innocence.'

'You support your father because he's your dad,' Jackson said, gruffly, as if cross with Mark.

Mark, a bead of cold sweat on his brow, stared in disbelief at the man gesturing toward the door. The meeting was over; Jackson was reading something else on his desk. Mark hurried away.

What kept Mark loyal to his father was pragmatism and not sentiment; Bill wasn't a murderer, but he wasn't entirely innocent either. He had met somebody, things hadn't gone well and bam, knife in the chest. Nothing premeditated, which the judge pointed out in his summing up, but the jury had rejected the plea of self-defence in favour of murder, not even manslaughter. The witness, a mate, or perhaps a bystander who had gone along, was real because he was consistently mentioned by people who knew people, and so on. But there was no name or description. A man more than likely. Deidre insisted that because of this one person there was some other story to be told.

Perhaps this man had done it and stitched Bill up. Unlikely. Bill would have named and blamed the other guy and, in any case, there was no physical evidence to support the theory another person was present at the crime scene. Then, what if this man had seen it happen, and for some reason refused to cooperate by hiding evidence that backed up Bill's side of things? Criminals fell out. It was plausible. But Bill's refusal to acknowledge the witness to Mark and any of the solicitors appointed to look after his case was the stumbling block to proving his innocence. He hadn't implicated anyone else and in every interview had claimed he'd acted alone.

It riled Mark to the point of fury that his father protected criminals. Where was family loyalty? Why couldn't he just plead guilty, do the time and then come home to Deidre? A new man. Chastised. Penitent.

Tick-tock, tick-tock. Mark had to focus on work. Waiting for news over the next few days would be horrendous, and, in the meantime, Mark wasn't going to tell either Deidre or Ellen a thing until he was certain of the facts.

14

Ellen

Ellen vaguely recalled mentioning Freddie to Mark, but why he had come up in the cringeworthy telephone call with her brother was a mystery. The memory fog worsened over the week, forming droplets of images and snippets of dialogue. Unable to fathom the workings of her own mind, on Friday, for the first time that week, she went running.

A warm weather front drifted over the city, drying out the puddles and sodden patches of grass. She sent a text to Nicky and arranged to meet him after work for a run at the Imperial War museum. They jogged around the small park, navigating a path between the shadows and the street lights. The evening air was bitterly cold and Ellen's fingers thickened with numbness.

To compensate for the lack of communication with Mark she kept up a breathless and cheery banter with Nicky who ran as if he was on air; bouncing off the pavement while she lumbered from side to side.

'So you're undecided about Mark still?'

'I'm wary. We haven't talked since that night.'

'Hardly surprising. You were pissed. Had your first blow job. Didn't enjoy it—'

'Nicky!' She checked around. 'It wasn't even that, okay. I wish I'd never told you.'

She halted; bent over and pressing her hands onto her bent knees, she snatched a few extra breaths. That night remained hazy; she had woken in the morning confused and hungover, not quite remembering what she had said to her brother, probably something stupid given his reaction. Nicky called by and had done what Mark had failed to do and hugged her, dusted her down and told her she had been silly and not to worry. She should concentrate on work and, from now on, she was only to run with him.

Nicky jogged on the spot. 'Then it's water under the bridge.'

Standing up straight, she flicked her hair out of her eyes. 'It doesn't feel like it. I got drunk after we'd done it and I told him to leave. Thank God, he did. He was fine about it. For a while I felt…'

Nicky stilled. 'What?'

'Elated. Thrilled. Then the alcohol kicked in and I started crying.' She cringed, wishing she could huddle under the branches of a tree and pretend her voice wasn't carrying in the wind. Jogging in the open with a shameless Nicky wasn't such a great idea.

'Sex can do that.'

She scowled and Nicky's grin disintegrated. She leaned toward him.

'It wasn't sex. I had my knickers on the whole time,' she said quietly.

His nostrils flared as he inhaled sharply. 'Good. Keep them on. Now, what about Mark?'

'I guess I owe him an apology. Dragging him out of bed to listen to me bawl.'

'He tried, I suppose, give him credit. He doesn't sound like the kind of person who deals with women often. Unmarried? No girlfriend?'

'Possibly. He's kind of secretive.'

They started jogging again. 'He probably needs a good lay then.' Nicky smirked out of the side of his mouth.

She stumbled over a kerb and nearly lost her balance. 'Oh, please, Nicky. Why bring that up? Is it always about having sex?'

'No, it's not,' he said. 'I'm getting it, so it's not an issue. It's people who don't get it who have the issue. I'm telling you, the world would be a better place if it lost all this inhibition about sex. It's fun. Relaxing.'

'If you know what you're doing,' Ellen muttered. Freddie would argue it was exactly the opposite. Less time thinking about it or doing it cleansed the soul, and so on.

Nicky suddenly flagged. 'I'm done. Need a drink. The Red Lion is around the corner. Fancy a drink?'

They dropped down to a walking pace and headed towards the street. 'Is it a gay pub?' she asked.

'Gays are everywhere, so probably. Bikers are, too. You should get to know a few.' He winked and she laughed.

The pub was warm, and her hands tingled as the blood rushed back around them. Topics came and went, his work, hers and Nicky's new boyfriend. The coupling seemed serious and Nicky went coy every time she mentioned the other man. Ellen stared at the small amount of liquid at the bottom of the pint. Life was changing, Nicky would replace her with his new-found love and she would see him less and less. Everyone had their lives to live and perhaps it was time to move on.

She would call Mark about living with him, but not yet. Let the decision sit for a couple more weeks.

As for Freddie, it had become a weird necessity to confess things to him and although she despised herself for needing him, she couldn't help it, so she would tell him about the man who had dropped his trousers.

Faceless Freddie had no presence in her life beyond his online persona. It didn't matter because there was something appealing about having a long-distance friend, even one that sermonised. It gave her a little buzz knowing she had a hold over him, just as the cuts had done years ago.

I'm kneeling on the floor ready to confess.

She meant it as a joke. However, she was on a beanbag.

Confess what?

She spelt it out. From beginning to end. The horror and awe of watching a man lower his pants. Her fascination with it. Her shame that it thrilled her.

She expected a slapped wrist.

You had a near miss. Move on. She had no time to assimilate the dismissal; Freddie was typing fast. We really should meet up.

His proposal was nothing short of a bombshell. Her heartbeats raced and her fingers danced, slipping over the keys. Where?

Come to Dublin. Spend a few days here.

Why?

I've been making enquiries and there's a chance for you to join a dig near Wicklow. Bronze age.

Seriously? Anything to improve her chances of winning a place at university. She was starting to look at courses again.

It's not the same as a university. It's paid work including accommodation. I've put in a good word for you.

When?

Next month. Can you get the time off work? A few weeks?

That soon!

I'd quit work to do it. No joke. Sod her boss and his uselessness.

What about Mark?

What about him?

Does he know about me?

No. A scant mention when drunk didn't count.

Why not?

I didn't see any point in telling him. You're over there. I'm here.

Perhaps you should.

She froze. Freddie had surprised her three times: no lecture, an offer and now cosying up to Mark.

He's busy. I still haven't moved in with him. I will soon. He's seeing a solicitor about Dad. If I tell him about you, what do I say?

That we're friends. Do you think all friends meet in pubs or workplaces? It's just how we met that bothers you.

You don't normally show an interest in Mark. Or meeting me.

I don't think your behaviour with that man was appropriate or healthy. Perhaps if you met me, you'd trust my opinion more. Start by telling Mark about me.

That we're friends?

That's the truth, isn't it?

No sweetie, she noticed. In fact, it had been a while since he had called her that. Recently, he had treated her with greater maturity, less banter and less humour. She was growing up. She wasn't a teenager anymore and maybe he was hearing the adult in her words and actions.

I'll think about it. What's the Z stand for?

I'll tell you, if you tell him.

Ellen was more worried about telling Nicky. Mark was probably too busy to care that much about what she did online. Nicky met people all the time that way, but he had rules about how to go about it, and going to Dublin, unaccompanied, was probably breaking one. Who should she tell? Nicky, her friend and confidante, or Mark, her brother and soon-to-be flatmate?

Freddie sent her the details and a form to fill in for the accommodation: a hostel on the outskirts of Dublin. She held off returning it. Instead she battled through another week at work. Her boss, Hugo, was insufferable, flapping about everything and barking orders. She had to throw together a brochure at the last minute for a new client and he picked it apart.

'If you gave me more than a few days' notice,' she said under her breath.

While eating a hurried ham sandwich, she spilled mustard on her skirt. Hugo accused her of looking drab. The others in the office simply rolled their eyes, chewed on their gum and soldiered on with the project. Ellen bit down a retort about him being a misogynist. She was so close to quitting.

In the midst of the mayhem, Mark rang. It was late, past six o'clock and she was stuck in work.

'Ellen.' He sounded breathless, as if he was running to catch a train. 'We need to meet. I've got something to tell you.'

'Mark, I'm up to my eyeballs.'

'It's important. I'm on the way to see Sophia. The appeal; she's got fresh evidence. Can we meet, this evening? I'll pay the taxi fare.'

Hugo had left, leaving her and two others to sort out his mess. She didn't have to stay. She could come in early and finish things off. New evidence? Ellen was aware of the finer details of that day, so what evidence was Mark referring to?

'Yes.' She folded the brochure and slotted it into a drawer. 'Your place, I assume?'

15

Mark

The call to meet Sophia came through by the end of the strenuous week, during which he had refused an offer of a night out with Julianna. She had not been happy with him anyway. Moody git, she declared during the telephone call, accompanying the comment with half-hearted laughter. He hadn't told her about the witness either.

Sophia's office was hidden away on a backstreet east of the City. Mark checked his watch; the appointment was scheduled for five o'clock. He went straight from work, keen to hear the news. The meeting had been arranged by Sophia's assistant, who apparently knew nothing about the case when Mark attempted to question her. He wasn't one for praying, but he hoped that there was good news waiting for him.

The cab drew up outside the bleak building. The wooden window frames were shedding paint – flakes of grey collected under the sills. The filthy glass was barely transparent, the interior hidden behind blinds. Inside, some investment: the tasteful decor was minimalist and untarnished by pollution.

'I'm here to see Sophia Crawford. I have an appointment.' He was sweating; a habit that was becoming increasingly problematic, along with the persistent stabbing sensation along his forehead. His overcoat was unnecessary and the briefcase a burden to carry.

'You are?' the receptionist asked, picking up the phone.

'Mark Clewer.'

'Hi, Sophia, I have a Mark.... right.' She hung up. 'You can go straight to her office. Third door on the right down that corridor.'

There were tagged dockets, yellow pads of notes and a swathe of documents piled on her desk. The computer hummed and the wall clock ticked aggressively. Sophia operated in a working climate that Mark wouldn't be able to tolerate. He wondered how Luke coped.

She blushed and pushed a stack of papers to one side. 'I know. Luke wouldn't stomach it, the mess. At home I'm very different.' She pointed at a chair. 'Please sit, Mark.'

Mark took off his overcoat and hung it on the back of the plastic chair.

'Luke's chambers at Lincoln Inn are so grand compared to this place,' Sophia said. Her attempt at small talk failed; he said nothing. She twirled a pen with agitated fingers and cleared her throat with a fake cough.

The ache behind his eyes strengthened and the fluorescent lights glared. He examined his shaking hands with their chewed fingernails, hating that he couldn't control his feelings. 'You've got bad news, haven't you?'

'Sorry. Let me fill you in.' She kept her eyes on the documents. 'The witness is an old friend of your father's. He was with Bill on the night... well, he was there—'

'So why didn't he come forward?'

'Because he was loyal to your father,' she said carefully.

'Loyal? By keeping his mouth shut and letting Dad sit in prison for years!' Mark folded his arms across his chest.

She picked up a piece of paper and smoothed it flat in front of her. 'Your father was arrested, tried and convicted of murder. The murdered man was important. His death caused a war between the gangs, retributions, other killings until things settled down. Bill pleaded not guilty to murder and the lesser charge of manslaughter and claimed self-defence. He was found guilty of murder and the judge indicated in his summing up that there was no evidence of pre-meditation: a mitigating circumstance.'

'I know all this,' Mark said, impatiently.

'A life sentence with a minimum of ten years. However, your father has maintained his innocence so no early parole on licence is likely. The courts have it in their power to increase his sentence.'

'Increase? What are you getting at?' Mark swallowed a mouthful of bile down. So far, things were heading in a terrible direction.

'The witness kept his mouth shut because his evidence, if presented in court, would have been seen by the defence as hostile. He would not have made life easier for your father by blabbing about that day. He wanted to protect your father. He's moved several times, to keep out of trouble, and lives in London now. Luke and I went to meet him in a pub. I'm sorry, Mark, but your father isn't an angel.'

'I know. He kept bad company. He worked hard though, there was always money, food, clothes.' His voice trembled and his heart pounded. Surely she wasn't implying his father was guilty of murder?

'Luke is good at cross-examining. The man wouldn't speak at first. Tight lipped. We talked about knowing the truth. That you, your mum, and Ellen, had a right to know the truth. That if what he had to say was never going to be heard in a court of law, then it should be said for your sake. He remains loyal to Bill, but they haven't spoken since the court case. He remembers you as a teenager. He saw you at a distance coming and going from your home. He never visited Bill if you or your sister were home.'

'I went out a lot,' Mark said quietly. Sophia hadn't mentioned where Deidre was during these visits.

'They got sucked down, Mark, sucked down into another world. It wasn't simply about petty thieving. Bill Clewer was the right-hand man in a gang that controlled an entire housing estate. He was very aware of what was going on. It might have started out differently, who knows, but he was drawn into something much bigger. Uglier.'

'Oh, God, no.'

'They were foolish, he admitted that. Bill considered giving it up; he wanted a fresh start so he could put you through college.'

Mark had heard countless times about his father's unachieved ambitions in life.

Sophia avoided eye contact. 'It wasn't unplanned, the murder. Your father always intended to kill this man.'

His throat narrowed, choking him. He loosened the strangling tie and gasped for breath. 'I don't understand… There was an argument… and they fought.'

She poured him a glass of water; her hands shook like his. 'He went to negotiate, on behalf of his boss, some deal involving girls.

They needed girls for prostituting. Bill wasn't in the car. He leaned through the window, and without warning, stabbed the man in the heart. The other knife was planted by your father in the dead man's hand. This witness, who was the lookout man, hid behind a wall and watched. Afterwards, he panicked and ran for it. He's been on the run ever since, both from the police and the gangs.'

Bill had gone with two knives, not one. If that evidence had been presented in court, it would have sealed his fate. The defence had been adamant that Bill brought one knife and he used it in self-defence.

He pushed the glass away, unable to swallow a thing, and buried his head in his hands. Nothing made sense. 'I don't believe it. I can't believe it. He's lying.' He refused to shed angry tears.

'The witness sounded very convincing. We recorded the conversation. He didn't know that we did. Luke, though, insisted we should. If I played it to you, you'd hear it in his voice, Mark. Don't though. Don't listen to it. It won't help you.'

The ticking of the wall clock punctuated the silence, reminding him in all that time, eight years, Bill had never said anything other than to reiterate his innocence. He had maintained a fabrication for whose benefit? Squaring his shoulders, Mark took a deep breath.

'My father has being lying to me, to Mum for years. Why?' He raised his hands, then dropped them into his lap.

'Who knows. Denial is a powerful emotion. As strong as grief and anger. You can believe he's determined to end his criminal activities. Yet, he killed a man. Hardly the actions of somebody trying to escape the life.'

'I can't believe he cold-bloodedly murdered somebody. My dad! I know he's a rogue, a likeable rogue. Bright, in his own way. He blessed me with his intelligence but wasted his time at school — more interested in sports than education. He taught me to be honourable, even while he shifted stolen goods.' Mark laughed. 'Honour amongst thieves, that kind of thing, like owning up to things, and protecting your friends and family. I lent my support to his charade of an appeal because of that and for his sake, more than Mum's. He told me he wanted another chance to prove himself.'

'Perhaps he wanted you to be what he had failed to be.'

'Christ, I don't know. I don't want to know. I don't want anything more to do with him. If this witness goes to the police and the sentence gets increased, then so be it. The bastard deserves it.' There was within him what Julianna would recognise: a hot-blooded soup of anger and disgust. 'I've got to tell Mum it's over. How am I going to tell her?'

'Wait,' Sophia said. 'Until you've accepted this yourself. Don't tell her when you're angry and bitter. She'll be devastated, won't she?'

Alarm had paled her complexion to marble. He inhaled deeply and unclenched his fists. Control, he needed to control his emotions. Nothing would come of anger, but more anger.

'Thank you, Sophia. At least I know the truth. What do I owe you, for your time? Luke's too.' With horrifying ease, he became that numerically driven accountant again.

'Please, don't worry about it... I'm still tying up some loose ends with regard to the information this witness provided.'

'No, I insist. I told Jackson I would pay you and I, unlike my father, am a man of my word. As far as I'm concerned there is nothing more you need do. Don't waste your time.'

She told him she would bill him by post. 'I'd like you to visit me and Luke for dinner with some friends. Bring your sister. We can introduce her to somebody with good connections.'

He looked at her blankly. Connections to what? He wasn't thinking about socialising at the moment. He couldn't put his mind anywhere sensible that didn't inspire anger. 'Sure,' he said vaguely.

They shook hands and she opened the door for him; she wanted him gone. 'Sorry that it's all turned out bad for you.'

'Please don't apologise.' He put on his overcoat. 'You've succeeded where others had failed. I'm grateful. Goodbye.'

The noise in the outer office didn't register and he ignored the fluttering eyelashes of the receptionist. He walked aimlessly for several blocks before hailing a black cab, wondering how to tell Ellen. She had a right to know the truth.

16
Ellen

The room smelt of roses. The aroma was subtle, but there, lingering in the air. There weren't any vases in the flat. She followed Mark into the living room where Mark stuffed a twenty-pound note into her hand.

'For the cab.'

She scrunched it into her pocket. He poured her a glass of wine and handed it to her. They sat, glasses perched on their knees, and he sighed a few times.

Worn out and lost, he was out of sorts in every way: scruffy pair of jeans with holes over the knees; a faded t-shirt with blotches of sweat under his armpits – old sweat, she reckoned; smudges of greyness under his eyes would worsen with the sleepless night he had yet to have. He fidgeted with the stem of his glass, spinning it with his agitated fingers.

'So?' she said, inquisitively. Better have it over.

'Dad committed murder, not manslaughter. There was no self-defence. It was premeditated and unprovoked.' He glanced in her direction. 'But I guess you're not upset by any of this.'

'No, not really, but I'm not pleased. Why would I be? Dad screwed us both over. What happened at the solicitors?'

He told her about the eye-witness who had held back from giving evidence to protect Bill from worse charges. He might not have saved Bill from a guilty conviction, but he had probably lessened the sentence by keeping silent.

'No motive provided. Dad banked on getting that self-defence plea, but he didn't leave enough evidence inside the car to support his false confession. All he had were two knives. One for him, one for the victim to hold, wiped free of his fingerprints.'

She nearly dropped her glass. The base landed on her lap and she managed to salvage the spillage with a brisk wipe of her sleeve. There had been two pockets sewn into the coat. She said nothing – what was the point? Mark knew now what she had known since she was eleven years old. Bill Clewer was a cold, calculating criminal. The judge's two key sources of mitigation were Bill's remarkable previous lack of convictions and the supposed spontaneity of the killing.

'He lied, Ellie. Lied and lied. He promised me… He.' Mark's voice broke. He slumped like a sack of potatoes and downed half the glass in one go.

She stretched out to touch his shaking hand, then changed her mind. Those fiery eyes brimmed with anger. Such suppressed rage wasn't healthy, and she should know. It sent a shiver down her spine seeing him like this: so like her.

He wiped the back of his hand across his mouth. 'You know what really pisses me off? It doesn't make a jot of difference. This appeal was never going to free him. So why, why fucking why drag it out for years? He could have pleaded guilty and got some miti-gation and a shorter sentence. I was willing to go with this damn appeal because I had this thing in the back of my head that he was decent. I never saw him as a heartless assassin.'

Ellen sipped her wine. She didn't want to get drunk here. Later, maybe. 'He hoodwinked a few people,' she said quietly. 'If he had his reasons, he's keeping them locked inside with him. You've got your closure.'

'I don't get it.' He hung his head and sloshed the wine about in his glass. 'Sophia couldn't explain it either. Denial is like grief, she said. And he's been holding on to it for eight years. I've got to tell Mum all this.'

She didn't want to be in the flat when that happened. 'Well, don't be surprised if she refuses to believe you. She's incapable of chang-ing her lies as well – the pair of them are made for each other.'

'What do you mean?'

'Oh, come on. She had to know about Dad, what with all those men coming to the house. Arguments they had about where the money came from. She turned a blind eye in the end and stuck by him because she spent so much time lying for him, she couldn't speak the truth. And she liked having the money.'

'How would you know? You hid in your room.'

She ground her fingernails into her thighs, right on top of her scars. No, not again. Mark's bitterness wasn't her fault. While she might have stayed out of sight in order to protect herself from seeing things, Mark had been kept occupied and deliberately distracted by their father's legitimate hobbies; things that wouldn't raise eyebrows. Mark had been adept at gluing himself to the better side of Bill.

She spoke with as much neutrality as possible. 'Tell her. Then forget it, and don't go looking for a reason, you won't find it.'

He finished his wine. 'So. That's that.'

'Not quite. I've got my own news to tell.'

'Oh?'

She reeled in the excitement. 'I've got a chance to go to Ireland and join a dig. It includes accommodation and some pay. I'm waiting on confirmation.'

Mark's eyebrows shot up. 'What about uni?'

'It can wait. Experience is just as important.'

'How did you find out?'

'I've a friend over in Dublin with contacts. He's called Freddie.'

'Freddie. You've not mentioned him before now.'

A hazy conversation echoed in her mind. Perhaps she hadn't mentioned his name. 'Why should I? It's not as if you show any interest in me. I'll have to quit work—'

Mark's reclining pose shifted into a rigid one. 'What? How long is this for? When?'

'Next month. And I don't know exactly how long. I don't care about work. I can get another job when I get back. Which brings me to your offer. I'm going to hand in my notice at work and on the bedsit and pay the last month off. Then I can move my stuff here to your spare room while I'm away.'

He blinked several times. 'You're going but dumping your things in my spare room. That's it?'

'Yes.' She nodded defiantly, then swiftly softened her voice into sweet contrition. 'If you don't have other plans for the room.'

He rose and carried his glass to the kitchen table. 'I've got a girl-friend.'

The scent of roses. She had been right. 'So this works better for you. Not having little sister around?'

Mark's face was an admirable portrait of neutrality. 'My offer for you to live here remains. I prefer her place.'

Things made more sense in the light of finding out he had a love interest. 'You're moving in with her?'

He laughed. 'No. We're not in that kind of relationship. We're friends with benefits.'

She called Nicky her friend without benefits.

Ellen handed Mark her wine glass. 'Finish it. I'm not in the mood.'

He caught her sleeve. 'Wait. There's something else. Sophia has invited us to her place for dinner.'

'Oh, no. Not another Razzles, please—'

'We should go and say thank you for her effort. Luke's too. I'm sure her fee will be discounted. Luke is Jackson's brother.'

She had nothing to thank them for. 'I'll drop her a postcard.'

'Ellen, they're inviting a professor you should talk to. It might give you another option, instead of going to Ireland. A good word from an eminent academic, yes?'

Freddie had given her a good word, too. However, if it shut Mark up and let her store her things for nothing at his place then she'd go. 'Okay.'

She confessed again. The compulsion to serialise her life into brief snippets continued to evolve and, back at home, she typed it out for Freddie to read.

I told him. Mark, that is. He wants me to meet somebody else, a professor.

He doesn't think you should come here?

He doesn't think I should ignore a Haynes offer. Mark's been given the name of an alternative who I should meet.

Your brother shouldn't decide for you. My name is Freddie

Zustaller. See, I'm good on my word. Is Mark? I think you know the answer. I'll let you decide.

He'd attached a drawing, an old map of Wicklow. It was annotated with jottings and marks about possible trenches and geophysical points of interest. Something real, tangible: a lure, and it worked a treat. One day she would control everything, be in charge of a major project and earn a reputation that was worthy, instead of contrived with the edge of a razor.

Ellen's fingers curled into a ball and she punched the air. The truth was she knew exactly what she wanted to do. Freddie had filled the void and if anyone deserved the recognition, it was him. She couldn't wait to meet him, touch him. Yes, even that. She would happily go where he sent her.

17
Julianna

Mark rolled off Julianna and flopped onto his back. She lay her arm across his chest and curled the black hairs around her fingers.

'This thing with your dad has really upset you.' She'd listened over dinner to Bill's story. She had hoped Mark might put aside his anger in the bedroom. Clearly not. It clung to him: a straightjacket of raw emotion.

'I'm sorry, I've not been good company.' He sighed, labouring the exhale.

'I don't mind.' Shuffling closer, she pressed her warmth onto him, hoping for a better response. But, nothing. He sighed, again.

'Your mum must have taken it hard.' She was surprised Mark hadn't regaled her with a woeful tale about his mother's response to the news.

'Haven't told her.'

She snapped one of his hairs and he slapped her hand away.

'Don't. She's in this bubble, why pop it? The longer I hold off the better. She'll be impossible to handle. Weeping, wailing. Gnashing of teeth. She can tell Dad then. I'm not going to see him. Ever. I'm considering burning his letters.'

Beneath her steady hand, she felt his heartbeats, the rapid knocks on his breast. The burning, she assumed, would be meta-phorical. 'How did Ellen take the news?' she asked gently.

'Indifferent. If she cares, she can't be bothered to show it. I doubt she does. In any case, she's moving on.'

'You mean moving in?' Julianna sat up. Mark remained rigid. He pulled the sheet back over his lower half, hiding his failure.

'Nope. She's going to Ireland to do some field work. As in real digging in the dirt. She's going to dump her stuff at mine for the duration.'

'Wow. How long will she be gone?'

He folded his arms across his chest. The arrangement of limbs was uncomfortably defensive and unnatural in bed. 'Does it matter? She's excited. It's more interesting than her job and they'll give her somewhere to live out there.'

Julianna drew her knees up and hugged them. 'Sounds fun for her. Who is they?'

He screwed his face up. 'Dunno.'

'She met someone?'

'I don't think so. Dunno. She's got this friend, Freddie, I think she called him. He's out there helping her.'

Julianna frowned this time. 'She's not met him?'

'I don't think so. No, she said she hadn't.' He rubbed his eyes. 'It's her life.'

Mark's interest in Ellen's life had peaked and fallen away. Julianna wasn't in a position to judge. She barely spoke to her own sister, although that was more to with envy than belligerence.

'I'm sure she'll be fine,' she said. What that meant was up to him. If he wasn't worried about his sister, why should she be? Something else was bothering him. He had heaped countless things on his plate in the last few weeks.

'I'm sorry. I'm probably tired. Busy day at work. Which reminds me. I've been given this assignment and it turns out to be pretty complicated. I could do with your analytical mind.'

'You think you've got a terrorist network?'

'No.' He skipped over her attempt at humour. 'A problematic Jackson Haynes acquisition. He's asked me to go through some irregularities.' Mark waved two fingers in the air to indicate the speech marks. 'Can you come by my office first thing tomorrow?'

'Sure.' She kissed his cheek. The wiry bristles grazed her lips. Humour hadn't lifted his mood, so she tried a different tactic. 'You're good at this job, you know that. You don't need me.'

'Once, maybe...' He stared at the lampshade above his head.

'Come on.' She swiped his arm with her knuckles. 'That business in Manchester, you caused the collapse of a corrupt accountancy firm.'

He covered his face with his hands and groaned. 'People lost their jobs. I betrayed my boss.'

She snuggled closer to him again. 'What was his name?'

'David Henderson. The senior partner in the firm. Haydocks was his baby.'

'Must have been worth his while: laundering money, dodgy deals.'

'Let's say he had these.' He spread his fingers out and stabbed them in the air. 'Pies.'

Henderson had to be a specialist in money laundering and not just a casual operative. 'Oh, more than one?' she asked.

'I found six clients with dubious accounts.'

'Six!' What a treasure trove. 'Why wonder you went into hiding. Didn't you want to take the credit?'

'I worked there for three years – my first job. Dave was my mentor. I wonder sometimes if he thought I was going to help out, become a crook like my dad. Perhaps he let me find the money. I don't know. I left. I didn't want to be implicated.'

'Oh, I guess that's always a risk if you blow whistles.' She pursed her lips. 'So, these clients, who were they?'

'Names. Just names and accounts. It was complicated. He'd covered his tracks and I didn't suspect anything for three years, until...' He yawned and stretched his arms above his head.

'Yes?' She twirled a few chest hairs again.

'Swedish... no Norwegian. Redningsmann, something like that. Redder: that cropped up too. It made me curious – those two: Redningsmann and Redder accounts were the biggest. Look, I drank a lot for a few months, trying to work out what to do with what I had found out. Then I panicked when Dave started bombarding everyone with questions. He was under pressure from somebody, probably the dodgy clients getting twitchy. I handed in my notice and decided to tip off the police, anonymously. Hardly the actions of hero. Dave knew something was up, but by then, a few of us had resigned from Haydocks; it helped cover my back.'

'You weren't going to help the police?'

Mark examined his fingernails. 'I don't exactly feel comfortable talking to the police. My family is known to them. It was easier not to get involved. They had all the clues they needed to arrest Henderson for money laundering.' He flung back the duvet. 'I should go.'

He grabbed his pants and left Julianna stranded on the bed.

'Sure you don't want to stay?'

'No, thanks, sweetheart.' He disappeared into the bathroom.

The endearment felt wrong. They weren't sweethearts, or darlings, or honeybuns, or whatever stupid phrase came to mind when they kissed. She'd not even considered calling him anything other than Mark. She was on a fence, somewhere between lover and friend. It didn't help she was wearing her detective hat too. Mark didn't seem the slightest bit curious about the criminals he had upset. Probably because it reminded him of his father. Somewhere, a hive of angry bees had been stirred and the fallout had to have been considerable and sufficiently intriguing to engage an outsider like Jackson.

Mark stuck his head around the door. 'Oh, and I'm taking Ellen to dinner at Luke and Sophia's. So we can say thanks. You don't mind?' He had a toothbrush in his hand, one of the few items he had left at hers, along with extra strong condoms and a stash of espresso coffee beans.

'No, why would I be?' She squirmed. She was bothered, but then, if he had turned up with the not-quite-a-girlfriend, it might be awkward. Luke was a Haynes and the Haynes family were a spy network in their own right.

Julianna ran her eyes over the documentation Mark had provided, along with a steaming mug of coffee.

'Lots of complex client relationships. Does seem suspicious, Mark.' Julianna sipped on her drink.

He ran his hand through his hair, ruffling it into a few indignant spikes. She could happily smooth them down. But she didn't. They were in his office. Instead of touching, they talked strategy. A little after half past nine his office phone rang.

He reached out with his hand, then snatched it back. 'I'll let it ring. It's Mum.'

Seeing how he fought with himself, she wished there was a way to help ease his pain. His concerns about his father's guilt weighed heavier than ever, dragged down by the need to know why Bill had lied. Unlike her previous job, she no longer had access to criminal records or other intelligence systems. But she knew somebody who had contacts.

Chris Moran stabbed at his keyboard with two fingers. Occasionally, he would scowl and hit the back space a few times. She hid a smile behind yet another sociable mug of coffee; perhaps she should switch to herbal teas… the grin spread at the unlikeliness of changing her habits. Coffee and the punch bag both remained essential. Poor Chris: computers weren't his friend. Some years back, Chris had been an armed police officer, he patrolled streets and ate sandwiches in his squad car while he undertook countless surveillance operations. The switch to private security was the result of a gunshot wound. He had lost the tip of his forefinger. However, he could still type with it.

The weekly catch-up meeting was something of a formality. Most weeks neither of them said much and since Julianna wasn't doing any protection work, he had even less to say.

'I'm working with Mark on something for Mr Haynes,' she said, emerging from behind the mug with a sombre expression.

'Okay.' Chris continued to batter his keyboard.

'Mr Haynes has taken quite an interest in Mark, hasn't he?'

Chris ignored the bait.

'Given what Mark did in Manchester, I'm surprised the boss took him on,' she said.

He ceased pecking at the keyboard, pushed it to one side and folded his arms. 'I don't read minds, Julianna.'

'His first accountancy job. He shopped his boss to the police. Mark told me about it. It's not in his personnel file. Now, knowing how Mr Haynes is about who gets near his wife, the omission is odd.'

'Meaning?' Chris shuffled a few random sheets of paper about on his desk.

'Why the cover-up? He's ideal for the job he's doing and has proved he can investigate fraud. Yet, given his experience, there's no mention of Haydocks on his file. It's like it's been scrubbed out.'

Chris stilled his hands.

She had his attention now. 'He uncovers this fraud, very extensive and involving several companies, passes the info to the police and then bolts. He ends up here, employed by Haynes, who I know is aware of what he did, but Haynes doesn't seem perturbed.'

'Whistle blowing isn't against the law,' Chris said. 'Henderson is the one behind bars.'

Chris was unsurprisingly well-informed about Haydocks; she hadn't mentioned Henderson.

'I guess the police in Manchester could have found Mark, questioned him, but they're still wading their way through the huge amount of information Mark leaked. They let him go. Haydocks would have been on his resume and I assume you followed the breadcrumb trail and pieced together the timeline. Mark was the obvious contender for dishing the dirt on Henderson. So why not leave it on record? A badge of honour and an explanation for why Mark got the job here.'

Chris's nose twitched. 'Haynes has his reasons.' A cop-out answer and it only stoked Julianna to push harder.

'Did Mark do more than he's letting on? Was he involved?'

'Look, Julianna, trust me, Mark isn't a crook, and neither is Haynes. Mark simply blew apart something big. Way bigger than he probably intended.'

'Mark doesn't know the full consequences of what he did. But Haynes does. So it has to have affected Haynes personally. Mark uncovered a network of phoney companies.'

Chris leaned across his desk, lowering his voice, which was unnecessary. They were alone. 'One name came up. It's relevant to the threats.'

Julianna stiffened. 'The threats against Haynes. Against Hettie?'

Chris nodded. 'Jackson immediately sought a means to get Mark here, in this building, without raising suspicions. You understand? And he made sure you two met.'

'He orchestrated our relationship. I guessed that.'

'He ensured you were interested in Mark. He doesn't care that you fuck each other. He knows you'll be his ears and eyes. But Mark hasn't a clue what he got himself into.'

Although her cheeks flushed hot when he revealed he knew about their relationship, she was more alarmed by the implication she was supposed to be protecting Mark. The extent of Haynes interference was far-reaching.

'Mark hasn't mentioned any threats.' Their conversations were mostly wrapped around innocuous topics because Mark shied away from intrusive lines of questioning.

'Once they know he's implicated, he'll be on their radar. You know they won't let him get away with it. Millions frozen in bank accounts because of the raid on Haydocks.'

'His sister? His mum?'

'There's a limit to how far Jackson can stretch resources without attracting attention. The boss is a target, and you know about Hettie. If we surround Mark's family, it will arouse suspicion. I don't think he's a target – there's no evidence and you've not commented on any unusual activity.' He raised his eyebrows, expecting her to confirm.

Julianna couldn't think of any occasion when they had been together that indicated he was being watched. He hadn't talked about harassment either. 'If you followed the breadcrumb trail, then they could, but in the opposite direction: to here.'

'Let's hope they're too busy protecting other assets to worry about Mark or his family.'

'I haven't met his sister. She's leaving London soon.'

'What's her name?'

'Ellen Clewer.'

Chris wrote it down on a scrap of paper. 'Is she aware of what Mark did?'

'No, I don't think so. What about their father?'

Chris leaned back in his chair. 'Ah, William Clewer. He's not going anywhere for the time being, especially now his appeal is over.'

'How did—'

'Luke told Mr Haynes, who told me.' The Haynes family network worked quickly.

'Mark has no sympathy for his father. Fury, more like it. His dad lied a lot.'

Chris smirked. 'And probably still is lying a lot.'

'Meaning?'

'Gangs. It's all about money and gangs. Rivals and allies. They're all stabbing each other in the back.'

She swore under her breath. 'What doesn't Haynes know? He's pushed me to find stuff out by dangling Mark in front of me.'

'You're astute. It's why Haynes likes you. He likes Mark, too. He's taken him under his wing. But Jackson Haynes style, you know?'

She didn't know. She wanted to know but probably not first hand. 'So you don't think Mark is under any immediate threat?'

Chris shrugged his shoulders. 'Guess that's for you to find out.'

'I'm the one piecing everything together, aren't I?' She rose to her feet. 'What's the name that came up at Haydocks?' she asked.

'Redningsmann.' Chris scribbled it down and handed her the note. 'Run it through a translator and you'll see why it grabbed Jackson's attention when he read the reports that came out. He doesn't think it's a coincidence. He would like you to prove him wrong, if only for both of your sakes, since that's where you've invested your interest.'

She ignored Chris's smirk and stuffed the note into her jacket pocket. She didn't need the paper; Redningsmann was already stashed in her memory. Now she was about to find out why. It wasn't the only name Mark had mentioned. There was Redder, too.

18

Mark

Bev and Tulip were vegetarians. Ellen was delighted. It helped break the awkwardness that came when strangers met for the first time. She had already drunk two glasses of wine by the time another couple arrived. A sanguine Ellen poured herself a third glass. Caroline, a plump lady with letterbox glasses said little, unlike the weathered Derek, the mysterious professor of archaeology.

'I'm driving,' he said, when Ellen passed him the wine bottle. He handed it to Mark, who helped himself to a small measure. Sobriety wasn't a requirement, but Mark wasn't in the mood for alcohol.

Mark envied Luke's generous apartment, especially the simplicity – each room seamlessly folded into one another. Sophia summoned them to the dining table. Luke adjusted his misaligned fork before sitting down. Mark accidently knocked his onto the floor and apologised.

'I'll get you a replacement.' Sophia dashed to a kitchen drawer. 'Don't worry.'

Mark had been on edge for days; he was on borrowed time. Deidre's desperate messages had increased in frequency and she had even threatened to come down on a train. He had reassured her he was alive, and very busy. It had placated her for the time being.

While Mark took time to open up to people, Ellen possessed qualities he had not noticed before. She helped in the kitchen, collected up the dirty dishes and kept the sometimes stilted conversations going. Razzles had been a disaster, but dinner with Sophia proved a success up until the dessert course. As Luke topped up wine glasses, and Sophia and Tulip talked about the best recipes for cheesecakes, Ellen fell apart in slow motion; her capacity for alcohol tolerance was breached. She stared unfocused with a familiar glassy-eyed smirk, and burped.

'Oops, sorry.' She covered her mouth and slouched, almost on the cusp of slithering beneath the table top. Throughout the meal, she'd showed no interest in Derek's lengthy digressions into the world of archaeological research. Mark was peeved with her and bored of Derek.

'I'm going to Ireland to do some field work.' She raised her glass to her lips.

'Oh, where?' Derek enquired.

Startled, she spluttered, 'South of Dublin, near Wicklow. Bronze Age site.'

Derek's wrinkly forehead formed trenches. 'I wasn't aware that there's an active Neolithic site near Wicklow.'

Ellen blushed. 'I'm only going for a short while. Just to help out. It's a new thing. I've a friend, you see. One you won't know because he's Irish. I think.' She tossed the napkin on her plate and patted her streamlined stomach. 'Stuffed.'

'I'm more interested in coastal archaeology,' Derek said. 'I'm overseeing a few projects across the country, including one in Scotland. We could do with some keen helpers there too.'

Mark winked at Ellen. Say something, he mouthed.

'I don't like the seaside.' She slurred the consonants into one another. 'Don't remember any decent holidays by the sea.' She'd regressed back to the childish attention seeker of old. She ignored Mark's warning glares. He had judicially kept out of the conversation and Luke seemed content to listen diplomatically with the same watchful eyes as his older brother.

The table was cleared and the coffee maker switched on.

Ellen tottered into the kitchen. 'Let me do the coffee, Sophia, you've given us such a lovely meal. It's the least I can do.'

Sophia politely declined the offer.

'I'm so grateful to you and Luke, you know, for Dad,' she lowered her voice, but not enough for Mark's keen ears. 'Naughty Bill Clewer.' She giggled.

Mark cringed behind his cupped face, hoping that shrill whoop of glee wasn't the reason for Derek's gruff expression. Sophia adeptly steered his sister toward an armchair. 'I'll bring you coffee,' she said.

Mark intercepted Sophia on route to the kitchen for a private conversation. 'I am so sorry, Sophia. She's not taking this business with Dad well. She doesn't talk to me about it,' he whispered, checking over his shoulder. 'She gets drunk.'

Sophia pressed her hand over Mark's. 'Don't worry. It's a big thing to come to terms with. I'm sorry it didn't work out for you both. She'll come round eventually.'

He joined the others around the coffee table.

Luke stared up at the ceiling. Bev had managed to engage Caroline in conversation. In a bubble of contentment Tulip helped herself to every one of Sophia's recipe books. The motley gathering offered Mark nothing and Ellen, who was supposed to be benefiting, had formed an unbreakable alliance with somebody else miles away. The loyalty she demonstrated to this person remained a mystery, but he didn't particularly care as long as it kept her happy. The evening might have gone so differently if Julianna had accompanied him.

Luke bent to speak in Mark's ear. 'Could I have a word in private.' The tone of Luke's voice reminded him of another man.

'Sure.'

They went to Luke's immaculate study where the law books were lined neatly on dust free shelves above Luke's barren desk. The pictures on the wall behind him were abstract barring one, which was a watercolour. Mark recognised the artistic style.

Perched on his desk, Luke cleared his throat. 'I wanted to say I'm sorry about your father and that we didn't bring this matter to a happy conclusion. The contrary in fact.' He spoke with a legal ease, the kind of tone Mark had heard many times when dealing with his father's case.

Mark wasn't prepared to discuss Bill. 'Well, I know now. So it's done and dusted.'

'Well, not quite. The tape recording,' said Luke, 'the witness's confession of your father's guilt. What do you want us to do with it? Keep it in case you want to hear it, or your father does. Or destroy it?'

Mark had given little thought to the condemning evidence. His first reaction was to destroy it and forget everything. He scratched his chin. 'I haven't spoken to my mother yet.'

'I see. You think she'll need to hear it?' Luke asked.

The answer to that lay in Deidre's stubbornness. 'I don't know, to be honest. Can we leave the decision for now?'

'No problem. It's your decision though. I'm allowing you this out of respect and because you're Jackson's friend. I should turn it over to the police.'

'Thank you.' Why was he thanking Luke? His father benefited, not him. The witness's loyalty to Bill was commendable; Mark's was slipping away to nothing. He pivoted on his feet, ready to leave when Luke spoke again.

'Don't blame those around you for what you've found out.'

'What do you mean by that?'

'Ellen. You two are okay?'

Surrounded by do-gooders; their pretence at sympathy infuriated him. Hierarchy he could respect; wisdom and experience too. But Luke wasn't his boss.

'Yes, of course we are,' Mark said curtly, then seeing Luke's bruised expression, he laced his voice with regret. 'Sorry, it's been a stressful time for me. Thank you for your time and everything. I can handle Ellen. She's my sister.'

'Understood, Mark,' Luke said, his face stony and unmoved. The damage was done.

Mark took Ellen home. The already frigid atmosphere cooled further in the taxi.

'There was a chance there,' Mark said. 'Derek. Scotland. It might have been the beginning of something for you and you blew it.'

'I'm going to Ireland. It's all arranged.' She shrank into the dark corner of the cab as if cowered. But her livid eyes reflected the passing streetlights. She wasn't upset, she was angry, and he suspected she had deliberately used her drunkenness to foster resentment between them. It was a pity that her attitude had caused collateral damage with the other guests.

'Then I hope it works out for you.' He stared out of the window until the cab drew up outside his flat.

Having filled a glass of water in the kitchen, she walked past him and slammed the spare room door shut behind her. Mark sat on his bed, head in hands. He wasn't cut out for being a big brother. Or a son. He couldn't handle either of those roles.

19
Mark

A week later, Ellen had moved some of the bulkier things into his spare room, stuff she wasn't going to take with her to Ireland. He had given her a spare key and she deposited the boxes while he was at work. Their paths hadn't crossed, and she left notes on the kitchen table.

Sophia wanted to return Bill's appeal papers to Mark. He decided Ellen wouldn't take well to seeing them alongside her stuff. He had politely put off Sophia with some feeble excuse. Once Ellen was gone, he would arrange for them to be collected.

He spent another night with Julianna. He planned to spend more time there. Waking up, he patted the cool dent on her side of the bed. Julianna had already left for work. She survived on less sleep than him and often worked out in the cellar downstairs before breakfast. It was a claustrophobic space with a punch bag and mould growing on the walls.

He clambered out of her bed just after seven and dressed. Jogging down the street to the bus-stop, he dashed into the mini-market and bought a Mars bar for breakfast. Coming out of the shop, chocolate bar stuffed in his mouth, a car passed him. Waiting for the bus, which was late, he saw the same black BMW circle three more times around the block. A private taxi? It didn't have license plates for carrying passengers. Each time it drew close to the kerb, it slowed and crawled in the traffic, annoying the vehicle tailgating it. A car horn sounded, and the BMW sped away, screeching its tyres and swerving between the parked cars. The old lady next to Mark in the queue complained about reckless drivers and the need for speed bumps. Mark agreed.

Mark mentioned the incident to Julianna that morning in his office. She was collating the spreadsheets on the interim report for Haynes' latest acquisition.

She paused, her fingers curling around a paper clip. 'Seen it before?' she asked sharply. 'The car?'

'I don't know. Why would I remember one car?'

'Private number plate?' Bent over the table with her eyes down, she stiffened.

'It had four doors and dark windows, okay, that's the sum total of what I remember. I was agreeing about the speed bumps. Somebody got knocked over a week ago.'

'Where?' The paper clip flew across the table.

The punch bag had failed her that morning. 'Outside the shop. What's with the third degree?'

She shrugged and retrieved the paper clip. 'Just that you should be careful, that's all.'

He touched the back of her hand, leaned over and kissed her cheek in a rare show of affection. 'You're very sweet. But I'm a big boy and can take care of myself when it comes to crossing the road.' At work, they were strictly professional and maintained a cool distance from each other. But that approach would become harder once his project was finished; she would be assigned to something else, which was probably for the best.

Her cheeks were pink. The poor paper clip was twisted out of shape. 'I hope so,' she murmured.

'Let's review where we're up to,' he said.

'To sum up: small subsidiary owned by larger company who look more profitable than they should. We could spend time digging up further issues but to my mind this acquisition looks rocky.'

He agreed. 'I'm not convinced that their cash flow projections are accurate. We need more time to determine what's going on.'

'You suspect fraud, don't you? Fiduciary fraud. They're making false tax returns. Ring Neil.' Neil, the chief negotiator, was in charge of the project.

Neil had been quick with his decision: the acquisition shouldn't go ahead. He contacted Diana, Jackson's PA for an appointment. Later that day, five of them, including Mark, but not Julianna, trooped up to the top floor and presented themselves at Diana's desk.

'You'll have to wait,' she said, tapping her watch. 'He hasn't finished the last meeting. You're early anyway.'

'Better to be on time, isn't it?' Neil said. The meeting had been arranged at short notice. Neil hadn't expected to be seen so quickly.

'Probably, given the mood he is in. Definitely not a day for bringing him bad news.'

Neil went slightly pale. 'We don't exactly have good news. Any reason why he's being irritable?'

Another PA perked up from his desk behind Diane's. 'Obvious. Something this long.' He indicated a short distance between his hands, 'And she screams a lot in the night.'

'Ah, not his wife I take it,' Neil said, cheekily. Mark smirked.

'Doesn't he have two houses?' asked Paolo, an intern with freckles and a tight-fitting suit that wouldn't impress Jackson. 'Can't he simply sleep at the other one?'

'Some father you'll make,' Diana muttered. 'Go and wait over there.' She waved them away to the seating area of the lobby.

Mark settled himself next to Neil on the sofa.

'I've never been up here before,' said Darren, Neil's protégé, a likeable man with a goatee beard and a crooked nose. Mark found it hard not to look at his nose.

'That's what happens when you're promoted,' said Neil. 'You get to find out if you have a head for heights.'

'I've never met him either,' said Darren, 'in the flesh.'

'Do you think you're going to become his friend or something?' Neil rolled his eyes. Mark kept his head down.

Darren fidgeted. Paolo preened his hair back and Duncan, who hadn't said a word, was reading through the documents, internalising everything as if he was about to be tested on his numbers. All of them, barring Mark, were lawyers and contract specialists. They weren't surprised that Neil was recommending pulling the plug on the deal.

'Oi, you're wanted.' Diana jerked her head toward the double doors.

Mr Haynes was by the window, looking down at the street. The sun, shining through the tinted glass, was low in the sky. He drew the blinds back across. He was without a jacket or tie, and he wore a wireless headset. He removed it, sat at the head of the table and drummed his fingers as he waited for them to join him.

Neil adjusted his tie before speaking. 'Mr Haynes, we've reviewed everything, especially Mark's input and we can't recommend going ahead with this acquisition. Too many discrepancies in several areas of operations.' Neil handed over the summary sheet he had compiled with Mark's help.

There was a pause while Jackson ran his finger down the bullet points. 'Okay. I agree, will end the due diligence and call off our interest. I don't want to waste any further time on this.'

There was a collective sigh of relief around the table.

Time meant money in Jackson's world. He spent a few minutes running through their findings. Darren continued to fidget, and Paolo had developed a stutter. Mark wanted to laugh. Jackson wasn't that intimidating, not when you knew him, but then Mark had had a privileged start at the company. He crossed his legs and settled back in his seat.

'You don't agree, Mark?' Jackson said sharply, his eyebrows bunched together above his nose.

'With pulling the acquisition? I agree whole-heartedly,' he said, uncrossing his legs. 'I would like to know what they're hiding and why. I don't think we've fully answered why things don't add up.'

'That's not our job, Mark. However, if you think you're close to finding the truth, you have to the end of the week. Then we walk away.'

Neil gasped and shot a glare across the table at Mark.

'Problem, Neil?' asked Jackson.

'No, sir.'

'This is just for Mark to deal with. Your team can bow out. I want a final report though. That it's, gentlemen. I have other things to deal with today.' He rose and so did everyone else.

Mark waited by the table as the room emptied. 'Mr Haynes?'

'Yes?' Jackson was back at his desk.

'I could do with Julianna's help still, on this.'

Jackson leaned back and his leather chair creaked. 'Could you now?' He grinned. 'All right. I'll speak to Chris Moran. Keep her freed up for you.'

Mark blushed; a stupid response and immature.

'Is that all, Mark? Because I haven't the time to arrange opportunities for you to meet your girlfriend.'

Mark stepped backwards, stumbling against a chair. He knew! The man had eyes everywhere. Had Julianna told Hettie? Possibly. Did it matter? Probably not, as long as he kept his head down and held on to his position in Jackson's inner circle.

'No. Just that I wanted to say your brother has been very helpful. And Sophia, too. They're a lovely couple and... my sister and I had a good time the other week and...'

Jackson picked up a pen. 'I'm glad. Now clear off, Mark.' Jackson's lip curled slightly as he delivered his dismissal.

Mark hurried out of the office, head down and clutching the report.

He was late home. Having delegated himself an additional piece of work – digging up the dirt on the failed acquisition – he would have to burn the midnight oil. Dropping his briefcase by the front door, he removed his overcoat and kicked off his shoes. In the bathroom, he washed the city grime off his face. Looking up, he caught his reflection in the shaving mirror. He saw somebody else looking back at him; somebody he rarely met these days. A man, who from the other side of a protective glass, had begged Mark to help relieve his mother's suffering and to find a way for him to gain his freedom. A lying, devious man and Mark hated him, hated that they shared the same features – the bold eyes and narrow nose.

He sat at the kitchen table, fired up his laptop and ploughed through the figures one more time. Outside, the rain pelleted on the windows and car horns blasted. He rose to shut the blinds and, looking down, he spied a biker and his pillion rider perched on a motorcycle outside the building. The pillion passenger was looking right up at his window.

A shiver went down Mark's spine as he snapped the blinds shut. After the incident with the car, he was on edge with everyone around him, just as he had been before leaving Manchester. Everyone thought he was a crook because of his father. He would prove them wrong. He would champion the righteous and become a scrutiniser of facts and figures. Jackson had employed him to maintain his business ethics and Mark would uphold them.

Ellen would have to take a back seat while he cemented his friendship with Haynes. Possibly Julianna, too. She was showing a progression of behaviours he had not experienced with his previous transient girlfriends: an interest in his family, which wasn't unusual, but for Mark it was unnecessary. She might be an ex-copper and bodyguard, but it wasn't her job to protect him. He shouldn't have let things get that serious between them. She deserved someone better than him and not the liar who had told his mother there was no news. Perhaps that was why the man in the mirror haunted him.

He turned away from the window, stormed into the bathroom, picked up the mirror and smashed it on the floor. A pointless exercise as there were other mirrors in the house. However, it was amazingly satisfying seeing the shards ricochet off the tiles; some of his anger was captured in those slithers of glass. A calmness washed over him and he fetched the dustpan and brush. He should have a go at Julianna's punch bag. He laughed softly to himself – it was a good enough reason to stay with Julianna. It would do for now.

20

Ellen

Monday

Ellen scrutinised the charity pile one last time. She didn't need all those towels. Or a fruit bowl. Or the backgammon set she had bought at a flea market because it looked pretty. Those impulsive purchases had proved themselves inconsequential or unnecessary. Abandoned on the roadside, they received their eviction notice; the van would arrive to take the bags away later that day.

Preparations sped along. She had resigned from her job the previous week and by utilising outstanding holidays, she entered the last week of work. To her embarrassment, her colleagues immediately set about organising farewell coffee and cakes for Friday morning, which she didn't want. Her boss walked past her desk without saying a word.

Pangs of anxiety hit her hourly as she continued to clear her flat. Packed, emptied and repacked, the suitcase bulged. She couldn't decide which significant objects of life should be squished into the cheapest, biggest suitcase that fell within the airline's weight allowance, which wasn't generous. According to Freddie, there was a washing machine in the hostel and a fully equipped kitchen. She imagined the place would be like the student accommodation she had never lived in, but still might one day, if her plans achieved fruition. Little steps, she reminded herself, rather than giant leaps.

She had texted Nicky and suggested a morning run on Wednesday to help with the nervous energy that kept her awake at night. She still hadn't told him about her change of plans – the one that had begun with living with big brother, and now involved going abroad. His reply was tardy. He was out of town, taking a small vacation with his new friend. The apology was sweet. Their paths hadn't crossed recently, and she felt his presence slipping away through her fingers. As she paved her future with concrete actions, her past crumbled into dust. She abandoned the idea of a run.

Her dreams had to lay elsewhere, fashioned by her own ambitions and decisions, and free from the influence of her family. But still, she slept fitfully and questioned her judgement, especially her rejection of Mark and his connections, and the few friends she had who might offer a neutral opinion. Instead, she had searched for information about the dig and, like Derek, she unearthed nothing.

Hello. The word echoed into the digital void and she waited. No response, so she carried on typing. I can't find the location of this dig? Why? Is it not registered?

Freddie was an owl and the reply appeared later in the evening.

It's not publicly listed because the landowner doesn't want people crawling over his fields with metal detectors. Sorry don't know any more. Not my area of expertise. I'm sure everything will be explained when you arrive. Remember to bring your passport and banker's card, so we can set up an account for your pay and have you bought the ticket?

Yes, and yes. Heathrow to Dublin. Friday evening.

It was already Wednesday – two nights to go. The level of excitement ratcheted up every time she chatted with Freddie. His enthusiasm bolstered her nerves. If she couldn't sleep tonight, she would have to drink herself there just for medicinal purposes. She hadn't drunk alcohol since the dinner at Luke's.

Garth will meet you. He's a good friend and I trust him. He'll come with Alicia, the archaeology student I told you about. They'll come to your room at the hostel, so don't go wandering off when you arrive. Alicia is keen to meet you and tell you more about the project. I'll take you out for a meal once you've settled. Something to celebrate your arrival.

Freddie included an email address for Garth. Ask him for more details. Thanks for the photograph you sent. I know this is the first time I've seen you, and I'm honoured by your faith in me.

You, too. You're younger than I thought. I had this idea you were an old catholic priest.

The photo he had sent earlier in the week was a head shot of a bearded man with red hair and black framed glasses that betrayed his myopic vision. He wasn't a looker. What had she expected? Another suave Nicky with body builder muscles.

Seriously? Me? I suppose I allow my religious persuasions to rise to the surface sometimes. Now I have to confess something to you.

What? Her stomach churned.

I trained as a social worker. I know you don't like us, so I kept it quiet. Can you forgive me?

She laughed, her fingers racing over the keys to relieve him of his worries. I forgive you.

Phew! So we're all set to meet this weekend. I hope you're excited.

Yes, yes. A string of emojis animated the line of text.

Her mood swung upwards.

One more thing, Ellen. Tell your mother. She deserves to know that you're moving on. Finding happiness.

Her hands slipped off the keyboard. The seconds trickled past. She hadn't spoken to Deidre in months. The last time, they had argued about visiting her father. Ellen had refused to make the journey.

Ellen. Make peace.

She closed the laptop lid. Freddie was keen on reconciliation, especially recently. If his long-term goal had been to reunite the family it was admirable, but unachievable. She would explain things when they met, fill him in on the missing details, then he would understand her bitterness and anger. For now, she would play along.

The blocked number was listed in her contacts. A daughter shouldn't block her mother's numbers, but she had. Deidre had tried to trick her with new SIM cards. She had even used neighbour's numbers. After a few months she had given up the ruse.

Tapping the screen of her mobile, Ellen dialled the home number, the landline. It rang and rang, and she heaved a sigh of relief. She was out.

'Hello?' her panic-stricken mother yelled out of the tiny speaker.

'Who's there? Is that you, Bill? It's not your day for ringing. It's very late. How have you managed—'

'It's me. Mum.'

'Ellie? Is that you?'

'Yes.' She gripped the phone tighter.

'Ellie. Is there news?'

'News?' She moved into the kitchen with the phone still close to her mouth.

'Yes. About the appeal. Mark hasn't contacted me in ages. Why is he so selfish? Eh? You must see him in London. The pair of you—'

'Mum, please, shut up and listen.'

'Oh, I see, like that is it?'

'I'm going to Ireland for a few weeks. It's archaeological work and I'll have the chance—'

'Ellen, I'm sure it's very exciting for you, but when is Mark going to call me about Dad? He's lost weight again. Do you know how hard it is to see him like that? Wasting away.'

She poured the wine out of the bottle into the glass and it spilt over the rim. 'Sure, Mum. He's going to slip between the bars and break out.'

'This is why I don't speak to you.'

The mobile shook in her hand. She couldn't hold the rage in. Mark should have done the deed, but he had missed the chance and had gifted Ellen the opportunity. She steadied her hand. 'The feeling's mutual. Well, I do have news. The appeal is over.'

'Over, what do you mean? Mark hasn't—'

'He can't bring himself to tell you. He's a coward. So I'll tell you.' She took a quick mouthful of wine to bolster her nerves. The room was hotter than ever. Winter had no impact on her horrible bedsit and she couldn't wait to leave it. 'Dad's witness said nothing because he saw what Dad did with his own eyes and that was murder a man in cold-blood and try to make it look like self-defence. Dad took two knives.'

'You're lying,' Deidre said. 'You wicked—'

'Child, yes. I know. You shouted those words at me many times. But I'm not as wicked as Bill Clewer. I guess he didn't ask you to sew those extra pockets in his coat, did he? For gloves? Beer bottles. Knives?'

The line clicked followed by the hum of a broken connection. 'Goodbye, Mum,' Ellen said, softly.

Opening the laptop, she sent Freddie a message.

It's done. I told her. We're fine. Everything's good. Now, tell me, what are the pubs like over there?

Oh, sweetie, they're the best, but then I'm biased.

21
Julianna

Wednesday Evening

Julianna opened the front door and greeted Mark with a lengthy kiss that left his ears a shade of pink.

He licked his lips. 'Honey?' he queried.

'Honey and mustard pork chops.'

He slipped past her and deposited a corked bottle in the kitchen. 'Delicious.'

She poured him a glass of wine. When Alex had brought home an extravagantly priced bottle, she had frowned upon it. How perspectives changed when the right man stood in the kitchen offering to help chop the onions. Before he had arrived, she had offloaded the pin-stripe trouser suit, and donned leggings and a baggy jumper that hung off one shoulder. If he expected bra straps, he wouldn't find them.

However, Mark showed no interest in slipping his hand under her clothes. It disappointed her, but she said nothing. After the meal, he fetched his files and scattered them onto the dining room table amongst the dirty dishes and wine glasses. They had two days left to explain the irregularities Mark had uncovered.

'What do you think Mr Haynes will do with the information, assuming we find something illegal?' she asked, circling dates with a red marker pen.

'Send it to the appropriate authorities.'

'People's jobs could be at stake, but you know that.' There was no need to mention Haydocks.

Mark tossed his pen down. 'So what? It's their choice to involve themselves in illegal activities.' Still a raw nerve.

'No excuses?' She topped up her wine glass. Mark covered his with the palm of his hand. One glass and he had stopped drinking.

'None.' He eyed the bare flesh of her neck and his fingers twitched.

'And with me? What if you found out I lie about things?' She hadn't told him about her conversation with Chris, nor the threats to the Haynes, nor the potential links to Haydocks.

'Why would you lie?' He gathered together his files. 'And about what?'

'That I wasn't interested in meeting your sister, for one thing.' Part truth. She was concerned enough to want to meet her.

'You don't need to meet her to know that she's okay. Ellen can look after herself. She's determined to make her own way in life,' Mark said with unguarded annoyance.

She would have to try harder. 'But you said she drinks too much. That she has this self-destructive streak. Doesn't that concern you?'

Mark fingered his wine glass. 'I can't do anything more for her,' he said quietly. 'I never could back then, so why should I now?'

There was something almost mean in his tone. She had heard it a few times now. She was starting to worry about this invisible Ellen. Reacting to something showing in her face, Mark softened the hard lines around his forehead and eyes.

'Don't worry,' he said. 'She's going to Ireland this weekend to start new life digging up old bits of stone and pottery. If she's happy, then who I am to stop her? She's got this friend and he's the one telling her what to do.'

'You haven't met this friend of hers?'

His impatience was showing through the veil of politeness. 'No. But she's known him for a few years. She's not your problem. None of my family is your problem.'

Julianna shifted backwards in her seat. Mark's dismissal of his sister was icy, uncaring, and unlike him in many ways. 'No, you're right, it isn't.'

Jackson wanted her to solidify connections, ratify them with evidence. He wasn't interested in the periphery of Mark's life, and Ellen easily fell into that grey area. Given Mark's gruff response, she had probed enough for one evening. The lie went unchallenged.

His broad shoulders loosened, transforming him from edgy to calmer, friendlier. With no resentment, and clearly tired, Mark slouched in his seat with his shirt tails hanging out, oozing desirability. The shift in attention to her was a welcome interlude. He didn't need alcohol, he needed her, that was obvious from the way his eyes tracked her every move.

'What do you want to do this evening?' she asked. 'In the bedroom, I mean.'

'I know what you meant.' He grabbed her hand. 'Let's go find out.'

He surprised her. She'd not seen him so keen for a while. He was making a point, that he was able to push aside his troubles and concentrate on her, and what she wanted. He also animated a gentler side and one that she might come to like. Afterwards, he spooned his body around hers.

'You're a very sweet lover,' she said into the darkness. The word 'lover' tasted delicious in her mouth. She hadn't intended to call him that.

He mumbled, a strangely courteous, 'You're welcome,' as if he had provided her with a service, then he fell asleep.

Coffee beans were scattered around the coffee machine, which was cold. She swept them into her palm and picked up where he had left off. He was talking, somewhere, his voice carrying up from below. She was surprised he managed to find reception down there.

She hovered near the cellar door.

Mark spoke hoarsely, as close to tears as a man might come and not shed them. 'I'm not a coward, or impotent. And I'm sorry Ellen was the one to tell you.'

He might have slept next to Julianna undisturbed, but come the morning, he had woken to the persistent trills of his mother's texts. Ellen had broken the silence, not him.

'But what she said is true. He's guilty, Mum.'

Only his mother could ruin the start of a day. Julianna understood what was going on. What Deidre lacked was guile; the cunning of an intellectual mind. A sledgehammer was Deidre's approach. According to Mark, her neighbours and friends would never know this side of her. They were party to her kindness, the sweet wife of a wronged man, who popped around for tea and left hours later, her bruised ego rescued by their sympathy.

'Mum, it's the truth,' Mark said, hoarsely. 'He took two knives with him, he planted the other. It was pre-meditated.'

Mark's patter of pacing feet stopped; Julianna edged away from the door, keeping her shadow out of the stairwell.

'You knew he was in with the crooks. What did you expect? You can't go on thinking he's going to be found innocent. You'll have to go see him and tell him to change his plea, take the advice of the parole board, and hope he gets out on licence eventually.'

An unwelcome wave of nausea lodged itself in her stomach. Mark was probably feeling much worse.

'An alibi?' he said, despairingly.

Deidre wasn't seeking a simple denial of guilt, she was suggesting perjury.

'Mum, that isn't going to work; he argued for self-defence. He admitted he was there.' There was a soft thump. He had landed a gentle blow.

The punch bag was strung up and ready to be battered. Her therapy was in his easy reach, and not hers. She hadn't realised how enticing it might be to somebody else, and she had spoken so often of her need to the point Mark had questioned whether it was appropriate – what if she lost control and used something else?

'Mum. That is it.' He hammered out the words into the icy basement. Down there he could shout, believing Julianna was asleep upstairs. 'He's guilty! If I can accept the truth, you can too. I'm not going to see my father again. He lied to both of us. I'm finished. Done. I've got a life and I'm not wasting it on him. Or you.'

She contemplated whether he wanted rescuing, but down there wasn't the best place to comfort him. It was horribly like a prison cell.

Something smashed, the impact of an object against a harder surface. What that was, she guessed, had been in his hand. The aggressive thump of fist against leather was a familiar sound. She winced; she was tempted to call out and warn him, but he would find out she had been eavesdropping. Instead, she removed herself back upstairs and hid under the bedcovers, pretending to sleep.

He detoured round the bed and slipped into the bathroom. Rising for the second time, Julianna returned to the kitchen and continued the quest to make coffee, the one he had abandoned so furiously. While the machine bubbled, she descended into the cellar. The light illuminated glittering pieces of something shiny... little shards of broken plastic.

She placed the coffee mugs on the bedside table, and while he remained occupied, she rifled through his trouser pockets hunting for the rest of the phone. The screen was shattered, the casing badly cracked. The shower door creaked. She dropped the damaged mobile back in his pocket.

He stuck his head round the bathroom door, and smiled, gloriously, as if nothing had happened downstairs. 'Hi. Mmm, coffee.'

'You're up early.'

'You don't mind, do you? I went into the cellar and punched the shit out of that thing.' His knuckles were red. He had found out the hard way.

'You should have bound them.' Why the pain? A stupid question because she used it in the same way.

'I realise that now.' He examined his hands.

'I'll get you some ice.' Just before she reached the door, she glanced over her shoulder. He wiped the condensation off the surface of the mirror.

She froze to the spot. He held the razor to his neck. It shook for a second, then he shifted it up higher, to his upper lip. 'Bitch,' he growled. 'Bitches, the pair of them. Well, screw them.' He scraped the razor along his jawline and rinsed the blade under the tap. Unperturbed, he smudged the spot of blood along the hardened edge of his chin.

Julianna retreated, carrying with her a bitter taste, and it wasn't coffee. Alex had called her a stupid bitch when she had found out about him. He had landed on the pavement and screamed abuse at her. The difference this time was blame: Mark's family had tipped him into a darker place, and it was getting harder to follow him there. She wasn't sure if she wanted to anymore. The thought of giving up on him, which she would revisit throughout that day, brought with it a realisation. Her feelings toward Mark had changed.

Julianna said nothing to Mark about his mobile, and in turn he provided no explanation for his assault on the punch bag. She applied ice to his knuckles and the pair of them danced around the reasons. Short on time, they drank scalding coffee and then ate toast in the car. Her clapped out vehicle was one of the few allowed in the building's underground exclusive car park. As soon as they walked into the lobby, he pecked her on the cheek and dashed up to his office while she descended into the bowels of the building to speak to Chris.

The BMW had proved to be a false lead. It was an unmarked police response vehicle cruising the area.

'I'm sure he's not a target, Julianna,' Chris said. 'There's no evidence they've traced Mark, or his sister.'

Even if the BMW was a red herring, she wasn't convinced. Against her better judgement, the temptation to invite Mark to move in with her rose a notch. He wouldn't agree; Mark valued his independence above her. They had chosen to navigate the meandering course of their relationship around their physical needs, not emotional ones.

Julianna circled Chris's desk. 'I just don't like it. It's like the quiet before a storm. And there's an innocent girl caught up in this, a girl I haven't even met.'

Chris tapped on his keyboard and scribbled something onto a piece of paper. He thrust it at Julianna. 'Go see her. Why do you need Mark's permission?'

'You had this all the time?' She stared at the address. It was south of the River Thames. The phone number for the job she no longer had.

'Only recently.' Chris cleared his throat, awkwardly. 'It was scribbled on a business card and tossed in amongst the files Mark sent to Sophia. Presumably he had referenced his sister as a potential witness. Sophia was going to contact Ellen directly, but Mr Haynes put a stop to it. Said deal only with Mark. He didn't mention you.'

Sophia had kept Jackson in the loop, or more likely Luke had. Jackson Haynes was monitoring the situation more closely than

Julianna had realised. Over the previous week, with the help of Chris's extensive resources, she had uncovered the significance of the name Redningsmann and the revelation alarmed her. If Jackson's assumptions were correct, then the man who had laundered money with the help of Mark's old company Haydocks, and who was likely to be seeking the person responsible for exposing it, was also behind the threats to Hettie; a dangerous criminal who ruled over a successful syndicate of organised gangs. She had teased apart the threads, identifying a few common strands, and they pointed further back in time. This, she believed, was where Jackson wanted her to go. Follow the money and the people, and she might acquire more information than the police and Chris combined. It would do a great deal for her reputation and standing if she proved the existence of these connections.

Secretly, she enjoyed delving into the mess Mark had left behind. It was probably why protection work lacked appeal, especially being at the beck and call of others and having little say in how she should spend her day. Protocols stymied Julianna's natural inquisitiveness. Being a bodyguard was nothing like the movies.

Recently she had ferried Hettie to the art gallery and waited for two hours while Mrs Haynes caught up with the latest plans for the new exhibition. Julianna spent the time drinking coffee in the cafe across the street. Unlike Tess, who devoured books, Julianna couldn't read. She had trained in surveillance, so that was what she spent her time doing: people watching. She wondered what lay behind the little scenes played out over coffees and croissants: angry exchanges, lovers kissing, mothers berating small children, babies demanding milk and men talking over laptops about sales figures. Her own life had never grounded itself in daily routines of family matters. Mark was similar in that respect. He detoured conversation around personal issues and homed in on work.

She stuffed the piece of paper Chris had given her in her pocket. 'I'm driving Mrs Haynes tomorrow afternoon?'

'Yes,' Chris replied.

'I'll try to see her after that.'

'I don't know what you'll achieve. This family is so screwed up. I've told him to stay out of it, but Jackson feels responsible.'

Chris rarely referred to his boss by his first name; he had let his feelings rise to the surface, which was unwise for a man in his position. Julianna sighed. 'You're not going to tell me why, are you?'

'No. It's personal. That's the problem with all of this business. It's too damn personal.'

Nothing more needed to be said. The web of connections revolved around the same people, the same origins. She had calls to make and no time to hassle Chris.

She and Mark spent the Thursday night apart, which was a necessary interlude. So far she had been kind of mercenary with her curiosity. What they both needed was a spell away from the office. After she had visited Ellen, and plugged a few more gaps in her knowledge, she and Mark could have a gentle heart-to-heart. It was time to drop the pretence that she wasn't that interested in him. She had to keep it sensible and not indulgent; no romantic overtures, which wouldn't impress him. He possessed aptitude in the bedroom, undeniably pleasing for both of them, however, what had won her over wasn't his flair for sex or his dogged investigative skills, it was his determination to stay out of his father's criminal affairs. With luck, by emphasising that honourable quality she could raise the awkward situation with his mother and sister, and find a way to diffuse the anger. Julianna wasn't expecting resolution, but she couldn't go on sitting on the side-lines watching the family implode. She was guaranteed to lose Mark if he chose to ignore what she was close to unravelling.

On Friday, Mark insisted she came with him and jointly present Jackson with their findings. She baulked at the idea of the trip to the top floor.

'You've done the leg work. I would have nothing to show if it wasn't for you,' he said. 'Come on, you're more than a driver. You know you want this recognition.'

Jackson already knew plenty about Julianna's potential – he had manufactured her secret assignment. But Mark was right. She needed to impress him as much as possible.

If Jackson was surprised to see Julianna appear alongside Mark, he kept quiet. He offered them a seat and a drink, which they both declined. Jackson hijacked Diana as she popped in to drop off files. 'Coffee. Strong and black.'

She glared at him. 'Give me two minutes, will you? My feet haven't touched the ground since you turned up.'

The repartee was reassuring. Jackson was in a good mood.

'We'll have to make this snappy; I want to leave for Fasleigh,' Jackson said. 'So tell me what you've found out.'

They presented their findings succinctly. The best clue was the discovery of a blog by a previous client of the company who had lambasted his investors for losing his money in a mediocre deal. They tracked down the investment cited, and it should have given a very good return.

'They're skimming off then.' Jackson folded his arms across his chest.

Mark nodded. 'There are probably other unhappy clients out there, but this one was keen to spill the beans. There's definitely something fraudulent going on. The tax office has already been alerted to under paying—'

'I know – get shot of the evidence by flogging the company off to me. Well done the pair of you. Your findings will be passed to the authorities and they can decide what to do.'

'Thank you,' said Mark. 'Should I tell Neil to send them packing?'

'Oh, no. That will be my privilege. Perhaps put a cat amongst the pigeons too. I know the board member who initiated the sale. Don't like him.'

Julianna didn't pity the man. A Jackson Haynes-style assassination was exactly what he deserved.

'Have a good weekend, sir,' Mark said.

'What about you?' asked Jackson.

'Oh. A quiet one, I think. Very quiet.'

Jackson turned to Julianna. 'That's a pity, isn't it?'

Julianna felt her cheeks flush with heat. 'I'm busy driving your wife. I'm picking up Sophia after work and taking her to meet Mrs Haynes for the journey to Fasleigh.'

'My brother and Sophia are staying with us at Fasleigh tonight. Luke will be late.'

'I'm on call for the whole weekend.' It meant she couldn't drink.

'Then hopefully you'll have a quiet weekend too, because I've nothing planned.'

The opportunity was there then to make her case for going forward together in partnership. Mark had a right to know what Jackson had contrived, and how that meddling had benefited them both.

'Quietish.' She winked at Mark and he blushed.

22

Mark

Friday Lunchtime

Since he was owed for the extra hours worked, Mark clocked off at lunchtime and headed home to a chilled bottle of beer. The door to his apartment was ajar. He stuck his head through the gap and listened. He held his breath, wondering if this was how it might happen – accosted in his flat and murdered. Retribution was close on his heels, and, one day, it would catch up with him. He was grateful to Jackson for the introduction to Julianna, and whether it was engineered or not, he no longer cared to worry about the distinction. He hoped Jackson's contrivances hadn't insulted Julianna's intelligence to the point she might reject him. There were companionable benefits beyond the obvious sexual ones; if Julianna had been with him, she would be armed with a karate chop. Unfortunately, she was on route to pick up Sophia.

Whoever was in his flat, they weren't quiet. There was a heavy thump accompanied by a high-pitched girlish squeal. With a sigh of relief, he opened the door wider.

'Ellen? Is that you dropping off things?' He had forgotten she was making her last delivery.

She came out of the spare room with the tip of her thumb between her lips. 'I dropped a box on it,' she mumbled through the sucks.

He slipped his overcoat off his shoulders and left it hanging off the back of a dining chair, keeping his back to her. He wasn't keen on having Ellen in his flat – his embattled feelings skewered by her ill-timed conversation with their mother.

His resolve shattered when he turned to face her smug features. 'You know who I spoke to this morning?'

'Mum.' She snorted. 'If you wanted to tell her, you should have.'

He planted his hands on his hips. 'Did you enjoy it? Rubbing her nose in it rather than letting her down gently?'

She crossed the room and clicked her fingers inches from his nose. 'I dropped it like a bomb. It was wonderful. I'm sorry you didn't get to enjoy it for yourself.'

Mark wanted to slap her face. 'Why do you hate her so much?'

A frisson of disgust traversed her face. 'Oh, you're such the good son, aren't you? And a hypocrite. Dashing off to uni, finding work, giving her money. Me, the little sister, forcing her to be a mother by slicing myself. Bad girl. Terrible daughter. I bet you answered Dad's letters. I burnt every single one he sent me or returned them to sender, unread. '

He had never witnessed the bleeding cuts, only the scars. He thought he had seen all her scars. 'You're no different to her. You wanted the attention. You deny it, like she does. You're a perfect pair. Why wonder you never got on, you're too alike.' The tussle grew uglier and nothing like those they had as kids.

'Oh, you imbecile. You don't have a clue, do you? She despises the power I had over her. All I had to do was open my mouth and destroy her, and him. She only cared about me because one little squeal on my part to somebody in authority and the secret was out.'

'What are you talking about?' Secrets come at a cost. He was starting to appreciate what that cost was to Ellen. She pleaded emotional poverty when it came to demonstrating love, but happily became a glutton when somebody else offered her affection.

She dragged his coat off the back of the chair and stretched it open, exposing the inner lining. He went to grab it off her, but she scuttled backwards. 'Mum was good at sewing. She made me a dress once, when I was small and sweet enough for her. She also stitched things into Dad's coats for him. Pockets at the back for the little packages of coke or heroin, then ones up his sleeve for the notes. The best two, one on either side, were long and thin. Perfect for knives.'

Mark leapt forward and snatched the coat out of her hands. He bundled it into a ball and threw it across the room. That was her secret? Those bright little eyes of hers had dazzled back then, and again as she revealed her complicity in hiding Bill's guilt and Deidre's malign involvement.

'Get out!'

The colour drained from her face. What did she expect him to say? 'Mark... I didn't tell you because—'

'I spent eight fucking years chasing after false leads. Wasting money on expensive lawyers. I paid to have independent forensics go over the fingerprints. And you, you selfish bitch, knew he carried knives around with him. Did you know he took them on the day?'

A tiny nod. Her eyes filled with tears. 'Please, Mark. I was dependent on them. I was torn in two. I hoped Dad would plead guilty to murder so I didn't have to speak up. For God's sake, I was eleven years old. A child.'

'Back then, yes. But you grew up. You thrived on the attention back then and I bet you still do. This whole trip to Ireland is about you, your escape. You don't even know who you're meeting, do you? Well, go ahead. Find yourself in Ireland amongst the bogs and limericks and dance a jig while I carry on picking up the pieces.'

'Shut up!' She backed away from him. 'Just, shut up. I wanted to, I so wanted to tell you. But where were you? And as for our parents. She, that useless mother of ours, bullied him. Did you know that? Nagged him. Told him to steal more, buy more. She snorted coke off the coffee table with him. She pushed him to go higher, bigger. When he whispered that they needed little girls, innocent ones, she shrugged it off. Said he should do it if it brought in more cash.'

The blow when it came wasn't physical. Mark had waited years for somebody to knock him out or shoot him, perhaps as he walked down a quiet back street – a motorcyclist, or a jogger, somebody would make his hit and bam, Mark Clewer, gone, the victim of a vengeful gangland killing orchestrated by a nameless boss. He was wrong. His sister had landed it; she had assassinated him.

The adrenaline crippled. If it came with excitement, he swam in its power, but not this painful drench. He doubled over and his elbow knocked against the table's edge. 'How did you—'

'I listened whenever I could. You'd be out playing football or chatting up Mrs Asani's brown-eyed daughter. You were rarely home. Then one night, I woke with a belly ache and stood outside their room and listened to that conversation. I never cuddled up in bed with them again.' The spite had gone from her voice. Her culpability had failed to span the chasm that had always been between brother and sister, and now it stretched them further apart.

'You could have said something,' he said bitterly. Gullible, weak-minded, pathetic: the words would be Mark's epitaph.

She crept towards him and her shoes squeaked on the hard floor. 'Who would have believed me? Dad was this big bad guy and met other bad guys. I was scared, Mark. He took you to watch football. Such a bright kid and never once did you question why he spoilt you rotten, kept you occupied and blind. He overlooked me. I'm just a girl.'

He felt dizzy. Sick to the pit of his stomach. Stunned, he couldn't think or speak.

'And yes.' Ellen sneered. 'I told her, bloody right I did. It's called revenge. Sweet, isn't it?'

'Go. Just go.' He waved toward the door. 'I don't care what you do. It's your choice. I'm not going to pretend I'm interested. I'm not the grown up in your life. You are.'

'I'm flying out this evening. My things—' Now, she had the gall to ask him.

'If they're still here when you get back, you'll be grateful.' Her things wouldn't be a hindrance, only a reminder of this lasting fall-out.

'I will, honestly. I'm not angry with you.' She scooped up his jacket and straightened it out, folding it over the back of the chair. A small act of mitigation and a pointless one.

'How nice for you,' he said. 'You didn't think of me at all. Well, I won't think of you. I wish I'd never laid eyes on you.'

She picked up her handbag and fished out a piece of paper. She left it on the table. 'You don't care, but this is where I'm going. His name is Freddie Zustaller, and I do know him. I've a taxi waiting below to take me to Heathrow.' She hurried past Mark.

Just before she reached the door, he spun on his heels. 'Did you ever love them?'

'Of course I love them. But what do you think it costs to keep a secret like that? School was hell. I was the butt of jokes, constant teasing — the daughter of scum. The boys leered and expected me to drop my knickers. Nobody was a good role model. So love? No, I didn't stop loving, or even hoping. But respect and admiration? I have neither of those for Mum or Dad. I'm sorry you see things differently.'

The door shut behind her, quietly. Ellen was gone, possibly indefinitely and he wanted to mourn the breakup but it wasn't happening; the feeling of loss wasn't forthcoming.

He ignored the beer bottles and poured a large measure of whiskey out of the decanter. His hand shook as he swallowed. It burnt a line down his throat and he spluttered. He picked up the piece of paper, scrunched it into a ball and threw it in the bin in the kitchen. If Julianna contacted him, he would blow her off. He would rather be alone for the weekend. She couldn't contact him anyway. Nobody could — his mobile phone was bust, he had no landline and his laptop was in a drawer at work.

He laughed and laughed until tears poured down his cheeks.

23
Julianna

The last place Julianna wanted to be on a wet afternoon was stuck inside a car. Even though it was a luxury vehicle, she wasn't comfortable being cooped up. Her twitchy legs needed exercising. There were other drawbacks: when she drove, she didn't get to choose the radio station. She was a taxi driver without any perks.

Her first pick up at 4 p.m. was Sophia Crawford, long term girlfriend of Luke Haynes, and close friend of Hettie. Sophia's office was in Aldgate. A narrow building slotted amongst other equally unremarkable facades that stretched along the street. She waited outside at the appointed time. Hooting the horn was forbidden, as was texting to alert anyone of her arrival. Julianna couldn't demand a passenger hurry up. Her time wasn't precious; it was already paid for.

Sophia dashed out of the office under the cover of an umbrella. Julianna held the rear car door open for her. She didn't need to be told where to go, she had the itinerary printed on a sheet. Holland Park, then onto Fasleigh, far outside the city. The children had gone on ahead with the nanny in a car driven by Tess, hence the need for an extra driver. The family was gathering for the weekend.

Before collecting Hettie, she and Sophia had half an hour alone in the car. Julianna itched to ask Sophia about Mark's father, but it wasn't her place to initiate conversations. Her analytical mind buzzed with a barrage of questions, especially about the mysterious witness Sophia had successfully tracked down. The minutes ticked by, wasted minutes. She tried a smattering of random coughs and tapping her fingers on the steering wheel.

'So,' said Sophia, dropping her mobile out of sight, 'done any more investigations?'

Julianna avoided a wandering cyclist with a gentle swerve before answering. 'Yes, just finished one today with Mark. Dodgy investments, skimming profits and tax evasion.'

In the mirror, Julianna saw Sophia sweep her hand over her head in a mock gesture. 'Beyond me.'

'Your clients aren't into that kind of thing, I guess.'

'Mine? Er, no. It's mainly petty, repeat offenders. Never their fault, of course. Always the police that stitched them up. I'm their agony aunt, a shoulder to cry on.'

'Couldn't do that myself.' Julianna was the tough arm of the law. The cynic in her would listen to those sob stories and pitiful excuses, and shrug them off.

'Neither can I sometimes.' The laugh was half-hearted. 'Taking responsibility is sadly not part of a criminal's psyche. They feel forgotten by society, and will take what they can. To be honest, I can't blame some of them.'

'Except the violent ones?'

'Yes, except them.' Sophia's voice drifted away behind the roar of a motorcycle.

Julianna decided to use the acknowledgement. 'Mark's father must have been a disappointment?'

'For Mark, naturally, but I wasn't the slightest bit surprised to confirm his guilt. The evidence Mark passed on to me was pretty damning.'

'If you don't mind me asking, how did your find that witness? Eight, nine years, have passed, and nobody else managed.' Julianna twisted her head for a fraction of a second, and caught hold of Sophia's blue eyes.

The rain had stopped. She switched off the wipers. The traffic outside went quiet, almost distant.

'Oh.' Sophia cleared her throat. 'It's one of those things, you know. Who knows who.'

'You know the witness?'

'Me, personally? No. He moved south and disappeared for a long while. One of my clients knows him. As you can appreciate, these people, men mainly, are in and out of prison, and they build their networks. It's like a tangled web, interconnected through key people or events. So, you follow one name, you're led to another, then another.'

'I understand.' Julianna relied on a similar network of informants, private investigators and law enforcers to bridge the gaps, allowing her to ask questions without the keeper of the information ever knowing who was the actual originator of the question.

'I have a client, let's call him John. A little speck when compared to the big players, but none the less, an ear to the ground type. He likes to lay it on thick about his importance. Frankly, he's a little dim, and unreliable. I've represented him several times and he's often failed to turn up at court or pay his fines, so I got the blunt end of the magistrates' wrath and refused to represent him again.'

Julianna edged the car forward, listening intently, her eyes on the car in front, her ears directed to the passenger. Sophia's casual style of storytelling was effective. Whereas Luke was accustomed to commanding a courtroom, Sophia's job was to soften the magistrates before her clients reached the judge and jury.

'He happens to be one of the guys who knows Mark's witness. Call him Reg. These two guys aren't friends, but they know each other. I offer to take John back as my client, because he likes me and I'm getting him lenient sentences, or so he thinks, and in return, he arranges a meeting between me, Luke, and Reg. Luke wouldn't let me go on my own.'

'Wise man. I'm surprised, all that sounded easy.' Julianna puffed out her cheeks. Eight years squandered because the previous solicitors had focused on the wrong city.

'Oh, God, no. It took eight years because Reg is petrified. So was John because both of them know who Bill killed. It took lots of back and forth, firm reassurances, then a change of plans, and a new location.'

'But Reg coughed up the information.'

'He didn't want to. He was ready to walk out the door. I had to milk his sentimentality, which was obvious given his loyalty to Bill. You see, please don't tell Mark, but I convinced Reg that Bill would be hit, taken out, if he was released on bail or freed. Better in than out. Reg told us what had happened off the record; he would never say it in court. So we recorded him to be on the safe side.'

'That is a possibility, about Bill's safety.' Julianna suspected Bill had been kept safe in prison for a purpose. 'He might decide to snitch, give up information, but not while he had a chance at getting out on appeal.' Circumstances had changed, though.

'Possibly. But my suspicions were right about Bill. He's guilty of murder, not manslaughter. He took out this big shot's cousin.'

'He did?' This was something new.

'I plied Reg with beer. This cousin, the one who met Bill Clewer, was the negotiator. Bill's lot needed girls. Girls, meaning kids. These scumbags aren't fussy about age.'

Julianna knew this. 'These scumbags have no names?'

'They had aliases. It didn't help Bill's case that he refused to give up any real names. According to Reg, from the moment the meeting was arranged, Bill intended to assassinate him. Reg tried to talk him out of it. Bill wouldn't say why; whether it was personal or something he had been told to do, but Reg thought that it had to do with it being young girls. Bill has a daughter, doesn't he?'

'Yes,' Julianna said quietly. A daughter who knew nothing about any of this. Nor Mark. More things to explain over a carefully crafted weekend of wine, sex and gentle soothing of his ruffled angst.

'Reg doesn't feel responsible for what Bill did; he was just the lookout. But now, he's worried again.'

'Worried?'

'I gather the murder caused a bit of a war amongst the syndicates. The big bad boss had to go into hiding abroad. He's back now, of course, and recruiting. Reg is keeping his head down.'

'Don't blame him.' Holland Park was a few streets away. She'd found out more than she'd expected.

'He says they patrol the streets on bikes, these guys who work for him, picking up girls that way. The silly girls love the leathers, the tattoos. Boys, too, of course. They befriend them, make them their best mates and sweet talk them. It's grooming. Slow and leisurely, so as not to raise suspicions. Then, they encourage them to leave home, take them to houses and bring them men.'

'Shit. Excuse me.' Mark had mentioned bikers. But she couldn't remember the context of the conversation. It was one of those tiny snippets that passed between them when they ate together or chatted in bed. Life was full of them, things tossed around with little idea of their use until they came back later, stripped of detail.

Sophia laughed. 'No, it's fine. I'm so used to the bad language. I have to roll it back when I'm with Luke. He's all upper crust. Jackson isn't. I think Jackson sees a different world because of Opportunitas. I like helping, especially the trafficked girls. They're the victims of this trafficker gang, this deliverer.'

Julianna's foot slipped off the brake and she nearly collided with the car in front. She curled fingers around the steering wheel.

'Who?' she said, too urgently.

Sophia's voice lost its sweetness. 'John and Reg shit bricks every time they mentioned his name. The Deliverer.' She chuckled, innocuously. 'Ridiculous, like they're talking about the Godfather. They've never met him, only go-betweens, and he uses lots of aliases, so he could be like a phantom.'

He wasn't a phantom. He existed. Julianna was sure of it and she scowled in full view of the mirror. Sophia leaned forward in her seat, poised to ask a question. Julianna turned the radio up, breaking one of those neatly written protocols she kept stuffed in the glove compartment, and Sophia shuffled back into the creaking leather and stared out of the window.

The whole business made her feel sick. Mark had to be told about the deliverer, the other criminal enterprise ruined by the Clewer family. She drew the car up outside of Hettie's house and glanced at the dashboard – half past four. She had to drive the women to Surrey, then bring the car back again. There was no point ringing Mark to arrange to meet him, his phone was out of action, and she still had to track down Ellen, find out what the girl knew.

Hettie dropped a bag into the boot without Julianna's assistance and slid into the seat next to Sophia. The two women air pecked each other's cheeks.

'Luke will bring your present later. He's stuck in court and it's in his car,' Sophia said.

'Oh, no worries. Jackson has already gone ahead of me. I think he's cooking something special with the kids...'

Julianna tuned the chatter out. She tried hard not to worry about

Mark and, in any case, what were the chances of something happening that specific evening? Weeks had gone by since Sophia had spoken to Reg and John.

She needed strong coffee, the kind that left the taste buds in no doubt they had been assaulted. Then maybe some sex with Mark to soothe his worries, and hers, then whisper into his ear how she had unravelled the knotted lines of his past and where they all led. Not to Bill, or Haydocks, but Haynes and Opportunitas, and the mission Jackson had given himself to destroy the trafficking networks and their money, the money that belonged to the likes of Redningsmann.

She still didn't know why Haynes was a key player. His crusade was a personal mission, the origins a secret. Chris would know, and one day, she hoped she would have the trust of Haynes like Chris. With luck her prowess would solidify her role in Chris's investigation team. For now, she was defined as Hettie's protection officer. Julianna glanced in the mirror. Poor Hettie was surrounded, constantly watched and given very little privacy beyond the walls of her home.

The bricks and steel of the city sank away into muddy fields and quaint villages. She turned off into a lane. They were a few minutes away from Fasleigh House.

Her passengers were laughing.

'Why do you care, Hettie? You have gardeners, hundreds of them, probably.'

'Two actually. They'll be complaining about the weather. It's either too wet or too cold to dig. Whenever I track them down, they're in the greenhouses, warming up.'

Too cold. Too wet. Who went digging in the winter when the summer was the perfect time? Driving through the gates of Fasleigh House, a gut-wrenching realisation struck her core. Julianna had it all wrong — the threat was immediate.

The lights of the house were a blur, children squealed with delight and Jackson's voice cut through them to welcome his wife home.

Julianna stayed in the car with the engine running. The rain was back, thundering on the roof. She had to make a decision: either she handled it all on her own or she told Jackson. If she screwed it up on her own, the price would be high, too high. If she roped in

Jackson and it turned out to be a wild goose chase, then she would lose his respect.

She thumped the steering wheel and turned off the engine. With her jacket pulled up over her head, she dashed to the front door and leaned against the doorbell.

Hettie opened the door. A small child was perched on her hip.

'Julianna.' Hettie eyed her cautiously. Evey babbled and drooled.

'I'm sorry about this, Mrs Haynes, but I'm stuck to know what to do and I need Mr Haynes's advice.' Julianna followed Hettie into the kitchen. She had seen the interior of the house only once during her orientation tour. From then on, she had never gone any further than the gatehouse, except for that evening when she had betrayed the Haynes' trust.

Noah was under the kitchen table with a set of dinky cars making "brum brum" noises. Sophia, with her head down, joined in, leaving her face obscured.

'Baptiste? What brings you here?' Jackson leaned back on the worktop and folded his arms across his chest.

Julianna wished the scene was less domesticated. She would prefer his office, even Chris's subterranean one. Jackson in his jeans and a rugby shirt was too comfortable. The aroma of warm bread and cakes played havoc with her senses. 'It's about Mark and Ellen, sir. Especially Ellen. I think he's going after her this weekend.' She shifted her eyes in the direction of Hettie.

Hettie retrieved her son from under the table.

'Please take the kids to another room, Hettie,' a grave-faced Jackson said.

She didn't question him and left the room with both children, the protesting boy pulled along with a firm grasp.

'What's happened?' Jackson came over to the table, where Sophia sat bemused, but wise enough to keep quiet.

'Mark's sister is going to Ireland. Mark's letting her dump her stuff in his apartment. She's quit her job and I think she's moving out of her flat soon. She's been arranging this trip with somebody Mark has never met. I don't know his name. But you can guess who I think he is.'

'Go on.' Jackson's forehead creased into troubled lines. He slid an untouched glass of wine away from him.

'She's supposed to be joining an archaeological dig. It's the winter, sir. Who organises a new dig in the winter? Who invites somebody like Ellen, who lives alone, is vulnerable, and has little experience of professional archaeology?'

'She's going out there without a chaperone?'

'Alone, that's definite.' The space around Julianna shrank and the air was stricken with tension. The stilted conversation communicated more than words. He was processing everything she said and more.

'When?' he asked.

'I'm not sure, but it could be soon.'

'Ring Mark. She's his sister.'

'His phone is broken. He doesn't have a landline and he's not responding to emails either.'

Jackson turned to face Sophia. 'I thought you'd lined up Derek to talk to Ellen?'

'She rejected Derek's offer to go to Scotland before he had a chance to make it,' Sophia said. 'She's adamant that this is what she wants to do. Mark's attempt at dissuading her backfired.'

'What about contacting Ellen?' Jackson asked.

'I don't have her number, but...' Julianna rummaged in her weighty handbag and retrieved a crumpled piece of paper. 'I do have her address. Chris gave it to me. I've not had the chance to visit her. I've never met her.' If she had, maybe things between Mark and his sister might be different, possibly congenial, and not requiring punch bags.

'And Mark has done nothing to prevent this relationship or find out who she's going to meet?' Jackson's mask of containment slipped, exposing rancour.

'I don't think so.' Julianna had unwittingly dug a big hole for Mark to fall into, but given the gravity of the situation, there was nothing she could do to mitigate it. 'They aren't talking much. I think his mum found out about the appeal ending from Ellen, not Mark. He didn't want to tell her until he was ready, so Ellen did the deed. I wouldn't be surprised if she relished doing it. When he found out, he smashed his phone.'

Jackson straightened up fast, startling both Sophia and Julianna. 'For fuck's sake, what was he waiting for?'

'I don't know.' That Mark hated talking to his mother seemed too facile an excuse to tell Jackson. Sophia twirled her finger around a gnarl of wood stain. The tips of her ears were pink. The news Julianna had delivered was ruining everyone's evening.

'I'm sorry, Sophia,' said Jackson. 'We'll have to celebrate your announcement another evening.'

Something more was on the cards than a simple birthday celebration. Jackson hated time wasters. Julianna neither wanted Ellen to be at risk, nor did she want to be setting off alarm bells for no reason. She had spoilt the weekend regardless of the outcome.

He called for Hettie, who returned child free, and drew her into his arms. 'Something has come up. It's foundation business. It's important. I wouldn't go if it wasn't.' He kissed her forehead.

He fished out car keys from his coat pocket. 'We'll take my car. Gary can pick up the one Julianna used.'

Jackson reversed the Porsche Panamera out of the garage, flicked a switch on a remote and opened the main gates. Julianna clutched her handbag on her lap and closed her eyes. Waves of nausea penetrated, breaking down the illusion of control. This was action, wasn't it? The very thing she craved.

'Calm yourself, Julianna. We'll find her,' Jackson said coolly. 'Punch in her postcode.'

The task completed, she rubbed her throbbing temples.

'There's a bottle of water in the glove compartment,' Jackson said.

She pressed the cool plastic to her forehead then swallowed a few mouthfuls to ease her dry throat.

Their roles were switched. Jackson was driving her, and he was quite a smooth driver considering he preferred chauffeurs. He picked up speed, clearly prepared to risk breaking the limits.

'You don't know Ellen, so why the concern?' Jackson asked.

'Because deep down Mark cares about her. Mark had offered Ellen a home, but once Sophia uncovered the truth, they failed to support each other. They never have perhaps. Blood isn't glue. Relatives aren't always friends.'

The traffic started to build up and Jackson hit the brakes.

'You love Mark?' The Haynes' bluntness was notorious.

Julianna looked out of passenger window. 'I don't know. I have this connection to him. My ex, you remember Alex Woodfall, he was such a self-centred git. Charming and generous with his friends, but he didn't think of me much.'

'Alex, yes, I remember him. A dickhead.' Jackson snorted, so derisively that Julianna laughed. 'You can do better,' he added.

'Is Mark better?' She fingered the buttons of her jacket, treating the question as her own. 'He makes me feel alive, I guess. I've really enjoyed being with him, working with him. We do stuff...' She was probably blushing.

'You could be good for him too,' Jackson said. 'Mark's speciality is doggedness, when correctly motivated. I suspect it comes from his mother, although he wouldn't take kindly to that comparison.'

'No, he wouldn't. I don't think his mother is dogged. More likely possessive, of him, his attention. A narcissist.' Julianna checked the time – just past six o'clock. Ellen could have already left the country.

They fell silent for a while, Jackson concentrating on the road. The streetlights dazzled.

'Was I wrong to involve you?' he asked. An awkward question. His face stayed in the shadows, along with his thoughts. There was nothing to read, or judge, just like when he had been in the back of the car when she had driven him and Hettie to the clinic.

'You wanted me to overhear you, though, didn't you, sir? It was deliberate.'

'Don't hate me for that. I think you've enjoyed finding things out. It's been useful for me too, having my suspicions confirmed; the links made concrete. I had no firm information to establish how everything fitted together. The murder and Haydocks's downfall happened years apart, which still doesn't make sense unless Bill... Well, that's what you're working on.'

She didn't have an answer. Had Bill really pushed Mark into Henderson's crooked arms. If he had... poor Mark. A double blow. Then there was the matter of Jackson's involvement – at what point had he decided to act? She hadn't discussed any of this with Mark.

'You've known since Mark joined your company, haven't you,

that Haydocks laundered money for Redningsmann?'

The shadows on Jackson's sculptured face remained the same, unprovoked by her direct question. His voice was equally unconcerned. 'I spoke to the police. I wanted to know if any of the clients might be linked to other businesses in the area. I've subsidiaries in Manchester. That name of that fraudulent client was sufficient to draw my personal attention. Mark had left Haydocks before the police could speak to him, and it served me to keep him out of the way. But I only had this one name, Redningsmann, and I knew of others.' There was a pause while Jackson negotiated a tricky roundabout. She left it to him to break the silence.

'Unfortunately, the police weren't forthcoming due to ongoing investigations. It made sense to bring in Mark; I'd no reason to suspect him. I had recruiters pick up on ex-Haydocks employees and screen them, offer a few of the promising ones jobs. The bad apple, Henderson, shouldn't ruin lives of good apples. Mark might have stayed at Daneswan, getting his confidence back, beavering away on minor accounts, except for what happened next. Mark bumped into Hettie, and as you well know, Chris found out about Mark's father. You could say my curiosity spiked. You know from the conversation in the car that Hettie is aware of Mark's connection to Haydocks, since it's no secret and within the scope of my business to keep a watching eye on known fraudsters.' Jackson glanced in Julianna's direction with his sharp pair of eyes. Too sharp; she flinched. 'But she wasn't told about Bill.'

Julianna had told Hettie. But Jackson went no further with his rebuke. 'And the appeal?' she asked.

'I kept an open mind, for a while. It proved short-lived. Mark has to deal with the fallout from that too.'

Mark was already in a bad place and they were about to make it worse. Her weekend plans were rapidly tumbling into a blackhole. She would have to show him how to punch harder without breaking his knuckles.

What she didn't know was part of Haynes' past. 'The Haydocks client was what caught your attention though, not Mark or Henderson. Redningsmann is Norwegian for deliverer.'

Jackson nodded. 'As I said, we know of other aliases, but that one was a new one.' A brief smile crossed his lips. 'Mark certainly unleashed a swarm of frightened bees at Haydocks.'

Julianna sensed another possible wrist slapping. She had drawn somebody else into Jackson's game. 'I took advantage of my time alone with Sophia in the car. It's what started... Sophia told me the witness to the murder referred to a malevolent person, the Deliverer, and I think she noticed my reaction.'

Jackson balled his fist and smacked it on his thigh. 'I don't know the details of what Sophia uncovered. She's the Clewer's solicitor. She only told me that they'd found the witness.' He perpetuated the silence for longer this time. 'She doesn't know about the threats, where they come from. I didn't want her unintentionally revealing anything to Hettie. They're very close. She's going to be family.' Jackson spoke into the glare of lights and kaleidoscopic raindrops snaking across the windscreen, his thoughts out in the open when previously he had kept them to himself. Under different circumstances, such faith in Julianna should have brought her pride. But not today. He sighed. 'Perhaps involving her was a mistake. It's why I needed an outsider, someone like you with no ties to my family.'

'Sophia brought an end to those futile appeal attempts. In his way, Mark is grateful. She doesn't know what makes Mark's case special to you. I think she deserves to, because what Mark uncovered isn't trivial.'

'You're right. This business of the Deliverer goes back further than Mark's involvement. To when Hettie was young.'

The last piece of the jigsaw. Between them, they were solving the puzzle. 'I don't want to intrude, sir. I know that she's precious to you...'

'You should know more – I dropped you into this mess. Hettie was adopted, which you know. A good family with enough money to support her creativity. She needs that outlet. When she was six, her birth mother slashed her wrists in the bath. Hettie found her.'

The handles of the pram. Jackson had calmly reacted to the fuss, knowing the injury was superficial, and protected his wife at the hospital from intrusive questions that might reveal the real nature of her affliction.

'Oh, my God. Her fear of blood—'

'Yes. It's from that time. I must have appeared uncaring from where you sat. I was cross with Lara for making a poor decision about the ambulance. She'd been briefed, I thought.'

'Chris informed me of the fear, but not the reason why. Perhaps Lara missed—'

'Blood is the trigger,' Jackson said sharply. 'It doesn't matter now. The point is, she fears the emotions it might awaken. So she protects herself by locking down – a form of catatonia. As a child she was taken into care and swiftly adopted. It helped her heal.'

'I understand. Her birth mother brought her up alone?'

'Divorced, alone, unsupported and a lot of debt. A hard time for them both. She got into drugs and then they came for her, the loan sharks, and forced her into prostitution. She obviously hated it. She spiralled into this darkness and took her own life. I met Hettie years later at a party. Young, vivacious. I'd no idea how fragile she was beneath that exuberance. I want to keep her safe. Always. The charity idea was one way I could help Hettie come to terms with her past. I set up Opportunitas, hoping to save people from this never-ending cycle of a life of poverty, drugs and sexual exploitation. It snowballed and became a crusade to find out who was behind these pimps, the gangs, the traffickers. The detectives I employ are successful, and consequently, I'm hated and threatened.'

'Hettie doesn't know who's behind these threats.' A statement of fact. Julianna had seen the emails and letters including the horrific images they tried to send her. Chris's team intercepted the lot. Hettie was cocooned behind a ring of protection. Jackson's commitment to take care of his wife depended on her trust in him and a marriage built on devotion to one another. Julianna had misunderstood marriage. Love was one thing that gelled a couple, but trust and loyalty underpinned it. Alex might have loved her in the beginning, and she had loved him for a time, but neither of them had worked to build on it.

'I fudge the truth,' Jackson acknowledged. 'She acts as if it's money that necessitates the bodyguards and the other measures I put in place. She could work it out, I know, but her instinct for now is to protect herself, and the kids, so she doesn't. You know, the things they want to do to her have nothing to do with money. They want her to suffer.'

'This Deliverer, is it one person?'

'There's one man behind the worst gang. We don't know his nationality. We know little of what he looks like – rumour has it his face is scarred. He uses this alias and versions of it. His online persona might be utilised by a network of handlers who seek out vulnerable people. So it's a representation for a particular purpose, but Chris and his team have unearthed enough evidence to prove this one man has a personal interest in seeing me and Hettie destroyed because of Opportunitas. I won't shut it down. I won't be defeated. Too many rely on the safe houses and support.'

The impact of the foundation's work had forced a new tactic – follow the money. Julianna moved the timeline to nearly three years ago. 'He laundered his money using Henderson's help. Mark uncovered the scam at Haydocks and assets were frozen. What Mark doesn't know is that his father killed the cousin of Redningsmann.'

'If it is him, my nemesis, the Deliverer, Ellen is walking into a trap. He's been waiting years, knowing what Bill did but leaving him in prison to rot. Mark's crusade was about the money, and that really hit hard, so he decides to act. It's about punishing Mark, and Bill, and the best way is to sell his sister into sexual slavery.'

A wave of shivers stung Julianna's skin. It all hung together if the final piece was Ellen's entrapment. 'It works *if* Ellen told them Mark's behind the breakup of Haydocks and revealed herself as his sister.'

'How that came to happen...'

Mark had shown so little concern. Ellen chatted with this guy for such a long time, in secret. How clever. And patient. Why wonder Mark hadn't been worried by Ellen's news. The evening traffic finally thinned out, and Jackson, sensing the alarm in Julianna's voice, picked up speed.

'This man doesn't rush,' he said. 'He's the ringmaster of a long-playing circus game. But I think it's reaching its final stage for Mark. Let's hope Ellen is simply going on a dig in Ireland and your nervous antennae is twitching unnecessarily.'

Julianna's instincts had been off-kilter for some time. She would like it to be way off for Ellen's sake; the girl wasn't even the original target; that was Mark.

'You wanted me to get involved with Mark so I could protect him and keep an eye on him.'

'Yes. I used you and I've no regrets. I set this all in motion, Julianna. I created this monster and his hatred for me. The police, other charities, local councils, we all work together. My money provides safe houses and repatriates the most vulnerable. Haydocks was used to control where the money went, the way it was laundered. I bet he's regretting using Henderson.'

'You said Mark needs to find out the truth, piece things together. But why? Why wait for Mark to find things out? I think, to be blunt, sir, you've played a game with him for too long.'

'That wasn't my intention. I assumed Mark would be the target for vengeance, which is why I erased Haydocks from his record, kept the police away, and brought Mark to where I could keep an eye on him. My headquarters is well protected by security systems, Daneswan wasn't. And Mark has you. Don't you think that helps him? What Mark has yet to realise is where his father fits in.... was joining Haydocks done with his dad's blessing or… We're here.'

She squeezed her handbag: a heavy leather one that weighed a ton. She had chosen it on purpose. 'He'll find out soon, won't he?'

'Yes, I'm dropping you off. See if you can find her. Ring for back up if you need it. If she's here, bring her to Mark's place. Watch your back. I'm going over to speak to Mark, break the news to him that his sister is the likely target. What's his address?'

She told him and he entered it into the GPS. She spoke, 'Please, don't... he's easily upset.'

Jackson's pupils were dark pinpricks in a sea of blue. 'I intend to upset him. He needs to start asking the right questions, not about his father's guilt, which is a distraction, but about why his father became that man, an assassin. He's evaded the truth for years. As for Ellen, she's his younger sister, and you know what I feel about family. It's everything to me.' He released the door lock and she climbed out. The wheels spun and he was gone.

The name next to listing for flat 3A was E. Devera. Had Chris given her the wrong address? She buzzed and waited, but there was no answer. She tried again. The other the occupants of the building were listed with their flat numbers and individual doorbells. One stood out: Jed Redder, 4A, the flat above Ellen's.

That lump in her throat returned. Redder was another translation of the Deliverer. She instinctively pressed the buzzer for 4A.

'Yes?' the voice crackled. 'Who's there?'

'I'm trying to find Ellen Devera in the bedsit below you. Do you know her? It's important.' She waited, her nose to the glass of the door. If somebody came out, she would whiz by them and in.

Nobody came.

'Who are you?' the disembodied voice asked.

'My name is Julianna Baptiste. I'm a friend of her brother, Mark.' It was a gamble. He would either ignore her or let curiosity win.

The main door released. 'Come up.'

The door to 4A was already open and the first thing she saw was the wall opposite, which was covered in posters of bikers. Bikers with long hair and tattoos, and plenty of black leather, macho poses, and some bare chests too. She tensed, remembering what Sophia had said about the Deliverer using bikers to recruit.

The man stood in the kitchen, his hand resting on a motorcycle helmet. He wore a black leather jacket. The apartment was a tip.

'What do you want?' he asked.

Julianna stayed by the door, on the threshold, half in. She kept her escape route open.

'Jed Redder?'

He shook his head. 'No. I'm Nicky. Jed's my half-brother. He used this flat until a year ago.'

How to spot a liar? By their eyes. 'The name tab says it's Jed Redder's.'

A flutter of his eyelashes, but he stayed with her gaze, matching it. 'Call me lazy, I haven't changed it.'

'You're Ellen's friend?'

'That's me.' He wasn't smiling. 'And you're Mark's?' He put both hands on the helmet. A posturing threat or to steady his hands?

'Do you know where's she gone? Shopping? Visiting a friend?'

'Why do you care?'

A touch of sarcasm. He slouched a fraction, too. Gaining confidence? Julianna wasn't sure.

'Because Mark needs to see her.'

Amongst the abandoned clothes and beer cans were dumb bells. It explained his bulk. Plenty of brawn, but not beyond her abilities.

'I haven't seen her all week. I've been out of town.' A weak shrug. Now he was uncomfortable, agitated. Was he colluding with somebody?

The black helmet reflected the spotlight above it. She shifted her handbag off her shoulder. 'You like bikes?' There were magazines strewn across the coffee table and another helmet on the sofa.

'I like bikers.' The shadows under his eyes lengthened as he leaned forward. 'What's it to you. You said you want to find Ellen.'

'How did you two meet?' She stepped over the threshold of the doorframe, giving her arms room to move, her legs kick space.

'Nosey, aren't we?' he said with a sneer. 'She never mentioned your name.'

Because Mark had never told Ellen.

'So you don't know where she is?' Time was precious now. She wasn't in the driver's seat waiting to be told what to do. She had to act, make decisions. The knots in her stomach contorted painfully. If this was her chance to prove herself, she couldn't have picked a crazier situation. The man who looked like he could steam roller his way over her could be the man behind Ellen's disappearance. He could be one of those who used the deliverer alias to tempt girls into a trap. Had he befriended her, moved in above her flat and slowly, insidiously tricked her?

He lifted the helmet. Beneath it was a sheet of paper. 'I know where she's gone. So I'm wondering why her brother doesn't. Because he should know. He should care very much where she's gone. Don't you think?' Fiery anger lit up his eyes.

'Shit,' Julianna muttered. She was too late. Ellen had left. But at least she would get to beat the crap out of the man who set her up.

The door to the bathroom opened. Walking towards her and adjusting the zipper of his leather pants was another man, just as brawny as Nicky. 'Nic?' The newcomer lifted two bushy eyebrows. 'Who's the chick?'

Now, she had to take on two men. The odds weren't great.

24

Mark

Mark sprawled, spider legged, on the settee with a newly opened bottle of beer in his hand – his third that evening. Surrounding him were numerous handwritten notes on prison paper and the shredder he had borrowed from the office. If he'd had a fireplace he would have burnt them. Letter after letter, promising Mark so much and delivering so little. The anger expelled in each ribbon spewing out of the machine was satisfying. He shoved the slithers into a waste bin.

Bill had portrayed his mundane life in intricate detail. He had lashed out at the inedible food, the inadequate fitness facilities and described his fleeting attempts at improving them. There was the comings and goings of his cell mates, the constant threat of violence and the conspicuous drug taking. Mark had no sympathy for those things, because Bill had chosen that way of life before he had even gone to prison. The letters were a pointless diary of an inconsequential life.

Turning page after page of his father's spiky handwriting, which gifted him with new hindsight, he realised that Bill had said nothing about his crime, in particular the appeal. The absence of pleas of innocence were obvious. He had been conned and the person to blame wasn't Ellen – she had never read her father's letters. He wished he hadn't said those things to her. He hadn't even accompanied her to the airport to say goodbye. The more he replayed their furious conversation, the greater the remorse, and the more he drank.

The buzz of the doorbell barely cut into his dulled mind, but Jackson's voice bellowing out of the speaker did. 'Mark, open the fucking door or else you're fired.'

Mark shoved aside the pile of letters and staggered to the security panel. He released the downstairs entrance door and unlocked his own. A few seconds later, Jackson appeared, nostrils flared and unusually breathless. He slammed the door shut behind him and circled the space between the kitchen and lounge.

'Where's Ellen?' Without a suit and tie, Jackson had lost his executive edge. His usually coiffured hair was flattened with rain, his eyes sculptured by tired lines and depth – Jackson had acquired a different energy. The urgency with which he bounded into the apartment continued as he paced, frowning at the bottles and the shredder. No apology was given for his abrupt arrival.

Mark, in his bewilderment, blustered. 'What are you doing here?'

'Your sister. Where is she?' An agitated Jackson was unsightly, an affront to his boss persona. Mark's anxiety escalated.

'Gone to Ireland. Like she said she would. A flight this evening from Heathrow. And it's her choice. I told her to go if she wants to.' He slumped down on the sofa and reclaimed his beer bottle. Jackson kicked the shredder to one side and loomed over the indignant Mark.

'Listen, Mark. Sober up. Who has Ellen gone to meet?'

He wiped the top of the bottle with his sleeve and lifted it to his lips. Why the urgency and why did it matter to Jackson?

'Who? I don't know. Some bloke she met online. She's been chatting to him for years.' Lovers, perhaps, who knew? It happened that way and why would he put a stop to it when she had shown no interest in his friends or the opportunities he had presented to her.

Jackson's hand shot out and snatched the bottle out of Mark's hand. For a second he looked as if he might smash it down. Instead he dumped it on the coffee table. 'Think. A name. Something.'

'Freddie.' He hadn't paid that much attention. 'Stupid name, not the slightest bit Irish. Freddie Zuss. Zustaller.'

Jackson dragged his fingers through hair, the colour drained from his face. 'Shit, shit!'

The spectacle of his fraught boss circling the room, cursing, was almost too much for Mark's churning stomach. He swallowed, hard, and, with burning throat, stumbled over his words. 'Wh- what have I done?' He had done something terrible, whether he intended to or not, and whatever it was went beyond the argument he'd had with Ellen.

'Zustaller is an alias. The name means Deliverer in German.'

'I haven't heard of it.'

'You've heard of Redningsmann. A Norwegian name. It means the same thing.'

Haydocks! Everything in his life came back to that one decision. He had been sober and confident when he had made it. A different man. Idealistic, too, his morals governed by a need to distance himself from his father. He stirred from the nest of empty beer bottles and crumpled letters and slowly rose to his feet.

'Tell me,' he said succinctly. 'What do you know?'

Jackson's expression was pained. 'I didn't know for certain, not until Sophia finished up the appeal case for your father. I hoped... I hoped I was wrong. I'm sorry, Mark. The man your father murdered was an associate, a relative of Freddie Zustaller, who for years has run a trafficking ring. Zustaller sent his cousin to negotiate a deal in Manchester. Your father killed that man and in turn was arrested, probably betrayed by somebody in his own crew as a result of the aftermath. Zustaller went into hiding, but he protected his money. He gave it to Henderson. He let Haydocks manage it.'

'No.' Mark gasped. 'No, God, no.'

'If it's Zustaller she met online, this is his revenge. He wants to punish you in the only way he knows. He will have her met by strangers and quickly drugged. They will feed her drugs until she's addicted, then sell her to the highest bidder. She will disappear into the ghastly underbelly of our lovely civilised world and within a year she will be probably be dead.' Jackson grabbed Mark's arm to steady him. 'Sit. It's not too late. If she's only just gone. We can catch up with her. She must have told you where she was going.'

He blinked the tears away before they could fall. 'We argued. She told me things about Mum and Dad I didn't know—'

'We don't have time to go over your misgivings. An address, her mobile number?'

He choked on the laughter. The irony of an accountant who could remember reams of spreadsheets but rarely bothered with phone numbers. Why, when there were apps to do it for you!

'I never bothered to memorise it – she mainly called me. It's listed on my phone's contacts. Except, my mobile is broken. I smashed it.'

'You've not written it down? Backed it up? Jesus, Mark, you're an idiot. What about your mother; would she know?'

'No, I'm pretty sure Ellen's number comes up as private and she changes it regularly to keep Mum off her back.' Mark sprang to his feet. 'She wrote an address down on a piece of paper, the address in Ireland. I threw it in the bin.' He dashed to the kitchen and emptied the contents onto the floor.

He spread out food cartons, half-eaten chips, biscuits wrappers and apple cores. The smell tortured his delicate nostrils; a warning sign of an impending assault, something he wanted to avoid at all costs. He inhaled deeply through his mouth. Amongst the litter were coffee grounds and split liquids, which had blended into a brown soup. He rummaged through the detritus of his life, scattering it across the tiles.

'It has to be here somewhere....' He spotted the scrap of paper and fished it out. 'No!'

Jackson snatched the note out of Mark's hand. 'I can see the name. It is Freddie Zustaller, but the address is covered in stains.' He held it up to the light.

'Can you read it?'

'No. The ink is smudged.' Jackson sighed. 'We'll have to try another lead. Let's hope—'

He'd given a spare key to Ellen. He had also given one to Julianna. When the key turned in the lock, he prayed it was his sister and that she had changed her mind and realised how foolish it was for her to go all the way to Ireland to do the things she loved when she could do them here, where somebody could watch over her. The door swung open. Mark, on his knees, surrounded by rubbish, held his breath.

It was Julianna. Her wet hair was matted onto her face, her cheeks flushed red, her body buried inside an oversized black leather jacket with studs down the arms. She panted, leant on her knees, struggling to catch her breath. Behind her was a thickset man in illustrated leathers carrying two motorcycle helmets. He, too, was breathing heavily and spraying raindrops.

'Is this the brother?' the brick-shaped man asked, pointing at Jackson.

'No. That's my boss,' she said.

'Then, this is Ellen's brother.' The biker pushed past Julianna and scrutinised Mark.

'That's him.'

Julianna's face was flushed with the heat of exertion, but there was also a peculiar blue tinge around her lips. She looked frozen stiff, as if a coil of steel was compressed inside her, ready to explode. The man next to her matched Jackson for height. Haynes rocked back on his heels. Being in control was the essence of his authority, but since Jackson had arrived at the flat, his highhanded presence had gradually eroded. Now he stood, perplexed, and indecisive. Mark battered aside the threat of humiliating tears; this chaos was all his own fault.

The beefy man grinned from ear to ear. 'He's sat in a pile of shit. Probably where he belongs.'

Julianna nodded. 'Possibly. Let's find out.'

25

Julianna

It was Ted's rather tactless sense of humour that resolved the tension at Nicky's flat. By calling her a chick, then jovially accusing Nicky of turning to the dark side and cheating on him with a girl, Ted inadvertently ended the standoff. Nicky's drawn face brightened. The wall posters took on a new meaning. Nicky wasn't a gangster, he loved men on bikes. Literally loved them. His hostile stance, the antagonism towards her arrival, was a defensive response to her own aggressive interrogation. She had played him wrong.

The handbag was lowered, the strident edge to her voice softened and she explained the reason she was there. Ellen was in danger. She was unequivocal in describing the situation. If they didn't find Ellen, she would be handed over to traffickers and vanish. Nicky thrust the piece of paper at her.

'She never told me she was going or anything about this,' he said. The letter was addressed to him and signed, Ellie. 'I've not heard about this man. If I'd known, I would have put a stop to it. Mark, this ass of a brother, practically told her to go. Start a new life out there. Look at what she wrote!'

Ellen's account of her conversation with Mark was terse and angry. She accused Mark of colluding with her parents while ignoring her. He had missed the signs, she wrote.

The scrawl indicated haste and she had pushed the note under Nicky's door. Nicky was especially upset that she hadn't said goodbye to him in person. Ted rested his long arm on Nicky's shoulders and gave him a squeeze. The use of the motorcycle was Ted's suggestion.

The call to Chris was scrapped. By the time Moran made it across the river, Julianna, mounted on the back of Ted's bike, would be there in quarter of the time. Nicky was desperate to help. She took his mobile number and promised to keep him up to date.

'Stay here. If she changes her mind, you're the person she'll come back to.'

'I'll kill him,' Nicky said, bluntly.

She hadn't the time to find out who he meant.

The journey to Mark's flat was exhilarating, frightening and cold. Nicky had given her an old jacket; a smaller one he once wore before he had started weight training. The sleeves were too long, but it was better than her flimsy coat. Arriving at the block of flats, she gained access with the key Mark had given her and ran up the stairs to his floor with Ted panting on her heels.

She nearly collided with her boss.

'Baptiste,' Jackson growled. 'Who is this?'

'This is Ted. Ted meet Jackson and Mark.' Julianna said. 'Nicky might love bikers, but he can't ride bikes. Ted brought me here. Quicker than summoning Chris. Scarier too. Boy, Ted, that was some ride you gave me.' She thumped Ted's arm; her knuckles cracked against solid muscle. In hindsight, it was fortunate she hadn't gone up against Ted.

Seeing Mark on his knees, bewildered, surrounded by the rubbish, she wondered if an irate Jackson had tipped the lot on him. But Jackson wasn't near Mark, nor was he paying him any attention. He was focused on Julianna, and not her boyfriend, if Mark was still that. Maybe what she felt toward him was disappointment; an unpleasantly familiar emotion that reminded her too much of Alex. However, although Mark had failed to bond with his sister, he wasn't entirely to blame for Ellen's predicament. Ellen had ignored common sense and inflicted danger upon herself; those things weren't strangers to Julianna. Mark had to get off the floor, out of the shit, as Ted so rightly put it, and show some backbone.

Julianna reached into a pocket and held up a sheet of paper. 'She wrote Nicky a letter. She caught a flight this evening and she's supposed to go to a hostel in Bray to meet somebody called Garth. I've got the address and a flight number.'

The colour drained from Mark's face. 'She told this to Nicky?' He scrambled to his feet.

'I nearly punched his lights out by mistake. There was some confusion. It turns out that it's possible to have the surname Redder and not be connected to a criminal underworld.'

'What?'

'Nothing, just a red herring, they happen. Give him his dues, Nicky was being cautious and didn't want to give me the address until he was sure I could be trusted. The letter paints you in a poor light. What did you say to her?'

'I was mad at her and said things, but I didn't cut her off, honestly, her things are still here.'

She wasn't convinced. 'She thinks you're a moron, her words, not mine.'

'There's no time for family sagas.' Jackson whipped out his phone and snatched the paper out of Julianna's hand. Chris Moran was kicked into action.

'It's the so-called Deliverer again. He's after Mark Clewer's sister. She is totally ignorant of the danger and boarding a flight to Dublin from Heathrow.' Jackson paced as he briefed his security chief. 'The company chopper? Log a flight plan from London to Dublin. Arrange transport and accommodation at the other end.' He hung up and tossed Julianna his car keys. 'The helipad. You drive, I've more calls to make.'

'Me?' She clutched the keys to her tight chest. Adrenaline was good. Strong heartbeats. Focused mind. Her father would tell her to channel the energy, not fight it.

'You two will go to Dublin and find her. Bring her back. If you don't find her, don't come to work on Monday, Mark. Your family is what matters and you'll not come back until you've done everything you can to put this right.'

Mark nodded and blinked. No Ellen, no job. The threat, if it was truly that, worked. He darted about his apartment collecting things. A coat, wallet and driving licence to validate his identity.

'Passport. Do you have yours?' Jackson asked her.

'Yes, sir. On me as required.'

Mark raised his eyebrows. 'You do?'

'I'm obliged to carry identification at all times.' But she checked inside the deepest compartment of her handbag and ran her fingers along the textured cover to be certain.

'Move, we've got to get to the helipad.' Jackson harried them with a swoop of his arms.

Their speedy preparations had an audience of one: a bemused Ted. Mark shook his hand and winced as Ted squeezed back in reply.

'Ted, thank you,' Mark said, extracting his throbbing fingers. 'Please let Nicky know we'll do whatever we can to get Ellen home safely.'

Julianna started to shimmy out of the leather jacket.

'Keep it,' said Ted. 'Won't fit Nicky again.' He grinned. Julianna could appreciate why Nicky liked that smile.

During the journey to the helipad, Jackson rattled through a string of phone calls. To his wife to say she was not to worry. To contacts he had through Opportunitas to start looking up possible leads in Dublin. As for the number Ellen had left for the hostel, Jackson cursed profusely. 'It went straight to an answer machine. Probably a dummy number or they only answer known callers.'

Julianna pressed her foot down on the accelerator.

Moran met them at the helipad departure area.

'The helicopter?' asked Jackson.

'On standby,' Moran said. 'A flight plan has been submitted.'

'Good, take these two over there. I want them in Dublin as soon as possible. Put this through my private account, not the company one.'

'When you've found her, and I pray that you do,' Jackson said to Julianna quietly, 'bring her to Fasleigh House. Not Mark's.'

The implication was obvious; Mark couldn't be trusted to look after his sister. Not now, perhaps never. Jackson had read what Ellen had written in the letter to Nicky.

26

Mark

Friday Evening

In the car, on the way to the helipad, Mark told Jackson that he would do anything to put things right. Jackson grunted an acknowledgement. With his boss in the front seat of the car, he had held back from saying anything personal to Julianna, words failed him. He had been selfish and inconsiderate, wrapped up in his own world of misery and anger, and she deserved better.

Jackson went home after dropping them off – he had his own commitments – and he delegated his powers to Julianna. Moran reminded them that they shouldn't involve the Garda unless they had to. 'Keep it low key as possible. In, then out. Hopefully this is a simple extraction operation and doesn't require additional specialist support.'

Mark dug his nails into his palms and pretended he hadn't heard the frank conversation between his girlfriend and Moran. Neither of them talked about plan-Bs, such as what happened if they didn't find his sister. From then on, as they boarded the helicopter, they were on their own.

Under other circumstances, a helicopter ride would thrill Mark. The helicopter took off with an unpleasant lurch and the seat harness gripped his waist, yanking him back into the leather seat. The nausea ebbed and flowed, and his empty belly yielded a bitter taste in his throat. There was nothing to enjoy about the journey.

Helicopters might be on Julianna's bucket list for all he knew – she showed no signs of sickness. He couldn't bring himself to ruin her fascination by talking. Only as they approached the city lights of Dublin, did she tear herself away from the skyline. She grasped his hand and he looked at her. Her expression exemplified pity.

He pulled his hand away. She said something, but the whirr of rotating blades drowned her out. She activated a mic and her voice arrived in his headphones. 'You've been irresponsible with Ellen, but it wasn't your intention to harm her.' There was nothing subtle in Julianna's sharp tongue.

'Why didn't I just listen to her? I treated her like a child because I only knew her as a child. I took her to a nightclub, a dinner party, stuff you do with a girlfriend, things I should have done with you. She refused to talk about our parents; I really could have tried harder to find out why. I'm a piece of shit...'

'It's not your fault. The chances of you going to work for Haydocks, the connection it had to your father—'

'Oh, please, don't make this one of those profound karma things. It isn't like that.' Ellen had her secrets and he had one too. He had been too ashamed to mention it to Jackson.

The helicopter lifted, rattled by invisible air currents. Mark drew himself up in his seat. 'I didn't always ignore my father's advice.' Before deciding to shred the correspondence, he had a read a few of the earlier ones. Bill had written every month or so, and when Mark was in his final year at Oxford and hunting for jobs, he had taken keen interest in his choice of degree, unlike Deidre.

'Dad suggested Henderson.' He watched Julianna's face for a reaction. He hadn't lied, rather because it happened a long time ago, he hadn't appreciated the significance until that afternoon.

The helicopter tilted and Julianna lost her balance; she slid and collided against him. She steadied herself using her hand on his leg.

'Your dad knew Henderson?' Julianna righted herself, but left her palm resting on his thigh.

This time, he didn't push it away. 'Surprising, I know, given Dad kept most of his ill-gotten gains in secret stashes.'

'Who gave the name to him?'

Mark shrugged. 'I've been wondering about that ever since Jackson told me about Haydocks and Zustfaller, whatever his name is.'

'Why didn't you tell Jackson about your dad and Haydocks?'

Mark smirked. 'I think he already guessed, don't you? Why the interest in me and my father if it wasn't about the money? It's always about money. In any case, I've destroyed the letter. I suppose it counts as more evidence of my father's guilt.'

'Bill gave you Haydocks.' The piece of information was filed away, she understood the significance. Mark was a pawn. But whose?

Mark frowned. The obvious thoughts were racing through his mind. 'Most large accountancy firms have hundreds of clients. Only a handful of Haydocks' were involved in illegal activities and Henderson managed those accounts. The only obvious way Dad would know about a bent accountancy firm was from another crook. I just find it hard to believe that it's a coincidence.'

'See, don't knock karma.' She squeezed his leg. The weight of her hand was reassuring.

Maybe he and Julianna still had a chance to come out of this intact. A partnership of some kind even if it meant starting afresh. The more he thought about Ellen's desperate bid to be an archaeologist, the more he appreciated why. Scraping away the dirt, uncovering harmless objects, she was safe. The things she found, no matter their original purpose, would not threaten her. Julianna craved something different, a more visceral approach to digging up the past and finding the truth. Alex's deceit had been a cruel blow and it had knocked her confidence. Yet, here she was, giving up her time and energy to find his sister. She'd proved herself to him, and hopefully Jackson. Her ambitions lay somewhere and he fancied she wanted in to Opportunitas itself. Whatever her original motives for spending time with Mark, whether self-serving sex or raw ambition, she'd rediscovered herself.

'You've not lost it,' he said softly, covering her hand with his.

She furrowed her eyebrows; his words were lost to the engine noise. However, she smiled. The first one in a while. 'We're coming in to land. Pop your ears.'

27

Ellen

Ellen arrived at the hotel by taxi. 'Is it a hostel or a hotel?' she asked the driver. The sign outside blinked: "Vacancies".

The driver continued to roll his cigarette. 'Depends. If you were told it's a hostel, it's a hostel. It's not my kind of place. But they say it's better than most for what you need.' He took her money and drove off.

The suitcase weighed a ton. She'd carted it through bus terminals, airport lounges and the taxi rank. The flight unnerved her because she'd only flown once before and that was to Jersey for a rare family holiday prior to the downward spiral of Bill's criminal life. Throughout the flight to Dublin, she'd gripped the armrests, turning her knuckles white. The man next to her played on his tablet. She'd none of those kinds of luxuries. She kept her phone turned off to conserve the battery life.

The skinny guy at the reception desk didn't raise an eyebrow at the time – a little past ten o'clock. He shook his head when she asked if a Freddie Zustaller, or the other names she'd been given, had left a message. After signing the registry book and snatching the key out of his spidery hand, she wondered if Freddie had given her the wrong address.

'Money?' He kept his hand out – dirt was etched into the creases of his palm. 'The deposit. Twenty Euros.'

She fumbled in her purse and handed him the note. 'Is there a kitchen?'

'At the end of the hall. No room service.' He chuckled. 'We don't provide anything but you can use it. There's Sammy's cafe a street away if you're wanting breakfast. It's popular enough.'

'I guess I'll wait for the morning.' She hadn't the energy to tackle an unknown kitchen.

He jerked his head at the entrance. 'I'll keep an eye out for your friends. Send them up when they come, shall I?'

'Thank you.'

A creepy grin split across his face. The hostel couldn't be more than a stopover. Freddie said the dig was in Wicklow to the south and there was a chance to live somewhere closer. The receptionist said something else to her, but she ignored the unpleasant sentiment and gesture.

The feeling of wrongness was heightened when she entered the musty bedroom. The wallpaper had curled away in places under the cracked coving and a threadbare patch of carpet was stained with heel marks. If the mattress served any useful purpose, sleep wasn't it. It creaked as she rested the suitcase on the bed and groaned when she moved it back off again. There was nowhere to hang her clothes and only a chest of wobbly drawers. Abandoned in the back of one was a dusty Gideon New Testament dated 1987 on the inside jacket. The room might have been cleaned, but not with anything that left a sheen. She winced at the salmon pink bathroom, its grouting decorated with black ribbons of mould. Having peed without sitting on the seat and washed her hands in the cracked sink with a squirt of liquid soap she carried in her handbag, she decided to email Freddie and seek some advice. The lack of both signal and wi-fi stymied the idea.

She lay on the bed with her hands pressed to her sides and chewed her lip. The ceiling was stained with yellow rings of cigarette smoke. She tasted the lingering tobacco on her tongue. Trying hard to dismiss the nagging worry that she'd misunderstood Freddie's plans, Ellen closed her eyes and hoped the morning would cast the room in a friendlier light.

She wasn't the slightest bit sleepy. A surprising level of cacophony impinged: stomping footsteps; giggles, then a shriek; the hoot of a car horn; a door slamming. She burrowed her face into the stale pillow. More footsteps running, this time along the corridor. A knock. Whispering. More doors closing; their latches clicking. The percussive sounds rumbled on until a woman screamed, the cry muffled by doors and walls. Ellen shot upright, held her breath while her empty stomach churned. She expected something in response to the rumpus: a siren.

An unearthly silence was born, and it stretched on and on. She waited for something to puncture it, reassure her that she wasn't in a dump of the worst kind. But she was. The hostel was a shit-hole. Freddie had picked the cheapest place for her because he knew she was on a shoestring budget. If he had checked it out first, he wouldn't have allowed her into the place. All those lectures on personal safety and Freddie had broken his own rules. Without him to guide her, she had to make her own decision; she would leave in the morning and find somewhere more suitable.

She curled into a ball under the musty counterpane. Shivering, her teeth chattered. She couldn't contemplate undressing, and the decision had nothing to with temperature and everything to do with fear. A deep yawn forced her eyes shut. She hovered in an in-between place.

Hammering stirred her semi-slumber. She slipped her feet onto the carpet and crept towards the door. There wasn't a peephole. She chanced it – hoping for a late visit from Alicia or even Freddie. Perhaps he would take her someplace else. And apologise, too.

The couple – a leather-clad man with oily hair combed back into a long tail and a skeletal woman – barged into the room and blocked the exit. The door slammed shut behind them.

Ellen stumbled backwards, and collided with the end of the bed. Where the hell was Freddie?

28
Julianna

Dublin was freezing. They dashed across the tarmac to the covered reception area, completed the formalities with a sleepy-eyed official, then stepped out into the darkness.

'Come on,' Julianna said. 'Moran has arranged for a driver and car.'

It was nearly midnight. Mark staggered on his tired legs. Julianna chivvied, plucking at his sleeve. 'There! There's a man with my name on a board.' She waved at the driver.

The man recognised the name of the hostel. 'Not the sort of place a tourist should go to,' he said. 'It's a piss hole.'

Julianna asked him to pick up speed. Mark's complexion was a shade short of puce. He was a good bedfellow, but not a reliable sidekick. Not yet, anyway. She fancied teaching him a few things about nerves and pressure, like breathing, keeping it steady and under control. It wasn't fair to criticise him. Anxiety lurked in the raked pit of her stomach, fed by necessary adrenaline, which sharpened her senses, honing them ready. Not so for Mark, who seemed to be battling something more debilitating than the cold. He had closed his dark haloed eyes and pressed his quivering lips together. What would he say to Ellen when they found her? He should definitely apologise. And listen to her; a lesson both siblings needed to learn in order to heal the rift between them. Jackson clearly thought it was beyond them.

The driver was prattling. 'Doxies use it,' he said with too much relish.

'What about students?' Julianna asked.

'Out here? Tis a long way from the colleges. You do know what a doxie is?'

'Yes,' she said, despondently.

Mark lowered the window and blasted the interior with icy wind. Drawing the lapels of the leather jacket up higher, she waited for him to realise his mistake. Goose bumps formed on the back of her neck and her muscles stiffened. Whatever Mark needed to feel, it wasn't helping her prepare. She cracked her knuckle joints, leaned across him and closed the window. He stared for a moment at her, then looked away.

No one spoke until they arrived at the hostel on the outskirts of Dublin. Mark wrinkled his nose at the neon lit sign. 'This isn't a hostel. It's more like a hotel.'

'Pay by the hour,' the driver said. 'It hasn't changed much in years. Garda ignore it unless there's trouble, so it keeps itself unappealing. That's its beauty.' He laughed. 'I guess your friend isn't familiar with the area. She shouldn't be here on her own.'

'Can you wait?' she asked the man.

The driver drummed his fingers on the wheel and peered at the dim street, the garish "Vacancies" in the hotel window. 'You know you're dealing with shite coming here. There are better places. Ireland isn't—'

'I know,' she said; every city had its rough spots. 'Please, just wait ten minutes or so. We're trying to help her.'

He shrugged. 'Ten minutes.'

Julianna wasn't optimistic.

The pencil thin man behind the reception desk lacked a name tag. The loose shirt, unbuttoned at the top, was creased in the wrong places. Two dopey eyes with their half-drawn eyelids peeped out from under a mop of greasy hair. He stank of tobacco, and something sweet, almost musty.

He picked up the registration log, placed it on the desk before them and rattled off the rates. Mark blanched; she thought he might keel over.

'She can't be here,' she whispered to Mark. 'I mean, why would Zustaller ask her to come here when it's so obviously the wrong kind of place. She'd walk out, wouldn't she?'

How gullible was Ellen? She'd lived in London for a year, grown up on a rough estate, she wasn't daft. How Redningsmann, or

Zustaller as Ellen knew him, had contacted her was unknown. It was in Opportunitas' interest to close down those conduits, which explained Jackson's ongoing interest. However, what drove Ellen to come to Ireland was more about what she was leaving behind; it was about escaping her past and hoping for a better future. Two powerful motives that might blinker her common sense.

Mark drew himself upright, making use of his six feet. 'I'm here to find somebody.' He shoved his face right up to the other man's nose. 'Are you going to help or not?' Mark finally understood the urgency.

The receptionist slowly scratched his chin, unperturbed by Mark's rudeness. 'It's late. Anybody in particular?' He lit a cigarette, blatantly defying the no smoking sign behind the desk.

'Yes, Ellen, her name is Ellen Clewer… I mean, Devera.'

The receptionist scanned down the list of names. 'Yep, arrived and checked in. Gone out again with a red-head, swinging happily on his arm.'

'Gone!' Mark's knees buckled.

Her mouth was sealed shut, blocking her screams. The screams that nobody in the building would bother to investigate, nor would they care about the bangs and shouts. Ellen was in exactly the right place for lassitude and disinterest. The man pinioned her head between his hands while the woman taped Ellen's eyes, sticking her eyelashes together. Pain spiked in her jaw; the tape refused to split open.

Had Freddie really patiently cultivated her friendship and trust for three years for this day? It didn't make sense – why her when there were more vulnerable girls to be tricked: a whole hotel full of potential victims? Freddie wasn't behind this nightmare. It had to be an opportunistic snatch. Perhaps she had been spotted entering the hostel alone. The man on the desk with the rabid breath had eyed her, noting her accent with a wry smile. 'We love the Brits here,' he had said, and winked.

What a fool she was. How stupid and naive. Deidre was right; she had led a charmed life, barricaded in her bedroom, refusing to deal with the outside world.

Leaving her trussed up on the bed, they ransacked the room.

Her presence thrilled them. She heard things through her frantic breathing and thunderous heartbeats: her bag was unzipped, and the contents scattered.

The woman laughed.

The man snapped his fingers, impatiently. 'We only need her passport.' There was no trace of an Irish accent.

'British girl?' The lanky receptionist rested his elbow on the ledger. The nonchalance was infuriating.

'Yes. You're sure she's gone?' Julianna leaned over the counter, rustled up an unblinking stare from her copper's armoury and used it to pin him down.

'Blonde thing with humongous tits.' He cupped a pair of imaginary breasts. 'Works up the street.'

'No, that's not her,' Mark said. 'Brown hair and eyes. Slender build.'

'Oh her. Yep, still upstairs. Popular she is tonight. You're the second couple to want to see her. So she likes couples.' He chuckled, and winked.

She grabbed his collar. 'Which room?' He weighed nothing. She lifted him up onto his toes and he squirmed satisfyingly, like a worm on a hook.

'Twenty-two,' he gasped. 'Second floor. What's the rush? She couldn't have finished with the first lot yet.' She dropped him, and stepped between the counter and Mark, who was charging forward with a raised fist.

'No, Mark,' she said. She snatched his flying arm and spun him around on his toes. 'He's just the gatekeeper, he's not got a clue. We're wasting time here.'

She bounded up the stairs two at time, slipping on an uneven step near the top before recovering her balance. Mark followed, calling for his sister in a desperate tone.

Twenty-two was locked. Mark rattled the door handle and pounded on the door. 'Ellen, open the door. For God's sake, it's me.'

Julianna pressed her ear to the door: muffled voices and scampering. She inspected the rusty lock and hinges – the top one was loose.

'You realise I will probably break my leg doing this.' She moved away from the door. 'Step back, Mark.' Being a black belt in karate had to mean something on a day like this.

She raised her heel and unfurled as much power as she could muster, channelling the energy with a focused kick and landing the flat of her booted foot by the weak hinge. It rattled and the wood splintered, but the door remained steadfastly shut. She repeated the process twice more until, with her strength nearly spent, the door flew open and ended up hanging off the last hinge.

Mark was frozen for a second, unable to move. Julianna barrelled past him. There were towels scattered on the bathroom floor; signs of a struggle. She raced into the heart of the room. The girl on the bed, who was much smaller than Julianna had anticipated, was curled up, lying very still and possibly unconscious. She was bound with duct tape around her wrists and ankles. Her mouth was covered and her eyes too. On the bedside table was a bottle of clear liquid. Standing over Ellen with a syringe close to her arm was a man, and next to him, a wan-faced nymph with scabby cheeks.

'Don't come any closer.' His black hair was tied back into a mangled ponytail. A white scar ringed his neck and each of his cheeks was pitted with tiny craters surrounded by wiry whiskers. It was a face she would never forget. The woman tottered on her heels and spoke to the man in a foreign language.

Julianna preferred not to fight; she was bone weary and unsure what she might unleash in her fractious state. But Moran had said no police, no other agencies who might complicate the extraction. 'Get out,' she said, foisting vehemence into her voice.

'Or else.' The man laughed. The syringe dripped its contents on to the bed. He edged towards Ellen's exposed arm. 'Stay back.'

'You heard her, get off,' Mark said, his hands balled fruitlessly at his side. Mark had no clue how to punch.

The petite woman backed into the corner of the room and cowered. Julianna bit the bullet and launched herself at the man, knocking him away from Ellen. With her fists and feet flying, she jabbed and stabbed, blow after blow. He attempted to feint and box with her, but her martial art techniques were quicker and smoother. If this man represented everything she loathed and hated, then he was her new punch bag. The tactic worked. While Mark protected Ellen with his body, Julianna unleashed her version of hell, one not even her father would recognise, certainly not her mother who preferred yoga. What brought Julianna to this moment had nothing to do with her upbringing, nor was it about photos stuck to parched leather; she struck the flailing stranger because she enjoyed giving some payback, even somebody else's.

She pinned him to the floor by her straddling thighs, and he twisted beneath her, bucking with his hips. Her tempered fists were losing their impact, so she battered his head against the bottom bed post until he lost consciousness. Gasping for breath, Julianna shot the diminutive accomplice an angry glare and the woman bolted through the broken doorway. It was the fleeing woman's terrified expression and Mark's pleas, 'You're killing him,' that successfully countered Julianna's blows. She stopped, suddenly aware of her bloody knuckles, the soft unresponsive body underneath her knees, the morass of congealed features that once was an ugly face, now even more so. She slid off him onto the floor, leaving him prone, and shifted her attention to the bed.

Were they too late? Was Ellen sufficiently incapacitated she might need medical help? Mark touched Ellen's cheek and the girl flinched.

'It's me, Ellie. You're safe.' Mark picked at the tape over her eyes, peeling it off.

Ellen blinked in the light. Her tears formed shallow pools that spilled over onto her alabaster cheeks.

'Mark.' Julianna staggered to the side of the bed. 'We need to be quick. We've got an unconscious man, a broken door, and drugs to explain. Let's get moving.' The adrenaline high smothered the familiar pain in her unclenched fists. She would worry about the consequences later.

'Sorry, luv, going to have to tear these off quickly.' He ripped the duct tape away and Ellen winced.

'Mark.' She shook violently, and stirred from the nest of his arms, as if awakening from a bad dream. 'I thought I'd come to the wrong place—'

Julianna, gently re-establishing some sense of normality, took Ellen's elbow, and steadied her. 'Can you walk?'

Ellen nodded. Julianna crouched by the man. She listened to his shallow breaths, observed, with unpleasant satisfaction, the bubbles of blood dribbling out of his swollen mouth and judged him thoroughly incapacitated. She had done this. She had never beaten a person unconscious; it was easier to do than she imagined. She rifled through the pockets of the man's coat and retrieved Ellen's passport. They collected up the rest of her scattered belongings and stuffed them back into the suitcase.

Mark guided the wobbly Ellen down the stairs. Confused and disorientated, possibly concussed, she required support. Julianna wheeled the cumbersome luggage behind them. Other than a few doors opening then quickly shutting, nobody disturbed their retreat.

'Did they inject you?' Mark asked Ellen.

She rubbed her arm. 'No. I don't think so.'

'That was quick.' The skinny man on the reception desk grinned. Julianna strode past the counter. 'Hey, what about my cut? You bitch!'

To her surprise, the taxi driver had waited. He waved, grinning briefly before realising something wasn't right; Julianna pulled down the sleeve of the conveniently oversized jacket and hid her hands. Bundling Ellen into the back, Julianna gave a destination near the airport.

'Right, I'll avoid the Garda then, should I?' He pressed his foot down without waiting for an answer. Wisely, he said nothing further for the rest of the journey.

'We're going to stay the night in a hotel, then fly back early tomorrow,' Julianna said to Ellen. The company helicopter was scheduled to return at seven in the morning with or without them, after which they had to rely on commercial flights.

Ellen nestled in Mark's arm and he stroked her hair. While her pitted eyes were shut, his were watery and unfocused. His actions were mechanical and unlike the way he soothed Julianna. Naturally, physical affection toward his sister was different. But, still, she thought, he could try to offer Ellen the kind of comfort that came from the heart.

Julianna gave the driver a generous tip. He nodded, wryly. 'Better place.'

The hotel was standard airport fare, no luxuries but functional and clean, and compared to the hostel, it was palatial in its plainness.

They were assigned two adjoining rooms, one with a double, the other a twin – she and Mark would not sleep together. Ellen flopped onto the double and instantly fell asleep.

Still riding the high of the fist fight, Juliana ordered food via room service for her grumbling stomach. While Mark fretted about Ellen, there were other things to do and with a deep breath, she dialled a number on her mobile. As expected, Jackson was awake too.

'We've got her. She seems to be in shock. I don't think she's been drugged.' Julianna paused to listen to his instructions. 'No, I don't think she needs a doctor. She's asleep. I had to take somebody down. A couple had come for her. They spoke something Slavic.' She glanced over to Mark. 'She's traumatised. Confused. Mark is obviously upset.'

'He should be. Remember to bring her here.' Jackson's distant voice crackled. If he was relieved, it was difficult to tell. She hoped he was. He had better be. She had nearly beat a man to death and needed her boss's support. There was a mess to clean up.

'Very good, sir. Tomorrow morning.'

She hung up.

'What did he say?' Mark asked.

'That we should come back on the chopper and bring her to him. He'll look after her. I mean, Opportunitas will.' Jackson was adamant that Ellen and Mark needed to work out their own issues before resolving their fractured relationship.

Mark peered around the door into the other room and checked on his sleeping sister. Satisfied, he returned and dissected a sandwich; the only meal on offer at that time of night.

'She didn't ask who you were,' he said.

'She will in the morning. In the morning, she'll want to know why we came. How we knew.'

Mark shut his eyes and put the half-eaten sandwich down on the table. Later, they lay on separate beds, the adjoining door wide open. Eventually exhaustion defeated Julianna, and she slept fitfully, troubled by dreams of the man with the ponytail – was he Freddie? Sadly, she doubted it; ponytail man was too young and from what Jackson had told her, the Deliverer kept a distance from his operations. It meant he was still in control and would be angrier than ever.

29

Julianna

Saturday Morning

Ellen remained in a state of shock throughout the flight to London. The stupor of fatigue kept her in a docile and convenient state for the journey home, and Julianna had a chance to evaluate Mark's sister. Petite, slender build, a hint of olive skin and walnut hair that bobbed around her neck as she moved. If there was a similarity to Mark it wasn't the tone of her skin or the colour of her eyes but the fullness of her lips and height of her cheekbones. A beautiful child in the body of an adult. Why wonder Zustaller coveted her.

As the grey dawn light seeped through the windows of the chopper, Ellen broke her self-imposed silence and started to ask questions. Awkward ones.

'I know it seems rude to ask now, but who are you?'

Julianna had been expecting that particular one for some hours and it was a measure of Ellen's trauma that it had taken so long to ask.

Stick to facts. 'Julianna Baptiste. I work for the same company as Mark. I'm one of Mr Haynes's investigators. This is a company helicopter.' She shot a glance at Mark, encouraging him to participate. He coughed nervously and looked away.

'Mr Haynes.' Ellen's eyebrows lowered into a thick line that met above the bridge of her nose. She fingered the leather upholstery. 'Why would he send a helicopter for me?'

'He's been very generous,' Mark said.

'What do you think happened to Freddie?' The helicopter pitched forward and Ellen grabbed her seat. 'Would they have got him, too?'

Julianna cringed a fraction. How to tell Ellen that she had nearly been sold into slavery by a man she thought was her friend?

Mark answered. 'He isn't who you think he is. You've been misled. How did you meet him?'

Ellen explained, taking them back three years to when she was seventeen and filled with rage and loneliness. She painted a story that began so innocently that only now, as she described how she thought he was a counsellor, a priest, a friend, did she begin to realise her naivety. Tears streamed down her face and Mark handed her a tissue.

'Don't say anything, not if it hurts this bad,' he said. 'All I need to know is at what point did he know about Dad?'

'Early on.' She sniffed and blew her nose.

Julianna inhaled deeply. For years, unwittingly, Ellen had fed Zustaller information about Bill's appeal. Of course Zustaller was happy for Bill to be locked up for murdering his cousin. He probably could have arranged for Bill to have an unpleasant accident, too. But, he hadn't. Perhaps Zustaller didn't want to reveal the extent of his criminal network by ordering a hit inside a prison. However, if Bill had been released, the story might have been different. So why had Bill maintained his innocence? Why risk leaving the relative security of a prison when the outside could be equally, if not more dangerous? Retribution had played out differently: abducting Ellen was Mark's punishment, not Bill's. Although Bill was hardly blameless, nothing untoward had happened until Mark instigated Haydock's downfall in Manchester. Jackson had predicted Mark would be held accountable, and once Zustaller knew his name, the Deliverer tailored his revenge perfectly.

'Ellen.' Julianna leaned toward the snivelling girl. 'You've heard of Haydocks?'

Ellen nodded.

'You told Freddie Mark worked for Haydocks. When?'

Her long eyelashes blinked as she concentrated on recalling what must be a complicated history of messaging between her and Freddie. 'After the wedding, when Mark went to that charity thing. I got drunk. I nearly slept with this man and Freddie was pleased I hadn't... Oh, shit.' Her head lolled forward into her palms and the tears returned.

Julianna's thin veneer of professional detachment splintered, and she wrapped her arm around Ellen's hunched shoulders. Neither woman said anything. It wasn't necessary. Mark stared into Julianna's eyes and he mouthed a thank you. Julianna thought his gratitude misplaced. He seemed unable to offer his sister any emotional support. Jackson was right – the girl needed a different mentor.

For the next two hours, Ellen remained uncommunicative, almost unreachable, swept away by the trauma of the last twenty-four hours and also, Julianna believed, a degree of shame at her gullibility. Like many young adults, Ellen probably considered herself worldly and invincible. Julianna had been just as naive at a similar age, falling for Alex's debonair charm.

The helicopter landed and they cleared the arrival procedures – the trappings of somebody else's wealth helped considerably. Julianna and Mark kept Ellen between them, supporting her as she swayed. Her dull eyes barely focused on anything. A car was waiting for them. Inside wasn't Chris, but Gary Maybank, his deputy and a reliable ex-copper whom Julianna respected.

The journey from the airport to Fasleigh House unfolded in parallel to Ellen's emergence from her state of shock.

'Where are we going?' she asked.

'Fasleigh House, Jackson Haynes's home,' Julianna said from the front passenger seat.

'Why there? I mean I would like to thank him of course.' Ellen peered out of the window.

'He's going to take care of you now, Ellen,' Mark said.

'Why him? Can't I stay at yours? What about Nicky. Oh, God, Nicky! I have to ring—'

'I've done it,' Julianna said. She had texted Nicky in Dublin. 'He's so relieved you're okay. He'll come and see you here, he promises.'

'You can't stay with me, Ellie,' Mark said. 'I'm not the best person for you right now. You need time away, doing stuff you like, and I need to sort out things, too. With Mum. And Dad. Jackson will keep you safe.'

From Freddie, Mark wisely didn't say. His nemesis, and Jackson's too, was hungry for revenge, more so than ever.

The car passed through the magnificent gates of Fasleigh house. Gary parked by the front door and straight away, Jackson appeared and opened Ellen's door.

Mark released her seat belt. 'I never intended for you to get caught up in all this. I wish you could have trusted me with your secret. I'm sorry, Ellen, so sorry. It's my fault.'

'You're fault? I let Freddie—'

'I mean, I started all this, not you. I failed you. More than any other person, I let you down. I ignored all the danger signs. I left you alone to deal with things back at home. I'm sorry. One day, I'll tell you everything about Haydocks.'

'Mark.' She opened her mouth and he pressed his finger to her lips. Julianna turned away and faced the windscreen. It was none of her business.

Ellen struggled to stand upright on the driveway. Jackson folded his arm around her shoulder, supporting her.

'I know you don't know me well, Ellen, and after what you've been through, this might be difficult to believe, but you can trust me. Come and see Hettie and the kids. They're always excited about visitors.' He guided Ellen towards the door. Gary had already dealt with the suitcase.

Jackson turned on the doorstep. 'Go!' he urged. 'I've got her.'

30
Mark

Gary Maybanks drove away from Fasleigh at breakneck speed.

'Your place?' Gary asked Julianna.

'Yes, please.'

The tension in the car was razor sharp. Mark had put Julianna in a dangerous situation, required her to fight for her life, and all he had done was stand there with sweat dripping down his back. He wouldn't blame her if she didn't want to invite him into her house and he expected she might try to find a way to dissociate herself from him. She was entitled to end things between them.

The silence was unending. With each mile, Mark's throbbing headache intensified, numbing his senses and altering his perceptions of light and darkness. What seemed dull, became vivid and colourful: sunlight bounced off car bonnets and targeted his eyes with searing brightness. Approaching the densely populated outer precincts of the city, the traffic became heavily congested and the noise thundered around the car. Mark felt sick and closed his eyes.

'This was meant to be my day off.' Gary slammed his hands on the steering wheel. 'My wife is so pissed off.'

Mark didn't know what to say. Jackson had arranged the cars, helicopter and hotel. The costs were mounting and he wouldn't be able to pay Jackson back on an accountant's salary. He sweated profusely.

'It's just an unusual set of circumstances,' Julianna said, her voice distant. 'I'll do a shift for you, Gary, make it up to you.'

Julianna was paying his debts, too. The misery deepened.

Gary parked outside her mews terrace house. 'Julianna, how could you afford this?'

'He's a successful commercial lawyer, my ex, but he sucked when it came to divorce law.'

Gary laughed.

Mark couldn't string a sentence together and Julianna said nothing, not even a goodbye. He was merely a passenger in the back seat, and she and Gary were used to ignoring the passengers in the car with diligent expertise. She opened her front door, crossed the threshold and closed it behind her without looking back at the car.

'Where now, Mr Clewer?' Gary asked. 'Home?'

Mark gave his address, yawned and slumped into an unexpected nap.

The jolt of the car halting outside the entrance to his apartment block woke Mark. As graciously as possible, he thanked Gary, who promptly drove off. Mark paused by the main door and fumbled for his keys. The fatigue in his muscles and the painful throbbing in his head reminded him he hadn't slept properly for over a day. As he leaned against the door, somebody shoved him in the back between his shoulder blades. Turning to complain, he was confronted by four men dressed in biker's leathers and carrying helmets. A gang, a herd of glaring eyes and snarling lips, and they stood shoulder to shoulder, with the exception of one younger man with dyed hair and a fierce expression. His hair was spiked up with gel and there were earrings in both earlobes.

'Nicky?' Mark backed further into the dark lobby.

'Yep, that's me,' said Nicky. 'I'm here to pay you a visit. Been waiting.'

'How did you find me?' Ted wasn't amongst them.

'Been here before. Ellen gave me your address. We scoped it out, Ted and I, a while back, because I'm curious like that when it comes to kids who live on their own, and Ellie is just a kid, isn't she?'

'What do you want?' The nausea intensified and his stomach shrivelled into a knot.

'Don't mind if we go for a chat. How about the basement?'

There was nothing in the basement except a broken washing machine and the bicycles belonging to the other residents.

He had no choice. Nicky grabbed his arm and propelled him towards the stairwell. 'Keep a look out,' Nicky said over his shoulder to the others.

31
Ellen

Ellen slept solidly for a couple of hours and woke up feeling refreshed, although stiff. She needed to move. With a boldness she had lacked in the hotel, she crept out of the bedroom and explored. The vast house had begun its life a couple of centuries ago. Consequently, the floorboards creaked beneath the plush carpets and a few of the inner walls bowed a little in places as if overburdened. Downstairs, the kitchen was unoccupied. Hettie was with Luke and Sophia, playing catch with the kids outside.

Ellen wandered through the house not daring to open closed doors – perhaps due to a lingering fear of what might lie on the other side. One was slightly ajar, and she peered through the crack. Haynes was behind a desk, reading something resting on his knee. The concentration was vivid on his face. As she tiptoed past the door, a noisy floorboard betrayed her. He called to her and asked her to come in.

The room was lofty with a wall of shelves housing leather-bound antique books that were probably for impressing visitors and not reading. On the wall, there were several framed pictures of contemporary landscapes. The artist had captured an urban scape with skyscrapers. She recognised part of the City from her daily sojourn into work – something she wasn't required to do any longer.

He followed the line of her sight. 'They're Hettie's. The advantages of having an artist as your wife, you get to commission whatever you like.' Jackson rose to greet her. 'Please, sit. You slept well?'

The chair faced the desk. It reminded her of visiting the doctor, but not the counsellor whom she had consulted at the request of social services. He had always put her on a couch surrounded by cuddly bears. Those soft, inert objects were supposed to comfort her. She had despised the man for treating her like a child. Freddie had never… she inhaled and cleared her dry throat.

'Yes. Thank you for helping me. The helicopter and everything. I'm very grateful.' She clasped her hands. 'I have questions.'

'Ask them,' he said kindly.

'Was Freddie ever real? A real person?'

Jackson paused before answering. 'Freddie Zustaller. His surname means deliverer in German. He isn't German. His nationality is no longer significant. He moves about Europe and rarely meets people face-to-face. He uses others to do his dirty work. Mainly Eastern Europeans or other ethnic groups. He's probably not in Ireland. If he is, he would be far away from where you were.'

'I don't understand. Who is he then?' Freddie had never stated his nationality.

'Zustaller is a career criminal who ran his shady accounts through a firm called Haydocks. You've heard of it?'

Ellen covered her mouth. 'Mark worked for them. He didn't do anything—'

Jackson interjected. 'No. Absolutely not. I never suspected him. Quite the contrary. Mark reported illegal practices to the police and the money was confiscated. Mark made a very bitter enemy. What I don't know is how Zustaller found you.'

She explained in a faltering voice how Freddie had tricked her by posing as a victim support counsellor.

Jackson pursed his lips. She waited for a rebuke, but it didn't come. 'I'm sorry, Ellen. Freddie's name was a cover for a sinister operation. Whoever you communicated with was after information about Mark and also your father. You were groomed to get at Mark.'

She opened her mouth, wanting to confess further, all the things she passed onto Freddie in her ignorance, but she shouldn't be apologising to Jackson for revealing information she should have kept secret. Somebody else deserved that apology.

'Zustaller is a trafficker,' Jackson said slowly. 'He sells women, men too, to others and on again.'

Prostitutes. She didn't need to hear the word – she knew what went on in that so-called hostel. Freddie had wanted to pimp her.

Bile stuck in her throat, layering the parched surface thickly with an acrid taste. The trembling was hard to control. She weaved her fingers, locking them into a knot.

'Would you like a drink?' Jackson asked.

She shook her head. 'He is, was, convincing.'

'Ah, don't judge yourself harshly. And, to be frank, given what we know, that is the charitable foundation I run, they are good at this. Zustaller would not have involved himself if it wasn't so personal. Would you say you were always dealing with the same person? In retrospect, is it possible that you were communicating with—'

'Yes,' she said. He waited as she pressed the heel of her palms against her wet eyes, hiding the tears that dangled on her eyelashes. 'Sometimes he treated me like a kid sister, other times friendly, calling me sweetie. Occasionally, he pissed me off. I thought he was a priest.' Dropping her hands, she laughed; the sound stuck in her throat and fizzled out. 'He told me he was a social worker. He knew I'm not a fan of them. Bizarrely, it convinced me that he was real... I didn't even question the details of the dig. A fake dig. It's so obvious now.' She slumped. How stupid she must appear to the man behind the desk – a chief executive who made important decisions on a daily basis and probably was a better judge of people than she ever would be.

Jackson moved out of his imposing chair and chose another nearer to her. She remembered him at the nightclub. A commanding presence; the host who circulated effortlessly, dipping in and out of conversations while she drank herself into oblivion. Across the expanse of the club, she recalled the blur of his face harbouring the two sharp pinpricks of his eyes. He had been watching her.

'Why are you so interested in me and Mark?' she asked.

He leaned back in his chair, and sighed. He spun the yarn out in a dispassionate voice. The efforts of Opportunitas in uncovering the network controlled by the Deliverer, her Freddie and his many voices. Then her father, Bill, who murdered somebody significant, deliberately provoking conflict. The tangle Mr Haynes described weaved its way toward her, she could sense the direction as the threads of his story came together. As for Mark, he unwittingly spoiled things further for Freddie Zustaller. She noted Jackson always called him Zustaller.

'He's got other names. It surprised me he used that particular version with you, because it's the one I first heard years ago, when I disrupted his supply chain. I had my suspicions.' Jackson tapped the tips of his fingers together, the lines of his forehead furrowed. 'But it was the witness that Sophia found and Julianna's investigations that made them concrete. Julianna in particular you should thank. She realised you were directly in danger and came to me for help. I mistakenly assumed it would be Mark who would suffer the consequences.'

'The needle...' How close it had come to slipping into her vein. She was supposed to have suffered.

'Drugs. Something to make you pliable and easy to transport. Eventually heroin so you would become dependent on them.'

Strange things started to make more sense. Freddie had asked her to tell Mark where she was going and he even insisted she spoke to her mother. Both conversations would have left clues to her disappearance. She wasn't supposed to simply vanish. Zustaller wanted Mark to know her awful fate.

Jackson's face softened. 'You're safe now. Both you and Mark have learnt a lesson the hard way.'

She blinked several times, processing too many emerging thoughts, but one in particular filtered through: Freddie had asked a great deal about Mark and Bill, about the appeal and whether it would be a success or not.

'I... I kept a secret. I shouldn't have done.'

'What secret?' Jackson asked.

'That I knew my father is a murderer. I saw the knives in his coat. I never told anyone.' She hung her head.

'But you told Mark before you left,' Jackson said. 'I saw the letter you left for Nicky. Julianna brought it to me as it contained the address in Ireland.'

Ellen closed her eyes. She had written some terrible things in that letter to Mark. Her reaction to Mark's benign response to Freddie's scheming was to accuse him of wilful neglect, of ignoring her self-harming incidents, and that he had aided her father's guilt and pandered to their selfish mother. She had spat words onto the page without considering why she blamed him and not herself.

'He didn't know about Freddie? Who Freddie is?'

'No, Ellen. He was beside himself with shock and despair when he found out what was happening. He's learnt his lesson, hasn't he?'

She opened her eyes and nodded. 'Yes. We both have. What do I do now?'

'Tell me about yourself.'

Ellen relaxed. Mr Haynes was quite an easy man to talk to. A passive, non-judgemental face, he occasionally prompted her with a question as he encouraged her to open up about her dreams, her aspiration to be an archaeologist. Her hobbies too.

'You like to run. So do I. Why not go for one or take a walk in the garden?'

'I don't have any running shoes. They're at Mark's.'

'I'll chase up getting your things from Mark's.' Jackson invited her to stay for as long as she needed and said that he could help her find work, something that she would enjoy doing.

Back in the spacious guest room with the view out across the impressive garden, she lay down on the bed, but failed to sleep, her mind buzzing with a strange sense of purpose, and trepidation. A fruitful combination, if she could work out how to utilise it. Jackson Haynes, her mysterious new benefactor was right; she had to keep moving.

The need to pound the ground and jar her bones until they ached was strong. The garden was one part of the extensive estate; beyond a garden wall there was a meadow and more trees. In the evening gloom she ran along the meandering gravel paths, which were laid out presumably for Jackson's benefit, and embedded with uplighters. Her Converse shoes weren't the best for running, but at least they were flat and water-proof.

Returning to the house, there was no sign of Jackson Haynes. She entered the sitting room and covered her mouth, muting the cry.

Nicky sprang up from the armchair and bounded over to her. Taking her into his arms he held her close, rocking her gently in his embrace.

'Okay, kiddo. I'm here,' he said. 'This Haynes guy filled me in on what happened to you out there. How you got out. You poor thing, so scary.' He squeezed her into a delightful hollow of muscular arms and a soft, sweet-smelling fabric. 'He told me to come and hug you. Well, that's what I said I'd do.'

'My apartment – I need it back.'

'It's already been let to somebody else. You know how quickly these places get snapped up. I'm only in mine because Jed had it first.' He drew her next to him on a sofa.

She bowed her head and fought back the tears. 'My things are at Mark's.'

Nicky briefly scowled. 'This Mr Haynes says he can have your stuff moved and stored here for now. You mustn't go there because it's too risky. Someone might be watching.'

Freddie? The man with the ponytail who had bound her? She shivered and Nicky draped his firm arm around her shoulder.

'I could kip on your floor, couldn't I?'

He tutted. 'Ah, shucks, honey, Ted has moved in. Cool eh? We're going to find something bigger. There isn't enough room for the two of us, never mind a guest.'

'What about me?' She sniffed. 'What's going to happen to me? No job. Nowhere to go.'

Nicky sucked in a breath. 'I don't know. I think you can trust this bloke though. His kids are cute. He sent a helicopter to rescue you. Quite impressive, eh?'

He squished her again. His bulk was so unlike anyone else she had ever met. He protected and soothed at the same time, the very combination she had lacked with her online relationship with Freddie, whom she had blindly followed, accepting his advice and foolishly gifting him all manner of attributes he didn't possess. Had Freddie really patiently cultivated her friendship and trust for over three years? It didn't make sense – why her when there were more vulnerable girls to be tricked? She still couldn't believe it.

Nicky eased away from her. Like Julianna, the knuckles of his right hand were red and swollen.

'What happened?' she asked.

He blushed and covered his injury. 'Nothing... I hit a wall. I was pumped up.'

'You should put ice on it.'

He brushed a rogue lock of her hair out of her eyes. 'I will, later. I have to go. I'm working extra shifts to pay for a deposit.'

She followed him to the front door. 'How did you get here?'

He shrugged awkwardly. 'Some friends dropped me off.'

'How will you get back? It's miles to the station.' She peered down the dark driveway. There was no frost or rain, but the wind was nippy and uninviting.

'The walk will be good for me. I need some fresh air. Look after yourself, kiddo. I'll ring you tomorrow. Okay?'

She couldn't persuade him to ask Haynes to arrange transport or a room for the night. Nicky's agitation grew and she waved goodbye.

Late in the evening, after she had helped Hettie put an excited Noah to bed, Jackson invited her into the study and the company of another man. Tall, like Jackson, he had buzz cut hair, wore khaki pants and a black sweatshirt. He resembled a commando. Jackson introduced him – Chris Moran, his chief security adviser.

Moran stared at Ellen's face. 'Feeling better, Ellen?'

In a short space of time, Ellen had become accustomed to her personal life, her name and state, being common knowledge to strangers.

'Yes. Thank you,' she said.

'Any luck?' Jackson asked Moran.

'No,' said Moran. 'Trail's gone cold again. I'm afraid there's nothing to follow, except your accounts, miss. The things you shared online.' He glanced at his boss.

'I can give you access, if it would help?' All those exchanges would be read and judged including the embarrassing level of detail she had given to Freddie and nobody else.

The big guy retrieved a small notepad from his pocket. 'If you don't mind. Passwords, too. I promise I won't share them with anyone else. It's likely he's deleted his accounts. But it might give us some more leads.'

She and Freddie had only spoken about her problems, a selfish discourse based on her needs and nobody else's. She wrote the account names and passwords down anyway. She had no plans to ever go near them again.

Moran, after dispatching a nod in Jackson's direction, departed.

'Yesterday, while we waited, Sophia told Hettie that you had a good time at her party and you met Derek; I'm going to suggest you follow up his offer.' Jackson handed her a slip of paper.

'Thank you. Yes, Derek. He was very friendly, and I was rather abrupt with him. I hope I didn't offend him.' Life from now on was going to be about making bridges, not destroying them. No more drinking, either.

'Hopefully he'll help you find work,' Jackson said. 'Opportunities.'

She felt a small pang of optimism. She would let it grow, but not too quickly, as it would have to be nurtured with the help of others. This time, she would let Jackson guide her. He seemed to be a good man and somebody to trust.

'Thank you.' The words of gratitude unstopped the dam she had built, the one that had begun when she was eleven years old at a newspaper shop. She wept, brazenly and loudly. Jackson wasn't embarrassed – he sat quietly. However, neither did he touch her or placate her by calling her sweetie. He passed her the box of tissues and waited.

32
Julianna

Julianna stared into her empty refrigerator. Saturday mornings was when she usually did her weekly shop and she couldn't be bothered to do it that afternoon. She ate an apple and drank coffee. Wandering ceaselessly about the house, she couldn't stop thinking about Mark; he had said nothing to her in the car. Was it because he was so consumed by his sister's brush with disaster, which was understandable, or that he had changed his mind about Julianna, now that he had seen her anger on full display? He had convincingly shut her out.

As required, she wrote a formal summary of events for Chris. She yawned and typed, skipped over the details of the fight, and merely stated she had disabled the man, when in fact she had beaten his face to a pulp. Pausing to digest the comment, she examined her bruised knuckles. Real flesh and blood, no matter how deplorable a person they embodied, was not the same as a punch bag. Alex never deserved that kind of anger. Relationships might falter and break, but rage never healed them. The punch bag had to go. Instead of freeing her, it fed her anger.

Her mobile rang. Mr Haynes was calling.

'How's Ellen?' she asked.

'No lasting injuries. She's sleeping,' Jackson said. 'I hope I'm not disturbing you, too.'

'No. I'm awake. Writing a report while everything is fresh in the mind.'

'Very diligent. It's what I like about you, Julianna.' Not Baptiste – a small, but significant shift. 'I want to say thank you.'

Julianna muttered an embarrassed acknowledgement. She waited, hoping the gratitude would take her somewhere better.

'I dropped you into this and you ran with it.'

'I did it for Mark, and Ellen, and you know that, sir.'

'I meant the bigger picture: Haydocks, Zustaller. I wasn't exactly forthcoming when I dangled the carrot. But I needed you to work it out independently. I'm too involved.'

'One last piece of information, sir. Haydocks. It was Bill Clewer who suggested it to Mark.'

'Ah.' Jackson paused. 'Makes sense, don't you think?'

'I suppose. He's not really clued into the significance yet. I think he will be. Then, perhaps he might want to visit his father again.'

'Mark will thank you when he's in a better place.'

The back of the car in a state of anguish was not a better place.

'Opportunitas needs somebody like you.' Jackson made the offer, the one she had wanted. It felt like an anti-climax. The price had almost been too high, and the big baddie was still out there, but at least Ellen wasn't with him.

'I would love to work for the foundation.' She injected a large dose of enthusiasm into her tired voice.

'Good. It will be piecework for now, a bit of casework to help you appreciate the technicalities. But it's a starting place. You'll still do your usual job alongside, but there'll be a pay rise. Understood?'

Her time would be in greater demand, but it would be worth it. After Ellen's close encounter, Julianna was keener than ever to hit back at the shady underworld she'd witnessed close up, and she guessed that the limitations of a charity was what Jackson meant by "technicalities".

Jackson told her somebody would swing by Mark's flat early in the morning to collect Ellen's things and take them to Fasleigh. She wondered why he was telling her. There wasn't much else to say. He said goodbye in his usual curt manner; he was still the boss. She wondered if Jackson would lose interest in Mark now that he had unravelled the mystery of Bill Clewer.

The report writing faltered and she drank more coffee. The mobile rang again. It wasn't Mark, but she wasn't expecting him to ring, unless he had made it a priority to go out and buy a new phone.

'Gary?' she said tentatively.

'Julianna, I wanted to apologise for sounding off in the car,' Gary said.

'What?'

'You know ranting. You three had obviously had some sort of horrendous misadventure and me being selfish and—'

'Christ, Gary, forget it. You missed out on family time.'

'You're alright?'

'Sure. Mark and I just need to have some down time.'

'Looked to me like Clewer has company for the afternoon.'

'What do you mean?' Julianna's stomach pinched. Freddie was still at large and Mark had gone back to his flat. How stupid of her! What had she been thinking when she left him in the back of the car in a dazed state – herself, and nothing else. Haynes assumed Mark had stayed with her, hence the request for access to Ellen's stuff.

'Well, four blokes in leathers were talking with him in the entrance to his flat.'

'Leathers?' Bikers. A bad sign. Julianna slammed down the lid of her laptop.

'Yeah, one with spiky blond hair.'

'Shit, *oh shit!* Julianna hung up without saying goodbye, grabbed her handbag and dashed to the front door.

Julianna drove precariously fast to Mark's, the car complained noisily, chugging and spewing fumes along the streets. Abandoning it on double yellow lines, she dug out his spare key from her handbag and took a deep breath.

'Please be there, Mark.'

Like last time, the apartment door was ajar. She shifted her heavy handbag off her shoulder, ready to swing it like a pole-axe. The defensive stance wasn't necessary: Mark was face down on the settee. He was extremely pale, sweating and trembling, and the collar of his shirt was nearly torn off.

'What did they do to you?' She crept towards him. 'Oh Christ, Mark, I'm taking you to my place. He doesn't know where I live. You're not safe here. I'm going to take care of you. And don't fucking argue.'

'Nicky won't come back,' he said feebly.

'I didn't mean Nicky. Zustaller lost money and you ruined his revenge. I should never have left you alone here.' She took charge, rummaged through the bedroom drawers and located plenty of clothes, toiletries, and anything else he might need for the coming days. 'Do you have a friendly neighbour?' she asked. He muttered a response.

The neighbours were in and happy to take her key. 'He's coming later this evening to collect a few boxes. He's called Tom Draper. Nice bloke,' she reassured the elderly neighbours.

She left a message at the Fasleigh gatehouse to tell Tom to contact Mark's neighbours for access.

'Come on.' She dragged Mark off the settee. He moved stiffly. As they passed Ellen's boxes, he rummaged in one and placed her running shoes on top.

'Running will help her. She finds it therapeutic,' he said.

Julianna wished he had shown such thoughtfulness on Friday. There was no point in regretting things. She would have to teach him how things should be done. She would ring her parents and tell them she was happy, safe and in love with somebody, even if he didn't know it yet.

Sitting cross-legged on the floor of her sitting room, Julianna held a spoonful of stew to Mark's lips.

'The odd thing is, Nicky said nothing once he got me down there. Probably because no words were necessary, and I couldn't think of a single thing to say to him.'

Mark hadn't read the letter Ellen had written. Jackson had confiscated it from Julianna and kept it. Given the anger in Nicky's eyes, it wouldn't have made much difference if Mark had pleaded that it was a terrible misunderstanding between the siblings, accusing each other of hiding the truth when neither of them understood a thing about their father. Mark was slowly realising his father was multi-faceted beyond duplicity.

She let him talk.

'I don't blame Nicky for hating me. I understand hatred and what it can do to dignity. Ellen is drawn to men who offer her a paternal shield. Zustaller might be the worst kind of con artist;

Nicky, however, is a loyal friend. A decent one, too. When he raised his fist, I closed my eyes and accepted I deserved the beating. Ellen's face has bruises.'

'But yours doesn't.'

'No. But there is a hole in the basement wall. My headache is down to this bloody migraine. I passed out in my flat.'

She had propped him up on her sofa under a blanket. The shivering had stopped.

'I thought you were concussed. I nearly called an ambulance.'

'I can feed myself,' he said with a quirky smile. She wiped his chin when the juice dribbled out of his mouth.

'I know,' she said coyly. 'I want to look after you.'

'Tastes nice.'

'Well, it's nothing special. Came out of the freezer,' she said.

'I really need to change out of these clothes. I think I stink.'

'You do smell ripe.' She laughed. 'I'll bathe you in the shower. Did you take the painkillers?' The migraine explained his silence in the car.

'Yes, nurse Julianna. I didn't realise the significance of my speech failing until Nicky pinned me to the wall and not a word came out of my mouth in protest.'

'Nicky didn't follow through, so I'm not going to either. I'm shattered and so are you. We're going to shower and go to bed.'

She took the empty dish away. The pleasant exchange masked all the things they weren't saying to each other.

'I want to apologise,' he said, in her bedroom an hour later. 'For everything. For not being honest about my feelings or emotional state. Keeping things from you and from Ellen too. I used you, both of you. I wanted help but was too proud to ask.'

'Mark, we've been using each other. I wanted to work for Opportunitas and this, you and your family, became my pet project for achieving it. Let's face it, we've been unable to articulate our anger at others. You're not Alex, and you don't talk to me like him.'

The room fell silent.

'I've not been gentle with you, when we've, you know…' he said quietly, easing himself upright and touching his temple, massaging it with his fingertips.

She quashed a chuckle. She didn't see it the same way. She had asked for sex to be like that – passionate yet detached from love-making. The way animals mated when in heat. 'I can over-power you, if necessary.'

'I witnessed that out in Dublin. You're quite violent when you have to be. How did you learn to do that?'

'Oh. I've been doing martial arts since I was a small child. Dad's an instructor and he started me young. Lots of competitions and he made sure I learnt to maintain discipline. Not go wild with it.' Except, she had in Ireland. Her father would be disappointed with the lack of self-control.

By the time she had undressed, the warm colours had displaced the cold tinge of paleness on his face. He smiled and this time, she let him embrace her. He had salvaged his relationship with Julianna, but what about Ellen? And Jackson? His presence in the company was a potential liability with Zustaller still in operation. Did he still have a job, and more importantly would Jackson consider him a friend?

She dreaded Monday morning. Jackson wouldn't wait long to give him an answer.

33
Mark

Monday

The message appeared on Mark's monitor the moment he fired up his computer. He stood for a few minutes mentally preparing himself by staring out of the window at the glazed offices situated on the other side of the bustling London street. Bright sunlight bounced off numerous glass facades, dazzling his still sensitive eyes. Ellen had been with the Haynes family all weekend. What had she told them?

He straightened his tie, headed for the lift and hit the button for the top floor. It was too early for Diana to shoo him into Jackson's office so he rapped his knuckles on the door.

Jackson gestured to Mark with a wave of his forefinger. 'In.'

Mark wasn't offered a seat. The formality didn't surprise him; it only disappointed. He hovered before the vast desk, waiting for Jackson to occupy his chair.

'How is Ellen?' Mark asked.

'Confused, tired,' Jackson said vaguely. 'She gradually opened up. Not about Friday, too early for her to deal with that trauma.'

Trauma – an appalling word. Mark swayed onto the heel of his shoes. 'She wasn't badly hurt? Drugs—'

'No drugs in her system. She'll heal quickly. She understands that she has to move on with her life. However, Zustaller is still out there. That has been hard for her.'

Mark swallowed a hard lump. His throat ached. 'Will he come after her? Me?'

Jackson picked up a pen, then let it go with a spin of his wrist. 'I don't know. He's a delegator.' Like me, Jackson didn't add. 'He plays a long game. He can't risk exposing himself too soon. I don't get the impression that he's impulsive. He's left Bill intact, because it serves a purpose to make your father sweat it out in prison, indefinitely. Punishment, not execution, is his style.'

'So… I shouldn't worry too much.'

His boss guffawed. 'If he wants you, Mark, he'll find some way, maybe not immediately.'

Mark felt the blood drain from his face. 'I'll have to move. Again.'

'I'd advise it. And Ellen, she'll have to leave London and go somewhere quiet, somewhere like Scotland.'

'I don't think she'll miss London, and Derek seems a decent guy.'

'Yes.' Jackson leaned back and the chair tilted with him.

'Whatever I can do to help, I'm here for her now.'

'The best thing you can do is leave her be, don't you think? You need to resolve a few things with your father. And your mother.'

'I'm not going near them.' Heartless maybe, but he was past caring. Pain shot across his forehead.

Jackson rose from his seat and came within an arm's reach of Mark. His pupils were black dots in a sea of blue; finely tuned, razor sharp around the edges. Mark flinched.

'I... don't want to speak to her.'

'You've always known your father's guilt, haven't you?' Jackson spoke with the enviable confidence of a boss in his place of power. 'You hoped he'd give up with the appeals. I bet he would have happily pleaded guilty and accepted his fate. But he didn't or couldn't. Your mother is behind all this, isn't she?'

The height difference was subtle, yet Jackson, though only a couple of inches taller, towered over Mark.

'I knew he'd killed a man. But I believed him when he said it was self-defence not murder. But yes, she walked all over him. Bullied him for years and years. I hate her!' He screwed his hands into boxer's fists.

Jackson stepped back, leaving Mark to expel a rasping breath.

'She made him the way he is,' he said, bitterly. 'He was a decent man once. But she's greedy, always wants more money for her clothes, nights out, whatever. He's no backbone; a gentleman with women, but he won't stand up to her. He started stealing or selling stolen stuff just for her. All that extra cash went into her pocket. We weren't poor. She's a selfish, greedy bitch.' He paused, seeing Jackson's reaction, the taint of grief in his eyes. True, it wasn't all her fault. 'Then everything went wrong. Wrong people. Wrong criminals. Wrong crime. She couldn't deal with it – her husband a murderer! What would her precious friends think? He has to be innocent for her sake, not his.'

'So here you are,' Jackson said, calmly. 'Outwardly the dutiful son, listening to his mother's rants while deep down you despise her and know you can do nothing for your father, who, behind bars, kowtows.'

Mark let out a cry of frustration. He turned away, placed the palms of his hands on the cool wall and leaned against it for support. He was right next to one of Hettie's beautiful compositions. Breathing heavily, he waited for the pain to ease.

'I'm coping,' he said, quietly seething. 'Was coping. But she wouldn't stop ringing me. That voice, over and over in my head. I think Dad prefers being in prison. He doesn't have to listen to her.'

'For the time being he'll remain there. Although, I'm inclined to hire a good lawyer for him and get him moved somewhere safe, so he can turn evidence. If he's safe, he might do it, but he isn't.' Jackson prodded Mark's shoulder. 'Think, Mark. Think of what your father did.'

Mark pivoted and rested his shoulders next to painting of river punters; a serene scene. 'The idea of young girls would appal him. So I guess he found out as much as he could about Zustaller's weak spots, killed the key contact to initiate a war and took the blame in the safety of jail. His only stumbling block was my mother and her insistence on proving him innocent. She nearly ruined everything.'

'I think your father knows Ellen found out the truth. For him, that was unfortunate, she was too young to cope with it. However, he hoped you would persist in looking beyond the evidence to see the connections, but I had to help you, prod you. And watch over you. Although I apologise, I didn't anticipate the threat to Ellen, who, out of misguided and confused love for Bill, colluded to keep the secret of his guilt. Your father, in his own way, remains a decent man. Remember that.'

The room descended into silence. There was no mention of Haydocks. The unspoken question remained: had his father sent him where the money lay hidden in the hope of destroying Zustaller or stealing it for himself, corrupting his son in the process?

He pressed his hand to the throbbing temple. The blasted curse was back with a vengeance. The slightest sound was amplified in his skull. The nausea, acute.

Jackson's voice was hushed, and catastrophically close, as if by Mark's ear. 'What happened, Mark? Did somebody beat you up?'

He shook his head, instantly regretting the sudden movement. 'Nicky was going to... he isn't really that kind of person. Ellen chose right with him. It's me. I've not been well.'

Jackson poured him a cup of water. 'Drink it all. You're white as a sheet.'

He swallowed the arctic liquid in one go, feeling it strike his wretched stomach and form a cold puddle. He looked at his feet, unable to take Jackson's searching blue eyes for another second.

Jackson gently patted his shoulder. 'Good grief, you're not going to be ostracised for what your father is or is perceived to be. That is your fear, I know it is. No, what you will do is stop living out the anger you feel towards you parents and concentrate on somebody more deserving of your attention. She's waiting for you. Don't deny it, you've fallen in love with Julianna. She certainly has with you.' He dusted down Mark's jacket with a brush of his slender fingers and straightened the necktie.

'You'll do,' said Jackson, stepping back with a smile. 'Take some time. Go watch the best of Man United's goals or whatever cheers you up, but perhaps you should seek out beneficial company. Plan a fancy romantic meal for her and tell her. Come back to work when you're ready.'

The heat rose into his cheeks. 'Thank you, Jackson.'

He strode out past the bemused Diana, and straight to the lift.

34

Julianna

Julianna usually typed quickly and with accuracy. However, not that morning. She ran her eye down the document, spotting a significant number of errors. She clucked her tongue and hit the backspace a few times with a furious stab of a digit. She should be feeling elated. It wasn't happening; the sensation eluded her. The reason why was probably the lack of closure. Or the drop, the potent hangover following a thrilling adventure, when life returned to normality with a bump. Both probably.

Compared to emergency helicopter flights to Dublin and rescuing a woman about to be sold into sexual slavery, Monday morning was tedious. She examined her bruised hands and sighed; they hurt, but not as much as other things. Why hadn't she said something before she left for work, just a word or two in his ear to soothe his troubled mind?

Her heart and soul had been kidnapped more successfully than Ellen's abortive abduction, and the culprit even managed to creep up on her.

'Julianna, could I have a word in my office. Thanks,' he said briskly, fiddling with the sleeves of his jacket.

She shut her laptop lid. 'Okay.'

The whites of his eyes were tainted by a little redness, the rest of his face was drained of colour though – the migraine lingered in some form. He shut his office door behind him, his hands still restless.

'What did Jackson want?' she asked.

They had anticipated separate debriefings. She had dealt with Chris's enquiries first thing. His concrete face had broken into a per-

functory smile and he'd issued a congratulations on her success, followed by a firmer rebuke for her excessive force. Face to face with
Chris, she had been more honest than in her report. However,
nobody with a pulverised face had been admitted to hospitals around
Dublin. Perhaps he'd walked out unaided, she had told Chris, who
had shared her optimism with a pessimistic frown. He wasn't happy
about the fallout either, but it wasn't their job to hunt down traffickers, only the women. As for Opportunitas, he accepted her changing role without a fight, which meant Jackson had already told him.

Mark flopped into his chair. 'He wasn't gentle with me. He
pushed me to see things. I'm allowed to hate my mother, it seems.
And I can declare my father decent, at least as far as motives, if not
the crime itself. Of course, it doesn't actually mean anything to have
Jackson Haynes sanction these things, but it helps to know he'll
watch my back, and Ellen's. She's going to Scotland. He offered
some reassurances about my future. It's good. My work here must
be my priority from now on.'

She rested her hands on his shoulders, gently massaging the rigid
muscles. He moaned, and cricked his head from side to side.

'And?'

'He's told me to go home for a few days and rest. I think I might
need some nursing care.'

'Do you now?' she said, dryly. 'From whom?'

'Oh, a certain Nurse Julianna. I'm sure she could do with a
break. He pretty much implied that. So here I am, in desperate need
of some love and attention.'

'Love and attention?' she said quietly, her heartbeat noisy.

'I love you,' he said, twisting his head over his shoulder. 'I'm
sorry, sorry that I made you wait for me to say this. I couldn't in
the car. I couldn't last night. I'm not great at saying these things—'

'Most men aren't.' She moved around him and perched on the
edge of the desk. Perhaps she had been hasty, too. Mark's safety
remained crucial. Zustfaller was unlikely to stop what he had
started. 'Move in with me.'

He raised his eyebrows. 'I'm not suggesting we should marry—'

'Pufft. Nor am I. I'm asking you to come live with me because
it's safer.'

'Safer?' He folded his arms across his chest.

'I'm a highly trained bodyguard.'

'I know. And, anything else?'

'A smooth lover?'

He laughed. 'I think we could try harder at that, don't you?'

She slid onto his lap. 'Fine. Dandy. Whatever it takes. I just want us to be okay again, like we were—'

'Before I bottled my emotions and let things slide.' He stroked her thigh.

She stilled his hand. 'Give yourself time, Mark. Go see your father.'

He puckered his lips and knotted his eyebrows. 'Dad, but not yet. Certainly not Mum.'

'No, not Deidre. She can wait. But Bill needs to know he's not lost to you. He wrote you letters; kind of sweet and old-fashioned of him. I would call him an old-style crook. Bad, but not psychopathic.'

'Nice of you.' He inhaled and rubbed his temple. 'Okay. I'll write to him, start things there, but nothing about Freddy, not until we're sure the threat is gone.'

'And your mum?' She collected her leaden handbag.

'She can wait. If I'm going to start mending bridges, then Ellen deserves it more than her.'

She concurred – an admirable idea. However, the only thing lurking unresolved was the Deliverer. What was he planning to do now that Ellen was safe and Mark was fully aware of the connection between Bill and Haydocks? Probably let loose all kinds of hell.

Part Two

RETRIBUTION

35
Mark

Spring

From the frisking down at the gate to the monotonous voices of the guards, the rituals re-enforced the strangeness of the place. Mark followed the signs and listened to the instructions. He had heard them all before. However, it had been a long time since his last visit and the appearance of his father shocked him: prison killed a man in slow motion, sapping his humanity and leaving only the bones of life.

The use of a communal visiting area forced Bill and Mark to speak in hushed tones. Mark didn't bother with pleasantries and hoped his face looked like thunderclouds.

'You're guilty. I traced the witness, and he confirmed it. But don't worry, he's staying silent. Don't waste any more of my life pretending otherwise. Come clean, Dad.' Mark leaned across the table, knuckles white and clenched. 'If you don't, I'm not coming to see you ever again.'

Dressed in an unflattering monochrome uniform, pale in his sunless skin and ragged around the eyes, Bill crumbled with sagging shoulders into a heap on his plastic chair until his chin nearly rested on the table. The room buzzed with voices, some loud, others like them, hushed and confrontational. He spoke so softly Mark had to cup his ear to hear him.

'I didn't want you growing up with a murderer for a father. Mum... she thinks it will ruin your chances in life.'

The cheap excuse didn't stand up – it was an old one and overly used. 'I prefer honesty to duplicity, Dad,' said Mark. 'Tell me, did you set me up with Haydocks? Did you want me to unearth the laundering?'

Bill jerked, levelling his head with Mark's. The flash of daylight that crept in through the barred windows lit up his eyes. There was the spark, the fight Mark wanted to see.

Bill licked his lips and glanced around. 'You found it? The money?' he whispered. 'It was you?'

Mark nodded. 'I cleaned them out.'

His father grinned. 'Good,' he mouthed.

'Why didn't you tell me, Dad?'

'Tell you what?'

'That Henderson's a crook.'

Bill perched on the edge of his seat and folded his body over the table, keeping his back hunched. He spoke to the table, not Mark. 'I wasn't sure, I suppose. Whatever happened, you'd have a job at Haydocks; a start in life.'

Mark scratched his chin and gaped at the explanation. It took a few seconds for it register. 'Seriously? That's your logic. Just dangle this lure and hope the bait works, that I'll been drawn into finding out the truth?'

Bill scratched his stubble. 'You're a canny lad. I had nothing to do with the money side. It was always others who handled that stuff. I took my cut…'

The prison jacket was too large for Bill. The weight loss was more apparent during this visit; when he shrugged, the jacket slipped off his bony shoulders. Bill's gaze swept around the room.

'The walls listen here. They listen everywhere.' He lowered his voice. 'If I pleaded guilty, they'd assume I was paid to do it. Get it? I'm not that kind of man, you know that.' His voice was fracturing.

'I know, Dad. It was because of the girls.' It would break his heart if Bill knew how close Ellen had come to being one of the lost ones. The way things played out wasn't all Bill's fault, even if he had planted Mark in Haydocks; it had been Mark's choice to blow the operation apart.

Bill found his voice again. 'I left you a breadcrumb trail. I knew your mum wouldn't lift a finger beyond begging for help. She's broken. I can't fix her. Once… maybe.'

The hollowness of his eyes intensified. Mark despised his mother even more for not seeing this man; afraid and dislocated from the world outside, and with Zustaller out there waiting, Bill was stuck in a grim hole of his own making.

'She's still hoping for some magical resolution to all this.'

'It ain't going to happen, son.' Bill settled back, appearing more relaxed.

Mark folded his arms across his chest. 'So, you're not going to co-operate with the police?'

'Nah,' Bill said, louder.

Mark closed his eyes. He felt no empathy, not unless it was creeping up on him in the guise of pity. But he couldn't leave his father believing there was no hope. He opened his eyes and leaned right across the table, seizing the attention of the lacklustre guard, who waved him back. Mark stayed poised, halfway, neither in his seat, nor touching his father. He spoke quietly. 'Dad. I've got a friend who's willing to provide you with a lawyer. And I mean a very good lawyer, if you change your mind and tell them everything, all the things you did back them, names, places, they'll give you protection. Hide you away.'

'I appreciate the offer, son. Tell your friend, thank you. But, I'm safer like this, ain't I?' He cocked his head toward the guards.

The guard coughed. Mark sat down. While Zustaller was at large, his father wouldn't take any chances. However, Bill's eyes sparkled, something Mark hadn't seen in years. He might not be released on appeal, but now that Mark knew the truth, Bill didn't need to pretend to be anything other than a likeable rogue who was caught up doing bad things and tried to do something good. His father never would be morally sound, but he wasn't evil or a monster. One day, Ellen would understand, too.

'Bye, Dad. Take care of yourself. The offer remains, if you want to take it.' Mark rose to his feet and held out his hand. Bill shook it with a firm grip.

'Thanks, son. You'll write, won't you? I do like letters.' He grinned; he had lost a tooth. Mark doubted it had fallen out of its own accord.

'Sure. I'll write.'

Mark's letters would be full of inconsequential things about football, the weather and maybe a little hint of what was happening outside. But not the ongoing mission to bring down Freddie Zustaller.

He left Manchester without visiting his mother. One day he might find room in his heart for her, but not yet, not for a long while.

His journey wasn't finished. Instead of returning to London, he turned north to Scotland.

36
Julianna

Julianna had bought a new car, a sporty BMW. Her rusty friend had been confined to the rubbish heap. The beamer wasn't a great car in the city, but driving to Cornwall to visit her parents, it purred like a new-born kitten. Unlike Mark's dysfunctional family, Julianna considered her family to be normal, reasonably affluent and broad minded enough not to judge her divorce or choice of career. Her father, a retired officer in the army, had left the forces to become a martial arts instructor, while her mother, an ex-army doctor, worked as a general practitioner in Falmouth.

She let Mark drive to Cornwall because his extra money helped with bills and allowed her the extravagance of buying a car. The journey was long, but worth it. He rolled his eyes every time she criticised his driving technique.

'I do have qualifications in defensive driving and high-speed evasion tactics.' She would have the return journey to scare him.

'Doesn't give you the right to tell me how to drive,' Mark said brusquely, while grinning from ear to ear.

Two months after she had invited him to move in with her, their relationship had grown in strength and his anger had diminished. The only issue to mar things was his relationship with his family. Julianna hoped visiting his dad would heal some of those stresses. She let him take the car to Manchester to visit his father. While he was there, he sent a text explaining a change of plan; he added an extra, considerably longer journey. He'd spontaneously decided to visit his sister.

Upon his return home, he handed back the car keys, apologising for the extended loan by way of a brisk, sheepish smile. Julianna supported the decision. Checking the car, she noted the mud splattered tyres and sand in the footwell of the passenger seat.

Fatigue was etched on his face. He pecked her cheek, cautiously. She could be patient.

She took his coat. 'Well?'

The details of his conversation with Bill slipped out over dinner, which he failed to finish. Mark was disappointed that Bill had refused Jackson's offer of help. She wasn't surprised. As he washed the dishes, she draped her arms around his waist.

'Don't fret,' she said. 'You don't have to forgive him, just know that he did it and the reason why. That's all. It's not as if he's wallowing in self-pity about it. Perhaps things might change in the future.'

'How?' Mark sighed. 'He'll always be watching his back in case of retribution.'

Julianna buried her nose in his shirt. He smelt of sea salt and something else, the legacy of the prison with its sweaty bodies and confined spaces. They both needed to watch their backs and each other. She hoped Ellen was safe up in Scotland.

'Tell me,' she said, leading him to sit on the sofa, side by side. 'About Ellen.'

'Going up there after seeing Tim in Manchester, it felt like the right thing. I couldn't answer Tim's questions about Ellen, like how's she doing. Felt bad about it. I stopped over in Edinburgh, not far from where she's living with Malcolm, and he told me where to find her.'

Malcolm was Derek's spy, of course. They were half-brothers. In return for free lodgings, Ellen provided rudimentary care for Malcolm by way of meals, doing the laundry and cleaning the house. She had arrived in Edinburgh with nothing but a familiar suitcase full of clothes and the address of a stranger. The rest of her things remained boxed up at Fasleigh House. If it wasn't for their trust in Jackson and his friend, Derek, they would have never countenanced the idea of her lodging with a man she had never met, especially after her experience in Dublin. Derek ran various archaeological projects in Scotland and northern England, but he wasn't just a professor of archaeology, he had ties to Opportunitas.

Malcolm was a retired surgeon. Julianna had been briefed by Chris. Only a handful of people knew Ellen's location, even fewer knew Malcolm's address. Ellen received cash payments to cover expenses – and her mobile number had been changed. Chris had told Ellen to stay off social media. She had been isolated, cut-off. But she wasn't a prisoner. Nobody was preventing her from returning to either London or Manchester. She was free to travel anywhere, even if her life was shaped by different people.

'She was out at a cove looking at a tidal mill, some marks on the rocks. Hard to see unless you've got a good eye for it. She's a neat artist, showed me her sketches.'

He described the landscape, the sodden turf, the wet sand and stench of seaweed. His sister, buffered by the sea breeze, happily working alone with her pad and pencils. 'I parked the car on the sea front – it's okay, not a scratch on it – and she climbed up to say hello.'

Had they embraced? Julianna liked to thing they might have done, but she doubted it.

Mark continued, his voice a little hazy and distant. He wasn't in the room with Julianna, but somewhere windswept and hopefully beautiful, especially for a man who had lived all his life in cities. 'We spent some time apologising.' He chuckled, but his eyes weren't smiling.

'Oh?'

'I told her I should have stood up to Mum. I should've asked the right questions, instead of assuming he was innocent. I didn't open up to Ellen, and I regret it.' Mark turned to Julianna. 'She sat in the car, and I thought, given how quiet she was, that I'd got things wrong. But it turns out, she's better at patience than me. She accepted it all without a harsh word.'

Julianna patted his hand. 'You're learning a different kind of patience.'

'Yeah, I suppose.' He puffed at his lips. 'Anyway. She apologised for not being honest with me about Dad, and Freddie. She's tired of hating.' His voice broke slightly. 'She asked me for help, to help her not hate them. I don't know if I can.'

There had been other conversations like that one, mostly by email. Jackson had suggested Ellen speak to a psychologist or a counsellor. According to Mark, she had scoffed at the idea. Nobody like that had ever helped her before, and wasn't that exactly how she had gone wrong with Freddie? She had politely turned down the offer. Julianna wasn't sure if it was the right decision, but Mark had agreed with his sister. The nightmares would go, and, eventually, Ellen would learn to let go of the blackness inside, the dread that woke her up some nights screaming. She never saw a person, just a thing, an entity. Julianna understood the origins of that nightmare – the bogey man never had a face, only a presence, which was why she had crafted one on her punch bag.

Mark blinked, recovering his voice. 'I told her what I thought. Dad's not evil. And she knows that, or why else did she keep quiet when she could have made things worse for him? He's a broken man, holding back from telling everything because he fears for himself, for us. If we can get him to turn evidence, he'll be free. But I told her we'd not see him again, because he'd be in a witness protection program.'

'What about Deidre?'

'Both of us agree. Mum doesn't care enough for Dad to follow him there. I don't think she knows how to.'

An honest appraisal. Even though she hadn't met Deidre, Julianna thought it accurate.

'Still. She wanted to know if she was wrong to keep that secret.' Mark met Julianna's gaze. Ellen wanted to be free of the guilt she had burdened herself with for years. Mark had accused her of making things worse, but now he knew that had never been her intention. She simply wanted to be a good daughter to at least one of her parents.

'By keeping it from the police, perhaps,' Julianna said diplomatically. 'But you can understand why she did it.'

'I just wish she could have trusted me more back then.' He shrugged. 'She cried when I told her that. It's hardly her fault we weren't talking. She misses London. Especially Nicky. But she insisted she has no regrets about the move north. She's working with geologists surveying the east coast. Plenty to do in those mud flats and rocky outcrops. She likes being outside.' Mark smiled. 'Even in the summer rain.'

Julianna laughed, then remembered. 'Not quite urban archaeology is it?'

'She says she's warming to the seaside, and I think I know why. She's met a man, Brett. Malcolm is okay with him, and I told her people have to trust, or we're always stabbing at each other's backs. It's a good place for her to start afresh, and she's told Brett everything. Had to get drunk to do it, she said. Can't blame her for that. Brett seems a decent bloke; didn't judge her. Easy going, by the sounds of it. I suspect she'll move out of Malcolm's place and find somewhere to live. She thrives in that calm space. Not like me… I'd go nuts.'

'Jackson has put his faith in these people. Let's hope that Ellen's location remains a secret.' She poured Mark another drink, then topped up hers with a generous amount.

The visit had been short-lived yet fruitful. Mark was simply reassured to find Ellen was happy. However, nobody knew Freddie's whereabouts. Things weren't safe.

'She still doesn't understand what I do for a living,' said Mark. 'Although it's brought danger to our lives, because of Haydocks and Henderson, she accepts it's my crusade, not hers.' He blushed, spinning the glass in his fingers. 'I kissed her goodbye.'

Julianna's eyebrows perched higher. 'And?'

'You really need to know?' Mark laughed, and it was genuine. 'A hug, too. One that lasted more than a second.'

He was pleased with himself. So was Julianna.

Her phone rang. She considered not answering it. Mark was in an optimistic mood.

'Hi, Graham.' She covered the mouthpiece. 'It's Graham Saddler, the useful ex-copper who helps out at Opportunitas.'

Mark acknowledged the name with a nod, and a frown. Graham's timing was bad.

'Julianna, just to let you now that lass I was supposed to meet, the one who was going to spill the beans on her pimp, didn't show. No sign of her anywhere.'

'Damn.'

'Yeah, sorry. I know you put some effort into getting her to talk. My contacts in the police have drawn a blank.'

'We can't force her. Thanks for trying, Graham.'

'My pleasure. Anything to help Jackson out.'

She ended the call. 'We're done. Just a little project I've been given is going nowhere. I'll switch the phone off.'

He rose. 'Well, I went somewhere and I brought the car back in one piece, just as I promised.' He held out his hand. 'Ellen thinks I've changed. Have I?'

She clasped his warm palm against hers and followed him out of the room. 'She should know. Both of you have.'

Gathered around a table, holding a glass of wine, eating a few nibbles and making small talk wasn't on Julianna's bucket list. Worse, the evening would probably be padded out by the trivia of relationship issues. However, because she remained curious about the Haynes, she'd accepted an invitation to play cards with Hettie, the woman whose life she was supposed to be protecting.

The threats had dried up since Ellen's crisis. Chris agreed with Julianna when she called it the calm before the storm; girls continued to disappear off the streets and out of the hostels at an alarming rate. Jackson's foundation was finite in its activities and constrained by the legality of its role in society. Julianna wanted to do more; playing friends with Hettie's inner circle wasn't part of her big plan.

Julianna's driving duties had recently increased. Chris still vetoed her other work, including helping Opportunitas, especially since Tess had been waylaid by personal issues, which meant Julianna had barely got her teeth into anything substantial since Jackson had invited her to help out.

The boredom of chauffeuring caused her to forget her primary purpose. When not listening to Hettie's entertaining tales in the back of the car, Julianna occasionally, when ordered, occupied a seat at the entrance of the gallery. Due to her prominent location, the visitors assumed she was an art aficionado. Rather than sitting on her assigned chair, she walked through the exhibitions, showing them the pictures, and handed out catalogues. It passed the time until Jackson turned up at the gallery in a surprise visit to view his wife's new paintings.

Chris witnessed Julianna with a small group of Japanese visitors doing her little impersonation of a tour guide. A disapproving stare was dispatched over their heads and she scurried back to her seat in a huff. When Chris and Jackson walked past her to leave, Jackson gave her an annoyingly perceptive grin and wagged his finger at her. Julianna squirmed uncomfortably in her chair.

Later, back at the company's HQ, Moran had hauled Julianna over the coals, reminding her not to engage in "arty farty chats about paintings". Just because she had spent time with the boss and his family, that didn't exempt her from a rollicking.

Julianna had arrived home despondent. Her salvation was Mark. He dispelled her misery with a sublime kiss on her lips, and a twinkle in his eyes. 'Forget it. Go have fun with Hettie, don't think about it.'

Julianna picked up her car keys, and the bottle of plonk she had selected from the shelves of the local supermarket.

Half an hour later, she slammed the flat of her hand on the leather steering wheel. 'What am I doing here?'

The seats were leather, and the dashboard flashed with all the latest instrumentation and the best satellite navigation system. She didn't feel out of place parked outside an exclusive area of the city. Indoors, she might feel different. She had never stepped foot inside the Holland Park house.

'Move,' she said in a tone reminiscent of her father's bark when he trained her to kick her legs as high as his throat, countless evenings spent in his customised gym where she had learnt to protect herself from an unknown, unforeseeable menace. She never questioned why it might one day be important.

She approached the iron gate, punched in the keycode for access and waved at the CCTV camera; the guy on duty would recognise her. She drummed her fingers on the gate until it swung open, then strode across the drive under the leafy trees. The doorbell chimed like any other, summoning her host. She straightened her sleeves and flattened the lapels of her coat.

Hettie waved her in. 'Julianna, come in, come in. You're the last to arrive.'

She kicked off her shoes. There was a neat line of footwear

along the wall from Jackson's hand-stitched loafers to a pair of boy's shoes. Using her toes, she straightened hers.

'I've bought a bottle of wine.' She held out the red.

Hettie thanked her and showed her to the kitchen, her bare feet pattering on the tiles. 'That's thoughtful of you. Jackson has a substantial wine cellar.'

The wine was a stupid mistake. She should have bought cake or chocolates.

Hettie put it on the kitchen worktop. 'Sorry, I sound ungracious. His wine collection is a little intimidating. I pick bottles up and put them back because I don't know if I'm about to throw back a hundred-pound bottle when all I want is to get a little pissed. So we'll open this one.'

'No, it's fine. Silly of me. I didn't know if I should bring anything or—'

'You don't have to bring anything but your company.' Hettie smiled. She could charm anyone with that smile. 'Please, Julianna. I know you're used to calling me Mrs Haynes. But I'm Hettie tonight.'

'Fine. Thanks,' she said awkwardly.

The kitchen was spotless to a clinical level of cleanliness, which made Julianna wonder if food was ever prepared on its surfaces.

'We're in the breakfast room. It's the sunniest room in the evening.' Her eyebrows bunched together. 'Thinking about it, it shouldn't be.' Hettie opened the bottle. 'You've not been inside this house, have you?'

'No, actually. I haven't. I kind of throw you out of the car, don't I?'

'I suppose you do.' Hettie led her into the adjoining room. There was, unsurprisingly, artwork mounted in polished frames and hung on meticulous walls. Everything shouted wealth, except the kitchen, which at least resembled some kind of grand version of normality.

The other two guests were nearly touching foreheads, nattering away in hushed tones. They broke apart when Hettie introduced Julianna.

'Hi,' said a thin woman with letterbox glasses. 'I'm Zoe.' She shook Julianna's hand.

'And I'm Eva,' said the other woman. Her hair was dyed red.

The roots were black.

The introductions completed, Hettie shoved the door shut with her hip. Hettie could wear anything and look graceful, even the casual attire of leggings and a low-cut sweater probably came straight out of a fashion magazine. Julianna had chosen straight slacks and a pin-striped top. She wished she had worn jeans and a t-shirt, like the others.

'Gin rummy.' Hettie offered Julianna a seat next to her at the table.

About them on the floor were boxes stuffed with toys and children's books. Unlike the kitchen, the breakfast room was lived in and family orientated.

'You shuffle too well, Zoe,' Eva said. She lowered her cards but didn't hide them well. Julianna concurred – Eva had nothing in her hand. 'Hettie says you're her bodyguard?'

She cleared her throat. 'Occasional bodyguard. Most of the time I do investigative stuff. Uncover financial irregularities, and other… stuff.' She glossed over the work of Opportunitas. Recently Tess had returned to work so Julianna was finally allowed a project of her own and, given the sensitive nature of the investigation, it meant reporting directly to Jackson.

'Which do you like best?' asked Zoe. 'Leaping into action at the wheel of a car or… fraud?'

Julianna hadn't leapt into anything since Dublin. 'Both, I suppose. I don't like being behind a desk too much.'

'She doesn't like driving me about too much either.' Hettie nudged Julianna's shoulder. 'Boring.'

'No!' Julianna said. 'It's not boring—'

'Don't lie. What an earth do you get from sitting in a car with a stressed mum and two screaming kids. Wine anyone?' Hettie asked.

'Gives you the chance to easily wipe snotty noses. Just a little, please,' said Julianna, accepting a couple of splashes in her glass. 'I'm driving back. I would be hung out to rot for drink driving.'

'You brought the bottle though,' Zoe said.

'I know, crazy choice of gift.' She seriously regretted the wine.

'I'll open the biscuit tin, something to soak up the alcohol.' Hettie prised off the lid and handed out biscuits.

'Do you ever drive, Het?' Eva asked.

Hettie scowled. 'Yes. A rarity but I do. I did a couple of weekends ago in fact. Something... well I had...' Hettie focused on the spread of cards in her hand and discarded one.

'You drove him?' Eva rested her elbows on the table and dropped her chin on her knuckles. 'Pray tell. What happened? Come on, tell us.' She had a sweet smile, quite girlish. There were no rings on her fingers, only a pale band where she had worn her wedding ring. Dishing the dirt on husbands was probably something Eva enjoyed. Julianna once had, but not anymore.

The tale began innocuously enough. They had been to the seaside and Jackson had accidently rubbed sand into his eyes.

'He let me drive home while he... Poor Noah was distraught. He thought Daddy was very sad about something because his eyes were watering. The car's an automatic anyway. I'm not incompetent.' Hettie won the hand with a whoop.

'While he what?' Julianna asked.

Hettie picked up the scattered cards. 'While he sat in the back with Noah. I moved Evey next to me.'

'In the back?' Julianna pictured Jackson's long legs. 'He didn't want you to drive, did he?'

Hettie shuffled the pack. 'I insisted. He was tired.'

'Noah?'

'No, Jackson. He won't admit it, like a petulant child. So I snatched the keys out of his hands and told him to sit in the back with Noah and have a nap.'

'Marvellous,' said Zoe. 'Just love it. Were the child locks on too?'

Hettie dealt the cards with a flick of her wrist. 'I played nursery rhymes. Noah sang. Loudly. Most unfortunate for Jackson. He was worried I'd forgotten how to drive. He worries too much. It's like riding a bicycle, comes back quickly when given the opportunity.'

Jackson wouldn't have slept a wink. And it wasn't the case that he simply allowed Hettie to drive as she had initially implied. Hettie had put her foot down on more than the accelerator.

The game resumed. Hettie kept her cards close to her chest, peeping at them from time to time. It was a reflection of her whole life, hiding things out of sight. Here, at least among friends, Hettie was revealing a different side and expecting privacy in return. Julianna rather liked seeing this version of Hettie.

Julianna glanced up to the double-glazed doors into the kitchen. Through them, she watched Jackson enter. Dressed in faded jeans and burgundy polo shirt, the man looked closer to thirty not forty. He padded about the kitchen in bare feet and put his empty coffee mug in the dishwasher. Nothing about his relaxed manner shouted chief executive. Pausing, he picked up an apple from the fruit bowl, then cocked his head, as if listening. He approached the double doors – Julianna refocused on her cards – and tapped on the glass. While taking a bite out of the apple and with a wag of his finger, he summoned Hettie.

'Excuse me,' Hettie said and followed her husband out of the kitchen.

'He's so gorgeous, isn't he?' Eva whispered.

'Too old for me.' Zoe sniffed her wine. 'This is a good bottle, Julianna. You should come again and share some gossip. You must hear them chat all the time in the back of the car.'

'I mainly drive Hettie, just her.' Julianna wasn't lying. Jackson had his own drivers.

Zoe shuffled the cards. 'Do you like driving?'

'Yes.' Julianna had learnt to drive at fifteen on a private road. She laughed and told the two women how she had driven up and down the straight stretch and performed a three-point turn at each end. 'I'm pretty good at hand brake turns.'

The conversation shifted away from cars and chauffeuring.

She had staved off their intrusive questions. It was another part of her training to deflect. She was never off-duty; her contract stated she could be called up any time if there was an urgent requirement. Her discomfort was entirely based around the knowledge she was in her boss's house thinking that at any minute he could snap at her to do something. He wouldn't, but the thought was there.

Hettie returned. 'So sorry. Jackson thought he heard Evey cry and, well, he's not always who she wants.'

She yawned and picked up her cards. They played, and talked, and none of it stayed in Julianna's head, which was strangely relaxing.

'Julianna should get a medal for driving you.' Eva swayed, then air pecked Hettie's cheek. The goodbyes lasted the length of the suave hallway.

'I'm sure she will.' Hettie winked at Julianna.

Julianna was the last to leave. As she slipped on her shoes, Hettie touched her arm. 'Sophia and Luke would like to invite you and Mark for dinner. Just you two. Luke asked Jackson.'

'I'll tell Mark. I'm sure he'd love to go.' She wasn't sure. The last time he had gone to Luke's, he hadn't enjoyed the occasion.

Driving home, Julianna played over the evening's events in her head. She had gone with an idea firmly planted in her mind that she wouldn't fit in and it had slowly unravelled all evening, which meant she and Hettie were becoming friends. How would Jackson view that development?

Mark was still up when she reached home and as she dropped her handbag on the stand in the hallway, he called out to her from the dining room table where he sat surrounded by documents, staring at his laptop screen.

'I thought you'd finished all that?' she remarked.

'Had one more look through the final report and decided to change a few bits,' he said, without glancing up.

'Control freak.' She bent to kiss his head.

'That's me, sweetheart. Though I prefer perfectionist: sounds better.' He rubbed his eyes and leaned back in the chair. 'How did the evening go?'

Julianna hadn't planned to relay the details of the evening to Mark but as she fiddled with a piece of paper, she relived some of the conversations, and it turned into a verbatim account.

'So,' Mark said. 'You brought wine when you shouldn't have bothered, you squirmed because they asked you about your job, and you managed to tell them nothing useful, and Hettie played at being Hettie.'

The spot-on summary grated. 'Yes. In a nutshell.'

'You're becoming friends with Hettie, her friends, and it makes you uncomfortable.'

Yes, damn it. Since he'd visited his father, Mark remained sharply focused. She felt like a blunt knife.

'I'm supposed to put my life on the line for her, and her kids. A year ago, I didn't think anything of it. I never expected it to get that serious.'

'Until Dublin.'

'Yes.' She stared at her shaking hands and rose to stand nearer to him. 'Now I know it is serious. I beat a man with my bare hands, and it felt good. What does that say about me?'

'It says you're good at your job and Hettie is lucky. So is Ellen.' He stroked her arm. 'I promise to excise your demons, Julianna.' He laced his fingers through hers.

She would tell him about the dinner invitation in the morning.

37
Julianna

Summer, Friday Morning

After the rather delightful dinner with Sophia and Luke, Julianna and Sophia ceased using the Haynes couple as intermediaries for organising their flourishing friendship. Julianna's involvement with Opportunitas further solidified the new, and, unlike with Hettie, uncomplicated friendship. By the summer she and Sophia were meeting every Friday, work permitting and they either lunched together or went for a brisk walk to clear their heads. The routine established, Julianna looked forward to her Friday lunchtimes.

On a promising summer's day she logged out of the office system and went walkabout with her friend in the warm sunshine. The topic of conversation was more serious than usual: Sophia's pro bono work for Opportunitas. Julianna was impressed by Sophia's dedication and had offered to help. Via emails and phone calls, Julianna had helped collate the evidence. There were others involved in the investigation, including Graham Saddler, who had assisted Sophia with background checks.

Graham had sent Sophia an email asking for information about one girl she had been interviewing.

'I went to see her, and she'd vanished,' said Sophia. 'The B&B where she was staying said she didn't come home one day. She'd managed to get a job in a cafe since she stopped working the streets and Graham thinks she's been enticed back again.'

'What about her pimp?' Julianna asked.

'Can't prove anything without the evidence. He claims to be her boyfriend. Which he so is not, or else he must have multiple girlfriends. What worries me, is this isn't the first time a girl has gone off radar. She's the fifth in two months.'

Julianna agreed, it was happening too often.

They rounded a corner, down a quiet side street back towards Sophia's office block; their usual circuit. As they strolled down the pavement chatting, they passed a black BMW; a stretch saloon familiar to chauffeurs like Julianna. The front window was wound down. Inside, the passenger was examining a street map.

'Ladies, please to help me?' The young man wore a baseball cap and reflective sunglasses. He smiled and waved at the map. 'I need to be here.' He pointed at a spot on the map.

Something wasn't right. She spotted a few niggling things: the car was an older model, but in good condition and it had a satnav. The tattoos along the passenger's arm were scripted with Cyrillic text. The driver's seat was empty.

'No satnav?' asked Julianna, keeping her distance.

'Kapput.' He shrugged. He wasn't a native English speaker. He opened the door and climbed out. 'Here.' He gestured again.

Sophia leaned forward. 'You're miles from there.'

Julianna reached out to touch her friend, to draw her away from the man. Out of the corner of her eye an arm flew past her and wrapped itself around Julianna's throat, pulling her backwards. Another coiled itself tight about her body. The masculine arms squeezed hard, expelling the air out of her lungs. The strap in her hand slipped through her fingers and she clung onto it. The handbag was as heavy as a brick and was her only weapon.

Sophia opened her mouth to scream. The man in the baseball cap slapped his hand over it and dragged her towards the car. The map fluttered to the ground.

'Shut up,' he snarled.

Julianna's eyes watered; she was asphyxiating. With the consciousness fading, the handbag fell to the ground. She weakened until, like Sophia, she was slammed against the car with her arms pinned behind her back.

Cold metal snapped her wrists together – handcuffs. Sophia's face was squashed against the window, her mouth open, gasping for air. She, too, was handcuffed. With her head spinning, Julianna was bundled backwards into the car and Sophia was catapulted into the seat next to hers. Julianna's eyes streamed. Her assailants' faces blurred into a diffuse arrangement of masculine features. She continued to resist, tossing her head from side to side. A rough hand slapped her face, then stretched a strip of duct tape over her mouth. Julianna kicked with her blunted heels. The young man grunted and, in reply, punched her stomach. Winded by the ferocity of his blow, she fought to stay conscious, vaguely aware he was binding her ankles. Once they finished trussing her and Sophia into packages, the men shoved them into the cramped footwells.

Pain, an occasionally useful nemesis, brought Julianna to her senses. Adrenaline, also reliable, pumped harshly into her bloodstream. Fright inveigled her; flight had to win, though. It had taken seconds for them to be snatched off the street. She started to pay attention and crushed the fear to the back of her mind. Had anyone witnessed their abduction? The quiet backstreet served its purpose; not a car or person happened upon their assault, even the windows of the buildings were shuttered by blinds.

The men spoke in an unrecognisable language. Baseball cap man returned to the passenger seat and the other one occupied the driver's seat. The car sped off.

Whimpering into her gag, Sophia was a frozen statue of white marble. Only her eyes seemed to respond. Taking deep breaths through her nose, Julianna pounded shock into a small ball in her stomach, where the pain was focused, and buried it there. There was no time for recriminations at her failure to fight off the men. Her friend needed her. She blinked, deliberately slowly, trying to reassure Sophia. They weren't dead. Whatever these men wanted, it wasn't an immediate death.

Still crammed into the footwell, she risked sticking her head between the seats, and caught a glimpse of the abductors. The man in the passenger seat in front of her was blocked from her view. The driver was in profile and the unflattering contours of his face triggered a vivid memory. The driver had two discerning features: a long black ponytail and a ragged scar on his neck. The last time they had met was in a hotel in Dublin where she had beaten him unconscious with her fists.

The annihilating impact of terror returned in abundance. For a few seconds, those images of his battered face consumed her. They carried with them anguish, hatred and fear, things that had no place when battling danger.

Sophia cried; the tears flooded her bewildered eyes.

The passenger in his baseball cap was speaking on the phone in English. Given the thickness of his accent, Julianna concluded they were an international gang. She also guessed who their boss might be; she didn't need to hear his many names.

'We've got her,' he said. 'And another.'

A pause.

'Don't fucking know.... Do you want her?' He produced a thick throaty laugh. 'Snuff flick. Sure, she would make good snuff flick. A, what say, a bonus.'

The men were laughing loudly and were distracted. Julianna eased herself up on to the seat but kept her head low. She slid toward the door release and tried to gently pull on it. The door refused to budge. A child lock. She nodded at Sophia.

Terrified, Sophia shrivelled further into the footwell. Julianna pleaded with her eyes. Time was running out. Although now and again they were stuck in traffic, soon they would hit the faster roads out of the city. Too fast to leap out of the car.

'You've not found him?' the baseball cap man asked the caller. 'He is at work. Stazki, here, wants both. He'll sell them.'

Ponytail man, Stazki, nodded and said something in his native tongue. The man in the baseball cap relayed a translation.

'She beat him. He wants them to beat each other. See who lives! He says she will. Weak man who hides behind woman. We speak later. Stazki wants Clewer. Get him. The boss will find out soon what he's done.' Baseball cap man hung up. The two kidnappers continued to talk in their own tongue.

The motive for their abduction was established, the likely outcome all too apparent, now was the time to act. However, throwing off the shackles of heavy traffic, the car accelerated hard and Julianna struggled to stay anchored to the smooth leather seat. She tried to encourage Sophia by jerking her head toward the other passenger door. Sophia's legs slowly unfolded, she perched her elbows on the edge of the seat and pushed her bottom up. There, precariously balanced, she fumbled with the door handle until there was a small clunk. No child lock. Sophia's widening eyes suddenly sparked with understanding.

The dashboard would light up with a warning light; it was a risk worth taking. Jump, Julianna pleaded soundlessly. Still keeping low, she lifted her legs onto the seat, knees bent to her chin, and there, foetal like, she held herself poised for the next stage. If Sophia made it out of the door, she would slide out and follow.

In the shadows, screwed into the corner by fear, the terror reflected in her glassy eyes, Sophia released the door catch. A little more weight was all that it needed.

The dashboard emitted a resonating beep. Sophia froze, childlike.

Julianna acted on instinct. Their captors within that millisecond started to turn, ignoring the road ahead. There was no knowing from her perspective what was behind the BMW, only the certainty that death was on the agenda if they stayed put, and opportunities unlikely for further escape. With the flat of her soles, she gave her friend one almighty jolt. Sophia tumbled backwards onto the street. Handcuffed, ankles taped together, and mouth sealed, the look of horror on Sophia's face encapsulated what Julianna felt. She had probably just killed her friend; there was no way of knowing.

Stazki swerved the car. The door swung back. As Julianna made the decision to gamble her own life too, a clenched fist hurtled towards her, striking her cheek; the collision of brute knuckles and soft flesh was impossible to avoid. The explosion blinded her vision, blocking out the interior, the bright sunshine. The twinned sensations of pain coupled to fading consciousness were extraordinarily calming in their simplicity because together they were a salvation of sorts. She tasted blood in her mouth and the cool air rushing into the cabin, brushing her stinging face. It was too late for a revival; the final obliterating blackness accompanied the door slamming shut.

38

Mark

Friday Afternoon

The screwed-up piece of paper flew over the desk, missed the waste bin and joined the collection on the floor. Mark was unusually bored. His last project was resolved and, sadly, lacked any improprieties. Some people were simply bad at paperwork and incompetence didn't justify prosecutions.

He glanced at his watch. The afternoon was drawing to a conclusion. What the hell, he decided, he would clock off early. As he powered off his laptop, there was a rap on his office door and before he could open his mouth to reply, it flew open. On the threshold of his office stood Gary Maybank and another member of the security team.

'Is this one of your flyby security checks?' Mark asked, without pausing in his paper gathering. The clear desk policy was religiously enforced.

'You need to come with us, Mark. Now,' Gary said brusquely. 'Mr Haynes's orders.'

Mark dropped the papers into a drawer. Gary, usually a waxwork of impartiality, looked flustered; the immaculate military appearance was slightly frayed in its execution. Mark had an equally unpleasant feeling in his belly; embryonic, but familiar: a pulse of anxiety.

'Why?' he asked.

'Jessop is here is to take you to Fasleigh.' Gary jerked his head impatiently towards the door. Black-clad Jessop was funereal.

'I asked why,' Mark repeated sharply. 'Fasleigh?' Jackson wanted him behind iron gates and a high wall.

'There's been an incident and your personal safety is at risk.' Gary held open the door.

'Oh no, you tell me more.' Mark planted his hands firmly on his hips and shot a fiery glare at Gary. Pleasingly, Jessop flinched. 'I'm not budging until you've said more.'

Gary nodded to Jessop and his colleague left the room to wait outside. Gary cleared his throat. 'There's no easy way to tell you this. Julianna was abducted at mid-day while she was out walking with Sophia Crawford. Miss Crawford managed to escape but Julianna is still missing, presumably held captive.'

Mark staggered against the desk. The embryo was now a rampaging monster about to be born. 'Abducted. By whom?'

'According to Miss Crawford, who was injured falling from a moving vehicle, the two men sounded Slavic. One had a black ponytail.'

Mark slumped into his chair. Burying his face in his hands, he groaned. Immediately, a fierce headache loomed behind his eyes. The shock blunted his mind and, for a few seconds, he was lost for words. Gary waited.

'Oh God no. Sophia, is she hurt?' Mark finally asked.

'Concussion and a broken arm. Julianna probably did her a favour by booting her out of the car. According to Miss Crawford, Julianna seemed to recognise who had taken her and decided letting Sophia fly out of a moving car was the better option. She was unable, I assume, to follow Sophia's flight.'

'Oh God!' The anguish spread to the pit of his stomach. He hugged it there, doubled over, attempting to crush it before it breached every part of his body.

'Mark,' Gary said gently. 'You have to go to Fasleigh. The security team are expecting you there. The men in the car mentioned your name. They want you, too.'

Mark was rooted to his chair. The thought of Julianna in pain was unbearable. Only he could touch her, breathe with her. Nobody else.

'Mark, come.' Gary grasped the door handle.

'No,' he answered softly.

'Please, you can't go home. Her house is compromised.' Gary

spoke like a copper; Julianna was supposed to be his colleague and friend. Mark envied his detachment.

'I'm not going home. You must be working hard to find her, so I'm staying here. I'll help if I can, I'm not hiding at Fasleigh, waiting for news. I want to know what's happening.' He rose to his feet, finding his legs firmer than he anticipated. Julianna often reminded him that adrenaline had its advantages.

'Mr Haynes insists you go to Fasleigh—'

'I insist I stay here. You can't force me. Now, I'm heading to the security office, and given I will be surrounded by protection officers, I can assume I'll be safe there. Yes?'

Gary sighed in defeat.

The security office was teeming with staff, the bulk of whom were on phones, checking computer databases, maps and other sources. The room was normally staffed by a couple of duty officers, now it buzzed with extras brought into help.

Mark turned to Gary. 'Her tracker app?'

Gary shook his head. 'The phone goes to voicemail and the tracker hadn't been activated.'

'She kept it in her handbag. If she was separated from it—'

'She was handcuffed.' Gary pointed an empty chair. 'Just sit, before you fall down.'

Having requested to do something useful, Mark became the redundant object in the maelstrom, unable to do anything productive. Without a task, he would go crazy.

Gary's phone rang. 'Sir?' He shushed the others in the room. Gary listened, then covered the speaker. 'According to Professor's Dewer's brother, Ellen is safe in Edinburgh. Chris is arranging somebody to guard her.' He removed his hand. 'No, sir, Mark hasn't gone to Fasleigh. He's still here, sir.' Johnson grimaced and held out the phone to Mark. 'He wants to speak to you.'

Mark took a deep breath. 'Jackson.'

'Why aren't you at Fasleigh?'

'I'm not sitting on my arse—'

'I'm not having you hindering the search for Julianna—'

Mark ignored the people around him, not caring who listened in. 'I'm not going to sit here and do fuck all.' He lowered his irate voice to a whisper. 'Could you if it was Hettie out there?' His question was greeted with a lengthy pause.

Jackson's usual confident tone was strained, stretched thin. 'Alright. Chris thinks Julianna is likely to be in Kent somewhere.'

He gasped. 'The Channel tunnel?'

'Possibly. It's as easy to smuggle people out as to bring them in. There's an all ports alert out for her. The Kent Constabulary are being very cooperative. Plus I'm being made aware of covert operations ongoing.'

'Covert?'

'I'm awaiting more details. Chris is liaising with the police. Europol have been alerted too. Lots of things are happening. Mark, don't do anything stupid. Stay put.'

'How is Sophia?' he asked.

'Not as bad as first thought considering she fell out of a moving vehicle into oncoming traffic. She's in shock. Given her account, this man who took them is in all likelihood part of Zustaller's gang.'

'Retribution for Dublin?' He remembered the bloodied body on the floor and the unconscionable rage in Julianna's face as she pummelled the man with her fists. To date, Julianna hadn't explained why she had reacted so violently.

'Julianna beat him up badly. It seems personal. Very personal. Sophia doesn't recall Ellen's name being mentioned. Yours was. However, she's concussed and somewhat confused. If they're still trying to find you, Mark, it means they might not have shifted Julianna out of our reach. Don't go anywhere without an escort. Understood?'

He faced the nearest wall. 'I'm very grateful, for all this. I can't bear to think—'

'Then don't. You're right. Find something to do. We'll get her back, Mark.'

Mark put the phone down. One question above all others puzzled him. Who knew the two women went for a walk on a Friday and the route they took? If he was Jackson, he would be looking for somebody in his own circle to blame.

The afternoon became evening and still no progress. Mark bore the frustration badly: pacing, peering over shoulders, hankering for the cigarettes he had never smoked but had inhaled for years as a child. He provided a list of people who might know Julianna's habits. A short list; Julianna liked her privacy. Everything was taking too long. Julianna's colleagues were determined, but the array of futile activities wasn't achieving much.

Food appeared from takeaways but Mark only managed to sip on water. Chris Moran arrived to work out a rota for the night, ensuring the team had adequate rest periods. Mark wasn't included.

Chris perched on the edge of a desk, his beefy arms folded over his chest and brought Gary up to speed in his gruff business-like voice. 'There's an undercover operation ongoing in South London involving Kent and Sussex forces. A gang of traffickers are operating out of a farmhouse. Attempts are being made to contact the undercover officer working with the gang. It's dangerous and could expose him.'

Gary chewed on a piece of pizza. 'This police operation has been ongoing for some time though. Julianna mentioned it in one of those intelligence reports Jackson had her write. Maybe she uncovered too much sensitive information and it led back to her?'

'It may be how they found her. I doubt it, as she's too crafty to put her name to anything. She uses aliases and indirect contacts.' Chris glanced at Mark. 'I'm pretty sure this is personal.'

'Her tracker?' Mark asked again.

'Sorry, nothing. And we believe her mobile has been disabled too.'

Mark rubbed his tired eyes. It was close to midnight. His optimism had never been strong, now it was in a rapid downward spiral.

With a snort, Chris jabbed his finger at Mark. 'You should eat.' He scooped up a cardboard pizza box under his arm and headed to the top floor where Jackson sought to maximise his influence with the relevant authorities.

The room fell quiet. Calls dried up and leads failed to materialise. The electronic tracker was still not active. The telephone next to Mark sang loudly and he jerked. It was Jackson's number. Tentatively, he picked up the handset. 'Yes?'

'Come up here and join me.' Jackson hung up before Mark could ask why.

39

Julianna

Pay attention to the details. Note each and every one because they save lives. The advice was old, probably from her days as a police cadet, and invaluable. The movement of the car – the constant accelerations and occasional hard braking – transmitted itself through her body. The crippling state of semi-consciousness kept her on the edge of oblivion. Her eyelids seemed glued shut – a blindfold. Searing pain shot across her forehead, its roots were where he had struck her.

The rumble of the wheels on the tarmac intensified, as did the cornering; they had left the city and were out in the countryside. She slid across the leather upholstery and with her fingertips, she clawed and hung on. How many miles and in what direction?

The car halted and the engine cut out. Doors opened. A rush of muggy humidity collided with acrid smoke in the cabin; the men had smoked incessantly the whole time. They dragged her out by her ankles, and she hit the hard ground, jarring her elbow and shoulder. The warmth of the sun beat down on her head; it wasn't the evening yet. She filed away the detail. An hour, maybe two on the road?

Without warning the tape covering her eyes was torn away. She screamed noiselessly into her gag, and, protesting at the harshness, she kicked out with her bound legs, hitting something. The small rebellion cost her another bruising blow and her head throbbed in a new location.

Breathe. She inhaled clean air through her nose and sneezed. Slowly, she blinked and opened her eyes. The sunlight blinded and she sneezed again, painfully, as she couldn't open her mouth to expel the air. Somebody, possibly the baseball hat man, hooked his hands under her armpits and yanked her up onto her feet. The man with the ponytail, Stazki, sliced the tape away from her ankles. She staggered to one side, nearly toppling over. Both men frog-marched her towards a bleary building.

Details. The devil is in the details. She forced her eyes to focus, horribly aware how her breathlessness mimicked her snapshot thoughts, both were rapid and short lived. The view, coming together from fragments, wasn't encouraging: lots of crumbling red bricks; rotten window frames boarded up with plywood; grey slatted roof tiles with several missing in places; untamed ivy clung to the walls while nettles, hollyhocks and other weeds strangled any other life. There was no garden, no fencing or footpath leading up to the doorway. On the horizon was a counterpane of fields and a small wooded area. The landscape beyond rose and fell gently; a typical English rural scene and hopelessly unpopulated. Surrounded by equally ruined out-houses, the derelict farmhouse was an angry blot in an otherwise tranquil location.

They pushed her towards the unlocked door with its peeling blue paintwork; one of them kicked it open and the hinges squealed in painful protest. The interior was gloomy except for the stream-lined shards of light that penetrated from outside through the thin gaps in the shutters, forming a ghostly pattern on the wall.

Once, years ago, the room had been a cosy kitchen. Now, there were no cupboards or worktops, only a square ceramic sink with no taps. A stained table was littered with crushed beer cans, take-away cartons and a couple of plastic carriers. Cigarette stubs ringed the two wooden chairs and boot prints trampled the dropped ash. There were more than two sets; a rota of guards? Against the back wall was a stack of bottled water and a black bin liner overflowing with rubbish. There was no light bulb attached to the wire hanging from the ceiling.

Details: an abandoned house with no electricity or running water. Which meant there would be no bills or records associated with the property. The place was utterly forgotten.

The dim light was easier to tolerate, and it calmed the rampaging pain behind her eyes. The two assailants who had grabbed her off the street remained her sole captors. Stazki, the man she had beaten in Dublin, was older than she realised and the pockmarked complexion, which was deeply tanned, implied time spent in warm climates. The scar on his neck was a jagged white line. He had carried it for many years, suggesting a long violent past. His companion was younger and impatient; he shifted on his feet and squeezed her arm in his pincer hold.

Stazki dropped something onto the table: her handbag! He had picked it up off the pavement. She allowed herself a tiny amount of optimism.

Stazki rummaged inside it and extracted her mobile. The back cover was off. Why hadn't he smashed it? He reassembled components, fiddling with the SIM card and battery, then tapped on the screen several times. She held her breath and waited.

Stazki held up her mobile, thrusting it at her face. 'Open.'

The lock screen was engaged. She shook her head.

The blow to her stomach brought her down onto her knees. Baseball man hoisted her up. Her insides would rupture with more blows like that. Gasping for breath, she unlocked the screen with a trembling finger. He quickly pulled up her contacts list and shoved Jackson Haynes's name – his business card complete with work address and corporate telephone number – under her nose. She nodded, acknowledging what he had found. However, Jackson's personal number was listed under a bogus name, as was Hettie's and a few other key people she chose to keep protected. A contacts list was a valuable commodity in the wrong hands. Her family's details she had memorised, including Mark and Ellen's.

Yes, details were important. Too important. Keep them safe.

Time to speak, so she cleared her throat a few times. Stazki ripped part of the tape off and she muffled a wince. Her raw lips cracked with thirst. 'My boss,' she croaked. 'I drive his air-head wife to the shops. I work for his security team. Nothing special.'

'Why send you to Dublin?'

'Mark Clewer is a sort of friend of his. Mr Haynes has a tendency to take pity on people. I was ordered to go with him to help.'

'You got the better of me,' Stazki said. 'I don't forget.'

'Sorry, I was obviously lucky with you. I wanted to get home.'

She shrugged. 'I thought I might get a promotion out of it. Didn't get it though.' She added more distance between her and Jackson, weakening the connection as much as possible.

'Now he's your boyfriend, this Clewer,' Stazki said.

'He's good in bed.' Stay away from him; she bit her tongue. 'Haynes asked me to keep him out of trouble.'

'You better be no trouble.' Stazki smashed the phone on the stone tiles and ground his heel into the screen. He placed the handbag on the table just out of her reach, then stuck the tape back over her mouth, smoothing it across her cheek. She jerked her head away.

She tried not to obsess about the handbag. She shouldn't draw attention to its contents. Her abductors hadn't mentioned the little device, and if they had seen it, they hadn't appreciated what it was. No bigger than her thumb, it resembled a key-fob and was stuffed in a side pocket. The handbag remained her only hope.

The younger man picked up a bottle of water and a carrier bag, the other pushed her towards a door in the corner of the room. Julianna teetered on the brink of a staircase leading down into a murky cellar. She nearly slipped on the uneven steps. The cellar wasn't cavernous and was partitioned off into rooms with a corridor down one side. A small amount of light seeped in through a ventilation shaft in the end wall. The floor was strewn with rubbish – bits of carpet, mouse droppings and leaves that had blown in through the vent.

They passed the first closed door and stopped next to the second. Stazki drew the bolt back and thrust her inside the room. Perhaps describing it as a room was being generous. It was a squalid space with bare brick walls, a filthy concrete floor and a low ceiling. The only source of light arrived through another small shaft barricaded with metal bars. Rainwater had one time pooled on the floor beneath the opening, leaving behind a dried-out green stain of algae and fungus.

In one corner, the furthest from the door, was a thin mattress, the kind that would typically be rolled up and taken on a camping trip. It was unlikely to offer any comfort or protection from the cold floor. Heaped on it was a tattered blanket and attached to the wall above, an iron ring with two metres of chain and a pair of manacles attached. There was also a bucket.

Baseball cap man trapped her arms to her sides while Stazki undid her handcuffs. He slammed her back against the wall, setting off dazzling fireworks in her head. By the time the flashing lights had retreated her wrists were shackled by the metal cuffs. Stazki stood over her, his foul tobacco breath mushrooming across her face. She stifled a retch. Using a bulbous fingertip, he touched her bruised right cheek and pressed harder. She winced, and her reaction triggered a grin that mirrored the shape of the crescent scar on his throat. The palm of his other hand rubbed up her belly until it touched one of her breasts. Julianna looked away and instinctively pressed her thighs together. He thrust his pelvis against her hip in a clear gesture of sexual predation.

'You are mine now,' he said, in a voice as coarse as his fingertips.

She tried to keep the terror at bay. Panic killed opportunities. Keep calm. A little bit of adrenaline was essential, but too much would overcome her. He exhaled into her grimacing face, using his personal stench to assault her further. The other man said something sharply. Stazki stepped back.

Julianna gasped and brought up her arms to protect her chest.

'I wait,' he said, with mock nonchalance. 'We go get your man. Then we leave England. You lucky that you are to stay fresh. Shame.' He frowned and added a small shrug. From out of the carrier bag he retrieved a battered apple and a grey bread roll. He placed them with the bottle of water on the mattress.

'See. We are nice. Sometimes. Be good.' He thumped his companion's back and they exited the room, laughing as they went. Their ugly duet of unintelligible banter continued outside the door. The bolt rattled, then slammed back in place. Footsteps faded until there was nothing save the distant call of birds.

Julianna sat on the mattress and cautiously removed the tape covering her mouth. Smacking her sore lips, she twisted the bottle top off and gulped down several mouthfuls. Some of the water spilt on her chin; she abruptly stopped drinking and screwed the lid back on the bottle. She had no idea how long the litre of water had to last. The paltry food she ignored.

There was some sunlight in the cellar compartment. The long summer days were beneficial; daylight was her only source of illumination. Night-time would be pitch black. The dank air was rife with the stench of mildew and cooling rapidly. She fingered the decayed sacking. For now, she would manage without the makeshift blanket.

She examined the walls. There were no large cracks or peep holes. Above her head were the wooden boards of the ground floor. Shards of light drifted through the cracks, which meant there was no carpet or rugs up there. The house was unfurnished. The ring was attached to the wall via a concrete fixture rather than directly into the bricks. She tugged on the chain, drawing all her strength into her arms as she pulled. But it didn't budge. The metal shackles were already chaffing and could easily break her skin. The locks would be difficult to pick. She didn't have a pin anyway. On the plus side, she was untouched and in reasonable shape. While she was capable of coherent thoughts, she needed to work out the possibilities. She had overcome Stazki before, but on that occasion she had caught him by surprise. He wouldn't underestimate her a second time, and there were two of them. He had ensured his accomplice was not a weak-willed woman who ran off when things started to go wrong.

The handbag was crucial; Julianna needed access to it.

For a few minutes, she granted herself a little breakdown. She hugged her legs and shed a few tears. Then with a deep breath, she shook herself out of the malaise, wiped away her tears and inspected the wall again.

She wasn't the first prisoner. There were scratches on one of the bricks – thin lines in a row. Back at work she had a list of young women who had gone missing. How many had curled up on the useless mattress? Too many. The cellar was haunted by the ghosts of fear and despair.

But the chains weren't just for Julianna and her lost girls.

Would they get Mark?

Do not think of Mark. Thinking of him in any capacity was painful and brought her close to an irreversible state of desolation.

If Mark was out of bounds, Alex wasn't. Would he laugh at her adventurous spirit now? Somewhere in Oxfordshire, he was living with her best friend. Two ex-friends happily domesticated. She pictured the scene: suavely dressed Alex bringing home flowers and boxes of chocolates, things she had considered sweet but uninspired.

She had not shown him much appreciation and occasionally she had spurned his traditional ways. How easy it was to belittle somebody and then allow that attitude to become the norm, letting it erode everything else with it. Alex hadn't been entirely at fault for their failed marriage; she hadn't opened up to him or made him part of her life. Locked in a cold cellar, an increasingly despondent Julianna reflected too deeply on past mistakes. She dragged her rambling thoughts to the present. Had she made another irreparable mistake when she shoved poor Sophia out of the car?

Julianna prayed her actions hadn't inflicted serious injuries or, God forbid, killed her new friend. For some reason, the two men hadn't bothered to pick Sophia off the road. Hopefully, Sophia would be in a hospital in London and a feverish hunt instigated to find Julianna. Jackson wouldn't let her go without a fight.

Jackson was her linchpin; the man held all the aspects of her life together. Through him, she had a chance to accomplish her ambitions, instead of living them out vicariously through other people like her military father or the other agents with whom she once worked in her previous job. Yet here she was, kidnapped in a pathetic trap and awaiting some gruesome fate because she had chosen to be one of Jackson's crusaders. The very excitement she had once craved was now holding her captive. It seemed she couldn't do it after all – be the kind of person who saved the day. Just thinking about Mark crippled her.

If she slept a little, then her strength would return. Maybe then she could stomach eating an apple and a piece of dry bread. She lay down on the cardboard-thin mattress and closed her eyes. Between the walls, something dripped incessantly – a disused pipe? Mice scrambled along the board above her head in an endless race. The cellar reeked of stagnant air. Her palpitating heartbeats added to the chorus of distracting noises.

The bolt was shot back across with a clang. Julianna jumped. She had been asleep; a lethargic slumber brought on by her battered head rather than the need for rest. The room was swathed in a sheet of blackness; she must have slept for some time. She sat and the sacking fell away. The cold penetrated deep into her flesh, mingling with the aches of uncomfortable muscles.

In walked Stazki accompanied by another man. Unlike Stazki, this man's face was hidden by a woollen balaclava. A squat person, his grim bearing was enhanced by dark jeans with a metal skull buckle on his belt, a shabby brown leather jacket, unzipped, and underneath, a white t-shirt that failed to flatter him; the newcomer carried before him a pot belly and lacked stature. However, when he bent his arm, the bicep bulged. In his grasp, held up high, was a gas lamp. The light flickered and macabre shadows danced along the imprisoning walls.

Julianna tensed, feeling the rise of paralysing fear. She shuffled backwards into the corner.

'Get up!' Stazki shaped his hands into boxer's fists.

The masked man handed the lamp to Stazki. He strolled toward Julianna and stopped a metre short of her. By then adrenaline had awoken the stiff muscles in her legs and she stood. He said something to Stazki and the light was brought closer.

'Julianna, a pretty name,' the masked man said. He had a strong foreign accent, but his English flowed easily out of his mouth.

Julianna said nothing.

In the dim light his pupils looked entirely black against the bloodshot whites. Bushy black eyebrows peeked through the eyeholes. His breath was sweet and minty, not like his compatriot, who reeked of tobacco. Stazki moved closer.

She needed every drop of willpower to fight the fear. The pit of it lay in her belly, while the edge of it, a bitter acidity, rested in the back of her throat waiting to spew out of her mouth. She held the nausea in check.

'Your man is surrounded,' the newcomer said. 'We can't get at him. As much as my friend here would like to have him, we're not going to risk delaying any longer. You will do. Just you unfortunately. Lowers the price considerably. But you're feisty. A fighter. There are men out there who like women who fight off men, and not just lie back and hope for the best. You will fight, Julianna. You are that kind, as my friend here knows. He's secretly impressed. Well, no, perhaps not, but I am. Will you fight, Julianna?'

'I'll do what I can to survive,' she said carefully.

'Ah. The ambiguous answer. I like it.' He leaned towards her. 'I wanted her too. Ellen. But Haynes has hid her too well. Poor girl never knew, did she? Once I found out she was the Clewer's girl, I invested five people, five pretending to be me, keeping her happy. Demanding bitch. Then she let slip her brother ruined Henderson, and I had to move my plans up. Couldn't wait any longer.'

He had confirmed his identity – Zustaller. The elusive villain was right there in front of her. The admission boosted her confidence. 'Five men to groom her.' She sneered. 'How inefficient of you.'

He snorted. The shadow looming over her lengthened as he leaned forward, speaking right into her ear. 'Four men and one woman. She called her sweetie. I watched. Added a little spark to the chat now and again. Kept things ticking over. I want her still. When I get her, I'll make her watch you.'

'How gallant.' Julianna risked much with her temerity, but the sarcasm was working. She snapped her shoulders back, presenting bravado instead of cowardice.

The balaclava failed to hide the pursed lips of a frown. 'Now do you need anything, besides your freedom? You will leave soon. Your travel arrangements are being finalised. It is not going to be very comfortable. I apologise in advance.' His eyes glistened under the lamplight; amused, not sorry.

The spike of confidence was counterproductive; she had to appear weak to actuate her plan. Drooping, she lost the boldness and hunched her shoulders. 'I'm cramping.' She laced misery into her voice. 'I know it doesn't bother you. But I've only the one pair of knickers and I don't want to leave here bloody. I have what I need in my handbag.' She pressed her palms together, mimicking prayer.

The pathetic touch worked. 'Get her handbag,' Zustaller said to Stazki. 'Not that blood would bother my buyer.' He laughed and circled a spot on the floor while they waited.

Stazki returned with the leather handbag, which had two compartments and a keyring sewn into the interior seam. Attached to the keyring was the moulded knob of plastic. Stazki held out the bag to Julianna, keeping his grasp on the lengthy strap. Julianna plunged her hands into the compartments; the heavy cuffs masked her actions. With one hand, she fished out a tampon and with the other she activated the silicone button secreted inside the plastic fob. No bleep or flash of light – the tracker was perfectly covert. She hoped the beacon was doing its job.

She held up the tampon, and joyfully witnessed their discomfort; both of them glanced away at the display of femininity, the very thing they espoused as her frailty, and that was their failing: a belief in the weaker vessel. Now, her anger returned, but this time she wouldn't direct the rage at Alex's betrayal. Her resentment belonged entirely to these men and their kind.

'We will leave you for little while, then we come back to get you. Try to eat.' Zustaller pointed at the food. 'It will rot if you don't and there is nothing else for you. My buyer isn't fussed about weight either.'

The men retreated out of the door with her handbag. She fumbled in the darkness and found the apple. Now it was worth eating; she needed the strength.

Another sliding bolt echoed somewhere in the cellar. There were shuffles of feet, a muted cry and a hard slap, then more cries and blows. She spat out the apple and covered her ears for the duration. It never crossed her mind there were others down in the cellar with her. One woman at least. The walls were thick enough to mask voices, but not cries. Her feeble protests eventually stopped. The bolt clanged again, signalling the end of the ordeal. A few minutes later a car engine roared outside, and wheels crunched on the gravel track.

There was nothing else to do but corral her fear and anger into the energy of resistance; the one thing she possessed that couldn't be broken. The opportunity to loosen it would come. She prayed it was when, and not if. In the empty silence, she waited.

40
Mark

Friday Night

Mark joined Jackson in his office a little after midnight.

'If you can't sleep at least have a shower and a change of clothes,' Jackson said.

The small en-suite bathroom was sufficient for refreshing aching joints. The sweatpants and matching t-shirt had arrived from somewhere, probably a nearby store and purchased by a member of the security team. Mark and Julianna's house was out of bounds in case it was being watched.

Mark and Jackson sat in silence around the conference table, fingering the handles of their mugs – the coffee had long since gone cold. A packet of digestive biscuits had been opened. The crumbs came from a broken biscuit at the top of the packet, the rest were untouched. Waiting was torture for Mark and Jackson was similarly afflicted with agitated impatience. Occasionally Jackson glanced at the clock on the wall, but mostly he alternated between tapping his fingers on the arm of his chair or pacing the length of the room. He had engaged every organisation or authority with whom he had influence. Mark was powerless and impotent. He pressed his palms together and raised his eyes to the ceiling in pseudo-prayer. He didn't believe in God, but this one day he wished he had some faith in divine intervention. Ellen was safe; if only it was true for Julianna.

The call that came through not long after four o'clock generated a burst of feverish optimism – Jackson ordered fresh coffee and tastier biscuits. Chris had informed Jackson that the tracker was sending out a signal and he was on his way to meet the police. Mark paced the floor for a while before collapsing in a chair. Nothing was happening fast enough for him. Jackson preferred to stare out of the window, arms folded, and watch the sunrise. The lack of further information blunted the initial excitement. The call merely signalled another period of waiting. Silence suited the temperament of both men.

At half past five in the morning the telephone in Jackson's office rang. Jackson leaned over and pressed a button. Chris's voice boomed out of the speaker.

'Sir. We don't have her.'

'We' meant the police. Chris Moran had relayed the location of the tracker's beacon to the local police in Kent, who had arrived ahead of him. Mark's head slumped and he clenched his fists in angst. Julianna had disposed of the punchbag; he wanted it right in front of him.

'What happened, Chris? You're on speaker and Mark is here,' Jackson said.

'The place was deserted. A derelict farmhouse with minimal furnishings. There are signs that the bedrooms were occupied by gang members. The place is basic; no plumbing or electricity. Totally off the grid. No evidence of women being held there. The police think it's a hideout and they left in a hurry. Personal items were abandoned.'

'And they're sure Julianna wasn't there?'

'Her handbag was found in the kitchen. The money had been pilfered, mobile gone but the tracker was still in place and transmitting. She could have been held there. The police have searched the place from top to bottom.'

'So, they've moved her and left the handbag?'

'That appears to be the case. There's something else, sir. It's not good. Pretty horrendous.' Chris spoke in smatterings, his words punctuated by rasps of breath.

Mark lifted his head. Across the room, his grey reflection bounced off the windowpane: beneath his sleepless eyes, shadows drew his cheeks into a stony pallor.

'Go on.' Jackson's body, like Mark's, was rigid and braced for bad news.

'There's the body of a man. Not a pleasant sight. He's laid out on the kitchen table and has numerous injuries. Dead and very recently, as in less than an hour or so. Probably done in a hurry as they departed. He's been recognised, sir, by the police. It's the undercover officer.'

Jackson lowered his head, hiding his face for a few seconds. A share of the burden of responsibility rested on his shoulders. He had encouraged the vice unit to utilise their officer to help trace Julianna. 'Shot?'

'Yes. The police are, well, upset about their colleague, especially the manner of his death. They're calling in extra officers to comb the area for any signs of the gang. But they have to be cautious now that they know guns are involved.'

'No Julianna?' Jackson reiterated.

'No,' Chris said. 'I fear she's been moved and without the tracking device. They're probably taking her out of the country, and quickly. They know they've a traitor in their midst.'

'Stay with the police. They're going to focus on finding the killers of their police officer. Julianna's predicament might lower in priority.'

'I fear so.'

Mark emitted a groan of pain. The hopelessness was profound and disabling.

Jackson looked across at Mark. There was nothing he could say or do. Everything that had happened was a consequence of Ellen's foolhardy trip to Dublin, and before that, their father's criminal past. The aftershocks continued to ripple on. Jackson generously turned away as Mark battled to keep his composure.

41
Julianna

Saturday 4 a.m.

Disturbed by a muffled nose, Julianna stirred from her protective foetal position on the mattress. Given the awakening sunlight, it had to be dawn. Her teeth chattered; the cellar was icy even on a summer's day. Lifting her head, she licked her cracked lips and listened.

A bang. The solitary noise echoed somewhere above her head. An inexperienced person might assume it was a car backfiring or a door slamming, or maybe a champagne bottle losing its cork under pressure. It was none of those: it was a single gunshot.

She waited, expecting more gunfire, but the only sounds were startled birds calling to each other. She hoped the noise signified the arrival of armed police in response to the tracker's beacon. Maybe the police had let off a warning shot. It seemed a convincing idea. But she dared not risk calling out.

The burst of energy she had stockpiled replaced the inertia of fatigue. She carefully stood and cocked her ear to listen. I'm here, she mouthed. Footsteps resonated throughout the cellar, punctuated by the ricochet of the door bolt.

Stazki, wide-eyed and sweating heavily. He stank of cigarettes and fried food.

'The police are here for me, aren't they?' she said, cheered on by his alarmed expression.

He strode over and slapped her face. 'No police, you stupid bitch. You're fucking trouble. Should've killed you.'

The slap was the last boost she needed. She was ready. He had come alone with no backup, but no police either, if he was to be believed. The only weapon was the chain: a potentially powerful one. She backed away from him, creating slack in the links; she tempted him closer with an arrogant smirk. When he raised his hand to strike her again, she twisted her hips and brought up her leg for a sideways kick. The sole of her shoe thrust into his ample belly with a worthy amount of force. Karate kicks were her speciality and her father had taught her to smash planks with the precision and power of those kicks. Stazki doubled up and clutched his stomach. Unable to speak, he grunted. With his head lowered, his scarified neck was exposed. She hooked the chain around it and yanked it.

Leaning backwards, she added her weight and strangled him. His knees buckled and he crashed down, dragging her with him. He thrashed about blindly and snatched a handful of her sleeve, tore it, then dug his fingers into her flesh. She ignored her pain, and his bulging eyes, and the crimson of his neck and cheeks. Instead, she focused on the door and freedom. Suddenly, he slumped and released her arm.

Julianna's cramping fingers let go of the heavy chain. He landed face down. She waited, half-expecting him to rise phoenix-like from the floor, and when he didn't, she knelt and searched him for the key to her shackles. His back trouser pocket contained a mangled packet of cigarettes, but nothing else. She heaved him over on to his back, and flinched at his grotesque appearance. Above his ugly scar, his lips had turned bluish, the skin of his cheeks blotched and purplish. The links of the chain had marked his throat with figures of eight. He moaned – a bubbly exhale – and opened his mouth to gasp for air. She hunted through his pockets and found the key.

Free of the hampering chains, she rubbed her sore wrists. The temptation to beat him to a pulp again was strong, almost overpowering. With him incapacitated, she could finish off what she had started in Dublin. Would Mark congratulate her? He had agreed with her reasoning when she removed the punchbag; violence was not the solution to her anger and nothing had changed. Mark's approval mattered more than ever.

She attached the shackles to Stazki's wrists and slipped the key inside her trouser pocket.

There was another bang. Another gunshot, then another and a barrage of angry shouts followed by more shots fired in rapid succession. Nobody seemed to be speaking in English. If they weren't the police, who were the intruders? She opened the door a fraction and peered down the length of the cellar corridor. The floorboards above her head creaked in time to cautious footsteps. Creeping down the grimy passageway, she tiptoed toward the stairs but as she passed the other door, she stopped. She couldn't leave her there, terrified and vulnerable. Julianna drew back the bolt and slowly opened the door.

There were two women, not one, and both were chained to the walls and hugging each other. They wore grubby floral dresses that were torn in places, their long hair was matted with filth, and their pale skin sallowed by undernourishment and darkness. The room reeked of urine. As she moved closer, instead of showing relief, both women stiffened. Julianna remembered in Dublin a woman had been used to help abduct Ellen. Their trust was so badly eroded she wasn't seen as their saviour.

She crouched and held out two palms. 'It's alright. I'm here to help,' she whispered. She showed them the marks left by her shackles, then produced the key. With a gasp, the older of the women released her companion, and offered Julianna her trembling wrists. She nearly said something, but Julianna quickly pressed a finger to her own lips and pointed up above them.

The younger girl was injured. There was dried blood on her lips and an ugly black eye. Julianna wondered if she had seen her photograph in a report. She might be one of the missing girls desperately sought by her parents. Julianna couldn't remember specific names.

'You need to be brave and try to walk,' she whispered.

The older woman spoke with a dry croak. 'She doesn't speak. I don't know where she comes from. I tried to protect her.' She held the other girl's hand. 'I'm Rita.' An Irish accent.

More footsteps. A loud shot echoed directly above their heads and the three of them bumped into each other. Somebody crash-landed on the boards above. Dust spewed out of the cracks and rained down on them.

'Come. Try to help her.' Julianna dragged the frozen girl up with the help of Rita. They steered her toward the door.

The cellar remained eerily quiet, untouched by the war raging elsewhere in the house. Huddled together, the trio inched their way along to the stairs. Rita and Julianna propelled the injured girl up the stairs. Reaching the top, Julianna propped her on a step and pushed the door open a fraction.

She held her breath, fearing the slightest exhale would signal their location.

A man lay on the kitchen floor in a stream of rippled morning light. Crimson rivulets poured out of a gaping hole in his head. Nearby was a handgun and the familiar baseball cap. He was twisted about his waist; arms one way, legs another, as if in the moment of his violent end he had pivoted and fired his revolver.

Nobody else, at least not in eyeline. She plucked up the courage to go further into the room, knowing that there really was no choice but to keep moving.

'Stay here.' Julianna crawled along the floor, avoiding the bloody puddle, and picked up the gun. There might be bullets left, but not many.

A floorboard groaned. Julianna leapt to her feet and spun on her heel, balancing herself. The man facing her was a stranger. He had tattoos spiralling his neck and exposed arm, and a pistol pointed at her. He stared, confused, his eyebrows knitted together. The hesitation threw her. Was this the undercover police officer? From the direction of the cellar door, the poor girl's terrified mewl escaped. His face hardened and he levelled the muzzle with Julianna's face. Her gun was tucked behind her back. There was no time for second guesses; she had to act fast.

She raised her weapon, aimed and squeezed the trigger hard in one fluid movement. The bullet smashed into his leg, just above the kneecap and splintered the bone. His startled eyes widened into plates, and with an agonised yell, he collapsed onto his back. While he writhed on the floor, she kicked the gun out of his hand, picked it up and pointed both weapons at his stricken face.

'Fuck you, bitch!'

Given his surprised expression, whatever was happening in the farmhouse it wasn't anything to do with her or the other two women. But hanging around to find out the real reason wasn't an option. There was a car key on the table. Stuffing one of the guns in the waistband of her trousers, she scooped up the key and signalled to the women to follow her closely. The younger retched as she hurried past the dead body. The sight of death bathed in sunshine gave all their legs a boost of energy. Freedom beckoned tantalisingly close.

The blue kitchen door was ajar. Behind them, the injured man fretted over his wound. Julianna kept the gun poised and ready to fire. Peeping around the door, she saw the black BMW, which had been used to entice her into a trap, parked on a stretch of concrete on the other side of the yard. There was another vehicle nearby – a large pickup truck. Both appeared to be unoccupied. The key in her hand was for the BMW. The distance wasn't huge, but she had to urge the frightened Rita and the girl to ready themselves for what might seem like a marathon dash.

'Run!'

The other two hadn't the ability to sprint like Julianna. Their legs staggered in slow motion as if tied down by invisible weights. Rita hauled the girl across the last few metres until they careered into the back of the car. Julianna activated the central locking and opened the rear passenger door. She bundled the two women inside and they sprawled across the seat.

'Get down!'

She climbed into the driver's seat. With her finger poised to hit the start button, another large car arrived on the scene. She ducked her head onto the passenger seat, where she had laid the guns. Panting, and unable to control her painful breathing, she prayed in silence to the God she had stopped believing in.

The other car's engine cut out. A door slammed and a man shouted something.

She lifted her head, just level with the dashboard and peered through the windscreen. By the open door of the farmhouse was a bald man surveying the dead body of the baseball cap man. She recognised his clothes – it was the man who had visited her in the dark, promising her a terrible retribution: Zustaller. From his jacket pocket, he produced a handgun. With no hesitation, he aimed it at the stricken man, who held up his hands in self-defence. The gesture proved futile. The shot rang out and he jerked in a death throe. The silhouetted Zustaller headed towards the cellar door and disappeared out of sight.

Julianna reached for the clutch. She scowled; she needed absolute control over the car and she wouldn't have it if only the tips of her toes rested on the pedals. Whoever last drove the car had gigantic legs. She wasted precious time adjusting the seat.

'Stay down. Whatever happens, keep down,' she told the other two before strapping on her seatbelt. 'Defensive driving course, you better be worth it.' She hit the start button for the engine and it roared into action: the cacophony that erupted into the quiet countryside was an unfortunate alarm bell. She shifted into first gear and the wheels squealed. First, she manoeuvred past the pickup truck, which was a challenge, there wasn't much space in the yard. Then there was the Audi, which Zustaller had arrived in. He had dumped it in the middle of the lane. More time ticked by while she drove up an embankment and steered around it.

She might have the keys to the shackles in her pocket, but there was no reason to believe it was the only set. As she turned the car down the unpaved road, the only route away from the farmhouse, in the rear-view mirror two men emerged from the house. Zustaller and his sidekick, Stazki; he had recovered sufficiently to give chase. Perhaps, she should have killed him.

Zustaller raised his weapon.

'Fuck.' Just as she floored the gas pedal the bullet hit the rear of the car.

The dirt track wasn't a good surface for grip and the rear-wheel drive BMW wasn't a great vehicle for off-road speed and stability. But neither was the sporty Audi being used by her pursuers. She bumped the car over potholes, willing it on, but the gap between the two cars shrank.

'Why not a bloody Land Rover!' She slammed her fist on the wheel, then switched on the fully functional satnav; the GPS displayed the vehicle's location on the fringes of western Kent, close to neighbouring Sussex.

The ensuing car chase unfolded across country roads, lanes and sometimes an open field. Julianna paid no heed to the silliness of the situation, how she, a desk bound intelligence officer, had finally achieved the kind of excitement a field officer only ever dreamt of experiencing. It wasn't fun. She was terrified and surviving on her instincts, especially her training in evasive car handling. Another car careered straight at the BMW, unaware of the danger, and she had to play chicken with it, causing the opposing vehicle to swerve and drive into a shallow ditch.

It didn't matter; Julianna wanted to infuriate other road users. Phone calls would be made to the police. Alert bulletins would be announced over car radios – a high-speed car chase across the Kentish countryside and she was the cause.

Why did Zustaller want to catch her? Was she that important? What had she witnessed that made them pursue her so remorselessly? The women in the back of the car clutched each other. Perhaps they were the reason for the pursuit. They had been in captivity longer than Julianna and might know significant information about their abductors: identities, trafficking routes, and the network of houses, ones like the farmhouse. Or perhaps it remained simple revenge, an ongoing reprisal without conclusion. She had beaten her adversary the first time with her fists, then strangled him, and now she was baiting them with a high-speed chase. Their repulsive sexual habits showed how little they cared for women. Julianna's strengths and her guile must epitomise that hatred in all its glory.

Her pursuers caught up with her and the rear-view mirror reflected their faces. Zustaller, the man behind Ellen's grooming and the target of Jackson's war on trafficking, was completely bald. The reason for the balaclava was apparent – a mottled red scar puckered one side of his face below his eye, as if a bullet had entered his cheek and left its mark. He wore a determined expression.

Approaching a sharp bend, she stamped on the accelerator. Braking hard, the rear end of the car slid sideways around the corner, almost spinning the vehicle around one hundred and eighty degrees. Turning the wheel in the opposite direction, the car clipped the hedge on the other side of the road. Julianna made use of heel-to-toe gearshifts, something she had been taught to do, but even with the seat close to the pedals, her foot slipped, the cogs ground and she missed a gear change. The action cost her a few metres of advantage over the pursuing car, and when the Audi slammed into the back of the BMW, her chin struck the steering wheel. The women screamed.

Locking her elbows straight, and ignoring the pain in her jaw, Julianna pressed her right foot down again. A stretch of road opened up before her. But that wasn't where she aimed the car. There was an open gate to the right and, with a last second change of direction, she squeezed the car between the posts. The satnav showed another minor road on the other side of the field. Skidding across the field of barley, she prayed there was another gate there. The Audi had turned too, continuing its relentless pursuit.

Flintstones flew up underneath the car and rattled against the chassis. Something hit the windscreen and chipped the glass, and she ducked instinctively. Straightening up, she spotted a wooden gate hidden in the hedgerow and picked up speed, intending to ram it. The wooden struts of the gate splintered over the bonnet and snapped off the left-hand mirror. Julianna braked hard and turned the car down another narrow lane.

She had re-evaluated her romantic view of car chases: they weren't glamorous. They were physically demanding and extremely uncomfortable. The car jolted every time it hit a pothole or rut, and the vibrations travelled through the steering wheel and into her aching arms. The combined effect of extreme braking and accelerating filled the cabin with the stench of rubber and fumes. The rev counter was stuck in the red and the angry engine wanted to change up when she changed down, but she was grateful she wasn't in an authoritarian automatic with its pre-programmed expectations of urban driving.

The girl was sick in the footwell. Julianna couldn't blame her; she was unwell, injured.

'He's right up against us,' Rita yelled into Julianna's ear. 'Do something.'

'I fucking know!' She had a good view of the stubble on their chins.

The two cars continued to tear up a network of poorly maintained minor roads. They shot through one small hamlet, sweeping up the roadside dust into a cloud, which prompted the postman to flatten himself against the door of his red van – a confetti of white envelopes flew up in the air.

How much longer? Julianna's headache was back with a vengeance and the rising sun dazzled her sensitive eyes. Exhausted, she struggled to make the quick gear changes and the car kangarooed across the country road: it too was giving up.

Where were the police, those comrade-in-arms she had once called her colleagues?

Turning a corner, she almost collided with a cyclist. Swerving, she was forced to crash through a fence and drive into a steeply inclined meadow that led down towards a creek. The wheels spun and slipped on the morning dew. It was like driving on an ice pan. Behind her, the Audi followed, but they were encountering the same problem with their vehicle.

It was her only chance. She put her foot down and accelerated.

'Do it. Go on!' she yelled. 'Chase me.'

The Audi picked up speed behind the BMW.

Julianna had boasted to Hettie's friends about her handbrake turns in a confined space. However, she had never done one in a field of slippery grass with molehills and invisible ruts.

The creek was directly in front of the car. 'Hold tight.'

She flung the steering wheel into a full lock. The car wouldn't answer at first. Julianna dare not look ahead and braced herself for the impact of landing in the stream. The car suddenly responded, almost tipping itself on to its side. It teetered for a moment on the edge of the creek, then the tyres discovered some kind of grip. The BMW's wheels spun for a second, before beginning the climb up the grassy slope. Black smoke billowed out of the exhaust.

The Audi carried on straight past her and at the last minute Zustaller attempted to make the same manoeuvre. The wheels locked and the engine shrieked. In the rear-view mirror, Julianna witnessed the Audi fly across the ditch. It pitched forward onto its bonnet, flipped over and missed the creek altogether. Instead, it somersaulted and smashed into a tree on the opposing bank.

Julianna wasn't going to hang around to see the outcome. They still had guns and for all she knew, given their scars, the two men were invincible and likely to walk away from the crashed car uninjured. She re-joined the lane at the top of the field. The cyclist was gone. Nobody was pursuing her, yet she couldn't stop driving like a maniac. The adrenaline rush refused to abate, and it created a strange euphoria. She laughed uncontrollably.

Coming in the other direction was a blue lit police car, its siren wailing.

'Please stop!' Rita hammered on the back of the driver's seat.

Julianna slammed both feet on the brake pedal; the engine stalled. She clutched the steering wheel, and panted, as if she had been running not driving. The police had finally arrived. She shut her eyes. For the first time in hours, she allowed Mark to creep back into her thoughts – the look of relief on his face, the smile he would give her when she walked into the house. She would carve that reunion into her heart.

'Armed police! Put your hands where I can see them.'

Julianna's eyes sprung open. Instead of walking towards the car, the policeman had ducked behind his vehicle. He held in his hands an automatic gun and wore a bullet proof jacket and helmet. Drawing up behind the BMW was another police car, blocking the road. The occupants scrambled to surround her car. One of the guns she had taken lay on the passenger seat, the other had tumbled into the footwell.

More demands for her to comply, and they weren't friendly shouts. The police officers were aggressive and jittery. The one in front was aiming his weapon directly at her head. She had just manufactured a high-speed chase – hardly the actions of a feeble victim. They thought she was part of the gang.

'Oh dear,' she muttered. Her tense hands ached so much they had glued themselves to the steering wheel.

Relief was replaced with a peculiar sense of disappointment. She turned to apologise to the women. She had let them down.

42

Mark

Saturday 6 a.m.

Mark crashed out on a sofa in the lobby of the top floor, the same spot where a few months ago he had waited with Neil. He lay on his back, stretched out with the crook of one arm blanketing his eyes. Jackson's office door was wide open. There was no news about Julianna. Mark was overhearing one half of Jackson's phone conversation with a member of his security team. What puzzled Jackson was the same thing that Mark wanted answering – who had betrayed her?

'Tess, have you compiled the list?' Jackson asked. 'Who's at the top of the pile?'

Jackson said something; Mark thought he heard, 'Ex-coppers.'

The security team was an amalgamation of vetted ex-coppers, army veterans and career security experts. If one of them had shafted his girlfriend, he hoped Jackson would throw them behind bars, preferably after he had used the bastard as a punchbag. Quietly, and out of sight, Jackson was on the warpath, hunting for his traitor, and Tess was his insider, working to find out who had exposed Julianna.

One call ended, then another began. Jackson spoke softly to Hettie, reassuring his fraught wife. Mark failed to hear the exact words, only the undulation of his pacifying voice. As for Ellen, she was safe, according to Derek's brother, whom Jackson had contacted around breakfast time.

Jackson joined Mark in the lobby, his low shoulders burdened by unproductive authority. 'Diana asked me once why I don't have a comfortable seating area in my office so that my meetings are in more relaxed environment.'

'And why don't you?' Mark asked from under his arm; he appreciated Jackson's efforts in distracting him, but they weren't working. He hid his eyes because the light blinded him. He had been sick twice in the toilet while Jackson was downstairs giving his team words of encouragement as a good boss should. Mark despised his own weaknesses. While Julianna suffered with fear, he had succumbed to a migraine.

'Snug seats?' Jackson laughed. 'Hard chairs keep my meetings short and on agenda. Nobody lingers with small talk when their arses are planted on rocks. Unfortunately,' Jackson sighed, lying back on the other sofa, 'it doesn't make for a pleasant waiting room.'

The two men fell silent again until a phone rang. Jackson's office line.

Mark reached the phone first. Chris Moran's mobile number was on caller display. Jackson let him pick it up.

Mark licked his dry lips and spoke into the microphone. 'Chris—'

'Mark!'

'Julianna!' Mark crumpled into a nearby seat while Jackson, his head bowed over the table, leaned on his white knuckles.

'I'm okay.' Julianna choked back a sob.

'Are you hurt?'

'No. Nothing serious.' She laughed a nervous titter. 'I almost got shot by the good guys, but Chris turned up like the cavalry and just in time to vouch for me. He wants me to go to hospital for a check-up.'

Mark wanted to hold her, see for himself that she was intact and untouched, but she was still miles away from him. 'You should go.'

'I want to be with you—'

Jackson interjected. 'Julianna, Chris will take you to the hospital where Sophia is. She will want to see you too. Mark and I can meet you there.'

'Sophia?' Julianna's voice crackled on the line. 'Is she okay?'

'Broken arm and a bump on her head. She's due to be released this morning.'

'Honey, go. I'll be there to meet you,' Mark said. The relief felt palpable, almost as unbearable as fear. Adrenaline worked its magic in many ways. 'I'm... I can't...'

'I know, Mark, me, too.' She started to cry. He had never heard her cry before. It ripped into his chest and crushed his heart.

'She's fine,' Chris's voice boomed in comparison to her weak one. 'Shock. I'll look after her.'

'We'll see you at the hospital. Thanks, Chris.' Jackson punched the call end button.

The drive to the hospital in the south of London was eternal. Every street elongated to the horizon and beyond. The traffic lights magically turned red every time they approached a junction, and nobody seemed to want to yield to let them pass. It was the final torture knowing she was waiting for him. Jackson followed in another car, giving Mark the privacy he needed to re-assemble his battered emotions. His chauffeur was appropriately silent.

In the emergency room cubicle, he rained kisses down on Julianna's pale face and she flopped against his chest until she had had enough of his affections and gently cuffed his arm.

'I was so afraid to think of you in case I went mad.' She plucked a loose thread off his t-shirt. Her fingernails were dirty, blackened with grime and a few were chipped or torn. She had fought or clawed at something. He smelt diesel, old tobacco and antiseptic wipes, things that were strangers to her. Tangled hair snaked around her face, but she couldn't hide the injuries: a vivid bruise on her cheekbone, another discolouration on her chin and a scratch above her eyebrow. Given the depths of the hollow shadows beneath her eyes, she had to be exhausted.

'I want to see Sophia,' she said, impatiently.

He gently kissed her forehead. Mark bet that for a brief while, she thought she had killed her friend and dreaded coming back to face Luke and Jackson.

'Soon,' he said, without letting her go.

43

Julianna

Saturday 8 a.m.

Julianna sipped on a glass of water and swallowed the painkillers the nurse had left.

Jackson appeared from behind the privacy curtain. 'You're one remarkable person, Julianna. I like to employ the best.'

Jackson was a different man that Saturday morning. Cautious in his mannerisms, his lips twitched as he shook her hand, then, changing his mind, he leaned over to kiss her unblemished cheek. She wasn't sure if she liked this version of him: tired, somewhat awkward, and possibly frustrated. He should be elated. She had probably killed Zustaller, Jackson's bitter foe, and the gang was in turmoil. Yet, he was anxious. Her kidnap had happened on a quiet London street and if she was in Jackson's shoes, she would want to know how that happened. She also owned him an explanation about Sophia.

'I'm not going to ask forgiveness for what I did to Sophia. It was a calculation I took at the time based on what I knew these guys are capable of doing. After what they did in the cellar of that farmhouse, I definitely made the right decision.'

Mark stiffened next to her. 'Jules, you said—'

'I wasn't touched,' she said, swiftly. 'I was, how should I say, inspected. If Sophia had been taken with me...' She grimaced and a shiver cascaded along her spine. Mark blanched into an even paler version of himself. With a thicket of stubble on his chin and eyes sunken into troughs, he looked dreadful. She had grown into her bruises since she had been locked in the cellar but hadn't lost the icy shivers. She clasped her grubby hands into a ball and hid the trembling.

'Tell me, are the other two okay?' she asked.

Jackson answered. 'Kind of. The doctors have sedated the younger one. She's an addict and needs help. I think she's a student and we're cross checking the missing list to see if she's on it. The Irish woman is singing loudly about her experiences. She'd been kept in a house in London for some time. A long-term sex worker, she was forced into a brothel. They were planning on shifting her abroad. The other girl joined her in the cellar a few days ago. Escaping on your own was a major achievement, Julianna, but to successfully bring two other captives with you is, as I said, remarkable.'

She didn't want praise; she wanted answers. 'There was a gunfight. I'm not sure if it was anything to do with me.'

'I'll tell you after your X-ray. Then let's go see Sophia and I'll explain. She wants to hear about your daring escape. We all do.' Jackson drew the curtain back.

'My kidnapper—' She reached out and caught his sleeve.

'I'm working on it,' he said. 'Chris is about to update me on things.'

After the X-ray, the verdict was given on Julianna's injuries: a mild concussion and bruising. She was discharged. Free to leave the emergency room, she and Mark went to see Sophia in her private room. Sophia was waiting for her discharge papers. Luke hadn't left her side since her mother had been sent home to sleep. Jackson was there, too, sitting in the corner.

The two women hugged until Sophia winced. Julianna perched on the bed.

'I know you think you probably took a risk in the car,' Sophia whispered into Julianna's ear. 'But thank you for pushing me out. I froze and—'

'It's okay. I made a snap decision and I don't regret it,' Julianna said firmly.

She described in a halting voice her escape and car chase. Her audience listened attentively as she pieced the fragments together. 'So, I drove batshit crazy, basically. Frankly, I won't complain about driving Hettie around boring London streets ever again.'

'Hettie is very lucky.' Sophia's left arm was in a cast from elbow to knuckles and a smattering of abrasions dotted one side of her wan face. There weren't any stitches visible, but according to Luke, she had grazed her back badly. Her dopey eyes had brightened when Mark and Julianna arrived, and she seemed content to lie on her side and listen.

Jackson cleared his throat. 'I've spoken to Chris, who's been updated by the police. They're still trying to piece it all together; the information uncovered is a gold mine. The location of the farmhouse used to hold Julianna captive was on the GPS of the BMW. You drove all over the place trying to escape your pursuers, but you ended up a few miles away from where you started in that derelict building; one very similar to the one Chris Moran arrived at earlier in the morning.'

'Two farmhouses.' Julianna's mouth formed an 'O' as she thought it through. 'One to keep the girls, the other for the gang to hole up in.'

'Exactly. The hideout where the officer was killed was unknown to the police; they doubt their man had been there before; he would have informed them somehow. It's likely he was taken there by force. However, the gang didn't suspect him of being an undercover policeman, they thought he was a spy from another gang.'

'Muscling in on their operations?'

'Something like that. Zustaller probably has many hideouts across Europe. Evidence collected so far indicates there are another three in the south east around London. Raids are ongoing at the moment. Your abduction coincided with this other gang attempting to snatch the girls from Zustaller's farmhouse. He probably got word of it while torturing that poor bloke. In the ensuing panic, he shot him dead and hurried to the farmhouse where you were being held. By then the shoot-out had happened, killing gang members on both sides. Four bodies were found, including one that fits the description of one of the abductors.'

Baseball cap man. She knew he was dead. The number of shots fired had been significant, but she hadn't realised there were so many killed. She had only seen the man she had injured and Zustaller finished off.

'So,' she said, 'he comes back and finds me leaving, gives chase until they—'

'Crash into a riverbank and tree,' Jackson said. He fished a piece of paper out of his pocket. 'Confirmation of identification of the two bodies in the Audi will take time. The man you beat up in Dublin is Roman Stazki and the other fits the vague descriptions we have of Freddie Zustaller. Let's hope it is him.'

'It is. He made personal references to Mark. To Bill. Even Ellen. It was a vendetta against Mark's family.'

'Zustaller bled to death. A branch had gone straight through him. He deserved worse,' Jackson said coldly.

Luke, whose quiet manner often left him to one side of the conversation, stirred. 'How did the police end up at the wrong farmhouse?' he asked.

'Chris said her handbag was there with the tracker inside. Why it was at that farmhouse isn't clear. What we do know is Zustaller's empire is crumbling. The rivals elbowing in, the police investigations, my foundation's work. He's too thinly spread and struggling to move the girls.'

Julianna spoke. 'Then he got reckless with a vendetta against two people who ruined a routine abduction in Dublin.' She glanced at Mark. 'Ellen wasn't a target this time.'

'I think Stazki initiated this act of revenge not Zustaller,' said Jackson. 'I can't see him being that reckless. I expect he found out what Stazki was up to and turned up in person to see you out of curiosity. They gave up on Mark. I'd put too tight a ring about him. Zustaller may be gone, but there are always others.' His quiet voice tapered into nothing, then his eyes lit up as he remembered something. 'As for your handbag.' He retrieved it from a plain carrier bag by his chair. 'Chris assumed you'd like it back.'

'Honey, the all-important handbag.' Mark grinned and passed it over to Julianna.

She unzipped a compartment. She stared at the contents for a few seconds before bursting into laughter, the shaky, tired laugh of somebody who had found the answer to a puzzle.

The smile dropped off Mark's face. 'What?'

'I had to activate my tracker somehow,' she explained. 'They had my handbag and I needed access to it. I took a gamble. I hoped they'd be squeamish about handling sanitary stuff. I told them my period had started, and I needed the tampon in my bag. So they brought it to me and I activated the beacon while fishing out the tampon.'

'Clever,' Mark said. 'What's the joke?'

'I only had the one.' Julianna delved into her handbag and held up a handful of tampons in their wrappers. 'They took it to the other farmhouse to fill it with supplies for me. All those nightmarish threats and they took the time to fetch me tampons.' She laughed, but it wasn't a joyful laughter. She wiped a tear from her face. She couldn't stop crying. Mark held her close.

Jackson leaned forward and touched Julianna's arm. 'I know you think if the handbag hadn't moved, the police would have come to the right farmhouse and the girl might not have been assaulted. But you know they wouldn't have got there in time. '

'I had to listen—'

'Please, Julianna, don't go there,' Mark said gravely, and she heeded his interruption – there was no point in replaying things over and over in her head, it would drive her crazy.

Jackson continued. 'Though it delayed your rescue and put you at risk in the shoot-out, the police were able to locate the second farmhouse with your tracker. Not only have the police being able to recover the body of their colleague, and his body would have disappeared without trace, they've found a mountain of information, data, maps, details of routes and most importantly a client list. In the coming days many police forces across Europe will be kept very busy ripping apart the dregs of Zustaller's network.'

'All for a pile of tampons.' Luke chuckled. 'I'd love to present this case in court.'

The nurse entered the room and paused in bemusement as laughter greeted her arrival.

The small convoy of cars pulled up outside Fasleigh House. Mark and Julianna, along with Luke and Sophia, would have preferred to be in their own homes, but Jackson, in an enigmatic and quite fierce fashion, told them they were to rest at his house until he received the all clear from his security team that none of the remnants of Zustaller's gang were after them. Julianna heard the executive bite in his voice. It still amazed her that he had the ability to snap orders at others and not lose their respect.

Hettie greeted her husband on the doorstep. Jackson lifted her off her feet with his embrace. Julianna looked away, somewhat embarrassed by the intimacy. They were her employers, a state of affairs she couldn't escape.

'Lunch is laid out; you must be very hungry.' Hettie swept them into the house with her busy arms. 'The kids are waiting for you in the snug.'

Hettie hugged Julianna with an overt display, almost squeezing the breath out of her. 'Oh, my dear. Thank heavens you're safe.'

She kissed Mark, too.

Julianna reclaimed him, wove her fingers through his and followed him into the house.

44
Mark

Saturday Afternoon

Mark, together with Julianna, Luke, Sophia and Jackson, ate in the kitchen. The spread was a cold buffet and easy food for queasy stomachs. Mark, unsettled by exhaustion, picked at his. Having finished playing hostess, Hettie slipped out of the room and joined the children.

Jackson piled the food high on his plate. 'I am so hungry.' He quickly reduced the mound while the others toyed with theirs.

'Why are we here, Jackson?' Luke asked. 'Something else is going on.'

'Can't hide a thing from you, can I?' Jackson winked.

'You were rather adamant we should remain behind your fences, so don't be coy.' Luke sharpened his tone.

'Alright.' Jackson leaned back in her chair and eyed the two couples. Julianna remained pale but her hands holding the cutlery were steady. 'Are you okay, Julianna?' he asked gently.

'Yes.' Julianna's stoicism was remarkable, and enviable.

Jackson tossed his fine linen napkin on to his empty plate. 'At the moment there's a frenzy of ongoing activity. People are moving, trying to cover their tracks and the enforcement agencies are casting many nets. Both Zustaller's gang, and the other trafficking gang, are in a state of flux. I find Zustaller's failure to control his empire ironic.'

A faint smile crossed Jackson's face. 'This is a man who acquired territorial gangs, like he tried to with Mark's father's in Manchester. His assets weren't just money, they were human. Rather like mergers and acquisitions, he built a business up from a base. But it appears he had no means to control his sprawling empire. There were betrayals and infiltrators from both rivals and law enforcement agencies. He stretched himself too thin and failed to contract to protect his interests. Not that I'm disappointed, but he was a crap executive.'

'But he's gone,' Luke said in an exasperated tone. 'But I'm here. So is Sophia. I thought you told me Sophia wasn't a target.'

Mark leaned toward Julianna and explained. 'After you two were snatched, and Sophia ended up in hospital, Jackson and Moran assumed Sophia was the target – her connection to a wealthy family makes her a potential kidnap victim. It was only after Sophia recalled the details of her attackers, did we realise she was never the intended target.'

Jackson's hearing was acute. 'Not then, but now she might be because, yes, it would appear that Zustaller is gone, so is one of his captains and the underlings are headless chickens. This is a rout, but it's not victory. Others will fill the shoes of the departed. The window of opportunity to strike will last a few days and then the rabbits will be back in their underground warren forming new gangs.'

'You can't keep us here indefinitely,' Mark said.

'No, I would like my house back, very true,' said Jackson. 'But bringing you here isn't due to the ongoing police operation. The surviving gang members are more interested in saving their own arses at the moment. However, there are others, who could make trouble. Who have made trouble. They're the hidden criminals, who outwardly appear normal, hardworking citizens and quite often pillars of society. They do their good deeds while behind the scenes they practise their criminal activities. They betray and inform. You must have wondered, Julianna, how Stazki came to find you so easily.'

Julianna said nothing.

'You've found something out?' Mark pushed his plate to one side, his appetite shattered once again. The headache, now dulled by painkillers, rumbled beneath his temples, threatening to return.

'I'm finding something out,' Jackson replied. 'While others concentrated on finding you, the pedantically thorough Tess has been following up other leads. She, Gary and Chris are the only ones who know what I asked her to do.'

'What leads?' Sophia asked.

'Those in Julianna's circle who aren't whom they seemed to be.'

Julianna gasped. 'My friends!'

'No, not friends. Your friends are steadfastly loyal to you,' said Jackson. 'A wider periphery of people.'

'Who?' asked Mark. 'Who wants to hurt us?'

'I'm awaiting confirmation. There are two key suspects. One works directly for me, the other indirectly. It is the latter that Tess is seeking further information about.'

'You're not going to tell us?'

'I want more proof. In the meantime, rest.'

'I'd like a bath,' Julianna said quietly. 'And clothes that fit better.'

The clothes Julianna had been given in hospital had been purchased in a hurry from a supermarket.

'I tell you what, while you two rest, I'll have Tom Draper drive out to your house and pick up some clothes for you. You can give him your house keys,' Jackson suggested. 'I'll get Hettie to show you to a room.'

Mark rose to his feet and wobbled. He should speak to his sister, but fatigue won out and he happily climbed the stairs. Julianna followed him. Tipping over onto the bed, and paying no attention to clothing, they lay side by side, their fingers touching, their breathing soft and secure in the knowledge they were safe. Later, when they stirred from a brief nap, they undressed each other and lay down again, this time closer and in such a way they could comfort each other with kisses and caresses. From there, they joined together until the whoops of children playing outside reminded them they weren't home yet.

In the garden, Hettie and Jackson played with the kids. It was a breezy day. Mark watched the family through a window: Jackson kicking a ball to Noah while Hettie perched Evey on her hip. So much laughter and joy. Mark crushed the envy. There was no reason he couldn't have that love in his life, if he wanted it.

Close to four o'clock, Jackson summoned him and Julianna to the kitchen.

'Jessop is going to be fired on Monday.' Jackson fiddled with the coffee machine. He had changed into a suit and tie. So official looking, it signalled a change in mood.

'Why?' Julianna asked, her eyes widening in surprise.

Jessop mainly worked as a security guard, patrolling the basement and manning the doors of the tall office block.

'He slept with an underage girl. And I don't mean a seventeen-year-old, I mean she's fifteen. Tess dug up the dirt on him and he became a suspect. However, although he has appalling judgement when it comes to picking up girls in pubs, nothing else warrants suspicion.'

Mark thought he had got off lightly, which meant Jackson was more interested in somebody else.

Jackson poured coffee into a mug. 'Julianna, did you ever tell Graham Saddler about your Dublin adventure?'

'Yes, I suppose I did, though not in great detail. I mean, I didn't provide the background of why Ellen was there.' She took a sip out of coffee. 'He liked to talk about the raids he went on when he was in the police. Arresting pimps, rescuing girls and I suppose I compared my experience to his.' Jackson stared intently at Julianna and she blinked. 'No, surely not. I mean, he was always kind-hearted and appeared genuinely concerned for the girls. Graham?'

'He's not who you think he is. Turns out Saddler left the force under a cloud. A fellow officer suspected he was interfering with prostitutes off duty. He certainly wasn't paying for any of their services. The other officer couldn't prove anything and, as Saddler was his superior, he felt vulnerable. Saddler saw the writing on the wall and took early retirement. This has now only come to light due to the gentle persistence of Tess.'

'And he came to work for Opportunitas as an advisor,' Julianna said.

Mark had met him at Fasleigh; the quiet police inspector who had said little. He gripped the handle of his mug tighter.

'Sophia mentioned that a few girls disappeared after Saddler had spoken to them.'

'Yes,' Julianna said, chewing on her lower lip. 'Only on Friday we commented on one not turning up for work.'

'All very suspicious. Tess check his expenditure; he has expensive habits: golf clubs and holidays abroad, lots of holidays in different countries. He has far more money than his pension warrants.'

'You're going to see him, aren't you?' Julianna said.

'Yes. Now, before he takes flight. Chris and I are going. I want the truth,' Jackson said.

Mark rose to his feet. 'Then we're coming too. Don't argue about it, please. I want closure on all this, we both do.'

Julianna agreed. The weight of fatigue lifted; she knocked back her coffee with one mouthful. 'Let's all go.'

An unusually pensive Jackson acquiesced to her demand, which surprised Mark.

Graham Saddler lived within easy reach and driving to his generously-sized house took no more than half an hour. Mark sat with Julianna on the back seat with his fingers interlaced in hers. Jackson was up front, next to Chris, the cast iron man who said little. The long summer evening would extract every last morsel of sunlight and add it to the residual heat in the air. Turning into a secluded sideroad in a leafy suburban village, Mark spied a silver executive saloon car parked up outside the double garage.

'Nice pad,' Mark said. The exterior was impeccably maintained with hanging baskets and tulips in the borders. The interior was hidden by Venetian blinds. The accountant part of his brain quickly totted things up. 'He couldn't have paid for this on a copper's salary.'

The former coppers in the car didn't disagree with his assessment. Chris scratched his unshaven chin. 'So unless a horde of ancient spinster aunts died on him, he has other sources of income.'

The quartet of visitors approached the front porch. The doorbell rang and after several achingly long seconds, the door opened. Saddler had gained weight. Grey belly hairs poked out between the stretched buttonholes of his creased shirt. His flushed cheeks and bald patch glistened with a sheen of perspiration. The low sun dazzled him, and he took a step back. Jackson filled the vacated space, and in moving forward, showed his face.

'Jackson,' Saddler said, his eyes widening further when he shifted his gaze to Jackson's companions. 'What—'

'What am I doing here or more to the point, what is Julianna doing here?' Jackson finished the sentence with his foot over the threshold. 'Good question. I'll come in and tell you.'

Chris and Jackson herded Saddler backwards into his own house. Graham blustered with annoyance. 'I'm busy.'

Julianna closed the front door and Jackson signalled to Chris. 'Look around.'

Saddler planted his stubby hands on his hips with agitated indignation. 'Wait a minute. You can't just poke your nose about my house and—'

'See what you're up to? If I was a policeman, it would be highly irregular, but I'm not,' Jackson said, almost pleasantly. 'Of course, you're free to call your former colleagues; I would welcome their presence.' He folded his arms across his chest and raised his eyebrows expectantly. Saddler dropped his arms to his sides in defeat.

The house was in a confused state. There were un-ironed clothes heaped about the spacious kitchen-diner and dirty plates and saucepans stacked on the worktops of the kitchen. Mark fingered an empty picture frame hanging on the wall. Something had happened and recently. Another empty photo frame lay on the sideboard surrounded by broken glass. The cat's litter tray was an unpleasant sight and Mark wrinkled his nose at the lingering odour. There was one fundamental absence in the house.

Jackson lifted a tea towel out of the sink. 'Where's your wife, Graham?'

'None of your business,' Saddler said. 'This is a fucking infringement of my rights.' He pointed his shaking finger at Jackson; his cheeks now fiery.

'She's gone, sir.' Chris trotted into the diner from the hallway. 'Her clothes are missing from the wardrobes, no toiletries, and other knick-knacks. Also, he's packing too.'

Julianna picked up something off the dining room table; it had been buried underneath the piles of washing. 'Your passport.' She handed it to Jackson.

Jackson thumbed through the immigration stamps. 'It seems you have a fascination with visiting, let me see, the Ukraine, Serbia. And Thailand.' He dropped the passport back on the table.

'Cheap beer,' Saddler said with a shrug.

'All in the last couple of years. You've been busy. Local girls not good enough for you or are your tastes too particular for them?'

Mark thought him too brash. Too confident. Julianna's hands bunched into fists. Chris cleared his throat and gestured to Mark to keep back. They were professionals and they were worried. He slid his foot and his heel hit the skirting board.

Saddler's hand disappeared under the nearest washing pile. Mark caught a glint of metal just as Julianna leapt forward. She careered into Jackson's outstretched arm. Mark was stuck by the back wall, Chris in the doorway and Jackson and Julianna to one side. They were fanned out and blocking the exit to the hallway. However, behind Saddler was the opened patio door. The blinds flapped in the breeze. An ugly silence descended.

Saddler raised the gun and pointed it directly at Jackson, who didn't flinch, which impressed Mark because his own legs had turned to jelly. The nauseating taste of fear filled the back of his throat. This, what he felt, was how Julianna had experienced all the previous night.

'Now who's in control?' Saddler chuckled. 'You'll regret turning up here unannounced. Yes, I'm leaving and to be honest I don't care what mess I leave behind.'

There was a window in the kitchen and as Mark's attention flitted around the room, a shadow blocked out the light for a second. He opened his mouth to warn Jackson but was distracted by an ear shattering bang. In the same instance, an invisible force slammed him into the wall. He had been punched, which given nobody was anywhere near him, was ludicrous. The violence of the unseen blow knocked the air out of his lungs. Pain seared down his side and he gasped for breath. The wall held him up for a couple of seconds, then his legs collapsed under him and he crumpled to the floor.

45

Julianna

Julianna had experienced such a burden of adrenaline in the last twenty-four hours, she was too numb to notice its renewed effects. She had seen those wild eyes of Saddler's before – the man at the farmhouse just before she shot him. This time she had no defensive gun, only her lightning responses. She lifted her leg as Saddler's finger squeezed the trigger. Her foot failed to make contact. However, the jab served a different purpose. The gun went off, but his inexperience showed. Distracted by her swinging leg, the shot missed Jackson.

A red inkblot rapidly seeped through Mark's t-shirt and rippled down his side. Chris froze; the chief bodyguard's aghast expression locked on Mark's bloody chest. Julianna started toward Mark.

'Don't go near him,' said Saddler, curtly. 'He can bleed out there.'

Pulsating with fury and hate, she wanted to tear Saddler apart. But the punch bag technique wouldn't work here – Saddler had the advantage. She let out a low cry of frustration.

Saddler returned the gun's sights to Jackson; his outstretched arm trembled and fresh beads of sweat trickled down his flushed face.

'Still,' Jackson urged Chris. Jackson's life was all about taking risks and he rarely screwed up. However, the risks he took were financial ones. Money was easier to sacrifice. People's lives were very different. She hoped he remembered her intuition wasn't as trusting.

Out of the corner of her eyes, she saw movement outside. Perhaps nothing more than the elusive cat, except it wasn't that small. Jackson's steady gaze fractured for a second too. What had he seen?

'You've made your point, Saddler,' Jackson said, regaining his composure with deft swiftness. 'Why don't you just go? Tie us up. We'll be stuck here for a while, and you can get away.'

'Shut up.' Saddler's eyes bulged. 'I have the gun. I get to decide. He'll pay me a bonus, especially when I give him her.' He jabbed his other hand at Julianna. 'So the news on the TV about the shoot-out and chase, it's all you?'

She nodded slowly. 'Why did you do it? Why did you give me to them?'

Saddler shrugged, mocking her with a touch of bravado. 'When I told Roman that you boasted about Dublin, he was furious. You humiliated him and it took weeks for him to recover. Roman had this idea to get his own back. Mark, I knew, lived with you, but he really wants you. I told him about your little walk on Fridays. It's bad practice, Julianna, to stick to a routine. You should know better.'

Jackson's blue eyes flickered, then returned to the gun. She saw the same thing – the movement wasn't a cat. She had to stop staring at the intruder on the patio or risk Saddler seeing her reaction.

As Jackson kept him talking, Chris edged toward Mark. Chris understood the significance of what was happening in the room and outside. He kept Saddler occupied with his small act of rebellion. Saddler frowned but didn't order him back.

Julianna joined in the distraction. 'How long have you worked for them?'

'Years. While I was in vice, other units too. So easy. I let them know when raids were on, when the girls needed to be moved about and they kept me satisfied in other ways – money, not girls. I'm not that cheap.' The smile was unpleasant. 'They hate your charity. Told me to get in there: infiltrate it and appear the generous volunteer and if I could send a few of the girls back to them, they would line my pockets.'

'So why are you leaving in a hurry?' asked Jackson.

Saddler rested his bottom against the dining room table, the gun steady, his stance obnoxiously confident. 'Since I can't raise anyone, I've decided to take a sunny holiday abroad until it all dies down. I was going to send my apologies for reneging on my commitments to your beloved Opportunitas, but since you're here, I can do it in person.'

'Your wife?'

A brief flare of his nostrils, then he laughed, a half-hearted chuckle. 'Left. Well, she's been leaving for years, and this week she packed up proper in a hurry. She'll come back for some photos of her family, but I've dealt with them. She'll want the cat, too; she loves that filthy fur ball.'

Mark inhaled sharply and his legs twitched. Blood trickled down into the crevices of the laminated floorboards. Time wasn't on their side.

'Stazki's dead,' Julianna blurted. 'So's his boss.'

Saddler snapped to attention and shook his head with disbelief. 'No.'

Another glance over her shoulder. Mark's eyes fluttered as he struggled to maintain consciousness.

She faced Saddler. 'That car chase, he smashed the car. Seen that in your news bulletins; two dead men in a car in a ditch? A bald middle-aged man with a puckered scar on his left cheek. I had a good look at him.'

'You're panicking, aren't you?' Jackson sensed a climax too. 'Things have been going wrong for a while, haven't they? What with infiltrators and rivals.'

Saddler's face slowly drained of colour. 'I told you to shut up!' The barrel of the gun shook.

'It's over, Saddler. Others, beside we three, know about you. The evidence is there ready to be handed over. You won't make it out of the street, never mind the country. The police have been called. Armed police.' Jackson lied with his double-bluff. Tess was probably the only one who knew Saddler's location; anybody else would take time to track them down.

Saddler's eyes narrowed in spite. 'Then I have nothing to lose if I do this.'

He squeezed the trigger.

The bullet went wide. Not due to Saddler's aim; he would have hit his target had the stance of his whole body not been shifted. The bullet ended up in the wall beyond Jackson's head.

'You bastard!' the woman screeched. Saddler keeled forward. The blood from his cracked head splattered across her face. He came to rest by her feet. 'He's killed my cat,' she said, tears flooding over her eyes. 'I came back for Delilah and he's dumped her in the wheelie bin.'

Jackson stepped over Saddler and removed the bloody baseball bat from Mrs Saddler's hands, then eased her down into a dining chair. Julianna grabbed a handful of the clean tea towels, knelt next to Mark and applied pressure to his wound.

'Ow!' Mark's eyes opened. 'That hurts,' he croaked.

'Keeping telling me that and I'll know you'll live.' She fought the temptation to drag him into her arms and hold him tight.

Chris rang for an ambulance and the police in that order.

Mrs Saddler stirred. 'Is he dead?' she said matter-of-factly. Her gaze blanked out the prone figure of her husband as if he was nothing but an inconvenient stain on the rug. The endpoint of the drama had been an anti-climax. Julianna in the end had done nothing heroic. Another wife had delivered the punch, and with an expression of emptiness, not hatred or anger. What Julianna had once feared to be was right there in front of her: a battered shell with no hope.

Jackson crouched and checked his pulse. 'No. But he may not regain all of his faculties.'

'I don't care,' Mrs Saddler said. 'He hurt me so badly yesterday. Thought he could threaten me with this.' She pointed to the bloody baseball bat. 'He's been cheating on me for years and I let him. I let him do things to me... and... he killed my cat,' she ended in a whisper, her shoulders hunched.

'Where did you go?' Jackson held her hand. His kindness was touching. His life was saved not by a highly trained bodyguard, but by a scorned wife.

'I went to a cheap hotel. I should do the ironing, I suppose.' She picked up a white shirt and crushed it with her manicured fingers. The shock turned to despair and she cried.

'You're a brave woman coming back here. I'll make sure you'll sleep in the best hotel.'

Julianna watched a once proud woman crumble. Another victim

to add to the day's list. But she wasn't one and neither was Mark. The bleeding had stopped and between her and Chris, they managed to make Mark comfortable. Although white and shivering, he was conscious and lucid. The bullet had grazed his ribcage. A bloody wound, but not deep.

Chris picked up the gun with a handkerchief and removed the ammunition before placing it on the worktop.

Sirens wailed, then screeched to a halt. The evening wasn't over yet. A crime scene had been created. Jackson and Julianna had found out the truth, but it had nearly cost Mark his life. She turned her face away from him, fearful her tears might make him believe he was dying. He reached up and tilted her head back to face him.

'It's alright, Jules,' he whispered. 'It's going to fine. We're going to get through this; I'm not leaving you.'

46

Julianna

Beyond midnight and into dawn, the owls had given up their hooting, so the birds took over with a chorus of chirping. Julianna lay on top of the guest bed wearing borrowed pyjamas. Next to her was Mark, similarly attired in a pair of Jackson's pjs, which hung off his shoulders. She held his hand. His wound had been stitched and the ribcage patched up with bandages. He had refused to stay overnight in hospital

'I'm going to write to Dad. Tell him what's happened, including you. And about Ellen in Dublin. Everything. Then, he'll know he's made a difference. What he set out to do eight years ago is over. Perhaps it might convince him to plead guilty and take up Jackson's offer.'

She nudged closer. Parts of her ached from fatigue and injury, parts of her ached for Mark. She had to be patient and wait for him to be ready. 'And Ellen?'

'She's in Scotland with Brett. I think she's actually going to be happy.' He squeezed her hand. 'I'm happy for her.'

Julianna's eyes drooped. 'I'm so tired. It's like a bomb has gone off in my head. How's the pain?'

Mark exhaled a gentle snore in reply.

By Sunday noon, they were both showered and dressed. Luke had already taken Sophia home. Hettie and the children were eating lunch in the kitchen. Jackson was ensconced in his study.

'Jackson wants to see you both,' Hettie said, spoon poised in hand while her daughter banged her grubby hands on her feeding tray. Hettie rolled her eyes. 'Don't worry, he's quite himself again, which is important, don't you think?'

She meant the status quo. Life needed normalising and quickly. No more wishing for adventure. It wasn't how the journey was supposed to be any more. Routine day-to-day things would become important again, like driving Hettie to the gallery. Whether Hettie needed protection was irrelevant; Jackson would always provide it.

Jackson wore a different uniform: grey pleated trousers and a light blue polo shirt, which was monogrammed with gold lettering. Seated behind his desk, laptop open and an earpiece positioned ready to take calls, he looked every bit the chief executive again. The father and genial host had been put aside – Julianna had no doubt they were paying a visit to their boss.

'Please, take a seat.' Jackson pointed at two chairs positioned on the other side of his desk. He removed his earpiece. 'You two look much better.'

'Thank you,' Julianna said. Mark was still pale and dosed up on painkillers, but she was free from discomfort – the iciness within had melted and the warmth had returned to her veins.

'In the last forty-eight hours numerous arrests have been made, here and abroad,' Jackson explained. 'In this country a dozen women and girls plus two boys have been removed from forced prostitution. Many others hopefully will follow. His big mistake was going to the farmhouse to see you in the flesh – he broke his own rules.'

'The two women held with me?' Julianna asked.

'They both would like to thank you in person, especially the family of the younger Portuguese girl who was taken from a train station not long after she arrived in London. They've been frantically trying to trace her.'

'I'd like to meet them.'

'Good. Saddler isn't in a good shape: comatose with major bleeding on the brain. I admit I underestimated his role in Zustaller's organisation. The assumption me and Chris made was that he was being blackmailed or manipulated in some way.'

'I still can't believe it. I wish I had been more curious about those girls vanishing. You assume it's the nature of their lives and the lack of stability. We're too complacent and uninterested sometimes.'

'You're being hard on yourself. Sophia is feeling guilty, too,' Jackson said. 'You can't be everyone's guardian angel.'

He slid his laptop to one side and leaned on his elbows, narrowing the distance between him and Julianna. 'Things are going to change for you, Julianna – it's unavoidable. Both Chris and I agree that you can't work as a protection officer any longer.'

She hadn't expected to be stripped of her bodyguard responsibilities. After all she had done for Haynes, the wealth of skills she had demonstrated, she was once again worthless. As she shifted to the edge of her seat, Mark rested his hand on her thigh and pressed her back down.

'I don't understand. Why?' she demanded.

Jackson held up a placating hand. 'You're too close to my wife. The role requires impartiality and no emotional attachments. Empathy taints judgement.'

'I don't think that's the case, sir,' Julianna said sharply.

'This isn't something I've decided lightly. My opinion was shifting before your abduction, and now it's immovable. You've been threatened by violent people, you've shot a man, and had your driving skills put through an extreme test. Your post-trauma status will require professional evaluation. I don't want you driving my wife, Julianna, or being her bodyguard. This is no disrespect to your powers of recovery; it is my personal decision and there is no negotiation.'

His points were horribly valid. Jackson the executive decision maker was back in residence. She slid backwards on her chair. 'Very well, sir. I respect your decision.'

'That being said, you're not out of job. You'll be given special investigations to carry out. You won't be working for Chris's team or in Mark's department. You will be working for Opportunitas full-time. We've rescued many women, recently and hopefully in the coming weeks. They're not all British, some are deeply traumatised, others are unable to trust anyone. Regretfully some are also mentally impaired. There are also families searching for missing loved ones. You will be tasked with tracing relatives for the women and children in the refuges. Also repatriating those who wish to go home. How does that sound to you, Julianna?'

Emotions, especially joy and relief, battled with incredulity; this was where she wanted to be – a woman with a valued role. 'It sounds a worthy job. Would that have been the option prior to my abduction?'

'It was one of two. The other was to give you more managerial responsibilities. But somehow I don't think that will appeal to you.'

She laughed. 'No, it doesn't.'

'Good.' Jackson leaned back in his chair. 'Ellen's staying up in Scotland, according to Derek. So, Mark, don't ignore your sister. Family is everything.'

'Yes, sir,' Mark said.

Jackson chuckled and rose to his feet. 'Stop calling me sir, at least outside of work. Hettie counts Julianna as one of her friends, which by default, means I am too. We share everything, as good partners do.'

Mark stood up and came over to offer his hand to Jackson. 'Thank you, Jackson. For everything you've done for me and Ellen. For helping me see my dad in a different light, for introducing me to Julianna. I'm very grateful to be counted as your friend.'

Jackson came over to a rather overcome Julianna and crouched down in front of her.

She finally found her voice. 'Strange world, isn't it? I thought you chose me because of Alex. I've struggled to let people into my life since him. So, I hope I can do this friendship justice. Thank you for finding me, for all you've done.'

'Julianna, you found yourself. Both in your remarkable escape and beyond. Don't judge yourself harshly. You're an amazing, resilient and confident woman and I can't think of anyone better to have about me and my family.'

Mark coughed awkwardly. 'We should go home then.'

A phone trilled and Jackson reached over to pick it up. 'Wait! Yes? Good, let them through.' He replaced the handset. 'Right on cue,' he said mysteriously.

He led the couple to the front door, calling out for Hettie at the same time. She appeared with Evey on her hip and Noah running about her legs, his chin plastered with vanilla ice-cream.

The door opened and Julianna was blinded for a moment by the bright sunshine. She shaded her eyes and peered at the car pulling up in front of the house. She recognised the make and registration plate.

She bounded down the stairs just as the car doors opened. There at the bottom step, she paused, disbelieving, and flung her arms wide open. 'Mum, Dad! You're here!'

47

Julianna

Autumn

It had been a few years since she had been in a prison and back then, it was usually a remand centre to interview a suspect in the company of another police officer. Not alone, like this morning.

Bill Clewer had Mark's eyes and, beneath their wrinkled shadows, Ellen's full lips and narrow chin. The composite of features blurred around his nose and eyebrows, which were thick and wiry. Neither of his kids had his rebellious hair, which coiled around his neck and poked out of his ears in spikes. He was something of a hairy gorilla, which was how Ellen had described him once. As he scraped his chair across the floor and under the table, he bunched his arms into a bundle and leaned forward. If she had expected a handshake, he wasn't forthcoming. She wasn't sure if she wanted to touch him, anyway.

'So, you're Mark's girlfriend,' he said, the smile creeping up his cheeks. 'Can I call you Julianna? Or Jules.'

She stopped him there with a frown. 'Julianna is fine.'

'So.' His voice rumbled in his throat. 'You've come to check me out?'

They were alone in a room, the privilege of special status afforded by the witness protection program. Bill was being constantly moved until his parole began. Then, he would disappear and not even Mark or Ellen would know where he had gone.

'I've come to ask a question.' She settled her hands on the table and wove her fingers together into a knot. Her back was upright, knees together and feet firmly flat on the floor. She wasn't afraid of him, but the defensive posture helped.

'Ask away.' He leant back in his seat and stretched his legs out. There was plenty of room under the table for his long legs.

'Mark is okay, by the way.'

He hauled his feet back and straightened. 'And Ellie?'

'They're both okay. Things have settled down, we hope. For you too, now that... he's gone.' She still shivered when she thought of them both mangled in the smashed car.

'Will she come and see me? Ellie?'

Julianna shrugged. His grey flecked eyebrows drooped before she answered. 'Maybe. She's happy where she is. In love, too. I'm sorry, Bill, but she doesn't need you. Don't you think that's a good thing?'

'I suppose,' he said. 'And Mark?'

'Mark will. He'll come and say goodbye.'

'Goodbye? I suppose.' He stared at his hands and sighed heavily, then looked up. 'Deidre is divorcing me.'

It was news to Julianna, and probably to Mark. His mother hadn't spoken to him in weeks, ever since the police had knocked on her door asking awkward questions about her supplying cannabis.

'She's not following you?'

He chortled, obviously not too upset. 'Deidre? No. She's not keen on the idea of disappearing at all. Once I turned into a super-grass, she gave up on me. The final straw, I suppose. I'm not the man she married.'

Was she now the woman he had married? Julianna didn't ask.

'So what's your question?' He relaxed into his seat, happy to clear up the family issues with a few brisk question and answers. Prison drained people into empty shells, then left them waiting for life to start over again – parole was edging closer for Bill.

'Thank you for seeing me,' she quickly said.

He shrugged. 'I'm always happy to have visitors.'

'You see when Mark last came here, he was vague about something and it bugs me, a little.' A lot, really, she nearly said. 'He's moving on and I'm the kind of person who likes tidy ends.'

Bill rubbed his rough chin. 'Sure.' He rolled his eyes northward, seemingly impatient, as if he was sick of interrogations.

'How did you know about Haydocks?' she asked.

He presented a revealing, knowing smile. 'Ah, Henderson you mean.'

'You met him?'

'Yeah. He and I used the same bookies. That's where we met, years and years ago. Chance encounter. He liked a flutter. Dogs, though, not horses.' He grinned. 'Won a few in my time.'

'And that's how you found out about Haydocks?'

His versatile eyebrows melded into one bushy line as he wrinkled his forehead. 'You mean the money? Nah.' He leaned forward, closing the gap slightly. On the other side of the door was the prison officer, ready to dash in if she needed him. She had flatly refused to have company. She could take care of herself.

'But you suggested Mark work for him?'

'I did. Mark, well, he's bright. He reckons it comes from me, but I'm honest enough to know I'm not that clever. It's that grandpa of his, Deidre's dad, who had the nous between the ears.' Bill tapped his temple. 'Having Mark go to Oxford was Deidre's goal, not mine.'

'She wanted him to be a lawyer.'

Bill laughed. 'She did. He's a numbers man. So I tell Henderson, the fat git,' – he patted his belly— 'nice on the surface, not so, underneath, but, I didn't know that at the time. I tell him my son is keen on the accountancy side, going to study numbers and stuff, and Henderson says, send him to me when he's ready, I'll make something of him.'

Julianna smiled. 'But not what he planned.'

'Aye.' Bill smirked. He scraped a fingernail noisily along the edge of the table. He wanted to say something, she was sure of it.

'And the laundering?'

Bill's cheeks went a little red. 'Didn't find out till I got the sentence. Totally out of the blue. I hears this name floating 'round the clink, how good Henderson is at hiding money, and blow me, I'd only gone and sent my son to work for him.'

She knew it! 'Coincidence? You set Mark up with Haydocks by accident?'

He nodded, sheepishly. 'Ironic, yeah? I thought I was giving my son a clean slate with Henderson. Though to be honest, I might have done it anyway, if I'd known whose money it was. But it was a surprise. I never told Mark when he came to see me; I made out it was intentional, kind of. Do you think he minds, not knowing the real reason?'

She had thought the sequence of events had originated with Ellen tumbling into the online grooming club run by Zustaller. Then, maybe it was Mark bumping into Hettie in the bar, or his sister in the cafe. He had a remarkable knack for finding women accidentally. All preposterous encounters, but none of them more so than Bill and Henderson betting on the same dogs long before either Mark or Bill had heard of the Deliverer.

Julianna released her fingers and pushed her chair back from the table. 'Your chance encounter in the bookies set off a string of events, Bill. But, if Mark hadn't gone to Haydocks, I wouldn't have met him. So, I'd like to think he's okay about it now that everything is out in the open.'

He caught sight of the ring. 'You're engaged!' he exclaimed. 'Let me see.'

She held out the hand and he nearly touched her finger with his; one of them was crooked, another was tattooed. 'Marrying you, is he?'

'Yes.' She couldn't believe it some days. 'I didn't think I could ever marry again.'

'It's good, marriage. If you get it right. Me and Deidre had it for a time, that thing, love, whatever people like to call it. Hang on to it. Don't let anything else get in its way.'

Bill's little advice was wise, if sad, coming from him.

'How did you meet my son?' he asked, rising to his feet.

'Not by chance. Somebody set us up.'

'Ooh.' He grinned. 'You should invite that person to the wedding.'

'I am. He's hosting the reception at his house.'

'Excellent.' Bill's smiley face crumpled. 'I'll not be there.'

'We'll send you some pictures. Okay?'

He beamed. A powerful smile. She recognised its nature. Warming. Welcoming. Bill, the likeable rogue, had a recruit to his side. 'Don't go yet, will you?' she said softly.

'I've got a few months left before they'll let me out.'

She nodded, leant across the table and pecked his cheek. 'Good luck, Bill.'

'You too.'

She swung her arms as she walked along the corridors of the prison. On the way out, she collected her brick of a handbag at the security desk and hooked it over her shoulder. She planned on replacing it. It was too heavy.

Acknowledgements

With gratitude to those who helped in the conception of this series. The writing of any book greatly depends on many contributors, their patience and advice. This book began life many years ago and wouldn't have been possible without my editor, cover designer, beta readers and the support of publishing professionals with knowledge and experience.

A special thank you to my parents for encouraging my writing endeavours over the last ten years as I carved a new path as a published author.

To my readers; thank you for your loyalty. Please consider posting a review if you are able.

Rae Shaw is a pen name for the author Rachel Walkley.

rachelwalkley.com

Rachel is based in the North West of England. She read her first grown-up detective novel at the age of eleven, which proved to be a catalyst for filling many shelves with crime books including police procedurals and historical mysteries. They grow in number whenever she visits a bookshop.

As well as crime, Rachel likes to unplug from the real world and writes mysteries that have a touch of magic woven into family secrets.